Michael Wood is a freelance journalist and proofreader living in Sheffield. As a journalist he has covered many crime stories throughout Sheffield, gaining first-hand knowledge of police procedure. He also reviews books for CrimeSquad, a website dedicated to crime fiction. *Time is Running Out* is his seventh novel.

twitter.com / MichaelHWood
facebook.com / MichaelWoodBooks

Also by Michael Wood

TIME IS RUNNING OUT

MICHAEL WOOD

One More Chapter
a division of HarperCollins*Publishers*
1 London Bridge Street
London SE1 9GF
www.harpercollins.co.uk

HarperCollins*Publishers*
1st Floor, Watermarque Building, Ringsend Road
Dublin 4, Ireland

This paperback edition 2021
First published in Great Britain in ebook format
by HarperCollins*Publishers* 2021

1

A catalogue record of this book
is available from the British Library

ISBN: 978-0-00-846062-4

This novel is entirely a work of fiction.
The names, characters and incidents portrayed in it are
the work of the author's imagination. Any resemblance to
actual persons, living or dead, events or localities is
entirely coincidental.

Printed and bound in Great Britain by
CPI Group (UK) Ltd, Croydon CR0 4YY

To Simon Browes
For replying to my disturbing questions with bizarre answers.
Let's hope nobody ever reads our text messages.

Chapter One

Vivian Harrison couldn't sleep. She sat up in bed, stared at the alarm clock and watched as the green figures changed from 4:22 to 4:23. She sighed. Next to her, her husband, Malcolm, was snoring gently. Why was he able to sleep when she couldn't? Bloody men.

Vivian listened intently to any sound coming from the next room. Most nights she heard muffled crying. She wanted to go in, hug him, tell him everything was going to be all right, but Malcolm told her not to. It caused her physical pain to see the torment this family was going through, hence the sleepless nights. And the indigestion. And the heartburn.

She threw back the duvet and swung her legs out of bed. It was a bitterly cold morning. She slipped her feet into her carpet slippers, grabbed her floor-length dressing gown from the bottom of the bed and wrapped it around her, tying it tightly at the waist. As she left the bedroom, she glanced back at her husband curled up in bed. He looked comfortable, warm, safe, and there was a hint of a smile on his lips. She wondered what he was dreaming about. She wondered how he could dream at all with everything going on around him.

On the landing, she walked slowly in the dark, avoiding the creaking floorboards Malcolm had promised to fix for the past fifteen years and never bothered to do anything about. Outside the spare bedroom, she stopped, placed her ear against the door and listened. There was an eerie silence. She could feel the powerful emotions emanating through the door. A whole universe was slowly dying in that room and she was impotent to do anything about it.

Since he'd moved in, Vivian's sleeping patterns had gone to hell. She managed a few hours a night, and they were fitful. Any hint of a noise and she was wide awake. She shivered in the cold and tore herself away from the door.

She tiptoed down the stairs carefully without turning on a light so as not to disturb anyone. While everything was quiet, everything was fine. Or so she believed. Once in the kitchen, she closed the door behind her and squinted as she flicked the switch and the room was lit up with a brilliant white light. She filled the kettle and turned it on. While waiting for it to boil, she leaned against the worktop and stared into space.

They'd had a lovely Christmas. Vivian had turned sixty on Christmas Eve, and what was left of her family had gathered round for a special meal cooked by Malcolm and her sister. She'd sat in the living room, surrounded by nieces and nephews and their children. Those too young to understand marvelled at the real Christmas tree and played happily with toys, huge smiles on their faces. Those who did know the recent history of the Harrison family sat awkwardly on the sofa, faces blank, not knowing what to say in case they put their foot in it.

Malcolm had presented Vivian with a diamond necklace for her birthday and the following day gave her a set of matching earrings. They were gorgeous, and she found herself smiling for the first time in months. On Boxing Day, they wrapped up warm and went for a long walk in the Peak District National Park, just the two of them. They stopped for lunch in a cosy pub and left all of their troubles at home, which, unfortunately, were still waiting for them when they returned. Vivian had gone upstairs to change, seen the door of the spare bedroom ajar, looked in and found him hanging by the neck from the light fitting. They cut him down and called for an ambulance. Malcolm performed CPR and brought him back to life just as the sirens were heard coming down the road. It was a depressing end to 2018, and it was going to be sad start to 2019.

The kettle boiled, bringing Vivian back to reality. She hadn't felt the tears roll down her cheeks but saw little splashes of them on the worktop. She wiped them away and set about making herself a strong cup of tea. She opened the cupboard above the kettle and took out a tin of biscuits. She'd overbought for Christmas, as usual, and there were plenty of snacks and treats left. It was times like these when worrying about calories and your waistline went out of the window. Chocolate was needed, and she had plenty to choose from.

———————

The kitchen door opened sometime later, and Malcolm padded in, dragging his feet along the floor.

'What are you doing up?' he asked her. 'It's still pitch-black outside.'

She looked up and saw her husband with wild grey hair,

his dressing gown half hanging off his shoulders and his eyes barely open. She giggled.

'I've never known anyone go to sleep and wake up looking like they've spent eight hours in a tumble dryer.'

He tried to neaten himself up. 'There's nothing wrong with being comfortable in your own bed. Still not sleeping?'

She shook her head. 'Would you like a cuppa?'

'I may as well, now I'm up.'

Vivian stood up and went to make another cup of tea. She'd almost finished the one she'd been drinking, so made a second cup for herself.

'I'm sorry I disturbed you.'

'You didn't.' He stifled a yawn. 'My mind must realise when you've got up and wakes me up. For some reason, I can't sleep without you next to me.'

'Ah, that's a lovely thing to say.' She turned to him and blew him a kiss.

'When you were in hospital for those three days having your shoulder done, I hardly slept a wink: tossing and turning, kicking the duvet off. I need to feel a warm body beside me.'

'You could have hired an escort,' she said with a cheeky grin on her face.

'If you'd have been away any longer, I would have done.'

She gave a throaty laugh and placed two mugs on the table. 'Then you'd have been in hospital with exhaustion.'

They sat at opposite ends of the breakfast table, Malcolm with his back to the door leading out to the hallway. Vivian watched while her husband rifled through the biscuit tin. They frequently exchanged jokey comments. They both had a dark sense of humour that only each other understood. Her smile soon faded though. Levity didn't visit this house for long.

'We can't go on like this, Malcolm,' Vivian said, her hands wrapped around the mug.

He looked up. 'I know,' he said softly.

'We need to do something.'

'Like what?'

She thought for a moment before shrugging. 'I don't know. Look, I know you said I shouldn't, but how about if I just call round this evening and have a word?'

'Vivian, no. It's got nothing to do with us. He needs to sort out his own problems.'

'But he's not doing it, is he?' Vivian said in a loud whisper. 'He spends all day in his room. He hardly eats. He never goes out. If she could just see…'

'Vivian,' Malcolm said firmly. 'It's over. His marriage is over. And the sooner he accepts that and moves on, the better it will be for all of us.'

His words echoed around the room. Vivian sat back in her chair. Her face a picture of sadness, worry and lost hope.

'It's not just his marriage, though Malcolm, it's everything else that's happened,' she said, a catch in her throat. 'He's lost his job, his home, his brot…' Her words were lost to her tears.

Malcolm jumped up and ran to her side of the table. He put his arms around her and held her tight.

'What did we do wrong, Malcolm?' she asked between sobs. 'We didn't neglect them as children. We didn't smack them or abuse them. We gave them everything they could want and look how they've turned out. One in prison and the other with a restraining order against him from his own wife.'

'None of this is our fault. We did everything right. *You* did everything right.'

'I don't know how much longer I can go on like this, Malcolm. It's making me ill.'

He kissed her on the top of her head. 'This needs to end,' he said. There was force behind his words.

He left the kitchen, opened the drawer in the cupboard in the hallway and came back with a cardboard folder in his hands. He sat back down at the table.

'I was going to save this for when things improved, but I don't think they're going to anytime soon.' He opened the folder and took out a brochure. 'I've booked us a holiday in Venice for next month,' he said, sliding it across to her.

Vivian blinked away her tears. 'What?'

'Happy early Valentine's Day.'

'But…'

'You've always wanted to go.'

'Venice? But you hate water.'

'I know.'

'You won't even cross the Channel on a ferry – you always make us go through the tunnel.'

'I'm aware,' he said, with a hint of a smile. 'However, I know you've always wanted to go, so we're going. I'll even go on a gonorrhoea with you.'

She laughed. 'Gondola.'

'That too.'

'Oh, Malcolm,' she said. Her whole face lit up. Malcolm smiled in return.

'I've got another surprise for you, as well.'

She looked up expectantly from the brochure. 'You're not pregnant, are you?'

'No, I'm on the pill,' he joked. He took out another brochure from the folder. 'I was thinking we could move house.'

Her eyes widened and her mouth opened in shock. 'Move? Why? Where to?'

'We've been through so much in the last few years. I saw this development online,' he said, pointing to the brochure. 'They're building new homes in Northumberland, near the coast. I've provisionally put our name down for a three-bedroom bungalow. They won't be built until the middle of next year, and I'll be able to take early retirement by then. I thought we could sell up here, have a fresh start. Just the two of us.'

He reached across the table and took hold of his wife's hand.

'You deserve it,' he said. '*We* deserve it.'

Vivian's face was one of surprise and amazement. 'I don't know what to say.'

'Thirty years of marriage and I've finally made you speechless. I never thought this day would come!' He laughed.

'What about…' She flicked her eyes up to the ceiling again.

'Vivian, he's thirty-four years old. He needs to take his own life by the horns and do something with it. We can't keep mollycoddling him.'

She took a deep breath. 'You're right.'

'I know I'm right. So, what do you think to this bungalow then?'

She opened the brochure and looked down at the computer-generated images of what the estate would look like.

'The main bedroom is en suite – you've always wanted an en suite,' Malcolm narrated while Vivian looked at the pictures. 'There's a decent-sized kitchen with a separate utility room. No dining room, but we won't really need one. And look at the size of the garden. You could finally have a vegetable patch.'

Vivian looked up with a huge smile on her face, which suddenly dropped.

'What is it? What's the matter? Don't you like it?'

Vivian froze. She didn't blink. She didn't move. She looked straight past her husband and out into the hallway. She started to shake. Tears rolled down her face as an expression of pure horror formed.

'Vivian?' Malcolm asked. He followed her gaze and turned around slowly. 'Jesus Christ!'

Standing in the hallway was their son, Jake. Tall and slim with an intense look on his face. His eyes were wide and staring. His arms were out straight. He was holding a handgun in both hands, which was aimed straight at his father.

'Jake, what are you doing?' Malcolm asked.

He didn't reply. He didn't move. A look of concentration was etched on his pale face.

'Jake, please,' Vivian cried.

'For goodness' sake, put the gun down. You're frightening your mother.'

Malcolm stood up and slowly approached his son.

'How did you get hold of a gun?' Vivian asked.

'Jake, I know you're going through hell right now, but we're helping you. We're doing everything we can for you. We've let you into our home and this is—'

A shot was fired. It was muffled, no louder than a sneeze. Jake's facial expression didn't change as the bullet hit Malcolm in the centre of the forehead. He fell to the floor with a heavy thud and was dead before he hit the ground.

Vivian, sitting at the table behind Malcolm, had been splattered in the face with the blood from his head. She was shaking and struck dumb with shock. She looked down and saw the dead-eyed stare of her husband looking back at her. On the table in front of her were the brochures that were signalling the start of the next chapter in their lives together. A few minutes ago she was happy, now… She looked up.

'Jake, please, no,' she pleaded.

Her son stepped forward into the kitchen, the gun aimed at his mother's chest. He fired once. The impact of the bullet caused her to fall off her chair and onto the floor.

Jake moved around and looked down at his stricken mother. She was still alive, gasping for breath, the pool of dark red blood growing bigger as it leaked into her dressing gown.

He aimed the gun at her and fired three more times.

Chapter Two

09:00 – South Yorkshire Police HQ

Detective Chief Inspector Matilda Darke was sat in Assistant Chief Constable Valerie Masterson's office. She was on her third coffee of the morning, and it still wasn't light outside yet. It was nine o'clock and the heavy clouds hanging over Sheffield were a harbinger of bad weather on the horizon. It didn't look like the cold winter sun would be penetrating it for a while.

Valerie leaned forward and switched on her desk lamp.

'I can't see a bloody thing,' she said, turning around and looking out of the large window. She rolled her eyes and turned back to the report on her desk. 'You've managed to cut overtime for the last three months in a row,' she said, surprised.

'You did ask me to.'

'I know, but you don't usually pay attention to what I say.'

'If I continue being insubordinate, you won't recommend

me for promotion in the summer,' Matilda said with a twinkle in her eye.

'I thought there was a reason behind it somewhere. So, you're itching to get into my shoes then?'

'I'll need a bigger size.'

'Nice things come in little packages,' she said. Valerie was exactly five feet tall. She was dwarfed by her huge desk and high-backed chair. She may have been small, but she had a titanic personality and commanded a magnificent presence wherever she went. 'What made you change your mind?'

Promotion for Matilda had been on the cards for a while, but she'd always ignored the idea. The last thing she wanted was to be sat behind a desk for eight hours a day, only reading about what was happening to the people of Sheffield in a report. However, recent events had forced her to change her mind.

'Me staying as a DCI is blocking other people from achieving more. Scott's passed his sergeants' exams but there's nowhere for him to go. I'd like him to stay within South Yorkshire Police as he's a bloody good detective. For him to move up, I need to move up. Besides, it would be nice to leave work at a decent hour in the evenings.'

'To spend time with Daniel?'

Matilda blushed. 'There are only so many times you can cancel a meal out before he starts looking elsewhere.'

'He's not, is he?'

'Not yet, but he's a man, he will eventually.'

Daniel Harbison was an architect who had helped make her new home habitable. He was also a close friend of her late husband's. Over the past year, they had grown closer. She hadn't wanted to enter into a relationship with another man following the death of James, but she couldn't ignore her heart, and her feelings for Daniel were growing stronger by the day.

'Sian was telling me the other day that you'd been spending more and more time together. Haven't you been away for a few weekends?' Valerie asked, coyly seeking gossip.

'One of these days I'm going to murder Sian,' Matilda replied as she reddened. 'Yes, we have been away,' she failed to hide her smile. 'Although...' She stopped herself.

'What?'

'Nothing.'

'No. Go on,' Valerie prompted.

'I think I'm starting,' she lowered her voice despite there being no one within earshot, 'the menopause.'

'Oh. What symptoms do you have?'

'Well, none really, but my periods are out of sync, and I came on this morning and it was heavier than usual.'

'Might be worth popping to see your GP.'

'I always associate menopause with getting old,' she said, deflated. 'I remember when my mum started with it – she made it sound like the end of the world. Then again, she's always been overly dramatic.'

Matilda's meetings with Valerie usually veered off to the personal side of things. They'd known each other for years and had been through a great deal together. When James died, Valerie gave Matilda all the support and time she needed before returning to work.

Valerie leaned back in her chair. 'The hot flushes were a tad embarrassing for me. I'd feel myself going bright red and the sweating ... good grief. I could feel it pouring off me. I remember once, me and Arthur...' Her face dropped. Her bottom lip trembled, and she put her head down to hide her emotions.

Matilda looked on. It was strange to see her austere boss exposing such raw feelings. 'How are things with Arthur?'

It was a while before Valerie answered. She swallowed hard a couple of times before looking up. 'No change.' She shrugged. 'We had an offer on the house at the weekend, which we accepted, and the bungalow is ready to move into. I just didn't see my life heading this way,' she said, a lump in her throat.

A year ago, Valerie was considering early retirement so she and Arthur could travel around Europe in a motorhome while they were still young enough to do so. Arthur had been retired for less than six months before he suffered two massive strokes that left him without the power of speech, movement or the ability to do anything for himself. They were now having to move from their farmhouse in Derbyshire to a generic bungalow on the outskirts of Sheffield.

'Are you still taking early retirement?' Matilda asked.

'I don't have any choice. Arthur needs round-the-clock care.' She took a deep breath and smiled painfully. 'I'll be gone by September, and I can't think of anyone I'd like to take my place more than you.' It was evident by the tears in her eyes that Valerie didn't want to leave.

'Will you be leaving your coffee machine, too?'

'You can piss off.' She laughed.

———

Matilda headed down the corridor towards the Homicide and Major Enquiry Team she oversaw. In recent months, and with a budding romance on the horizon, Matilda had started to get into shape again. She felt confident as she walked with her head high, her back straight and her shoulder-length dark brown hair flowing. She even had a smile on her face, which was something rarely seen unless she had several glasses of wine inside her and was picking plot holes in the Marvel movies with her best friend Adele.

'Ranjeet,' she called out to Detective Constable Ranjeet Deshwal, who was entering the HMET suite ahead of her. He stopped and turned around.

Tall, slim, incredibly good-looking and with a gorgeous head of shiny black hair, Ranjeet smiled and stepped towards her.

'How long is it until Kesinka's back at work?'

Kesinka Rani was Ranjeet's wife. They'd married after a whirlwind romance. She had fallen pregnant on their honeymoon and was due back from maternity leave any time now.

'Twenty-first. Two weeks yesterday.'

'Is she looking forward to it?'

'Absolutely. I think she's going stir-crazy.'

'Have you got childcare sorted?'

'Yes. My mum's looking after him three days a week and her mum the other two.'

'Excellent. How is little Hemant?'

'He's fine,' he said with a beaming smile. 'Not so little now. He's like a little rugby player, bless him.'

'Who knows, maybe you'll have a whole team at some point.'

'I'd love more. Kesinka isn't too keen. The birth was quite painful.' He winced.

'Wow. Who'd have thought squeezing an eight-pound baby through the eye of a needle would be so painful. Someone really should have mentioned it before now,' she said with a sarcastic grin on her face.

Ranjeet held the door open for her and Matilda entered.

The HMET team had shrunk slightly in the past year. The cruel death of DC Faith Easter had been a bitter blow. However, her replacement, DC Finn Cotton, had fitted in perfectly. With Kesinka off and DS Aaron Connolly no longer on the team, their number was depleted, but they were a strong team who worked well together.

DI Christian Brady was coming out of his office when he saw Matilda.

'There's a call for you,' he said.

'Oh. Who is it?'

'They wouldn't say.'

'What do they want?'

'They wouldn't say.'

'You're a mine of information, Christian.' She smiled. 'I'll take it in my office.'

'Line two,' he called out after her.

Matilda entered her small office in the corner of the suite. She closed the door behind her and picked up the phone. 'DCI Matilda Darke. Can I help you?'

'You're a survivor, aren't you, Matilda?' The voice was low and deep.

'Who is this?' She frowned.

'But what's the point of surviving, when everyone around you is dead?'

The caller hung up.

Matilda put the receiver down. She searched her memory to see if she recognised the caller's voice. She didn't. Putting it down to a crank call, she picked up her iPad and headed out into the main part of the suite where her team were waiting for her to begin the morning briefing.

Matilda cleared her throat. 'Right then, good morning,

everyone. Now, before we begin, I'd like us to take a moment to reflect on a piece of sad news I received yesterday evening.' She looked up to see a sea of concerned faces looking at her. 'As some of you may already know, PC Natasha Tranter has accepted DC Rory Fleming's offer of marriage, and I think we should all offer our deepest commiserations to her at this difficult time.' She couldn't hide her smile any further.

Cheers and hollers were heard around the room as those who didn't know stepped forward to shake Rory by the hand, ruffle his hair, and slap him on the back.

Matilda had never seen Rory blush before. It made her smile even more.

'Seriously though, congratulations, Rory. I hope you'll both be very happy together.'

'Thank you, ma'am,' he said, running his fingers through his curly dark hair.

'Bloody hell, Rory Fleming settling down,' Christian said, a beaming smile on his face. 'And they say miracles don't happen.'

'Single women all over Sheffield will be calling the Samaritans,' Sian said, kissing him on the cheek. 'Congratulations, Rory.'

'Yes, well done, mate,' Ranjeet said, slapping him on the back. 'Don't blow it.'

'Now, let's get down to business, shall we?' Matilda said once she'd basked in the glow of Rory's embarrassment. 'Sian, you've been conducting weekly meetings with the street workers. How are things?'

DS Sian Mills reached for a folder in her in-tray. 'It's all been quiet recently. There's nothing new to report. Bev was saying no other prostitutes have gone missing. It looks like the killer has gone to ground or moved on.'

In the past four years, six prostitutes had gone missing from Sheffield. One had been found murdered. Matilda was working alongside the women to help them feel safe on the streets while also trying to find the killer of Denise, and the whereabouts of the other missing women. So far, they'd hit a brick wall.

'Let's hope so,' Matilda said. 'Have you been in touch with other forces to see if they've had any go missing?'

'Me and Finn are working on that.'

'I've been concentrating on neighbouring forces and moving out,' Finn said as he flicked through his iPad, 'but I've found nothing locally.'

'Good. Now—' She stopped as the sound of the fire alarm broke out.

All eyes turned back to Sian, who was the team's fire marshal.

'I haven't been told about any test today,' she shouted above the alarm.

'Ok,' Matilda said. 'We all know the drill. Over to you, Sian.'

Sian had already reached into the bottom drawer of her desk and taken out her fire marshal's high-visibility jacket. 'Ok, people, leave quietly and calmly. Make your way down the stairs on the left-hand side and go to the nearest fire point,' she said as she put the jacket on and picked up her clipboard.

'Where is the nearest fire point?' Rory asked.

'I knew you weren't paying attention. Back of the car park. There's a very clear sign you pass every morning. Take nothing with you,' she called out to the rest of the team, competing with the noise from the alarm. 'Put your laptop down, Scott. Just leave the building.'

Matilda and Sian were the last to leave the suite. As she did

so, Matilda took one last, lingering look at the office to make
sure no one was left behind before turning away and heading
down the stairs.

―――――――――

In an orderly fashion, uniform and plain-clothed detectives
and civilian staff made their way out of the building and into
the damp winter air. All teams had to remain together for the
heads of each department to make a roll call.

'I hope the place doesn't go up,' ACC Masterson said to
Matilda in passing. 'I haven't had my new Gaggia a month
yet.'

'I bet you'll let me have it if it's fire-damaged.'

'If I get back to the office and I see it's been tampered with,
you're in trouble, my girl.' She pointed up at her with a wicked
smile on her face.

'I'm surprised you didn't bring it out with you.'

'The plug's behind the filing cabinet. I can't move it on my
own. And I know what Sian's like when she's in official mode.
She scares even me.'

They both laughed as they watched Sian directing everyone
to where they should be. She was in her element.

The building emptied and everyone stood back and looked
up. There was no smoke, no flames, no smell of anything
burning.

Rory searched the crowd and his eyes fell on his fiancée.
She held up her left hand and pointed to the ring. It was the
first time she'd worn it to work. Now everybody knew they
were engaged. He grinned at her and she blew him a kiss.

'Everyone knows now,' DC Scott Andrews said to Rory, his
best friend. 'No backing out.'

'I've no intention of backing out,' he said. 'Best decision I've ever made.'

'Any idea who your best man might be?' he asked, hopping from one foot to the other to keep warm.

'I was thinking of asking Christian,' he said with a sly grin.

'You better bloody not, Rory Fleming.'

'I was joking. Of course it's going to be you, you knobhead.'

They hugged.

'Great!' Scott smiled. 'I'll start working on my speech. I've got some embarrassing stories to tell about you.'

'I don't get embarrassed.'

'That's true. You've no shame whatsoever. We need to start thinking about a stag weekend. I've heard Dublin is great,' Scott said, his eyes lighting up. 'We could get a minimum of say ten people, get the ferry across and—'

There was a scream. Both turned around and saw a group of uniformed officers standing around someone on the ground.

'Rory!' Natasha shouted. She was squatting down, looming over a uniformed officer lying on the wet concrete. Her face was one of worry. She held up her hands to show Rory. They were red.

'What's going on?' Scott asked.

'I've no idea,' Rory frowned as he headed for his fiancée. He started in a walk before speeding up. He was almost at her when her whole body jerked. She seemed to have been hit by something. She fell to her knees and then to the ground.

'Natasha!' Rory cried as he raced to her.

'She's been shot,' someone shouted.

'What the fuck's going on?' another called.

'Someone's shooting at us.'

'It's a set-up.'

'Everyone, back inside the building. Right now,' Valerie shouted.

Pandemonium set in as, in a hail of bullets, officers and staff ran back towards the building. Glass in the windows shattered and bodies fell to the ground as people were hit. Screams rang out around the car park as everyone pushed and shoved to get to safety.

Rory was knocked in every direction as people headed for the building. He couldn't move. He remained, stricken, rooted in place as he looked down at the lifeless body of the woman he loved.

'Natasha?' he asked quietly.

Her eyes were open and lifeless. A pool of blood began to grow around her.

Rory sank to his knees. He carefully lifted her up and cradled her.

Sian froze. She held her clipboard to her chest and looked on in horror as her colleagues fled back to the safety of the police station. She watched as they started to fall. Tears pricked her eyes. She was powerless. She had no idea what was going on and fear took over.

'Sian, come on, we have to go back inside,' Ranjeet said. He grabbed her by the shoulder and pulled at her, but she wouldn't move. 'Sian come on. We can't stay out here.'

She looked at him with confusion. Horror was etched on his face. 'What's happening?' she asked, visibly shaking.

'I don't know. But we have to—' He didn't finish his sentence. A bullet hit him in the head, spraying Sian with his blood, brain matter and fragments of bone. He dropped to the floor at her feet. She opened her mouth and screamed.

Christian Brady ran towards her. There was blood on his white shirt and spatter on his face. He looked petrified. He grabbed her and pushed her towards the building.

Sian started running. She dropped the clipboard and tripped over it. She landed on the cold, wet ground, banging her head on the concrete. She heard the sound of more gunshots raining down on them. Something landed on her, pinning her to the ground. She screamed and scrambled to try to get up but couldn't.

She turned her head to look behind her. A body had fallen on top of her as it had been hit, trapping her.

'Oh my God!' she cried. She struggled under the dead weight to get free. As she pushed it off her, the body rolled over, and she saw it was that of her boss, ACC Valerie Masterson, looking at her with dead eyes.

'Valerie?' Sian reached out. Her hands were covered in blood. She held her by the shoulders and began shaking her. 'Valerie? No. No. Valerie, come on.'

Christian grabbed Sian and pulled her up. 'Sian, come on. We have to get inside.'

'That was Valerie. They shot Valerie. Did you see her?' She screamed hysterically.

'Just move.'

They ran for the building as another bullet flew past them, shattering a window.

Finn was at the door to the station. He held it open and practically pulled Christian and Sian inside.

'What the hell is going on?' Sian could barely talk through the tears. Her whole body was shaking.

'Are you all right? Are you hit?' Finn asked.

'No. I'm fine.' She looked down and saw all the blood on her clothing. 'It's not mine.'

Once inside the building, they stood back from the window and looked out at the car park. Bodies were strewn about where they'd fallen.

Sian looked around her. She took in Finn's wide-eyed disbelief, Scott's look of horror and Christian's blood-spattered face.

'Where's Rory? Where's Matilda?' she asked, panicked. She turned and looked out of the window. 'Oh my God, Rory's still out there,' she said as tears fell down her face. She placed a bloody hand on the glass and banged on it hard, shouting Rory's name.

'Sian, get back.'

A bullet shattered the window. Everyone screamed. Christian grabbed Sian and pulled her to the floor as they were all hit with shards of broken glass.

'Is everyone all right?' Christian called out.

Outside, Rory was cradling the dead body of the woman he planned to marry. He was rocking back and forward, crying loudly.

'I'm going back out there,' Scott said, standing up.

'Don't be stupid,' Christian said. 'You could get yourself killed.'

'Look how many we've lost. I'm not losing Rory.'

'Scott, don't!'

He ignored his superior officer's advice, opened the door and stepped out into the dull-grey morning.

The shooting seemed to have stopped. A heavy silence descended. Those who were able to had made their way back into the building. Scott looked down at the dead; bodies strewn about the car park and rivers of blood flowing. He looked back at the building, saw the broken windows, bullet holes in doors, blood splashed against the brickwork.

In the quiet, Rory could be heard talking to Natasha.

'You're going to be all right. The ambulance will be here any minute.' He was stroking her blood-matted hair. 'They'll make you better. You'll be all right. I know it.' Tears were streaming down his face.

He saw the ACC and Ranjeet and others he recognised but didn't know the names of. He was headed for Rory when he saw Matilda Darke standing still, looking up.

'Ma'am,' he said quietly. 'Ma'am, are you all right?'

'It's him.'

'What?'

'I know him.'

'Know who?' Scott followed his boss's gaze and looked up at the gunman on a building high up behind the station. 'Shit. Ma'am, we need to get back inside.'

'*What's the point in surviving when everyone around you is dead,*' she said calmly.

'What?'

'That's what he said to me.'

'Who is he?'

Matilda didn't break eye contact with the gunman. She didn't move despite Scott telling her to get back inside for her own safety.

The gunman squeezed the trigger. The first bullet hit Matilda Darke in the left shoulder. She staggered backwards. Scott ducked out of the way. Another shot rang out, and the second bullet took off the back of Matilda's head.

Chapter Three

A t Stannington Secondary School on Greaves Lane, the day was just beginning. The teenagers were filing into the building with their usual strolling gait, while the teachers were downing their coffees and preparing their lessons.

Chris Kean was tall and athletically built. He was handsome and many of the female students had a crush on him. They were barking up the wrong tree. He was in a committed relationship with Detective Constable Scott Andrews and living in a beautifully created two-bedroom apartment above the garage belonging to DCI Matilda Darke.

He entered the staffroom already looking harassed, and the day hadn't even properly begun.

'Graham isn't coming in again,' he said, slumping on the seat next to his colleague and good friend Ruth.

'Why not?' she replied

'Apparently he's still not up to it. What's that even

supposed to mean? I often wake up not feeling "up to it", but I still come in.'

'I'm guessing you're covering his classes today?'

'Yes. I was supposed to have two free periods today to get started on those mock exams. Bloody man. Why doesn't he just retire?'

'Graham Pinkerton is one of the most dedicated and professional teachers I have ever worked with,' Pauline Butters, the head of geography, chimed in. 'I will not hear a word said against him. You'd do well to take a leaf out of his book, Mr Kean. You've not been here five minutes – don't make any enemies.' She gave him a lingering glare before marching out of the room.

'That told me.'

'She's probably going to fill up the inkwells,' Ruth said with a smirk.

'They're dinosaurs, both of them,' Chris said. He took a deep breath. 'So, how are you?'

'I'm fine. Why?'

'No reason,' he said with a hint of a smile.

'Why do I get the feeling you're wanting to ask me something?'

'I was just wondering why you didn't return my calls last night.'

She turned to look at him with a steely glare. 'I had an early night.'

'Oh yes. Who with?'

She tried to hide her smirk, but it was difficult when Chris was in full teasing mode. 'I'm really sorry to disappoint you, Chris, but last night, I was alone. I had a headache, so turned my phone off and went to bed.'

'Oh,' his smile dropped. 'So, you didn't see Ryan then?'

'No.'

'Will you be seeing Ryan again any time soon?'

'What's the fixation you have with wanting me and Ryan to hook up?'

'It's not a fixation. I just want you to be happy.'

'Chris, I hate to break it to you, but a woman can be perfectly happy without having a man in her life.'

'A woman's happiness is predicated on *not* having a man in her life,' Julia Simms said as she passed them with a mug of strong coffee in one hand and a bacon sandwich in the other.

'See,' Ruth said.

'She's still bitter about her divorce. Don't listen to her. Not all men have secret other families—'

'Do I look all right?' Fiona Mayhew interrupted, turning from the mirror she'd been glaring into for the past ten minutes.

'You look lovely, why?' Ruth asked.

'My bloody hair's growing back in clumps. It's thick at the back and thin on top. I don't really want to go back to wearing a wig,' she said. There was a sad expression on her face. She'd only been back at work for two months following an intense course of chemotherapy to burn away the cancer in her stomach. She had lost weight and her hair, which gave her serious confidence issues, especially when faced with spiteful teenagers on a daily basis.

'I think you're gorgeous,' Ruth said. 'You've got colour in your cheeks and give it another two weeks and your hair will be thick and lush all over. You should definitely keep it short though – it shows off your cheekbones.'

'Do you think?' she asked with a rueful smile.

'Definitely.'

'Chris?' Fiona sought a man's opinion.

'I've always thought you were a very beautiful woman. And you still are,' he said with earnest.

'Ah, Chris, that's really sweet,' Fiona said, blushing.

'Why are you never that considerate with me?' Ruth asked.

'I am.'

'At the school Christmas party you said I looked like a glittery hooker.'

'No offence, Ruth, but you did,' Fiona said. She picked up her bag from the table. 'Must dash. Thanks for what you said, Chris.'

'I could go off her,' Ruth said playfully.

'Now, back to what we were talking about.' Chris grinned. 'You and Ryan—'

'Look, Chris,' she interrupted. 'Ryan is a lovely bloke. I like him a lot, but the last thing I need right now is another relationship. We've met a few times, we've had a few drinks, let's just leave it at that, shall we?'

'If you say so,' Chris said, sitting back and folding his arms.

'I do. Now, if you'll excuse me, I have algebra to teach to some kids who don't want to learn it and will never use it a day in their adult life.' She stood up and smiled and began to walk to the door, but turned back and leaned over Chris's shoulder and whispered in his ear. 'I'll tell you one thing; Ryan is a bloody animal in bed.' She kissed him on the cheek and headed back for the door.

Chris turned around, a huge grin on his face as Ruth turned back, winked, and left the room.

'I knew it,' he said to himself.

'Mr Kean, your class of year nines are waiting for you,' Pauline Butters called from the doorway.

'Thank you very much, Graham,' he said under his breath.

As he left the room, Chris took out his phone and sent a text to Scott:

Graham hasn't come in again. I'll be late home. Love you, xx.

Chief Constable Martin Featherstone didn't have any appointments until ten-thirty, so had decided to have a lie-in and a leisurely breakfast. After, he took his time in the shower and was wearing only his underwear and socks and was sat on the edge of the bed, buttoning up his white shirt, when his wife, Roisin, walked unsteadily into their bedroom. She stood in the doorway, leaning on her walking stick and slightly out of breath. When she saw her husband, she smiled.

'Is it wrong that I find you sexy dressed like that?' she asked, looking at him with her head tilted to one side.

'Not at all.' He smiled. 'I find you sexy when you're dressed in your paint-splattered decorating clothes.'

'You've never said before.'

'I thought you might think I had some kind of weird fetish.'

'My fetish is for men in white boxers and black socks showing off their sexy hairy legs,' she said as she sidled up to him and rubbed his thighs. She leaned down and kissed him passionately on the lips.

'I hope you're going to be like this when we're in the Lake District in exactly thirteen days' time.' He grinned.

'Will you be bringing your black socks?' she asked, looking him straight in the eye.

'Kinky.' He smiled.

They both laughed.

Martin stood up and reached for his trousers. He was fifty-one years old but looked younger. He had a full head of dark brown hair, a hint of grey on the sideburns, and no signs of any wrinkles, just a few lines around his eyes when he smiled. He was handsome and cut a fine figure as he stood in his uniform at six foot three.

Born and bred in Taunton in Somerset, he'd lived in Sheffield for the past twenty years yet still couldn't shake the West Country accent. He'd been chief constable of South Yorkshire Police for the last five years and enjoyed being in charge of such a huge force.

'What are your plans for the day?' he asked his wife as he looked into the floor-length mirror and tied his tie.

'Lunch with Diane at one, hospital for more physio this afternoon. That's about it,' she said forlornly.

'Are you ok?' He looked through the mirror at Roisin's reflection. She was sitting on the bed, her head down.

She shrugged her shoulders. 'I'm tired of being in so much pain. I'm so bloody bored. I want to go back to work, and I hate having to carry this sodding stick around with me wherever I go.'

Nine months ago, Roisin had been walking back to her car following an intense swimming session at Pond's Forge when she was jumped by a masked man and mugged. Thinking back, if she'd allowed him to steal her bag, she would have got away with a few grazes and bruises from hitting the ground, but she hadn't. She fought back and held on to her bag as if it contained her life's savings. The mugger punched her in the face. She fell to the floor but still gripped her bag by the handles. Her attacker kicked her several times in the stomach before taking to stamping on her leg. She screamed as she heard the bones breaking. Even when she relinquished the hold on her bag, the attack continued.

Roisin was in hospital for six weeks while the bones in her leg had to be reset and her knee reconstructed. She had to learn to walk all over again. Recovery was slow and frustrating, and as a trained physiotherapist herself, she made a terrible patient.

'I thought Diane said you could go back into work on a part-time basis and do some paperwork.'

'She did. That's what this lunch is all about. It's just… Paperwork, really? Can you see me sitting behind a desk, filling out sodding forms and making appointments?'

'It'll get you out of the house.'

Martin's mobile started ringing.

'I suppose it'll keep my brain ticking over – I'm sure it's disintegrating,' she said with a hint of a smile. 'I've started enjoying *Homes Under the Hammer,* for crying out loud.'

'Featherstone,' Martin said, answering his phone. He listened and his eyes widened in shock. His face paled and his mouth opened. 'I'll … I'll be right there,' he muttered before ending the call.

'What is it?' Roisin said, sitting up.

'There's been a shooting at HQ.'

'A shooting? Oh my God. Is everyone all right?'

'Valerie's been killed.'

'Oh no,' she said, slapping a hand against her chest.

'I need to go.'

Roisin struggled to get up from the bed and limped over to her husband. She held him by the arms and looked up into his eyes. 'Promise me you'll not do anything silly? I want you back here alive tonight. Promise me, Martin.' Her voice was shaking and full of urgency.

He leaned down and kissed her on the forehead. 'I promise.'

He left the bedroom without turning back.

Roisin sat back down on the bed and started to cry.

Chapter Four

A paramedic on a motorbike was on the scene within four minutes of the 999 call being made. Matilda had lost a great deal of blood, and as much as Scott tried to put his first-aid training into action, Matilda was flailing her arms around to get him off her. Shock had set in. The paramedic calmly took charge. He turned her onto her side, intubated her and stabilised her breathing as he barked orders to Scott to apply pressure on the open wound at the back of her head. Once Matilda was calm, he stepped in and Scott was able to stand back.

He looked down at his stricken boss. He could see her skull. He looked her up and down. Her clothes were covered in blood. There was so much of it.

'Is she...?' he asked quietly.

The paramedic didn't hear him. An ambulance crew ran into the car park and dropped to the floor to help their colleague. They spoke in a medical language Scott had no understanding of. It could have been Klingon for all he knew.

'Scott.' He turned as the mention of his name and the

slightest pressure on his arm. 'Scott, come on, let's get you inside,' Sian said.

He looked at her with wide-eyed bewilderment. 'She was shot.'

'I know.'

'Her head. It just...'

'I know, Scott. Come on, let's get out of the way.'

'I...' He turned to look at the building looming high over the car park where the gunman had shot from. There was nobody there.

He turned back and saw Matilda being carefully placed on a trolley and wheeled away towards an ambulance. Where she'd lain, a massive pool of blood trickled along the cracks of the tarmac. He waited until the ambulance doors were closed before he started to move away. He wondered if it would be the last time he'd see his boss and landlady.

———————

DI Christian Brady was in his office with the door closed. He'd been in the changing room and washed the blood off his face and put on a new shirt. With shaking fingers, he'd done up the buttons and ploughed towards his office with his head down, not wanting to make eye contact with anyone. The first thing he did was call his wife. His voice was shaking as he told her of the horror of what had just happened, and she'd burst into floods of tears, demanding he come home. If only he had that option. She made him promise to stay safe and keep in touch.

He'd had a brief chat with the Chief Constable, who'd put him in charge until he could get there. The Armed Response Unit had been dispatched, and the hunt was on for the gunman. Out of the window, he could see members of the

HMET looking sombre and forlorn. Matilda would have known what to do in a situation like this to rally the troops. He shook his head. He couldn't believe what he'd witnessed out there in the car park. Matilda had just stood there, frozen in fear. That wasn't like her at all. She didn't make an attempt to run for safety. Why? Was she putting herself in harm's way to save her team?

He closed his eyes tight and saw again the image of her being hit in the head by the bullet. She dropped to the ground like a stone and didn't move. Scott selflessly threw himself towards her and tried to stem the flow of blood, but there didn't seem to be anything he could do. She was unconscious and unresponsive when she was put into the back of the ambulance and driven away at speed. He wondered what was happening to her now. Oh God, he hoped she was all right.

He opened his eyes, took a deep, but shaking, breath and channelled his inner Matilda Darke. He needed to be the strong one now. He needed to lead this team into hunting for the gunman who had killed so many of their own. This was going to be a long day.

———————

Christian entered the HMET suite from his office. The atmosphere was heavy and sombre. Sian was sat at her desk, head down, tears streaming down her face. He went over to her and squatted beside her desk.

'I can't seem to stop crying,' she said, wiping her eyes with a saturated tissue. 'Poor Ranjeet. He's only just got married and become a father for God's sake. How's Kesinka going to cope? He stopped to save me. If he hadn't... If he'd carried on running, he'd have made it back.' She wiped her eyes again, rubbing them red.

'Sian, you can't blame yourself. Any one of us could have been hit out there.'

'I froze. I just … I couldn't move.'

'Sian, don't.'

'And Valerie. How's her husband going to cope now? And Matilda. Did you see what happened to her head?'

'Sian, look at me,' he said firmly. 'We have to be strong. I need you by my side to help. I can't do this on my own.'

'Where's Rory? He was so happy this morning.'

'Sian!' He grabbed her by the shoulders and shook her. 'Sian, you need to get a grip. You're not going to be any use to anyone if you're just going to sit here crying. I need you to focus.'

She wiped her eyes again, ran her fingers through her red hair and sniffled. She blew her nose and composed herself.

'You're right. I'm sorry.'

'No, I'm sorry. I shouldn't have snapped at you like that. Have you called Stuart?'

'Yes. I've told him what's happened. He's coming here to bring me a change of clothes,' she said, looking down at herself. She was still wearing her fire marshal's jacket over her white jumper, both of which were covered in blood.

'Good. Now, the Chief Constable is on his way in. He's going to be Gold Command and I'll be Silver. I really need your help, Sian. I've never been involved in anything like this before.'

'Neither have I. Normally, the ACC would be Gold and Matilda Silver. You and I would be Bronze.'

'Forensics are downstairs, and they've accessed the building where the gunman was shooting from. CID are trawling CCTV footage to see if we can pick him up. The first thing we need to do is identify the dead and inform next of kin.'

'Right,' she said, rubbing her eyes again. 'I'll get Finn on to that.'

'We're also going to need statements from everyone. Hopefully someone saw who was shooting at us. Are you going to be all right?'

'No. But I can fake it until I can get home.'

'That's what I plan on doing.'

_____

In the men's changing room, Rory Fleming was sat on a bench in complete shock. He had no idea where he was. His mind was trying to make sense of what had happened. He was happy. He was engaged. He was in love. Now he was covered in blood and his fiancée was dead. How did that happen in the space of a few minutes? Scott was filling a sink with warm water and dampening a flannel.

'Is he all right?'

Scott jumped at the sound of the voice. He hadn't realised there was someone else in the room with them.

PC Rix was standing in front of a row of sinks. His eyes were wide. He had the look of fear etched on his face.

'No, he's not,' Scott answered honestly.

The uniformed officer swallowed hard. 'Is there anything I can do?'

'Can you leave us for a few minutes? Make sure no one comes in?'

He nodded and headed for the door, not taking his eyes from Rory.

Scott had taken off his clothes. The suit was ruined. He'd been splattered with the blood of his colleagues. He was currently wearing a forensic suit until he could find time to go home and change into a replacement. But his first priority was Rory. With a facecloth, Scott was wiping his friend's face to clean it of blood spatter. Rory didn't react as Scott ran the wet towel over his cheek and along his forehead. It was clear he didn't feel anything.

'Rory, you need to take your jacket and shirt off,' Scott said, quietly. 'Rory, can you hear me?'

'Huh?' He looked up to his best friend.

'Your shirt. It's covered, mate. You need to take it off.'

He looked down as if seeing it for the first time. 'Oh. Right. Yes.' He shrugged his jacket off and began to slowly undo the buttons. 'Do you think she'll be all right?'

'Matilda? I'm not sure. I hope so.'

'No, Natasha. Do you think she'll be all right?'

Rory's face was blank. His eyes were wide and stared straight into Scott's.

'Natasha?'

'Yes. I mean, they'll look after her at the hospital, won't they? But she'll be all right. When do you think I'll be able to visit? Do you think Matilda will let me take this afternoon off?' He started to shake, as if he was cold.

Tears pricked Scott's eyes. He squatted down to his knees and held Rory by the shoulders. His paper suit crinkled. He could feel Rory's shaking body. 'Rory, Natasha was shot,' he said slowly and clearly.

'Yes.'

'She died, Rory.'

'She...?' A tear escaped his left eye and fell down his cheek.

Scott nodded.

'But we're getting married. I gave her a ring. She wants to get married in August.'

'I'm so sorry.'

'She died?' Rory asked, his face frowned in confusion.

Scott's tears began to fall, and his bottom lip wobbled. He was trying to hold on to his emotions for the sake of his best friend, but it wasn't easy.

'What do I do now?' Rory asked eventually.

Scott took a deep breath. He held his friend firmly by the shoulders. 'We find the bastard who did this. We tear this city apart, and we don't rest until we've got the fucker locked up.'

Rory nodded slowly. It was a while before he spoke as Scott's words slowly began to take meaning. 'You're right. I can grieve when we've caught him.'

'Exactly.'

'And when I catch him, Scott, I swear to God, I'm going to kill him with my bare hands,' he said with steely determination in his eyes.

Chapter Five

'DI Brady, isn't it? CC Martin Featherstone said as he entered the building.

'Yes, sir,' Christian responded.

'Walk and talk,' he said, heading for the stairs. 'What's the latest?'

'We have six confirmed dead so far, including ACC Masterson. Eight are at hospital with injuries, none of them life-threatening, except for DCI Darke.'

'How is she?' he asked, his face showing concern, but his voice was professionally strong.

'It's too early to tell.' Christian's reply was full of emotion.

They walked with urgent strides. Christian was not a short man, but even he found himself having to break into a trot to keep up with the Chief Constable.

'And the gunman?'

'Nothing.'

'Nothing?' He stopped and looked at Brady.

'We don't know who he is. Hopefully, he left something

behind on the roof he was shooting from. Forensics are up there now, and we're looking through CCTV footage.'

'Is this a terrorist attack? Have we received any phone calls?'

'Not that I'm aware of. I've got someone contacting other forces to see if they've had any incidents today, but so far, there have been none.'

'Have the media been in touch?'

'No. It's only a matter of time, though.'

'Ok. I'll deal with that.'

As they walked towards Valerie's office, they passed police officers and civilian staff, most of whom looked shocked by the events of this morning. The whole atmosphere of the station had changed. Everyone who worked here knew at least one of the dead. No one would fully recover from this.

'Do we know if this was directed at any one individual or the force as a whole?' Martin Featherstone continued.

'We don't know at the moment, sir,' Christian said, feeling more and more dejected with every negative answer he had to give.

'And the fire alarm was a hoax?'

'We assume so.'

'I'm not hearing any firm answers from you, Brady.' He stopped and turned again so he could look Christian in the eye.

'I'm sorry, sir. It's very early days, and we've lost a lot of officers. We're doing all we can with the resources we have.'

Featherstone took a breath. 'Of course. You're right. I'm sorry. Look, get your best people working on this. Keep me in the loop, and I'll handle the media and try to get more officers attached to this. Anything you need, let me know.'

'I will, sir. Thank you.'

Christian watched as the Chief Constable turned a corner. He then blew out his cheeks and turned on his heels to head back to his office. This was a nightmare scenario that even DCI Darke would struggle with. How the hell was he supposed to cope?

———

'Where is everyone?' Christian asked as he entered the HMET suite.

Sian was on her mobile. Judging by her body language and her hushed tones she was obviously making a private phone call. DC Scott Andrews was by the kettle, making a round of teas. It was clear even from the doorway that his hands were shaking.

Scott looked up. 'Erm, I don't know,' he said, his voice full of emotion. 'Rory's getting changed. Finn is around somewhere. I'm sorry.'

'Scott, are you all right?'

'No. I'm not,' he answered honestly. 'I've just seen my best friend's fiancée get murdered and while wiping her blood off his face, I had to tell him to try to be strong. And I have no idea what that even means. How do you remain strong when the people you care about the most are being shot at?'

Sian had ended her call. She stood up and went over to Scott, putting her arms around him.

'It's ok, Scott. What you said to Rory was the right thing. It may have sounded like bollocks to you, but it's what he needed to hear. It wasn't the words; it was the sentiment. You'll be there for him. We'll all be there for him.'

Scott held Sian in return. He leaned his head down on her

shoulder and began to sob. 'I saw Matilda's head… How's she going to survive that?'

Christian watched on. He'd never seen either of these two officers cry before or show their feelings to such an extent. It was hard to witness, yet it's what they needed to do in order to release some pent-up emotion to be able to continue working. He hadn't cried yet. He was sad, naturally, and when he called his wife from the station toilets to tell her what had happened, he'd choked on his words, but the tears wouldn't come. He felt angry rather than upset.

'Scott, why don't you take a step back for five minutes; go home and get changed,' Sian said.

'I can't even do that as the building's in lockdown. I'm not allowed to leave.'

Christian looked out of the glass door to make sure no one was about to enter. 'Look, you two, I really need you to help me out here. I've no idea how to lead this investigation. Until we get CCTV and anything from forensics, we're going to have to rely on the public phoning in, saying they've seen someone with a gun. I need your support. Please.'

Sian and Scott pulled apart. They both nodded.

Scott wiped his eyes. 'Matilda said something before she was shot. She was looking up at the gunman. I mean, she was really glaring at him. She said she knew him.'

'What? Did she say who it was?' Sian asked.

'No. All she said was that he'd called her.'

'He'd called her?' Christian echoed.

'Yes.'

'When?'

'I don't know.'

'She had a phone call when she came in this morning,' Christian said. 'She went into her office to take it. She wasn't in there more than a couple of seconds before she came out. She looked … I don't know, sort of pale.'

'Did she say anything?'

'No.'

'You think she might have been threatened or something?' Sian asked.

'She could have been.'

'But then why didn't she tell us?'

He shrugged. 'Maybe she didn't think it was a credible threat.'

'But it must have sounded credible because less than five minutes later we were all getting shot at,' Scott said.

Christian perched on the edge of Sian's desk. 'Scott, when Matilda was looking at the gunman, did you see him?'

'Not clearly. I was only really looking at the gun.'

'Do you know what kind it was?' Sian asked.

He thought for a moment. 'It looked like something Armed Response use.'

'A rifle?'

'I think so. He had it on like a tripod thing at the front. He was squatting behind it, looking through the viewing bit.'

'Sounds like a Heckler and Koch,' Christian said to Sian.

'Scott, think back,' Sian said. 'Can you remember anything about the gunman?'

'No. He was wearing a hat, a beanie. It was black, and he was wearing dark clothing, but I don't think he had a jacket on, as he looked slim, like he wasn't padded or anything.'

'Did he look young or old?'

Scott frowned as he thought. 'I'd say … young, I think. The way he moved though—'

'What do you mean?' Christian interrupted.

'When he shot Matilda, he moved very quickly away from the edge of the building, as if … I'm not sure.'

'Go on.'

'It was as if he knew exactly what he was doing. The way he put the gun away and dismantled everything, it was like it was second nature to him.'

'Like a professional?' Christian asked.

Scott nodded.

'Fuck me! We've got a sniper loose on the streets of Sheffield.'

'What does that mean?' Scott asked.

'It means he's not finished.'

Chapter Six

The paramedic alerted the Northern General Hospital from the back of the ambulance that they were bringing in a major trauma. He monitored Matilda's output and made sure she remained stable as they sped through the busy streets of Sheffield. He wasn't worried about the wound to the shoulder as, despite there being no exit wound, the bullet hadn't seemed to have hit any bone or major artery. The wound to Matilda's head required urgent attention. The skull had been fractured and if any fragments were lodged in her brain, it could drastically cut her chance of survival.

When the ambulance arrived, the team was waiting, and Matilda was wheeled directly into Resuscitation where the paramedic gave the handover to the team who would work to save her life.

'Forty-four-year-old Matilda Darke; a detective chief inspector with South Yorkshire Police. Time of incident was around nine this morning. Two GSWs. One to the left shoulder. No exit wound. Bleeding controlled. One, a glancing bullet wound to the left-hand side of the head. Depressed skull fracture. Pulse one-ten, tubed and ventilated. Oxygen ninety-seven per cent. BP maintained at over fifty. GCS on arrival was eleven, eyes three, motor four, verbal four. She was combative and disorientated and had to be restrained and sedated. Pupils fixed and dilated: left four millimetres, right three millimetres. Responsive.'

'Thank you. On my mark. One, two, three, lift.'

Matilda was transferred from the trolley to the bed where the medical team in Resus began to cut her out of her clothes and monitor her vital signs to make sure she was stable. Once the bleeding from her head was under control, the first task was for Matilda to have a CT scan to see the extent of the damage on her head and to the brain. A surgical team, including a neurologist, and an operating theatre were all on standby. They were all against the clock to save Matilda's life, and time was running out.

Chapter Seven

C laire Alexander rushed into the autopsy suite.
        'She's coming,' she said excitedly.

Home Office Pathologist Adele Kean stopped what she was doing and ran into her office. From the bottom drawer of her filing cabinet, she carefully lifted out a large box. By the time she'd removed the lid and carried it through to the main suite, her anatomical assistant, Lucy Dauman, had entered.

Adele burst into a rendition of 'Happy Birthday' with Claire joining in. Neither of them could hold a note and the noise resounded off the pure white walls, but the sentiment was genuine.

Lucy blushed and tucked her long blonde hair behind her ears. She couldn't stop grinning and didn't know where to look as she was serenaded.

Adele placed the box on a stainless steel table in front of them. Inside was a cake she'd had made by a baker she knew out in Dronfield. The cake was in the shape of a body on a slab. There were realistic-looking silver instruments along the side and a perfectly accurate Y-incision drawn down the naked body. It was ghoulish and in slightly poor taste, but it was made of cake, so that made it all right.

Lucy couldn't help but laugh. 'Oh my God, that is horrifying,' she said.

'I gave the cake maker an old photograph I found of a man on a slab. I asked if she could do something like that. I must say, I wasn't expecting her to be so graphic,' Adele said.

'That is truly gross. I love it. Thank you so much.'

'You're welcome. Happy thirtieth birthday, sweetheart,' Adele said, stepping forward and giving her a hug and kiss on the cheek. 'You'll get your present later. There's also a bottle of something very nice chilling somewhere very inappropriate that we'll have with lunch.'

'I really think you should see someone, Adele,' Claire said. 'You're getting more disturbed.'

'It's healthy to have a sense of humour in this job. Isn't it, Lucy?'

'Oh my God, if you look under his towel you can even see his...' Lucy said, taking a closer interest in the cake.

'Yes, we've noticed,' Claire said. 'I think we should keep an eye on that baker – she seems to have enjoyed herself far too much making it.'

'She did say it was rare to get such a project. When she does, apparently she likes to go that extra mile. I suppose it makes a nice change from knocking up a Victoria sponge.'

The phone in Adele's office started to ring.

'I'll get it,' Claire said.

'So, remind me, what's it like being thirty?' Adele asked.

'Well, I woke up this morning feeling fine until I opened Ben's presents. He got me a woolly cardigan, a set of knitting needles, a pair of comfortable slippers and the DVD box set of *Hetty Wainthropp Investigates*.'

'Oh. I'm guessing he's now in one of the freezers,' Adele said as she smiled.

'He said it was just a jokey present, and he'll give me my real one tonight. He's a sod. I'll have to think of something to do for when he turns thirty in September. The problem is,' she said, tucking her hair behind her ear again. 'Is it wrong that I liked the cardigan?'

Adele threw her head back and laughed.

'Adele,' Claire called out from the doorway of her office.

They both turned and saw the look of fear on her face.

'What is it?'

'There's been a shooting at the police station.'

Adele worked a great deal with all departments and staff within the building at South Yorkshire Police HQ and knew the majority by name. She felt the effect of a shooting like a slap in the face, and it was a very long minute before she was able to compose herself and spring into action. If she'd been called out, it meant that there were fatal casualties, including people she might know.

While she and Lucy assembled what they'd need, Adele kept checking her phone to see if Matilda had called or texted to tell her about the situation. Her phone remained silent. While this wasn't unusual, she felt a sense of foreboding creep in. She knew one day Matilda's luck would run out. She'd been involved in so many confrontations with killers and rapists but always managed to survive, albeit with a few bruises.

'Adele, I'm ready when you are,' Lucy called from the doorway. Her eyes were wide and her face pale. She, too, knew how grave this case was going to be if people they knew, who had attended post-mortems in this very building, were among the dead. This was going to be a memorable birthday for Lucy Dauman and for all the wrong reasons.

Adele jumped. 'I'm coming.' She quickly grabbed her coat and left her small office.

'Have you heard from DCI Darke?'

'No,' she said, tucking her phone into her trousers pocket.

'She's probably busy. A shooting at the station. I mean, it's just nuts, isn't it?'

'Come on.'

The drive took less than ten minutes, but it felt like forever. It was a dull and gloomy day. Clouds hung low over the city and a heavy mist was in the air. Adele sat in the front passenger seat, her mind whirling through the many possibilities that could have befallen her friend. She wondered who was among the dead; Scott was dating her son, Rory had recently proposed to his girlfriend, Ranjeet was a new father, Christian had two lovely daughters and Sian had four children and a husband who doted on her. Please God let them all be all right.

'Is it selfish of me to hope no one I know well has died?' Adele asked, breaking the heavy silence in the car.

'Of course not.'

'I was just thinking … We know so many of them, uniformed officers, detectives, civilian workers, but some we know better than others. Look at that PC who always seems to be the exhibits officer, the one with the lisp and the cute smile. I'd be devastated if he'd been killed, but then I'd be putting someone else in his place.'

'Adele, it's only natural to think like that. I was thinking exactly the same.'

'Really?'

'Yes. I'm hoping to God it's nobody I've met. I don't know how I'd cope if say Rory or Sian or Ranjeet had died. They're like friends, aren't they?' she said as she pulled up at a set of traffic lights.

Adele took her phone out and looked at the blank screen.

'Still nothing?'

'No. I was wondering if I should phone Chris and tell him.'

'There's no point until you know what's going on. I'm sure Scott's fine, but there's no point worrying him unnecessarily.'

'You're right.'

They turned the corner and saw the station up ahead. It looked as it usually did. Lucy parked, and they set about getting their things out of the back, slinging heavy bags over their shoulders, picking up forensic suits and packets of gloves and overshoes.

They walked slowly to the doors, but they didn't open as they should have done automatically. A uniformed officer was stood behind them.

'Dr Adele Kean and Lucy Dauman. I'm the pathologist,' Adele shouted. She was struggling under the weight of her bag and case, but dug her ID out of her pocket and slapped it on the glass.

PC Rix nodded and opened the doors.

'Sorry, we're in lockdown.' His face was ashen.

'What's happened?'

'There was a shooter on the roof of the office block behind us. He just opened fire.' There were tears in his eyes.

'Are there many dead?'

He swallowed hard and shrugged.

Lucy placed a hand on his arm; a sign of comfort, while Adele asked where they should go.

As they made their way to the rear car park, they walked along corridors in stony silence. The atmosphere felt heavy, as if the building was already in mourning. They exchanged frightened glances. They both knew they were about to enter hell.

As Adele stepped out into what counted for daylight in early January, she stopped and looked at the carnage. Bodies were littered about the concrete, lying in pools of blood. Shattered glass was everywhere, and a team of white-suited forensic officers were already marking the area with evidence tabs.

'Adele.'

She turned at the sound of her name being called and saw DI Christian Brady heading towards her. She felt an instant sense of relief. One officer she knew well was still alive.

'Christian, what the hell's happened?' she asked softly.

'What have you been told?'

'Just about a shooting. Where's…'

She didn't need to finish her question. Christian's eyes told her everything she needed to know.

'She was hit twice. Once in the shoulder and once in the head. She's been rushed to hospital, but … it doesn't look good.'

'Oh … my…' Adele buckled and dropped her bags. Christian and Lucy caught her between them. Tears were streaming down her face. She tried to talk but found she couldn't speak as the emotion gripped her throat.

'Why…? I mean, who's…? I don't…'

'It's early days, Adele,' he said, holding her firmly. 'We're going to work round-the-clock to catch whoever did this.'

She looked up at Christian's blank face through tear-stained eyes. 'Are you all right?'

He nodded.

'Who's dead?' she asked.

'From our team, we've lost Valerie and Ranjeet.'

'Ranjeet?' Lucy gasped, slapping a hand to her mouth. She'd always had a soft spot for the young DC.

'Oh no,' Adele cried. 'Where's Scott?'

'He's fine. He was with Matilda when she was shot, though. Adele, are you going to be able to do this?' Christian asked.

'I can give Simon Browes a call, Adele, if you want?' Lucy said.

It was a while before Adele answered. 'No.' She sniffled. She struggled to take a tissue from her pocket and wiped her eyes and nose. 'No. I'm fine. I can do this. I can. What about you, Lucy?' She turned to her assistant, who had tear tracks smudging her make-up.

'It's our job. We have to.' She'd obviously tried to sound confident, but her shaking voice belied her words.

The Crime Scene Manager told Adele where forensics had finished and directed them over to where two bodies were covered with white sheets. They suited up, taking their time to put on the blue suits, overshoes and gloves. They were in no rush.

Adele knelt down by the first body. The sheet was patchy with drying blood and a pool of it had seeped out beneath. She took a deep breath, steadied herself and slowly peeled it back.

Valerie Masterson was lying on her front, her head facing to the left, her eyes wide open. Her face was spattered with blood and her brown hair was matted where it had dried. A bullet had entered her neck. There was no evidence of an exit wound.

'Do we do post-mortems on them all?' Lucy asked, looking around at the covered dead.

'Yes. At the inquest, questions will be raised about how long it took for the emergency services to arrive. They'll want to know if any of them could have survived had an ambulance arrived a minute or thirty seconds earlier. We have to answer that question.'

'And could they?'

'Not in Valerie's case. It was a direct hit. The bullet entered the back of the neck and went into the brain. She'll have been dead before she hit the ground,' Adele said, sniffling. 'Lucy, give Simon Browes a call. I'm not conducting a PM on Valerie or Ranjeet.'

She covered Valerie with the sheet and stood up. She turned to look at the building. Windows were shattered, bricks were riddled with bullet holes. How the hell had this been allowed to happen?

———————

Sian was looking out of the window at Adele stepping around the bodies. As she pulled back a white sheet and Valerie's face was revealed, Sian baulked and stepped away from the window. Surely this was a nightmare. She felt numb. Her mobile on her desk started to ring.

'Stuart,' she answered. 'Where are you?'

'I'm outside. They won't let me in.'

'What? Why not?'

'Some young uniformed officer on the door said the building's in lockdown.'

She rolled her eyes. 'I'll come down.'

She ended the call and ran out of the room. She was

covered in blood. It was drying and sticky, and the metallic smell was making her feel sick. There was no way she was spending the day in a sodding paper forensic suit.

She ran into reception and saw her husband standing on the opposite side of the automatic doors, a rucksack in his hand.

'Can you let that man in, please?' Sian said to the young officer. Her question was polite, but there was venom in her voice.

'I can't let him in, ma'am, I'm sorry. I'm under orders,' PC Rix said, his voice quiet and shaking.

'That man is my husband. He's brought me a change of clothing, unless you want me to spend the rest of the day wearing the blood of my dead colleagues,' she said, her voice rising.

'Chief Constable Featherstone has giving strict orders than no one is allowed in or out—'

'I don't give a fuck what orders you've been given,' Sian interrupted, practically exploding. 'That man is my husband, and he's coming into the station right fucking now,' she screamed.

'Let him in, Constable.'

Sian turned to see CC Featherstone in the doorway. She gave him a brief smile before turning back when she felt the blast of cold air on the back of her neck.

Stuart barged into the building and grabbed his wife, holding her firmly against him.

'Oh my God, are you all right?'

'No, I'm not,' she cried into his chest.

'I've brought you some clothes. I don't know if I've brought the right ones. I just shoved anything in.'

'That's ok. Come on.' She headed for the changing rooms. As they passed CC Featherstone, she said, 'Thank you.'

'You need to show a little compassion,' Featherstone said to the uniformed officer when they were gone.

'I'm sorry. I…' he quivered.

'That's ok. I know you're only following my orders, but orders are there to be broken, *occasionally*, but don't tell anyone I ever said that,' he said, giving a wry smile. 'Are you all right?'

'I'm fine,' he said, despite the fact he was evidently not fine.

'No, you're not. None of us are today, but that's all right. What's your name?'

'PC Rix, sir. Justin.'

'Nice to meet you, Justin. Have you been on the force long?'

'A few years. I joined South Yorkshire Police in November.'

Featherstone gave him a weak smile and turned to leave.

'Sir,' Rix began. His voice was light and soft. 'Is it true, about DCI Darke, I mean?'

'Is what true?'

'I heard a couple of the women talking in the canteen say that she's dead.'

'She's in a very critical condition. It doesn't look good.'

Rix staggered back in shock, hitting the wall behind him. 'Are there many others dead?' he asked, his voice barely above a whisper.

'Six. So far.'

'Why did this happen?'

'If I knew, I'd tell you,' Featherstone turned and headed off down the corridor, leaving the young PC staring into space.

Chapter Eight

There were a couple of uniformed officers sobbing in the female changing rooms when Sian entered. She told them her husband was coming in and to get out. It was out of character for her to be so impolite, but today was an unusual day for everyone. Everything had changed and would never return to normal.

The moment they were alone, Sian collapsed in a torrent of tears. Stuart held her tight. He was a huge barrel of a man with a rugby player's build, legs like tree trunks and hands like shovels. He almost scooped his petite wife up, and that was precisely what she needed. Her cries were muffled as she pressed her face against his chest and let out all the emotion she was holding on to in front of her colleagues. They'd seen her cry before, but never like this.

'What actually happened?' Stuart asked when Sian pushed herself away and began drying her eyes.

'There was a fire alarm. We all went outside. And then, I don't know, someone just started shooting at us,' she said as she began unbuttoning her shirt. She wondered whose blood was on it. 'Oh Jesus, it's gone right through to my bra.'

'I've brought you one. You said to bring a full change of clothes, so I just grabbed whatever from each drawer.'

She looked at him and smiled. 'Thank you,' she croaked as tears pricked her eyes once more. She looked down at her body, at the knife wound she'd sustained last year. At the time, she'd thought nothing could be so frightening as getting stabbed. She had no idea something this horrific could happen. Not here.

'Is it a terrorist attack?'

'I don't know.'

'Was there a warning?'

'We're not sure. Matilda received a call a few minutes before, but … we're looking into it.' She took off her shirt and tossed it onto the floor. 'That'll have to be thrown away. I've not had it long.'

'How's Matilda?' Stuart asked. He'd only met her a handful of times so didn't know her, but he knew Sian held her in high esteem.

She slumped down on the bench and shook her head. 'I can't see her surviving. That second bullet took off the back of her head, for crying out loud. She dropped to the ground like a boulder.'

Stuart shuffled up next to her and placed a massive arm around her bony shoulders. 'Come on, you know Matilda, she's tough. She's been through so much. She's not going to let a little thing like a bullet finish her off. She's not the type,' he added a forced chuckle.

Sian gave a weak smile. 'She's not indestructible. Nobody is. Even if she does survive, I doubt she'll be able to return to work.'

'Think positive, Sian. That's what you're always telling the kids. The world is a bad enough place as it is without us being all gloomy and negative. If we think positive, then positive things will happen.'

'Today I've just realised how pathetic that sounds. What's the point in being positive when there are people around every corner trying to destroy things?'

'But there aren't. You're just saying that because of the job you're in and the people you come into contact with on a regular basis – the murderers and rapists. Most of us are decent people just trying to make sense of the world and do the right thing.'

'Trying but failing.'

'You can't think like that, Sian, especially today. You need to be positive to catch this man. You need to be positive for your team. You need to be positive that Matilda is going to pull through,' he said with determination in his voice.

She turned to look at him. 'When did you become so wise?'

'I've always been wise. I've just been saving it for the right moment.' He smiled.

She gave a genuine chuckle and fell into his arms again.

'Come on, you're no use to anyone sitting here in your bra. Get dressed, go out there, catch that man, and come home tonight. I've got the day off. I'll make us all a special meal and we'll sit down like a family for once, all six of us, and we'll celebrate being together.'

'But you've got tickets to that thing at the Sheffield United ground.'

'I'll give them to Rob at work. He can take his son.'

He kissed her on the forehead.

Sian felt herself softening. She could always rely on Stuart to say and do the right thing. They'd had their moments over

twenty-five years of marriage, like any couple, but despite
what happened in life, he was constantly beside her. He was
proud of her career, of what she'd achieved as well as having
and raising four children.

'I love you so much, Stuart Mills,' she said.

'I was about to say the same thing.'

'You love yourself, too?'

'I do, but not half as much as I love you.'

'I should elbow you in the stomach for a corny line like
that.'

'But you won't because I'm so loveable.'

He gave a silly grin, which made Sian laugh. She stood up
from the bench and opened the rucksack he'd brought with
him and began taking out the clean clothes. They'd wrinkled
while they'd been in the bag, so she wouldn't look her normal
pristine self, but it was only for one day. And there was
nothing normal about today.

Stuart stayed long enough to make Sian feel better. She was a
detective sergeant and therefore had people who would look to
her for guidance and advice. As the unofficial mother of the
Homicide and Major Enquiry Team, she was seen as the safe
pair of hands, the one who was calm in a crisis and cool under
pressure. As much as she didn't feel like it today, she knew
she'd have to fake it for the sake of others and fall apart when
she went home. Stuart would be there for her, like he
always was.

When she re-entered the suite, she saw a strange man
sitting behind Matilda's desk, which brought a lump to her
throat. Had the DCI been replaced already? She soon

recognised him as someone from the tech department who was obviously going through her laptop to see if she'd received any threats or demands that could provide background to the shooting.

She looked at Rory, who was sat at his desk, head down, in a world of his own. She wanted to go over to him, put an arm around him, comfort him, tell him she knew how he felt. The problem was, she didn't, and every time she tried to open her mouth to speak, more tears raced to the surface.

Screw it. If people couldn't cry together on a day like today, then when could they? She blew her nose and walked tentatively over to Rory's desk.

He was slumped in his chair. The smell of soap was coming off him. He was dressed in a black T-shirt and jeans, his suit having been ruined with the blood of his dead fiancée.

'Rory,' she said quietly, leaning down next to him.

He turned to look at her. His face was blank and pale.

She placed an arm around his shoulders as their eyes locked together. Neither of them could speak. There was nothing to say. Rory's bottom lip began to wobble, so Sian pulled him into a tight embrace.

Christian Brady entered the HMET suite. He saw Sian and Rory together and swallowed his emotions. He signalled to Scott to join him in his office.

'How are you?' Christian asked.

'I've no idea. I feel numb.'

'Understandable. Where the hell did you get that suit?' he asked, looking the young DC up and down.

Scott was dressed in a dark grey ill-fitting suit that looked a size too big for him. Scott was very conscious of how he looked, and his clothes were always fitted as if tailor-made.

'Aaron's always kept a spare one in his locker ever since he was vomited on as a PC. He let me borrow it. Maybe I should keep a spare.'

'You look like a teenager in his first suit heading for court.'

'It's been a while since I've been called a teenager, so I'll take that as a compliment.' He smiled painfully. 'Are you ok?' he asked.

Christian paused. He had no idea how he was feeling. He thought for a moment. 'The same as you, probably. Any news from the hospital?'

'Not yet.'

'No news is good news, and all that bollocks, I suppose. Anyway, Scott, I need you to go through the CCTV footage around the entrances to the station. The fire alarm that was set off was behind the custody suite, near the entrance to the car park. Now, if the gunman triggered it, he'd be caught on camera. See what you can find.'

'Will do.'

'I've heard back from forensics. They've identified the bullets as being fired from a Heckler and Koch MP5.'

'They're what we use,' Scott said.

'I know. Several forces around the country use them, including the Met. There are no distinguishing markings on the bullet, but we need to know if any are missing.'

'You think it could be one of our guns?'

'I don't know.'

'If it is, we could all know who the gunman is. Maybe he's a disgruntled officer or something.'

'It's too early to speculate. These guns can be found on the black market, the dark web, from someone dodgy in a backstreet boozer, but all avenues have to be explored. The most obvious one is checking whether any of our guns are missing,' Christian said firmly.

Scott nodded. 'I'll ask Finn to check.'

Christian stood up from leaning over the desk. He'd rolled his shirtsleeves up, his hair was unruly, and he looked shattered.

'Who have we got working on this?' he asked.

'Me and Finn. Sian and Rory when they're able to. It's not easy.'

'Featherstone is going to draft in some more from CID, but they've lost officers, too.'

'This is going to take some getting over, isn't it?' Scott asked.

'I don't think any of us ever really will, to be honest. Have the press picked up on it yet?'

'I don't know. We've got the TV on silent—'

The door opened and Sian popped her head in. Her eyes were red from crying. 'You'll never guess who's on TV.'

Christian rolled his eyes and followed them all out into the open-plan office.

On the large screen was the BBC News channel. A woman sat at a large desk wearing a conservative jacket and perfectly styled hair was talking direct to camera with a stern expression. In the background, journalists busied themselves in the newsroom.

'Turn it up,' Christian said.

'We can now go back to Sheffield and our North of England correspondent, Danny Hanson.'

'What the fuck!' Christian exclaimed. 'Since when was he on TV?'

Danny Hanson was the bane of South Yorkshire Police,

Matilda in particular. He was constantly following HMET's cases and managed to get several front-page stories out of it. He was eager, there was no denying that, but he was the kind of cut-throat journalist who would sell his own parents for a decent story.

'He called Matilda a few months back,' Sian said. 'He was bragging about how he'd landed a job at *Look North*.'

'This isn't *Look North*.'

'No. But he's here. The BBC use their correspondents as and when needed.'

Danny was stood outside South Yorkshire Police HQ, the main entrance in the background. He was wearing a dark designer coat open to reveal a blue check shirt. His hair was neatly ruffled, and he was clean shaven. His large brown eyes were dancing. This was his first time on a national channel, and he was obviously revelling in it.

'Earlier this morning, a gunman opened fire within South Yorkshire Police Headquarters, behind me. Eyewitnesses have claimed hearing as many as a dozen shots. Chief Constable Martin Featherstone is set to give a statement at eleven o'clock to give us the latest on this breaking story. So far, we have been given no figures as to casualties or if any officers have been fatally injured. However, several ambulances were at the scene and the local A&E department has been closed to non-emergencies. At present, all the press office is telling us is that there has been a major incident and the building behind me is in lockdown.'

'Why's he talking like a complete wanker?' Christian asked. 'It's only a few months ago he had a Yorkshire accent.'

'He's on television now. He's got to look and sound the part,' Sian said.

'I thought the BBC liked regional accents these days.'

'Not the Yorkshire one, apparently.'

'*Danny, is this being treated as a terrorist attack? Has the gunman been caught?*' the newsreader in the London studio asked.

'*We haven't been told anything to confirm or deny that. Hopefully Chief Constable Featherstone will give us more information in his statement. I have seen armed response officers and tactical vehicles leaving this compound. There has also been a great deal of police activity coming from the building behind the police station, which is an office block housing many local companies.*'

'*Has that office block been placed in lockdown?*'

'*Yes, it has. A cordon has been put in place and all traffic diverted. This is a serious incident that is unfolding by the minute.*'

'*Danny Hanson, our North of England correspondent, thank you.*'

The camera switched back to the studio and the newsreader's face softened as she went on to a different story. Christian muted it. The mere mention of the word *Brexit* was enough to raise his hackles.

'He's enjoying himself,' Scott said.

'Featherstone is giving a statement at eleven,' Sian said, looking at her watch. 'Have all the families been told?'

'Each department is dealing with their own officers. The Chief Constable said he was contacting Valerie's kids and Matilda's parents,' Christian said.

'Has anyone told Kesinka about Ranjeet?' Scott asked.

Blank faces and silence revealed the answer.

'Scott,' Christian said. 'You and Finn go round to see her. Break it to her gently. Tell her she'll get all the support she needs.'

'Me?' Scott asked. 'No offence to Finn, but I'd rather Sian come with me.'

'I need Sian here. I'm sorry, Scott. There's no one else.'

As much as the officers wanted to get answers to what had happened this morning, the majority were too shocked, stunned and numb to physically do anything. They wanted to band together, hug each other and talk about what they'd witnessed. However, time was of the essence, and more lives were in danger if uniformed officers and detectives didn't put their personal feelings to one side and concentrate on the task in hand.

All staff within South Yorkshire Police HQ had to give a statement as to what they had witnessed and as Christian returned to his office, he sat down and began to write his own. He picked up a pen and stared at it. It was a silver-plated Parker fountain pen, given to him a few Christmases back by his daughters. Despite him having trouble reading his own handwriting, he loved it and enjoyed writing with it. Holding it in his shaking right hand, he couldn't bring himself to write down what he'd seen that morning. Putting it into words made it real, and he couldn't get his head around seeing his colleagues gunned down in cold blood.

From the cracked window in the station, he'd watched as Scott Andrews bravely went out amidst the carnage. Matilda stood looking up. At what, he had no idea. Suddenly, a shot rang out. Matilda staggered backwards. Scott leapt out of the way. Another shot and Matilda—

There was a light tap on his door. He looked up. Sian entered the office with a mug in her hands.

'I've brought you a tea.'

Christian didn't say anything.

'The press is gathering outside,' she said.

'The Chief Constable said he was taking care of that, thank

goodness.' He leaned back in his chair. He looked out into the main suite, but his stare went much further. His eyes looked intense, but he wasn't seeing anything.

'I don't know what to do,' Sian said. 'There's so much to do, but I just … I don't know. You don't expect something like this to happen, do you?'

Christian shook his head. 'Every time I close my eyes, I see it all over again. I'm replaying it and thinking what I could have done differently.'

'It all happened so quickly. There was nothing more you could have done.'

'There was a PC in front of me. He was running towards the building. He was hit and fell to the ground. I should have stopped and helped him, seen if he was all right, but I jumped over him, Sian. I just left him.'

Sian stepped further into the office and closed the door behind her. 'It's human. Don't beat yourself up about it.'

'But I'm a police officer. My job is to protect others, to save others, and I didn't. I stepped over him and ran to safety.'

Sian sat in the chair opposite his desk. She reached across and grabbed his hands. 'You saved me. You saw me standing there, shaking like a leaf, and you stopped to help me. You saved my life.'

'But I didn't save his.'

'We can't save everyone.'

'I stopped for you because I know you. I didn't know this PC. I shouldn't be doing this job if I'm going to stop and choose who I help.'

'Christian, this is a situation none of us can prepare for. We can train, but we don't know how we'll react until it happens. You can't go over every detail and analyse it and wonder what you could have done differently, because you'll go mad considering all the various options. Don't beat yourself up, Christian. You're a good man and a bloody good detective.'

'I don't think I can do this anymore.' He looked at her with tears in his eyes.

'You can,' she said firmly, increasing her grip on his hands.

'I don't think I want to,' he said, barely above a whisper.

Chapter Nine

There were six confirmed dead from South Yorkshire Police HQ. That number was likely to rise as the day went on with several being treated for severe injuries at hospital, not to mention the grave danger Matilda Darke was in.

The bodies were transported to the Medico-Legal Centre at Watery Street on the outskirts of Sheffield city centre, where Adele and Lucy would begin the post-mortems.

Claire Alexander sat behind a bank of computer screens in the digital autopsy suite. She watched with a heavy heart as the side door opened and the first body was wheeled in on a trolley. There were many more out there waiting to go through the scanner. She tried not to think of who was in the sealed body bag, but it wasn't easy. Although she hadn't had much contact with the police officers from HQ, she'd heard Adele and Lucy talk fondly about them all. This was going to be a very sad day.

Claire was wearing oversized scrubs and her dark brown hair, now at shoulder length, was neatly tied back in a ponytail. The first body bag was on the scanner in the next room, waiting for the digital autopsy to begin, which would give detailed information on entry and exit wounds, the trajectory of the bullet, and whether it was still lodged inside the victim.

The door opened behind her. She turned and saw a grim-faced Adele standing in the doorway. Her eyes seemed glazed over, as if her body was present but her mind elsewhere. She was looking at Claire but not seeing her.

'Any news?' Claire asked.

Adele shook her head.

'Oh God,' she said, bowing her head as she cried. 'I can't believe this has happened.'

Adele stepped forward and put her arms around Claire, but there was no comfort or emotion involved. 'I know. It's shocking.'

Claire grabbed a tissue from her desk, wiped her eyes and blew her nose. 'You wake up in the morning and you think, "OK, I'll go to work, have a chat and a laugh with my colleagues, and wonder what's worth watching on TV tonight." You don't think that your whole world is going to be destroyed in the space of a few minutes.'

'I know.'

'You see things like this on the news and you feel sorry for those poor people. After a few days, the story vanishes from the screens, and you forget. You shouldn't, but you do, you get on with your own life. But what are those people feeling three days after the event, five days, a month, a year? You don't know that until you're living it.'

'I think we just have to take one day at a time,' Adele said, slumping down in the seat next to her, her head on her chest, her shoulders hunched, as if life was draining out of her. 'I can't believe Valerie and Ranjeet are dead. Ranjeet, I mean, he's only in his twenties, for crying out loud. Married just over a year and a new baby. How can you try and make sense of that?'

'You can't. It doesn't make any sense at all.'

'I sometimes hate what this world is turning into. For someone to attack the police like that.'

They sat in silence for a long time. Eventually, Adele seemed to come to her senses, as if she suddenly remembered where she was and what she was doing here. 'Shall we begin?'

With shaking fingers, Claire typed on the keyboard and the scanner in the next room came to life. The digital autopsy was a non-invasive post-mortem in which digital imaging technology, along with CT scans, was used to develop cross-sectional images for a full virtual exploration of the body. As radiographer, Claire would zoom in on parts of the body, turn it over, look deep within the tissue and organs, without physically touching the body and potentially destroying vital forensic evidence. Cause of death could be accurately confirmed in 75 per cent of digital autopsies, and that figure was rising as technology advanced. Adele would always be needed to perform full invasion autopsies, but the digital version was less intrusive and more respectful for relatives.

Adele hadn't asked which victim was in the scanner. As a skeletal image appeared on the screen, she could tell right away the body had been hit with three bullets. Once in the back, where the bullet was still lodged, once in the neck and once in the back of the head, where there were both entry and exit wounds. There was only one victim at the scene Adele had identified as having three gunshots. She was looking at the image of twenty-seven-year-old Detective Constable Ranjeet Deshwal.

'Oh God,' she said under her breath.

Claire cleared her throat. 'The bullet to the back of the head doesn't have as high a trajectory as the other two. I think we can assume this was the first to hit him.'

'Apparently, he stopped to help Sian. He was hit and went down in front of her.'

'Jesus Christ. The other two will have been where he was caught in the crossfire.'

'Where's the bullet imbedded in him?'

'It's lodged in the fourth thoracic vertebrae.'

Adele made a note.

There was a knock on the door, and Lucy entered.

'Adele, Simon Browes is on his way. He's coming up from Derby.'

'Thanks, Lucy,' Adele said without turning around to look at her colleague.

'Also, Matilda's mum's called and left you a message. She's asked if you can meet her at the hospital.'

Both Adele and Claire were alert and turned to Lucy.

'Has she said how she is?'

'No. But she'd like you to be there.'

'I suppose I could pop along while Simon does the PMs on Valerie and Ranjeet and be back for the others.'

'I can hold down the fort with Simon. Take as long as you need,' Lucy said.

'Are you sure?'

'Of course.'

'Right. I'll get changed.'

'Will you keep me informed?' Claire asked.

'Sure.'

'Wait, has anyone phoned Daniel?'

'Oh my God, I completely forgot,' Adele said, suddenly

remembering Matilda's boyfriend. She squeezed the bridge of her nose as she tried to remember if she had his number. She was pretty confident she had. 'Shit. I'm going to have to call him, aren't I? Is this day going to get any bloody worse?' she asked herself as she stormed out of the digital autopsy suite.

Chapter Ten

C hristian was marching down the corridor, back towards the HMET suite, when his phone vibrated in his pocket. He answered without looking at the screen.

'DI Brady.'

'It's Gavin Porter. Armed Response,' the deep baritone of Inspector Porter replied. 'None of our weapons are reported missing. All are accounted for. None of our officers are behind this attack. They've all been questioned, and all are on standby, waiting instruction.'

'Thanks, Gavin. Shit, I'm getting another call through. I'll ring you back,' he said as he answered another call. 'Brady.'

'Sir, it's Finn. I didn't know where you were, so thought it best to call you.'

'I'm right outside the suite and can see you picking your teeth.' He hung up the call and pushed open the door.

'Sorry, I've just had a Snickers,' Finn said. 'I've got CCTV footage from the entrance to the building where the gunman was shooting from. I can't be certain, obviously, but I think this is him.'

Finn swung his laptop around. The image on the screen showed a tall, thin man wearing a dark beanie hat, dark combat trousers and a black body warmer over a dark top. He was carrying a rucksack over one shoulder, which looked heavy. Finn pressed play. The man came out of a side entrance, looked around him before stepping out onto the street. He kept his head down as he made his way out of the frame.

'Take a screen shot and send it to my phone.'

'Will do.'

'Where's he heading?'

'I've followed him on a number of cameras but lost him as he gets to the city centre.'

'Does he do anything?'

'No. His head is permanently down. People sidestep him, likely because it's clear he's got this determination about him, if you ask me.'

'Hmm,' Christian mused.

'What are you thinking?'

'If you've just pulled off a shooting spree and managed to get away, why would you be walking with such determination, making yourself stand out from the crowds?'

'To get away.'

'But he has got away. He's disappeared into the city centre.' Christian ran his fingers through his hair.

'There are loads of cameras in town, sir. I could spend days getting footage of them all.'

'I know. Don't worry about it. Shit—' He stopped.

'What is it?'

'This just confirms what I was saying earlier to Sian. He's determined because he's got something else in mind. Another attack.'

'Are you sure?'

'When Scott saw him just after he shot Matilda, he said he looked like he knew what he was doing. He fired, packed up his gun, and headed off. He's got something else in mind.'

'Jesus!' Finn said under his breath.

Christian walked away from his desk. He chewed his bottom lip as he thought. 'Finn, get onto uniform and make sure they're driving round. We need a presence on the streets. I need to ring Porter back,' he said, selecting his number on his phone. 'I want Armed Response out there now.'

'Sir, if he is planning a second attack, shouldn't we let the public know?'

'If we knew where, yes, but we don't.' He looked up when he saw Sian entering the suite, but frowned when he looked past her through the doorway. 'Why are there officers hanging around doing nothing?' he said, commenting on the two uniformed officers standing outside the door. 'Sian, make a call, I want SY99 up in the air right now.' He pulled open the glass door to the two PCs. 'What are you doing?'

The female PC baulked at the force of Christian's questions. 'Sergeant Naylor asked me to give you this list of the injured and dead,' PC Zofia Nowak said, handing out a folded sheet of paper with a shaking hand.

'Right. Thank you,' he said, his face softening slightly. He looked to the other, much taller PC and raised an eyebrow.

'I was wondering if I could have a word, sir?' PC Justin Rix asked.

'It'll have to wait. I'm sure you have things to do. Off you both go.'

Christian closed the door and opened the piece of paper. His eyes scanned down the list of names. 'Jesus Christ,' he uttered. He closed his eyes to compose himself against the horror unfolding in front of him for a moment. He took a deep breath and released it slowly. When he opened his eyes, he felt a strong determination of what he had to do. Standing in the HMET suite, looking around him, these were his officers, his detectives. They were relying on him to keep his head when everyone else seemed to be losing theirs. He could do this. He could be the leader they needed him to be.

'Finn, get uniform to help you track the gunman's movements from the building. He's got to be in a vehicle of some kind. As soon as you've identified it, let me know. We need him found before he reaches his next target.'

'Next target? What's going on?' Sian asked.

'Sian, just get the helicopter in the air,' he instructed forcefully. 'Everyone, we're against the clock here,' he said to the room as a whole. 'It's been ninety minutes since he tried to kill us all, and we've already wasted valuable time. I believe he's a man on a mission and is plotting another attack. I hope to God I'm wrong, however, we need to be prepared. I want everyone in that building opposite interviewed,' he said, pointing out of the window. 'Somebody must have seen him entering or leaving. Monitor incoming calls – has anyone reported someone driving erratically or looking suspicious, or having driven through a red light? Check social media for talk of an incident of this kind. If it's a terrorist attack, there'll be chatter about it. If it's a lone gunman … well, that makes things trickier.' He fell silent and chewed his bottom lip, hoping to God this wasn't a trigger-happy psychopath acting alone. 'Don't stand there looking at me like a goldfish. Move, move, move!' he shouted.

He pulled his phone out of his pocket and looked at the image Finn had sent him. He leaned in, squinted and glared at the blurred photo. There was a familiarity about him he couldn't put his finger on.

'Who the fuck are you?' Christian asked.

His phone vibrated in his hand. It was an incoming call. He swiped to answer. 'Brady.'

'Sir, it's Lisa McGregor from the tech department. We've been looking at DCI Darke's office phone. The call that came through this morning was from a mobile phone that's still active. I'm sending you a map of the trigger points.'

'Thank you.' He hung up then made another call. 'Gavin, the call to Matilda's phone was made from a mobile that's still active. As soon as I get the coordinates, I'll send them over to you. I want an armed team out there, and I want that phone found. Any CCTV of the area needs to be scrutinised.' He hung up before Gavin could reply. An email had already arrived on his phone giving the details of the mobile. He forwarded it straight to the inspector in charge of Armed Response.

The location of the mobile phone was somewhere on Weedon Street, a long road not far away from South Yorkshire Police HQ. Armed officers ran to their vehicles and, under the direction of Inspector Porter's running commentary, headed for the scene.

On one side of the road were offices and industrial units, on the other was scrubland next to the River Don with Meadowhall Shopping Centre a stone's throw away.

According to the map on Porter's phone, they were very close by. He instructed them all to pull over and begin a fingertip search of the area, but to also be on the lookout in case the gunman was still in the area. The phone was stationary and had more than likely been dumped, but the gunman had already targeted the police once this morning. There was a real possibility this could be a ploy to lure a unit of armed response officers as bait. With a packed shopping mall a few hundred yards away, an unpredictable shooter on the run was the last thing the police needed right now.

Porter ran down the pavement with his team behind him as they looked for the location of the phone. They were almost on top of the phone, according to the map, but couldn't see anything on the ground.

'It's got to be on the wasteland,' he said, slightly out of breath. 'He'll have thrown it over the fence. Someone get a ladder.'

A ladder was brought out of the back of one of the vans, placed against the steel fencing, and, one by one, officers jumped over it.

'Do you want me to call for the search dogs?' a uniformed officer asked, shouting above the fast-moving traffic behind them.

'Not yet,' he replied. 'I've got a feeling we're not going to need them.'

'Sir!'

He looked up. An armed officer approached the fence, a rifle in one hand, a plastic bag in the other. He passed it to him through the slats.

Porter rolled his eyes. He took out his mobile phone and made a call. 'Christian, it's Gavin. We've found the phone. It's an old-style Nokia, switched on. It had been thrown over the fence on Weedon Street.'

'Excellent. Get it straight to forensics. They—'

'Wait,' Gavin interrupted. 'The phone is in a bag. It's in a sealed South Yorkshire Police issue plastic evidence bag.'

'What?' Christian asked.

'You know what this means, don't you?'

'The fucker's playing with us.'

Chapter Eleven

10:40 – Sheffield Parkway

Jake Harrison walked through Corker Bottoms Allotments with his head down. His face had a heavy expression and his lips moved slightly as he muttered to himself, going over everything that had just happened. He could see the odd person tending their patch in his peripheral vision but didn't want to make eye contact and invite conversation, even if it was a simple head nod or a good-morning. He took long strides. He blended into his surroundings with dark clothing, army-style trousers and heavy walking boots. His backpack felt heavy, full of his arsenal of weapons. He'd taken care of Matilda Darke. He just needed to throw the police off his scent, giving him enough time to get to his second destination. Once that was over with, he didn't care if a police marksman took aim and blew his brains away. It would be a happy release.

His first attack had gone exactly as planned, better even. By the time the fire alarm sounded, and everyone began filing out of the building, Jake was in prime position on the roof of the building behind, having gained access using a stolen key card.

From his vantage point, he had full view of the police station car park. He waited until the whole building had been evacuated, plain-clothed detectives, uniformed officers and civilian staff. He spotted Matilda straight away. He'd been watching her, following her, studying her for so long that he was seeing her in his sleep. He thought he'd be nervous, but surprisingly, he felt calm. He wasn't just after Matilda, he wanted to hurt the police. He wanted to deplete their number, have them struggle to cope with the loss of colleagues as well as the hunt for him. There was no way he was going to make today easy for them. His plan was to destroy. This day was going to go down in history as one of Sheffield's darkest days – no, by the time he was finished, the whole world would know about him. This would be one of England's darkest days.

He lined up the shot, aiming for a very attractive young uniformed officer and squeezed the trigger. The sound of the shot was muffled. He hit his target, and she dropped like a stone. There was a delay as those around her looked bewildered, wondering what had happened. He fired a second shot. He heard a scream, and everyone began running back into the building. Jake found himself smiling. The sound of panic and horror was like a rush of blood to the head. He aimed carefully and accurately and watched as people started to fall. It was like shooting fish in a barrel. For a moment, he took his eye off the ball, and it wasn't until he saw Matilda standing in the middle of the car park, actually looking up at him, that he remembered his whole reason for today was to kill her.

There she was, standing tall in her winter coat, dark hair flowing in the breeze. She wasn't hiding. She wasn't running.

Her face was blank, her eyes wide as she stood in the middle of the carnage. Her colleagues were dead around her, and she just stood, looking up at him, challenging him, almost.

This was too easy.

He looked momentarily from the viewfinder, and he was sure their eyes locked. He smiled, but she remained passive. Silence fell all around him, and he remained fixed on his target. She was making it so easy for him.

He lined up the shot and squeezed the trigger, hitting her in the shoulder. She staggered backwards, and he got her clean in the head with the second. He watched her drop dead to the ground, packed up his kit, and left.

He ran down the stairs quietly and calmly. He needed to leave the building urgently, to flee before he was surrounded, but he couldn't panic, as that would raise suspicion as well as cause him to make mistakes. He could hear the blood pounding in his ears. Every time he blinked, he saw Matilda's dead expression as she fell backwards. He pushed open the fire door to the office block and stepped out into the cold winter air. Everything was calm and quiet. A great disaster had taken place, and everyone was trying to make sense of the sounds they'd just heard before the reality hit. He stood still on the edge of the road and took in a lungful of polluted air. It tasted good. It tasted of a task well done. His brother would be proud.

He headed for the van he'd parked in a side street, far enough away so hopefully CCTV would lose him in the miasma of alleyways he went down to reach his vehicle, started the engine and made his way to his next target.

Jake Harrison had never felt more alive than he did right now. The world had dealt him a very bad hand. He'd been hampered at every turning. Society scorned him. His parents pitied him. His wife loathed him.

His brother had the right idea. Nobody fucked with a Harrison and got away with it. It was time to show everyone what he was truly made of. Today was the day he was going to sit back and watch the world burn.

———————

Past the allotments, Jake trudged over uneven ground under the cover of darkness provided by a thicket of trees. He would have preferred a clear day, but the weather in England, particularly in the North, was unpredictable. It was a dull, dank day. Heavy cloud hung over the city, and there was a fine drizzle in the air. On one hand, it kept people indoors, or in their cars, so there were fewer to see him stalking the streets of Sheffield. Unfortunately, it left him exposed.

The sound of the Parkway grew louder as he exited the trees. He looked around him, constantly keeping vigil. With the noise from the traffic whizzing by at sixty miles per hour, it would be easy to not hear someone close by watching what he was up to, or a police officer on his trail. No, he was sure they wouldn't have worked out who he was yet. He still had time on his side.

To his right was Harborough Rise and a handful of terraced houses. He walked along the pavement as if he belonged there; a regular member of the public going about his busy life. He paused as he took a step on the bridge. He took one last look behind him to make sure there was nobody close by. Up ahead, nobody was heading towards him. Traffic below was busy and fast-moving. The timing was perfect.

He walked onto the bridge and stopped over the lanes

running southbound. The noise from the vehicles was loud, and the smell of diesel and petrol clung to his nostrils and scratched the back of his throat. It tasted foul. He removed his backpack and squatted to the ground as he opened the camouflaged bag and scrambled among his weapons. He had three different variations of a Glock pistol, a Heckler & Koch he'd used at the police station, but he chose the SIG SG 552, which he'd managed to get from someone online who had connections with Derbyshire Police.

The SG 552 was a compact weapon. Jake unfolded it, inserted a spring-loaded cartridge and set the firing to a single shot.

He could feel his heart pounding. He thought his palms would be sweaty and his nerves would make his body shake, but he felt none of that. The moment he picked up a gun, he knew this was what he was destined for. He took a deep breath. He was ready.

He looked through the bars of the iron railings at the fast-moving traffic below. Cars, taxis, lorries, vans, coaches and trucks hurtled along. He wanted a car, preferably an Audi. He hated Audis and their drivers. They seemed to think they owned the roads and could do what they liked. Wankers. There was one up ahead. Light grey. Fingers crossed a sales rep would be driving.

Being right-handed, Jake steadied the gun with his left hand and put his right forefinger on the trigger. He couldn't afford to take too long in case a driver looked up and saw him aiming at them. He had the Audi in his sights and squeezed the trigger.

A bullet was fired. It cracked the windscreen of his target car and hit the head of the driver, who was thrown back in his seat. The car continued travelling but began to drift into the next lane. A Ford Focus beeped and swerved, slamming on its brakes. A car behind the Focus crashed into it. The Audi, still drifting, clipped a motorbike, which spun. The driver fell off and was run over by a white van whose tyres screamed as the brakes were applied. The Audi crashed into the embankment at speed, flipping it over. A Punto swerved to avoid crashing into it and ploughed into a Nissan, which then hit a Mercedes. It was carnage. Squealing brakes and the smashing glass and the crunching of metal filled the air.

Traffic began to slow down and stop as they witnessed the crash ahead. Someone will have called the police. Help would be on its way.

Jake watched from the bridge. He couldn't help but smile as he looked out at a sea of gawping faces. They were sitting ducks. He changed the setting to firing three bullets with a single touch of the trigger.

People started to get out of their vehicles, seeing if they could help the injured. Others started filming on their mobiles. Ghouls. They had to be taken out first. He didn't want to be captured on camera.

He raised the gun, aimed and fired.

Chapter Twelve

Detective Constables Scott Andrews and Finn Cotton were parked a few doors down from the Deshwal house at Heeley on the outskirts of Sheffield city centre.

It was a cramped-looking street with two rows of terraced houses either side, no front gardens and cars crammed into any available space.

'I've never delivered a death message before,' Finn said from the front passenger seat.

'I have, but never to a colleague.'

'How's Rory?' Finn asked, looking across at Scott.

He shook his head. 'I've no idea. He should go home, but I doubt DI Brady will allow it.'

'I still can't believe what happened. I was close to the building when the shots started ringing out. I just opened the door and ran in. I didn't think about anyone else.'

'That's perfectly understandable.'

'I just stood there and held the door open for people. I could have run out and helped. I saw Sian fall. I should have gone to grab her, but I couldn't.'

'Finn, don't beat yourself up about this. We can all say we'd be the hero under fire, but until it happens, we don't know how we'll react. Have you called your wife?'

'Yes,' he said, wiping his eyes. 'She told me to stay safe.'

'Well, make sure you do. I don't think I'll be able to do this more than once today.'

There was a knock on Finn's window. They both jumped and turned to see Kesinka's smiling face beaming at them. She was wrapped up warm against the elements, woollen hat, matching scarf and gloves and a thick winter coat. Finn opened the window.

'I thought it was you two. On a stake-out? I'll save you the bother. The drug dealer at number twelve has gone on holiday. Two weeks in Miami, lucky sod. Who says crime doesn't pay?' She laughed.

'Hi, Kes,' Scott said, sullenly.

'What's up?'

She took in Scott's blank expression and turned to Finn. His eyes were wet and darting left and right as he didn't know where to look.

Kesinka's smile dropped.

'Oh my God, no.' She put her gloved hands to her face, releasing hold of the pram she was pushing. It started to roll down the street.

Scott jumped out of the car, followed by Finn. Finn made a beeline for the pram while Scott grabbed Kesinka and pulled her to his chest. He held her tight as she sobbed loudly. He increased his grip as her legs buckled and she started falling to the ground. Her screams echoed around the neighbourhood.

From her handbag attached to the handles of the pram, Finn took out the house keys. He unlocked the front door and

Scott walked in slowly, pulling Kesinka with him, leaving Finn struggling with the pram.

———————

It seemed like an age before Kesinka stopped crying enough to look up. She was on the sofa with Scott next to her. Finn was in front of the fire, little Hemant in his arms, rocking him left and right as he made gurgling noises. Behind Finn, on the fireplace, a silver-framed photograph showed Ranjeet and Kesinka on their wedding day. It was a simple affair, nothing big and fancy as neither of them wanted a fuss. Ranjeet looked dapper in his fitted dark grey suit and dusky pink tie. Next to him, linking arms, was Kesinka in a cream floor-length dress. It clung to her in all the right places. Both of them grinned to the camera, having just declared their love for each other in front of their family and closest friends. They were happy. In a confusing and unstable world, they'd found each other among the madness and decided to share the rest of their lives together.

'What happened?' Kesinka choked. She held a cushion on her lap, cuddling it firmly to her chest.

Scott filled her in on the shooting. He told her how Ranjeet had stopped to help Sian. How he'd died a hero.

'St-stupid bugger,' she struggled to say as she tried to catch her breath between the tears. 'He never thought of himself, always other people. Look at what happened last year when we had those floods and he jumped into the river to save Ellen. I didn't half give him hell once I got him back home. And now look what he's gone and done.' She tore at a damp tissue.

She started to cry anew and fell into Scott's embrace.

'Would you like me to make you a cup of tea or something?' Finn asked.

Kesinka didn't react. Finn looked at Scott and shrugged his shoulders. He looked uncomfortable cradling a child.

'I loved him, Scott. From the moment I saw him, I loved him. It was his hair. So shiny, so thick and lush. And his eyes, deep and dark and smiling. He was gorgeous. I didn't think I stood a chance with him, but when he asked me out, it was like all the angels in heaven were singing. I've never met a kinder, more caring, loving, honest man. He really was the perfect husband.'

'I'm sorry, but I think Hemant might need changing,' Finn said quietly. He looked horrified at the prospect of having to change him.

Scott stood up and took the baby from him. 'I'll do it. Is everything upstairs?'

Kesinka nodded. Scott left the room holding the child, not even a year old, at arm's length.

'What am I going to tell his parents?' Kesinka cried, looking hopefully at Finn.

'We can do that if you want.'

'And what do I tell Hemant when he gets older?'

Finn sat down on the sofa next to her and put an arm around her shoulders. 'You tell him his dad was a hero, because that's what he was. He died saving people's lives.'

She tried to smile, but grief wouldn't allow it. The tears continued to flow.

'Why, Finn? Who would do something like this?'

'I don't know. I really don't,' he answered honestly.

'I'm supposed to go back to work in a couple of weeks. We joked about being a husband-and-wife team, solving crimes together like some kind of cliché TV detective drama. How can I come back to work now knowing my husband was killed there?'

She looked at Finn with tear-filled eyes, hoping for an answer. Her world had been destroyed. How was it possible for her to continue?

'I really don't know, Kes. Don't make any big decisions now. They can all wait. Just concentrate on yourself and the baby.'

Scott came down the stairs carefully, holding baby Hemant in his arms.

'I'm never doing that again,' he said with a look of disgust on his face. 'I'm not sure if I've put it on him correctly or not,' he said, handing the baby to Kesinka.

She took him in her arms and held the gurgling baby to her chest as she leaned her head on his and wept.

'He looks like Ranjeet, don't you think?' she asked, looking up.

'He really does,' Scott said. 'He has his eyes.'

'I suppose this is Ranjeet's legacy right here. He died young, but he left his mark on the world. I just have to make sure Hemant grows up knowing how brave his dad was and encourage him to follow in Ranjeet's footsteps, putting others first.' Her bottom lip was wobbling uncontrollably. Tears were leaking down her face.

'That's that best thing you can do,' Finn said, putting his arm around his colleague.

'It's going to be so difficult on my own.'

'You're not on your own,' Scott said. 'You've got the whole of South Yorkshire Police behind you.'

She looked up again and smiled, though it looked painful for her to do so. 'Will you guys do me a favour?'

'Anything,' Finn answered.

'When you catch this gunman—'

'Don't say it,' Scott interrupted. 'I know what you're going to ask, and I understand, because you're angry, but, please, don't.'

She paused, her eyes locked on Scott, before eventually nodding.

'We should be getting back,' Scott said gently.

'Is there anyone you'd like us to call?' Finn said, getting up.

'No. I'll call my mum, ask her to come over. She only lives up the road. She won't be long.'

'If you need anything, give us a call.'

'I will.'

Finn made his way to the front door. He left the house and seemed to visibly relax once he was out in the cool air.

Scott held back and waited until Finn was out of earshot. He turned to Kesinka.

'I'm going to catch him. And I'm going to kill him for you, and for Ranjeet.'

Kesinka smiled and placed a hand on his arm. 'Thank you, Scott.'

Chapter Thirteen

C hristian had three missed calls from his wife. He'd already phoned her twice and told her he was fine, but she'd obviously been watching the news and needed reassuring. He tried to placate her by telling her he was in control and knew what he was doing; that he was calm and dealing with the matter in hand. When he hung up the phone, he felt sick; he hated himself for blatantly lying to her. He looked up and through the window into the main suite, where he saw his officers struggling to maintain their emotions.

His officers? He supposed they were his officers while Matilda wasn't here, and judging by the state she was in when the paramedics wheeled her into the back of an ambulance, it would be a long time before she was back at work, if at all. Until then, he was in charge. What Sian, Rory, Scott and Finn did was down to him. As much as he'd sought more responsibility and hoped for promotion, he wanted it through his hard work, not to have it thrust upon him due to a horrific act of violence. Under this kind of pressure, would he be able to cope?

On the corner of his desk was a framed photograph of his wife and two children. It had been taken three summers back while they were on holiday in Disneyland Paris. They'd been saving for years, and for the kids it was the trip of a lifetime. Christian had taken the snap after the three of them had met Mickey and Minnie Mouse. The kids were beaming. He smiled at their happy faces. He came so close to dying this morning, to ruining their lives. The thought sent an icy chill down his spine. He always knew there was an element of danger in being a detective, but it hadn't fully hit home until now. Any one of those bullets could have hit him. It was pure chance that he'd survived.

There was a sharp rap on the glass door. He looked up and saw Rory standing in the doorway.

'Yes, Rory, what is it?' he asked, a catch in his throat.

'It's eleven o'clock. The Chief Constable is about to give a statement.'

Christian took a deep breath and left his office. Finn and Scott were still out delivering the bad news to Kesinka, so the room was practically empty. He joined Sian and Rory and they sat in front of the TV watching a picture of the front of the building they were in.

Outside the main entrance, a sea of reporters had gathered. Danny Hanson had fought for prime position at the front of the melee building up behind him. His cameraman was beside him and while Danny held his microphone aloft to capture the words the Chief Constable would be saying, he also had a digital recorder in his top pocket for his own private collection. His intention was to write a book one day. He tried to hide his smile. This really was the biggest story of his career so far. Who knew where his work on it could take him? He was picturing himself in a warzone, wearing a helmet and a bulletproof jacket with 'Press' printed on the back, giving a direct-to-camera report while British troops fought the enemy not six feet behind him.

Cameras started flashing, and he was pushed forward. He came back to reality from his daydream and looked up as the imposing figure of Chief Constable Martin Featherstone exited the building and walked to the top of the steps. He held his head high, shoulders back, a stern look on his heavy brow. His uniform was spotless, as were his shoes. He viewed the sea of reporters and cleared his throat.

Danny turned on the digital recorder in his pocket nonchalantly.

'Ladies and gentlemen, good morning,' CC Featherstone began. 'A little after nine o'clock this morning, the fire alarm sounded here at South Yorkshire Police Headquarters.' He spoke slowly and calmly, but there was a nervousness to his voice. 'All staff followed procedure and filed out of the building. Within minutes, an unknown gunman opened fire from the roof of a nearby office block, killing several officers and wounding many more.' It was obviously difficult for the Chief Constable to talk, as he had to keep stopping to swallow his emotion. He cleared his throat again. 'Among the dead is Assistant Chief Constable Valerie Masterson.'

Danny paled. He'd met with Masterson a number of times. He'd liked her. She was fierce, but she was fair. He found himself moved and the seriousness of the situation dawned on him. He wondered if any other detectives he knew were dead or injured. He wondered about Matilda Darke.

'At this stage, I am not going to reveal the names of the

other dead officers, as we are still in the process of contacting their families. The gunman hasn't been caught or identified. However, officers from the Homicide and Major Enquiries Team and CID are working together in this fast-moving investigation. We will, of course, keep you updated with any new information as and when we receive it. Thank you.'

Before he even finished talking, the reporters erupted and began asking a barrage of questions.

'Chief Constable, is this a terrorist attack?' someone to the left of Danny asked.

'We don't believe this was a terrorist incident, no,' Featherstone replied confidently.

'Has the force received any threats recently?'

'No. However, we're keeping an open mind and looking into that line of enquiry.'

Danny watched the Chief Constable's face intently. He was itching to ask a question.

'Should the people of Sheffield be worried?' another shouted from the back.

'The safety of the people of South Yorkshire is paramount. We believe this was an isolated incident, and while our numbers have been reduced today, and we have lost some well-liked, respected and dedicated officers, we are all highly professional and will not allow this to get in the way of performing our duties to the standard the public expects.'

Danny licked his lips. Not yet.

'What advice would you give to the people in Sheffield right now?' the reporter directly to the left of Danny asked.

'To remain calm. To go about their business as usual. But also to be vigilant. And if they see anything or anyone unusual, not to take action themselves, but to dial 999 immediately.'

Now.

'Chief Constable,' Danny began, raising his arm. 'Is DCI Matilda Darke leading the investigation?'

Their eyes locked and Featherstone's face paled. He opened his mouth and closed it again. His eyes darted left and right as he struggled to find an answer.

A uniformed officer came up behind him and whispered in his ear.

'I'm sorry, ladies and gentlemen, I'm going to have to leave this press conference for now. There will be updates later in the day. Thank you.' He made eye contact with Danny once again before turning on his heels and taking urgent strides back into the station.

Danny turned to the camera. 'That was Chief Constable Martin Featherstone telling us that a number of police officers have been killed including Assistant Chief Constable Valerie Masterson, who has served with South Yorkshire Police for more than thirty years. Back to you, Sophie,' he said, handing back to the studio.

He waited a few seconds before lowering the microphone.

'Something's wrong,' he said.

'What are you talking about?' his cameraman, Lewis, asked him.

'Did you see his face when I asked about DCI Darke? I bet she's been killed, and he's not saying.' There was a hint of concern in his voice. He tensed his jaw as he quickly thought about how he was going to uncover the truth.

'Why wouldn't he say? Who is she anyway?'

'She's a brilliant detective but completely fucked-up as a person, which makes her the perfect target to get a juicy story. Something's happened to her and he's not telling us the full story.'

His mobile vibrated. He fished it out of his pocket, smiled when he saw who was calling and swiped to answer.

'Hanson.'

'I have to be quick,' the caller began in a low voice. 'There's been another shooting. Sheffield Parkway. Gunman shot from the bridge.'

'Shit. Any dead?'

'Loads.'

'What can you tell me about DCI Darke? Is she dead?'

'I've got to go.' The line went dead.

'Shit! We need to go,' he said to Lewis.

'Where?'

'I'll tell you on the way. There's been another shooting.'

'Who was that?'

'Loose lips sink ships, Lewis,' he said with a grin as they made their way to the BBC van.

'We're not at war, Danny.'

'We so fucking are.' The excitement in his voice palpable.

Chapter Fourteen

Wakefield Prison

In 2017, Steven Harrison was given a life sentence for murdering six people in Sheffield. At the time of his killings, he was a serving police constable with South Yorkshire Police. He used his position to access information on people who had been released from prison who he thought hadn't served enough time for their crimes. He hanged his victims, believing he was serving them the justice they should have originally faced.

When DCI Matilda Darke discovered the killer's identity, he made sure she would remember him for life and murdered one of her own officers, DC Faith Easter, in front of her. She tried to save her from The Hangman's noose but couldn't. Faith's death haunted Matilda. Steve haunted her, too.

The press was all over the story. Serial killers are rare in England, so the story of one, especially a serving police officer, was a dream for the news editors. Steve Harrison, dubbed 'The Hangman', filled the front pages for weeks, and although his guilty plea denied the papers a gritty trial, it made the sentence hearing unmissable. The court was packed. Journalists and reporters lined the pavements outside. Roads had to be closed and extra police drafted in to deal with the deluge of people wanting to witness a life sentence being handed down.

At the sentencing hearing at Sheffield Crown Court, Steve stood in the dock, wearing his best Hugo Boss suit. He was clean shaven, his dark hair neatly combed, and he wore a splash of his favourite fragrance. His hands were cuffed behind him, his head was high, and he paid attention to every word the judge said to him – the other man calling Steve a 'degenerate narcissist with contempt for his fellow man' – before he was sentenced. The whole life tariff didn't come as a surprise, and he didn't flinch as his freedom was taken away from him.

'Is there anything you would like to say, Mr Harrison?' the judge had asked.

'Yes. First of all, thank you for your oratory, Your Honour,' he said, giving a little bow. 'To the families of my victims,' he began solemnly. 'I would like to say…' He paused and bowed his head momentarily as if caught up in emotion. He looked up. 'They fucking deserved it,' he spat with venom.

Cries were heard from around the court. The judge slammed his gavel and ordered the police to take Steve away, and as he turned around he saw DCI Matilda Darke in the gallery, looking down at him. They made eye contact. He slowly licked his lips and smiled. 'Matilda, sleep with one eye open. I haven't finished with you yet,' he screamed as he was led away.

The court rang with the echo of Steve's crazed rantings.

As the largest high-security prison in the UK, Wakefield Prison in West Yorkshire has often been dubbed 'Monster Mansion', due to the number of depraved and dangerous criminals who have been housed there over the years. From serial killers and murderers to gangsters and paedophiles, notable inmates have included Dr Harold Shipman, Ian Huntley, Mark Bridger and Colin Ireland.

Steve wasn't nervous. He wasn't frightened. He left his cell on his first morning with his dark hair slicked back, a swagger in his step and a smile on his lips. If this was to be his home for the rest of his life, he might as well make the most of it.

While sat eating his breakfast, he received a few lingering looks and several inmates seemed to purposely keep their distance. His reputation had obviously preceded him. Here he was, the great Steve Harrison, Britain's latest serial killer, whose handsome face had adorned many a front page for weeks. He was violent, sadistic, a cop-killer.

He chatted to a few inmates but knew they wouldn't become lifelong friends. He had no interest in the banality of most people and believed them to be limited in brain power. Conversations would be basic and dull. He doubted they'd spend their downtime reading the works of Dostoyevsky, writing haikus and finding new ways to expand their minds. In all honesty, Steve found Dostoyevsky hard going, and most of the haikus he claimed to have written he'd found online, but he gave the impression of an intellectual, and the tutor in the prison's literature-appreciation group was gullible enough to lap them up. He had the ability to bluff, and as long as people believed it, that was all that mattered. Steve was a master in manipulation.

Steve was also an incredibly handsome man. He was of average height, but of a muscular build. He had large, dark, twinkling eyes, and everyone remarked on his gorgeous smile, which they said lit up his face. When he saw his reflection in the mirror, he knew what they meant. He was good-looking. No, he was beautiful.

He caught the eye of several men in the shower as soon as he stepped in and made a play of showing off his body. He had no interest in engaging with sex with any of these blokes, but if they thought they had a chance with him, why not use it to his advantage. Within a week of being incarcerated, his cell was decked with all kinds of contraband. He'd even managed to get hold of a couple of memory foam pillows and a decent digital radio. And all he'd had to do was make eye contact and smile.

His charm soon began to waver, and when he gave nothing in return for the gifts he received, the inmates turned. He was set upon several times in coordinated attacks that resulted in him spending a few days in the prison hospital for bruised ribs, contusions and concussion. But it did nothing to dent his confidence. He still flashed the smile, he still strutted, and there were still some prisoners who gave him what he wanted when he asked in his own special way.

There were a group of lifers who had been at Wakefield long before Steve arrived who didn't take too kindly to him turning up and thinking he was cock of the walk. If being pushed down the stairs, beaten up in the exercise yard or attacked in the gym wouldn't wipe the smile off his face, they'd have to step up their assault.

One morning in November, Steve stepped into the showers, threw his threadbare towel to one side and stood under the lukewarm water as it rained down on him. He slowly ran his hands over his body, caressing himself. He knew he was being watched. He knew he was fulfilling someone's fantasy. If they enjoyed what they saw, that was their pleasure. Fingers crossed they'd thank him with something he could sell or put to use. He was about to soap up, when he felt a hand on the back of his neck. He was pushed forward. His head hit the cold tiles with a dull thud.

'You're a cocky cunt, aren't you, Harrison?' He felt the warmth of the stale breath as the words were hissed into his ear. The large, calloused hand gripped him harder around the neck. His legs were kicked apart.

'Jesus,' his whispered to himself. He knew what was coming.

A finger was inserted roughly inside him. He gasped.

'Oh God, please no. Please. Please. I'm begging you,' he said as he started to cry.

'Not so tough now, are you?'

Steve was turned around and slammed against the tiles. In front of him were four muscular men, all taller than him, all grinning with crooked smiles, showing off broken teeth and enjoying his terror. He was pushed to his knees and had a large erect penis thrust in his face. He closed his eyes tight. He heard the gang laughing and jeering as he was slapped around the face with it. He could smell it, taste it. He felt sick.

'Open your mouth, copper.'

Tears streamed down his face. Fortunately they were mixed with the water from the shower, so they couldn't see him crying.

'You either open your mouth or it goes up your arse. Your choice.'

He couldn't open his mouth. He froze. The man leaned down and squeezed his nose shut. Steve had no option but to open his mouth to breath. He gagged as the penis was thrust to the back of his throat. But he'd show them.

He clamped his mouth closed, biting down hard. He heard a high-pitched sound he'd never heard before in his life. He tasted blood.

Everyone backed off as the injured prisoner dropped to the floor, screaming in agony.

Steve opened his eyes and saw the thug on the floor, his hands between his legs, blood running through his fingers. There was something in Steve's mouth. He could feel it resting on his tongue. He turned and spat it out. It landed in a wet plop of shower water. He felt sick. He'd just bitten off a piece of a guy's penis. Steve stood up. He wiped the blood off his mouth with the back of his hand, drank from the shower head, swilled the water around his mouth and spat it out. He looked to the other three prisoners standing back, not knowing what to do. He smiled. 'Don't even think of fucking with me again. Understand?'

They nodded, their hands up in surrender.

Steve stepped over the stricken prisoner, grabbed his towel and walked slowly out of the shower room. If that didn't cement his position at the top of the chain of command, nothing would.

Two years into his sentence, and Steve was now a hardened prisoner. Nobody fucked with him again after the incident in the shower. The twinkle in his eye had long since gone, as had the winning smile, which had turned into a depraved sneer. He had no friends, no acquaintances, nobody to chat to or confide in, and he didn't give a flying fuck. He went about his work calmly. He showed the prison officers respect, though it pained him to do so, and he behaved as a model prisoner. But it was all part of the bigger plan.

Since just after breakfast that morning, Steve had retreated to the television room. There was an underlying smell of sweaty feet teasing his nostrils and causing him to grimace. He wasn't a fan of daytime television; baseless, dumbed-down entertainment aimed at the elderly and unemployable, presented by shiny-faced rejects not good enough for prime time. He turned to the BBC News channel and rolled his eyes at the mention of Brexit. He voted in the referendum and opted to leave. He could see the country would benefit more from being in Europe, but he wanted to enjoy the ensuing chaos of a leave victory. Now, he was bored with it. It wasn't chaos; it was annoying.

Steve looked at the time in the bottom corner of the screen. It was twenty past ten. Surely the police would have released something for the media by now. He was impatient and paced the room, biting his bottom lip and tasting blood. He'd woken early, excited, with a sense of trepidation. Steve had been indirectly brainwashing Jake for months. It had all be leading to this, to today.

He was alone in the room when an inmate entered and sat down. He picked up the remote and pointed it at the screen.

'Press one button on that remote and I'll break off every one of your fingers.'

'You're not even watching it,' the young inmate said.

A death stare from Harrison was enough for the other man to put down the remote. He picked up a well-thumbed car magazine instead and opened it at random.

Steve continued to stare at him. Eventually, the young lad looked up over the magazine.

'Fuck off,' Steve growled.

'I'm not doing anything.'

'If I have to tell you again, I'm going to roll that magazine up and shove it down your fucking throat.'

The inmate swallowed hard. He closed the magazine, slapped it down on the coffee table and left the room.

At ten-thirty, the newsreader announced there was some breaking news. Steve was all ears. He sat on the seat closest to the television. His eyes widened in excitement. He was almost drooling. A gunman had opened fire at the headquarters of South Yorkshire Police.

'Good lad, Jake,' he said to himself.

At eleven o'clock, the BBC News channel went live to South Yorkshire Police HQ. The building he used to work in hadn't changed much, and he felt a pang of something from deep within. He almost missed the place.

He watched with rapt attention as Chief Constable Martin Featherstone approached the microphone and announced to the waiting press that ACC Valerie Masterson was among the dead. Steve felt his face soften into a smile. She was a bonus hit. He never liked the way the short-arsed bitch strutted around the station like she owned the place. When Danny Hanson asked about Matilda Darke, Steve sat up. He reached for the remote and turned up the volume. It was a while before Featherstone began to answer, but before he had the chance, he was interrupted. But that was okay; his stony face had said more than any words could. Matilda had been hit.

'Jake, you're a fucking legend,' he said to himself as he sat back in his seat.

Chapter Fifteen

'What's this about another shooting?' Chief Constable Featherstone asked as he entered the HMET suite.

Christian had been talking on the phone with an inspector from Armed Response while his team waited for orders.

'A man has opened fire on a bridge over the Sheffield Parkway,' he said, looking grey.

'Casualties?'

'We don't know yet. I've just been speaking to Inspector Porter, sir. He and his team are on their way to the scene.'

'Same man?'

'We have to assume so until we know otherwise.'

'So, what are we saying? There's an armed man running around Sheffield shooting at random?'

'It would appear so,' Christian said reluctantly.

'Jesus!' The Chief Constable ran his fingers through his hair. 'I want an armed presence on the streets and a helicopter in the sky, Brady.'

'I've already taken care of that. SY99 are being diverted to the Parkway.'

'Good. We need to show we're in control of this, even if we're not at the moment. I want schools and hospitals placed in lockdown. Is there a football match tonight, do we know?'

'There's a charity event at the Sheffield United ground tonight,' Sian said. 'My Stuart's got tickets.'

'Brady, inform their security of the situation. Tell them no extra police officers will be available due to what's happened today and advise them to cancel.'

Featherstone turned on his heel and headed for the door. He stopped and turned back. 'Have you all contacted your families?'

There were nods of ascent from around the room.

'Good.' He left the room, taking his own mobile out of his pocket. With shaking fingers, he selected his wife's number and called. She should cancel her appointments for today and stay home. He couldn't face the prospect of her being hurt again.

———————

The ambulance transporting Matilda Darke from the Northern General to the Royal Hallamshire Hospital tore through the streets of Sheffield with lights flashing and sirens blazing. It pulled up, its brakes squealing, and Matilda was whisked straight into theatre where a team of specialists were standing by to save her life.

The shot to her head was not a direct hit. It had grazed along the side but, upon impact, the bullet had fractured her skull and the force of the bullet had imbedded some of the fractured bone inside Matilda's brain, causing it to swell to dangerous levels. The fragments of skull needed to be painstakingly removed if she were to have any chance of survival, and she was placed in a medically induced coma so the delicate procedure could take place.

Matilda lay on the operating table, her eyes closed, tape over each one. Her thick dark hair had been shaved. When she first arrived at the hospital, doctors had worked aggressively to resuscitate her, and they'd been able to maintain her blood pressure and oxygenation levels so that a CT scan of her head was possible.

When the brain is injured, it swells. However, as it is encased in the skull, the swelling has nowhere to go. As pressure inside the cranium increases, the more damage is done to the soft tissue, which, if the patient survives, can cause serious debilitating injuries. The only solution is to relieve the pressure, and fast, and that involves cutting open the skull.

Using a craniotome, a piece of Matilda's skull was removed. The noise, like that heard in a dentist surgery to extract a tooth, echoed around the theatre as the surgeon cut out a large section of skull. It was carefully detached from the brain and refrigerated along with several of the larger fragments from the impact of the bullet, which could be put back together like a jigsaw at a later time once the swelling had gone down.

'Blood pressure is falling,' a nurse said as she monitored the screen.

'This is incredibly nasty,' the surgeon said as he surveyed the brain. 'There would have been less damage with a direct hit. There are a great deal of tiny fragments of bone. Getting them out is not going to be easy.'

'What do you need?' a doctor next to him asked.

'Well, I know it's only early, but I wouldn't say no to a large scotch right now. Can we get some of this blood drained?'

'Suction.'

'What's this I hear about a second shooting?' the surgeon asked as he leaned down to try and pick at a small piece of skull with tweezers.

'Some bloke on a bridge over the Parkway opened fire,' a nurse said.

'Many casualties?'

'Plenty by the sounds of it.'

'It's going to be a long day. BP?'

'Still falling.'

'Have we enough blood?'

'Still waiting for cross-match. I've sent for some O-neg, and they're standing by.'

'She's a detective, isn't she?' the surgeon asked as he dropped a fragment of bone the size of a pin head into a metal dish.

'One of the best by all accounts.'

'Well, unless something miraculous happens, she's going to be looking for another job if she pulls through.'

'What are we going to do?' Scott asked.

Christian's face was a map of worry as he tried to think. The situation seemed to be spiralling out of control and he had no idea what do next. He needed Matilda.

'We need to get out there,' he eventually said. There was a sheen of sweat on his forehead. 'Sian, you and Rory stay here, coordinate what's going on with forensics and eyewitnesses. Chase up CCTV – it's taking too bloody long. Finn, Scott, we're going out to the Parkway.'

'We've just this second got back.'

'And seeing as you haven't had time to take your coats off,

you can go back out again,' Christian said, his voice raised slightly.

His phone started ringing, and he disappeared into his office to answer it while Finn and Scott exchanged worried glances.

Sian went over to the two young constables. 'Listen to me,' she said in hushed tones. 'I don't want you doing anything stupid, ok? Listen to what DI Brady tells you, and if you find yourself in a situation that is likely to get you injured or killed, get out of there straightaway. You've both got people who love you. They'll want you to go home this evening. Is that understood?' she said firmly.

'I'm going to give Susannah a ring,' Finn said. His voice was quiet as he tried to hide his emotions. He pushed up the frameless glasses on his nose, picked his phone up from his desk and went into the corner of the room to make the private phone call.

'I don't want to go,' Scott said quietly as he looked to check he wasn't being overheard. 'I'm finally happy. After years of hiding away and not wanting to say anything for fear of being made fun of, I've found a man I love and now I'm going to get shot.'

'You're not going to get shot,' Sian said, holding his clammy hand. 'Stay calm, vigilant, and don't take any risks. You're a sensible lad – you'll do the right thing.'

He took a deep breath. 'You're right. I suppose, if I was still single, I'd be more likely to take a risk. Being with Chris, it gives me a responsibility.'

'Precisely. I'll go and get the flak jackets for you and Finn.'

Sian headed off. Rory stepped forward.

'Mate, you all right?' he asked Scott.

'I'm fine,' he lied.

'Don't do anything fucking stupid out there.'

'It's the ones with the guns who'll be doing anything stupid. I'm staying in the car,' he said with a nervous smile.

'Will you do me a favour?' Rory asked.

'Anything.'

Rory stood closer to his best friend. His voice was low and urgent. There was a look of horror in his eyes that unsettled Scott. 'Don't put yourself at risk, obviously, but if you find yourself in a situation with the gunman, I want you to fucking kill him for me. For Nat.'

_____

'Shit!'

'Problems?' Sian asked as she walked by Christian's office.

'That was forensics. They've just analysed the mobile found at Weedon Street. There are no fingerprints, no call history and no serial number. It was just a burner phone. Used once then tossed away.'

'Why leave it on, though? Why leave it where we'll find it?'

Christian chewed on his lip while he thought. 'To distract us. To make us waste our time while he can get to the Parkway and kill more innocent people.'

'He knows what he's doing, doesn't he?'

'He certainly does. I don't mind telling you this, Sian, but I'm genuinely scared about what else is going to happen today.'

Chapter Sixteen

'Suze, it's me,'
     'Oh, Finn, thank God. Are you all right?'
     Susannah Cotton was glued to the television. She should have been working on her clients' accounts, as the deadline for self-assessment tax returns was looming, but the news of a gunman on the streets of Sheffield and her husband possibly in the firing line caused her to down tools, leave her home office and sit in front of the television to watch the newsreader with the awful haircut ramble on about Brexit before intermittently updating viewers on the breaking news with infuriatingly little.
     As soon as her mobile started ringing, she'd snatched it up from next to her on the sofa and swiped to answer.
     'I'm fine. You?'
     'Not in the slightest. Have you caught him?'
     'No. Not yet. Listen, there's been a second shooting at the Parkway. You're not going out at all today, are you?'
     'No. I'll stay in. Mum said she was going to come over, but I've told her to stay indoors.'

'Good thinking. Listen, Suze, I'm being sent out to the scene.'

'What? Why?' she asked, a tear escaped her eye. 'Shouldn't Armed Response go? You're just a DC.'

'I'm part of HMET. We have to investigate. I need to knock on doors, ask if anyone's seen anything.'

'Can't someone else go?'

'No. It's my job, Suze. I have to do this.'

'You'd better come home tonight, Finn Cotton.' She tried to sound positive and commanding, but she felt anything but. She was pleased he couldn't see her, as she knew the colour was likely draining from her face.

'I will.' He paused, and a silence developed between them. 'I love you, Suze.'

'I love you too, Finn.' She cracked and tears streamed down her face.

———

'Scott, what the fuck is going on? Our school has been placed in lockdown,' Chris Kean said. He was in the staffroom on a break. All pupils and staff had been told about a situation developing in Sheffield city centre and for everyone's safety they were to remain in school until further notice, all outdoor activities were cancelled and none of the senior pupils would be allowed out at lunchtime.

'There's been a second shooting.'

'Jesus Christ! Where?'

'At the Parkway. I'm going out there now.'

'You'll stay safe, won't you?'

'Of course I will. Listen, if anything happens to me—'

'Scott, please don't,' Chris interrupted.

'No, I need to say this. If anything does happen to me today, I want you to know that this past year has been the happiest of my life. I didn't think I'd ever be able to be so open about who I am, but with you by my side, I've achieved more in one year than I have in my whole life. I love you, Chris.'

'Oh my God, Scott, I don't know what to say,' Chris said. He ran his free hand over his cropped haircut. He wanted to cry but had to be strong for Scott. 'We have had an amazing year. I've loved every minute, but it's not over with yet. We've got so much left to do.'

'Have we?'

'Of course. We've got tickets to see Muse in Manchester in June. We'll stay there for the weekend and get pissed. We'll go on holiday in the summer – somewhere hot and exotic. And then there's your thirtieth birthday to plan for next year.'

Scott laughed. 'I'm not even twenty-nine yet.'

'So? A big celebration takes planning. Don't talk like you're saying goodbye, Scott. You'll be home for tea, like always.'

Scott heaved a deep breath. 'What are we having tonight?'

'I've no idea. It's your turn to cook.'

'It is, isn't it? How about my famous spag bol?'

'Sounds good. I'll pick up some wine and garlic bread on the way home from school,' Chris said, his lips quivering as he tried to maintain a smile.

'Right, well, I'd better be off.'

'Any news on Matilda?'

'Not yet.'

'Ok. I love you, Scott.'

'Love you, too.'

Chris ended the call and looked at his phone. The wallpaper was of Scott's smiling face grinning out at him.

'Is everything all right?'

Chris jumped and turned to see Ruth standing behind him. He shook his head.

Despite being several inches shorter than Chris, Ruth pulled him into an embrace and rubbed his back.

'There's been a second shooting,' Chris cried into her shoulder. 'Scott is being sent out to the scene.'

'He'll be all right.'

Chris pulled away and went over to the window. He looked out into the greyness. 'I can't lose him.'

'You won't. He won't be anywhere near the action. If there's a sighting, it's the Armed Response teams that go to these things, right? He'll be in the background.'

'You're right. I know you're right. It's just … it's scary.'

'It is. It's a bloody scary world out there at the moment,' she said, joining him at the window.

'Every time you turn on the news there's been another stabbing or gang-related violence or a terrorist attack. And nobody is doing anything about it.' He stood with his arms folded tightly across his chest. He sniffled back the tears. 'Politicians don't have a clue what's going on in the real world. Look how much money they're wasting on Brexit when it could be used better elsewhere like the NHS or to put more police on the streets. They don't have a clue and they don't care. They're only interested in what they can make for themselves.'

'Anyone would think you were dating a policeman.' She smiled.

Chris turned to her and cracked a smile. 'I'm right, though. We don't need a cabinet filled with Etonians from privileged backgrounds running the country who don't know what it means to struggle. I fucking hate this country right now, and I never thought I'd hear myself say that.' He kicked a chair over and stormed to the other side of the room.

'This is more than your political stance, Chris, isn't it? What's going on?'

Chris flicked the kettle on and took a deep breath. 'I want to ask Scott to marry me.'

Ruth's eyes lit up. 'That's brilliant news. What's stopping you?'

'I don't want to be married to a policeman.'

'Ah.'

Chapter Seventeen

At the Royal Hallamshire Hospital, Matilda's parents were waiting impatiently for news of their daughter but the operation had only just begun. They were in for a long wait, and neither of them thought they'd have the stamina for it.

Frank and Penny Doyle lived in a picture-postcard cottage in Bakewell in Derbyshire. When Frank had ended the call after being told their daughter had been shot, neither of them had spoken. They'd been expecting something like this to happen at some point. Thankfully, they'd been on their way to Meadowhall at the time and so were relatively close by. They were at the hospital within minutes.

Matilda's relationship with her parents wasn't easy. She was a daddy's girl and, although she didn't see him as much as she liked, she phoned and texted him often. They had a strong bond that went back to when she was very young. Her relationship with Penny, on the other hand, was stilted, to say the least. At almost every opportunity, Penny tried to get Matilda to rethink her choice of career. She hated her daughter being in the police force. She wanted Matilda to have a safe job – something dull and boring where she wasn't risking her life every day – to get married again and have a child. Rather than have to endure the same conversation over and over, Matilda simply kept away from her. Unfortunately, this meant rarely seeing her father.

Penny, heavily made-up and wearing designer clothing, sat on the edge of a hard plastic chair in a family room close to the operating theatres. She'd taken off her knee-length winter coat with the fake-fur trim and tried, with difficulty, to not chew on her perfectly manicured nails.

'It's strange how everything changes so quickly,' she said, breaking the painful silence. 'This morning, we got up, had breakfast as normal, and all we planned on doing was having a trip out to Meadowhall – hit the sales, have a nice lunch, back in time for tea. You don't think…' Her words were lost to tears. She pulled a small packet of tissues out of her leather handbag and carefully wiped her eyes so as not to smudge her make-up.

Frank was sitting by the door. He was tall and athletically built, having taken care of his body during his retirement years. He had a good life, money in the bank, and wanted to enjoy his free time as much as he could. Living in the countryside, he was able to get out for long walks and the local swimming baths were only a short drive away. He lived for his family. He loved his wife, despite her being high maintenance, and he doted on his two children. He didn't want much out of life, just happiness and good health for those he loved. Was that too much to ask for?

'Penny, have you phoned Harriet?' he asked.

She looked up. There were tears in her eyes. 'No. Do you think I should?'

'She'll want to know.'

With shaking hands, she fumbled in her bag and pulled out a shiny iPhone. She unlocked it and scrolled through her contacts, looking for their youngest daughter's number.

'I can't do it,' she whimpered.

Frank stepped forward. He sat down next to her and took the phone off her. 'It'll be all right, Pen. Matilda's a fighter. She's had to be.'

'She's never been shot before. Who survives a bullet to the head?'

'A lot of people.'

'But they're never the same afterwards. There could be all sorts of things wrong with her.'

'Penny, let's just wait to see how she goes in the operation. Whatever happens, we'll deal with it.'

Penny stood up and went over to the window. They were high up in the hospital, and on a clear day, the view was of the whole of the Steel City. Today, the low cloud was too thick to see through. It was oppressive and claustrophobic. She stood looking out for a long time. When she turned around to face her husband, black mascara had run down her face.

'I don't think I'll be able to deal with it, Frank. I'm sorry, but I don't.'

'With what?'

'Matilda. If she's brain-damaged or needs constant care. I don't think I can feed her, dress her, wash her, take her to the toilet. I'm sorry. I know this makes me sound like a bad person, a bad mother, but I can't see my daughter like that, Frank. And she wouldn't want me to. She wouldn't want to survive this knowing she couldn't be independent.'

'Penny, you're thinking too far ahead. We can't go making plans until the operation is over with. Stop getting yourself in such a state,' he said, holding her firmly by the shoulders.

'Frank,' she began, looking up at him with wet eyes. 'If they ask us to turn off the life support…'

'Penny, don't.'

'No, listen to me. If they ask us, we should let them.'

Frank let go of his wife and stood back. They'd been married for forty years and he'd always let her have her own way. As long as she was happy, he was happy. This time, he would fight her all the way.

Chapter Eighteen

DC Rory Fleming took over Scott's work when he went to attend the scene of the second shooting but he was struggling to concentrate. He kept hearing Natasha call out to him, holding up her bloody hands, then that bullet hitting her. Her eyes were still fixed on him as she dropped to the floor. How was he going to cope without her? He loved her so much.

'Shit,' he said to himself as he felt the emotions rise. He needed to get a grip. Nat's killer was out there and he needed to find the fucker.

He'd perused the CCTV footage from the entrance and exits of the police station and found nothing untoward. There was a question mark hanging over one man seen entering the station via the back entrance carrying a spirit level over his shoulder and coming back out again less than a minute later, just as the fire-alarm started. Had he been simply following procedure and heading for the nearest exit when an alarm sounded, or was there something more sinister about him?

Rory watched the footage again. He zoomed in. The man's eyes darted rapidly left and right as he left the station. He was wearing dirty clothes, jeans that had seen better days, a holey sweater with a high-visibility waistcoat over the top and a beanie hat pulled down low. His face seemed filthy and he had an unkempt beard. He could have been a workman, but Rory wasn't convinced. He looked too dirty to be a workman just starting. Surely he'd have washed before coming to work.

He picked up the phone and dialled the main reception.

'Alice, it's DC Fleming from HMET.'

'Hello, Rory. I was sorry to hear—'

'Yes, thanks,' he interrupted, not wanting to hear another round of sympathy about Natasha being murdered. 'Listen, can you find out for me if there was any building work booked in for today?'

'What kind of building work?'

'I'm not sure. Anything that would involve someone coming in with a spirit level,' he said, looking at the still image of the man on his laptop.

'Not for today. There was a bloke in on Friday to look at the central heating, but nothing else is scheduled.'

'Thanks, Alice,' he said, hanging up before she could say anything else. He called Sian over and told her to look at the footage.

'That's not a workman,' she said. 'That's McNally.'

'You're going to need to explain how you know that.'

She pulled up a chair. 'McNally is one of Sheffield's increasing number of homeless people. About a year ago I was out with my sister-in-law. We'd been to City Hall to watch a...' She looked at Rory. 'It doesn't matter what we saw,' she said, reddening slightly. 'Anyway, we were going back to the car when this bloke tried to mug us. From nowhere, McNally very kindly told him to leave us alone. Although, he was a little more forceful in his choice of language. Anyway, me and Liz bought McNally a drink as a thank-you and he told us all about himself. Whenever I see him outside the cathedral, I slip him a fiver. He's a lovely bloke.'

'So why did he enter our police station with a spirit level over his shoulder and leave less than a minute later?'

'You think he set off the alarm?'

'Possibly.'

'Print off his picture and update the board, then we'll go and have a wee chat with him. He always hangs around the cathedral around lunchtime, as it's busy.'

———

Sheffield city centre was subdued. People had heard of a gunman stalking the city and had decided to stay clear of crowded places. The January sales were in full flow, but the footfall was lacking. The cold, wet weather probably didn't help either.

Sheffield was still going through a period of regeneration. Dated concrete monstrosities were being demolished to be replaced by generic boxes. More shops were built but remained empty, and blocks of student apartments were being thrown up left, right and centre.

Sian and Rory, wrapped up against the elements, headed on foot for the cathedral. Sian's phone rang.

'It's Aaron,' came the reply once she'd answered.

DS Aaron Connolly had been a part of HMET since its inception but was forced to quit over an affair with a witness last year. Since then, he'd been working with CID on drugs busts and burglaries. Whenever someone was needed to attend a secondary school to talk about the dangers of drink and drugs or how to stay safe online while using social media,

Aaron was always sent. That was his penance for South Yorkshire Police being torn apart during a high-profile murder case at the Crown Court.

'Oh. Hi,' Sian said, a frostiness to her voice.

'I've been seconded to help.'

'I see. Well, welcome back,' she said, not sure if she meant it. 'What can I do for you?'

'I've been interviewing some of the staff in offices behind HQ, and although they said they didn't see anyone suspicious this morning, CCTV has shown a man gaining access to the roof. The thing is, he doesn't look like the bloke you suspect of setting off the fire alarm in the police station.'

'Well, I didn't think it would be the same person. It would have taken too long – by the time he'd reached the roof of the offices after setting the alarm off, we'd have realised it was a false alarm and gone back inside.'

'What I'm saying is, maybe there is more than one man on this.'

'That's what we're saying, too.' The man never listened. 'In fact, we're off to speak to a source now – a homeless bloke who goes by McNally.'

'What do you know about this "McNally"?'

'He's a harmless man who is down on his luck, like a lot of the homeless.'

'Really? You've looked him up?'

Sian hesitated. 'No,' she said.

'Well, I'm looking at his file now. Duncan Arthur McNally, born on the twenty-eighth of October 1989. No fixed abode. He's been arrested six times for drunk and disorderly, seven times for disturbing the peace and twice for drug dealing. When he was twenty-five, he was dishonourably discharged from the army for unruly behaviour.'

'Well, none of us know what these young men have to face in the army,' she said.

'Sian, you're not listening. He's ex-military. Who better to launch a sniper attack than someone trained with guns? Where are you?'

'We're heading to the cathedral to speak to McNally, as I know he's normally there around this time.'

'On your own?'

'No. I have Rory with me.'

'Don't approach. I'll send back-up.'

'Aaron, calm down. You're overreacting. I've chatted with this guy on many occasions. He's not a killer. He's not a sniper. He's a little mixed-up, but who isn't when you're sleeping on the streets. If you send armed officers and surround him, he'll clam up. Personally, I think he was paid to go into the station and set the fire alarm off. It's possible he's seen the gunman, but he won't tell us anything if he feels threatened.'

'I don't like this, Sian.'

'Personally, Aaron, it's nothing to do with you. You've been seconded back to the HMET. You're no longer a member and I have the final say on this.' She ended the call and put the phone back in her pocket.

'Aaron's back, is he?' Rory said, speaking for the first time since leaving the station.

'Temporarily, yes.'

'So, we're going to meet a man, unarmed, who was paid to help the gunman murder my fiancée?'

'Rory.' Sian stopped and turned Rory to face her. 'I know you're going through hell right now, but you need to put your personal feelings to one side until this is all sorted out. I know it's difficult, but you have to be professional about this.'

'How can I? I've lost my fiancée, Sian. I've lost the

woman I wanted to spend the rest of my life with, the woman I was going to marry, the woman who was going to have my children. How can I carry on like nothing's happened?'

'I'm not asking you to do that. I'm asking you to remain professional. By all means, cry, mourn, do whatever you have to do to come to terms with it, but while you're at work, you need to be a detective.'

'How can you be so cold after what you witnessed this morning?' he asked, looking daggers at the sergeant.

'Is that what you think I'm being?' she sounded hurt. 'I know you're going through a lot right now, Rory, but I will not tolerate you turning on me. I've cried buckets this morning. Ranjeet, a young man with a baby, was killed right in front of my eyes, trying to save me. I had to scrub his blood out of my hair. His child will never know his father. I'm devastated, horrified, shocked and appalled by what's happened, and I will relive his death every day for the rest of my life. However, I can honour him by catching the bastard who killed him. I'm not cold. I'm not calm. I'm screaming inside, but I'm fuck-all use to anyone if I allow that to show.' With that, she stormed off, leaving Rory behind.

'Sian, I'm sorry,' he said, breaking into a trot to catch her up. 'I didn't mean to snap like that. I just … I honest to God don't know how I'm going to come back from this.'

'You won't,' she said. 'I'm sorry, but you won't ever be the same person again. Neither of us will. You've lost somebody special in the cruellest way imaginable. From today, you'll be a different person. You will love again, and you'll laugh again, it'll just take time. But even when you've moved on, found love again and you're stood at the top of the altar waiting for your bride to walk down the aisle, you'll be feeling a different kind of happiness to what you would have felt had today never happened.'

Rory swallowed hard. 'Thank you.' His eyes glistened with tears. 'And I'm sorry, again.'

She rubbed the top of his arm. 'You don't need to apologise today, Rory. Just remember, you know me – I will never say or do anything to upset you, and I will be here whenever you need to cry or scream.'

'You're a good woman, Sian.'

'I know,' she said with a smile. 'If you ever want to recommend me for an OBE, I won't stop you.' Rory gave a genuine smile, but only briefly. 'Come on, let's go and see what McNally has to tell us.'

Duncan Arthur McNally wore dirty cargo trousers, scuffed walking boots, a dark red sweater with holes in it and a padded waterproof jacket that was a size too small for him. He had a khaki beanie hat pulled down low, sitting just on top of his eyebrows. He was twenty-nine years old but living rough on the streets of Sheffield had aged him terribly. His face was ruddy and wrinkled, his dirty-blond beard was wiry and unkempt.

It was a cold day and a harsh wind was blowing. He stood in the shadows of the cathedral opposite East Parade. He liked it here. It was central, so close to shops and offices where people made their way to and from work at lunchtime. He often made a few quid, enough to buy himself a sandwich and a coffee somewhere. It was also quiet, away from the main hustle, so he could be left alone with his raging thoughts.

Winter was a difficult time for the homeless, and although

there hadn't been many frosty nights and very little snow so far this season, temperatures had been cold, the wind had been strong, and rain had been heavy. He had no idea how much longer he could continue living like this. He ached all over from holding himself rigid at night against the cold. He'd had a cough for weeks that showed no sign of shifting, and the cut he'd gained from being attacked over Christmas by a group of drunken teenagers was refusing to heal.

'McNally,' Sian called as they approached.

Leaning against the wall of the cathedral, McNally had been away with his dark thoughts and he jumped at the sound of his name being called. He wiped his wet eyes with the sleeve of his jacket.

'Sian, you all right?' he asked with a quiet but gruff voice.

'I'm doing ok, thanks,' she lied. 'How about you?'

'Can't complain.' He smiled.

'Are you eating?'

'I am. I had a big fry-up in the market this morning. That'll keep me warm all day.'

'McNally, this is a colleague of mine, Rory. I don't know if you've heard, but there's been a shooting at our headquarters this morning. We've lost a few officers.'

'I'm so sorry,' he said, genuinely meaning it. 'Are you all right?'

'Physically, yes. The thing is, we've been going through CCTV and we found you entering our building via the back door with a spirit level over your shoulder.' Sian took out a printed copy of the image, unfolded it and showed it to him.

He nodded. 'Yes. That's me. I didn't shoot anyone though,' he said defensively. He tried to take a step back, but the cathedral was in his way.

'I'm not accusing you of anything. I know you didn't pull

the trigger. I'm guessing someone paid you to go into our building and set off the fire alarm?'

McNally looked from Sian to Rory and back again, then looked around to see if anyone close by was listening in to their conversation.

He ushered them to lean in close, so he could drop his quiet voice further. 'This bloke came up to me first thing, while it was still dark. He offered me fifty quid to just waltz into the station, set the fire alarm off and waltz back out again, bold as brass.'

'Can you remember what he looked like?'

He thought for a moment. 'Tall, thin, pale. His eyes were too close together for my liking. He looked shifty.'

'Did you ask him why he wanted you to set the alarm off?' Rory asked.

'I did. He told me to mind my own fucking business. His words, not mine.' He smiled to Sian.

'Where did you get the spirit level and the high-vis jacket from?'

'He gave them to me. He told me to dump them afterwards. I'd left my coat and bag round the corner from the station and threw the stuff in a bin nearby.'

'How did you get to the station?'

'He gave me a lift in his van.'

'What was his van like?' Rory asked.

'It was white. Well, I'm guessing its original colour was white. Like me, it needed a good wash,' he said with a chuckle in his voice.

'Did the bloke say anything to you on the way there?'

'Nope. Nothing at all. I tried making conversation, but he wasn't having any of it. He didn't even look at me; just stared straight out of the windscreen. His hands didn't leave the steering wheel once. He had a determined look on his face.'

'How did you get back into town?' Sian asked.

'I walked. Once he dropped me off round the corner from the station, he told me to give him five minutes, do the deed, then I was free to go.'

'Did you see what direction he drove off in?'

'No. I wasn't looking. Look, if I'd known he was going to shoot at you, I wouldn't have done it. I swear. You know me, Sian.'

'I do,' she said with a smile. 'Listen, we'll need you to give us a formal statement. I'll make sure you get a hot meal in the canteen, and we'll sort you out a change of clothes, too. Will that be all right?'

'Sure.'

As they headed off from the cathedral towards the station, Sian took a twenty-pound note out of her inside jacket pocket and discreetly handed it to McNally when Rory wasn't watching. He took it and smiled.

'Did you see any guns or anything suspicious in the van?' Rory asked.

'No. Although…'

'Yes?'

'When we pulled over behind where the station is, we went to the back of the van to get the spirit level and jacket, and I saw a uniform in the same box.'

'What kind of uniform?'

'A copper's uniform.'

Chapter Nineteen

The chaotic scene at the Sheffield Parkway looked like a film set. Vehicles were riddled with bullet holes, shattered glass covered the road and blue lights flashed off every surface. By the time Scott and Finn arrived at the scene, the injured had been taken to hospital, traffic had been diverted and the Parkway closed in both directions. Several of the dead still lay strewn about, white sheets giving them a final cover of dignity against the violent deaths they'd endured.

'Oh my God,' Finn said as he stepped out of the car. He looked around him. He shopped at the nearby Morrisons most weeks. He and his wife had driven along this stretch of road countless number of times. Seeing it like this was alien.

'Over here!' Christian Brady called out to them.

They both looked up and saw the DI on the bridge above, who summoned them to join him. On top of the bridge, the wind was stronger, the gale buffeting them as they walked. They were cold and exposed to the elements, and possibly to the gunman too.

Surveying the scene from above didn't lessen the impact of

what had taken place. In fact, it heightened it. Crashed vehicles seemed to stretch for miles as drivers had tried to flee the danger and caused more damage. A covered body was half hanging out of a car, shot dead while they tried to make their escape. It was a sad and painful scene to witness.

DI Brady was with Inspector Gavin Porter. Standing at five feet nine inches tall, Porter was dwarfed by the other three officers, but his all-black clothing, his protective equipment and the large gun in both hands gave him a sense of power and danger that made his presence much taller than the others.

Porter had been with South Yorkshire Police since he was young enough to join. Following his two-year probationary period, he immediately joined the Armed Response Unit. He'd always wanted to be at the forefront of the action and had policed many large events in the region from football matches to royal visits to protest marches. He prided himself on having never once fired his gun throughout his twenty-year career, but he'd been highly trained for every eventuality.

Scott glanced at him and took a step back. Despite being a detective and having come across guns many times in the past, he couldn't get used to them. He hoped he wouldn't live to see a day when all British police were armed. If it happened while he was still a serving detective, it would be the day he resigned.

'We've had a few good eyewitness statements so far,' Christian shouted against the wind. 'None of them could give us a decent description of the gunman, but the Audi down the embankment was the first hit. A perfect shot right through the windscreen and into the driver's eye.'

'Jesus,' Finn winced.

'Lucky shot or plenty of practice?' Scott asked.

'Look around you,' Inspector Porter spoke up. His

Yorkshire accent was thick and deep. 'There's eighteen confirmed dead so far and dozens injured through being hit, ricocheted off or other injuries, yet we've picked up less than sixty shell casings. This bloke knows what he's doing.'

'A marksman?'

'Or as good as. All of his targets were moving, and he managed to hit someone or something with practically every bullet. You've got a dangerous bloke out there. He needs catching fast.'

Christian nodded to Finn and Scott to move up the bridge for him to talk to in private.

'Guys, this isn't going to be easy,' he said quietly once they were in a huddle. 'We don't know where he's going to target next, we don't know his motive and we don't know what kind of weapons he has on him. He's already targeted the police; he could still come after us again. We need to identify him as quickly as possible.'

'How?' Scott asked.

'We need to work backwards. He obviously came here straight from the station, so what route will he have taken? I've phoned Sian, and she told me he paid a homeless guy to set the fire alarm off at the station, so he was waiting for us to leave the building with his gun aimed. He's organised. He's calm and he's fucking dangerous.' There was an urgency in Christian's voice, his body shaking. Scott wasn't sure if that was from nerves or the cold wind.

'What do you want us to do?'

'Armed police! Your house is surrounded.' A shout was heard from somewhere below the bridge.

'Brady, we've got something,' Inspector Porter said from the side of the bridge.

They ran down the steps from the bridge and the decline

towards the houses on Beaumont Road North. The row of terraced houses in the cul-de-sac were characterless, and judging by the toys abandoned in one front garden and a trampoline in another, home to families with young children.

Two marked police cars were parked haphazardly as armed officers in protective clothing ran from house to house, garden to garden and shed to shed to make sure the gunman wasn't hiding close by. Through a loudspeaker, instructions were being given for residents to remain indoors for their own safety. Curtains twitched in almost every window as frightened onlookers tried to see what was happening in their usually quiet neighbourhood.

One of the houses had turned their front lawn into a makeshift driveway. A dirty white transit van was parked on it. Several armed officers were standing outside of the front door, guns aiming at the house.

'There are people in there, but they won't come to the door,' an officer shouted towards Inspector Porter, his voice muffled behind his mask.

'How many can you see?' Christian asked.

'At least three adults in the living room.'

'Knock again and tell them to come out.'

The officer banged on the glass with a gloved fist. The noise echoed around the street. 'Your house is surrounded by armed police. Open this door and walk out slowly with your hands up. This is your final warning. I will break this door down if necessary.'

Christian looked nervous as he exchanged eye contact with Porter. Finn and Scott, wearing only flak jackets for protection stood well back.

After a long silence, the armed officer looked towards Porter.

'Your call, Brady,' Porter said in turn.

'Shit,' he uttered under his breath. 'I can't risk anyone losing their lives. Do we know whose house this is?'

'No. Either way, they're ignoring us. They're obviously hiding something.'

'Ok. Break in.'

'Go ahead,' Porter instructed his officer.

'Can someone get me a ram?' he shouted over his shoulder.

A heavy metal battering ram was brought out of the back of a police car. A tactical-support officer, dressed in identical clothing to his armed colleague, went up to the door. They both took hold of it and on the count of three swung it into the door. It opened with little resistance and armed officers entered the house in a barrage of yelled instructions.

Christian bit his bottom lip hard and frowned. He was waiting for gunfire, but none came. After a few minutes, an officer came out of the house and said it was clear for them to enter.

As soon as they walked in, they could tell why the residents were reluctant to open the door to police. The house reeked of cannabis. In the living room, three young men in their twenties were sat on a dated brown sofa, guns pointing at them from every direction.

'There are three bedrooms upstairs and two of them are full of the stuff,' an officer said upon entering the living room.

'Not our problem. Give organised crime a ring and get someone out here to deal with it,' Christian said as he left the room and the house. In a way, he was relieved. He hadn't wanted a gun battle taking place in a housing estate. On the other hand, the nightmare continued.

His mobile vibrated in his pocket and he dug it out. He listened, barely saying two words before hanging up.

'The station's had a call from someone at the allotments just down the road from here,' he said to Scott and Finn who were waiting outside the drug house. 'Before the shooting, he saw a shifty-looking bloke walking through the allotment. Go down and have a word with the witness.'

'Will do.'

Christian was about to take a deep breath when Inspector Porter called out to him. He turned around to see the heavily armed officer stride towards him. 'Right then, Sheffield Park Academy, Pipworth Primary School, Norfolk Park School and Prince Edward Primary School are all within a ten-minute walk from here. They've been placed in lockdown. How do you want to play this?'

Christian shook his head and released a heavy sigh. 'You know something, Gavin, I don't have a fucking clue.'

Chapter Twenty

A dele pulled open the double doors and entered the surgical ward of the Northern General Hospital. She spotted Matilda's mother pacing just inside the relatives' room.

'Penny,' Adele called out.

The woman turned quickly on her heels at the sound of her name being called. She had an expression of horror and worry on her heavily made-up face that softened, slightly, at the sight of someone she knew.

'Oh my God, Adele, thank you so much for coming,' she said, opening her arms.

Adele hugged her and felt the emotion well up inside her. If she hadn't had broken free, she thought Penny might have held on to her for the rest of the day.

'Have you had any news?'

Matilda's dad Frank stood up from the row of seats on the far side of the room.

'We haven't heard anything,' Frank said. 'She was in theatre by the time we arrived. They haven't told us any more.' There were tears in his eyes, threatening to fall at any moment.

Adele knew all about Matilda's relationship with her parents, and while Penny wore her emotions on her sleeve and had dried tear tracks on her face, Frank's concern seemed more genuine. He was pale, stony-faced, and had a look about him that suggested his entire world was crumbling around him. That wasn't far from the truth. Since James's death, his worry for Matilda had grown. He wanted her to be happy, but she continued to cling to the memory of her husband, and she was unable to move on. However, just as she was starting a new relationship with Daniel Harbison, as she was beginning to let the light back into her life, this had happened. As Frank stood up to greet Adele, it seemed to take all the energy he could muster. He was drained.

'They've sat us in this depressing family room and told us to wait. It is so suffocating in here, I don't know what to do,' Penny said. Her face had been wiped free of most of its make-up and her eyes were red from crying.

'What actually happened, do you know?' Frank asked. 'Nobody's telling us anything.'

Adele slumped down on a nearby seat. She waited until Frank and Penny sat before filling them in on everything she knew about the shooting.

'Oh my God. Who would do such a thing?' Penny asked, wiping her eyes with a tatty tissue.

'I don't know. Look, Scott told me that Matilda was shot twice. Has a doctor or anyone given you any more information?'

'All we know is that they're not too concerned with the bullet in her shoulder, but...' Penny couldn't continue. She fished in her oversized bag for a replacement tissue to the damp and crumpled one in her hand.

'There are bullet fragments in her brain, apparently,' Frank continued. His voice was slow, as if he was too exhausted to speak. 'They need to take them out. They've done a scan, and they know where they are, but they don't know if they'll be able to remove them without … damaging the brain further.'

'Jesus!' Adele said, putting her head down.

'Adele, you're medically trained, is there a chance she could be brain-damaged?' Frank asked.

Adele took a deep breath. She'd known Frank and Penny for more than twenty years – they were like a second set of parents. They'd be able to tell if she was lying or trying to placate them and would accept nothing less than the truth.

Adele could feel the rise of emotion building inside her. She'd been crying while alone and driving to the hospital. She cried in the police station car park when surrounded by bodies and at the mortuary. She always prided herself on being strong and in control, but today, she'd given in to her feelings completely. She was struggling to cope.

She swallowed hard and tried to keep the nausea at bay. 'That is a possibility,' she said. 'However, they won't know that until she wakes up.'

'Is there a chance she won't wake up?'

Adele nodded as tears fell down her face.

'So there is a chance she won't survive the surgery?' he asked.

She couldn't speak. She nodded again.

'Oh my God,' Penny's voice croaked.

'Have you phoned Daniel?' Frank asked.

'Yes. I called him earlier. He's in Nottingham. He's on his way back here now.'

'Good.'

Frank had met Daniel several times when he'd driven over to Matilda's house and he'd been there. He liked him. Penny had yet to meet him but both were relieved to see Matilda had finally found someone to make her happy following the death of her husband five years ago. It had taken a long while, but it seemed she had finally accepted that time doesn't stand still, and life goes on.

The three of them slipped into an awkward silence. Around them, hospital life continued as staff clattered down the corridors, trolleys rattled and lifts were called. They kept turning to look at the double doors of the theatre, wondering if and when they were going to open to be informed of Matilda's progress.

'Are there many casualties?' Frank eventually asked.

Adele nodded. 'Six dead in total including ACC Valerie Masterson. You met her, I believe.'

'Tiny woman with grey hair?' Penny asked.

'Yes.'

'Oh goodness. She was a lovely woman. Hadn't her husband recently been ill or something?'

'He had two severe strokes last year.'

'Good heavens. That poor family.' She thought momentarily, her eyes darting every which way. 'I've never liked Matilda being in the police,' Penny said as she wiped her red nose. 'I've been saying it for years. Do you remember when she told us?' She nudged Frank. 'You were pleased as punch. I just kept thinking... Well, I mean, when you look around you at the state of the world, I knew something like this was going to happen one day.'

'You can't know what's going to happen, Penny. If you fret and worry about every little thing, then you won't do anything with your life. You have to take risks. You have to take chances. It's called living,' he said harshly.

'It might be living to people like you and Matilda, but what about us poor buggers who are left to worry?'

'Worry?' Frank asked. He frowned as he turned to his wife. He raised his voice. 'When did you ever worry? All you ever did was nag at her. You constantly badgered her to leave the force and do something else. You'd have had her miserable in a call centre instead of happy as a detective.'

'At least she'd have been safe,' Penny snapped. 'Look what's happened to her in the last few years. Look what happened to her last year when she was knocked unconscious and driven into the reservoir? She could have died then.'

'Yes, and you don't let a day go by without bringing it up.'

Adele sank down in her seat, not wanting to get involved in a marital squabble.

'Why do you think she hardly visits?' Frank asked. His face had turned red in anger. 'Why do you think she rarely phones? Because she knows what she'll get from you. You've made it obvious for years that Harriet's your favourite.'

'What?' Penny exploded. She shot a daggered look at Frank.

'Matilda is less than a half-hour drive away and you've only been to her new house twice. And yet you'll happily do the two-hour trip to see Harriet and her kids. So Matilda's not married and doesn't have children. Who cares? Would you want to bring children into this fucker of a world right now?'

'Do you know why I don't phone and visit as often as I should?' Penny asked, standing with her arms on her hips in defiance. 'It's because I'm scared to death she's going to tell me how her day's been. I'm scared of her saying she's been shot at or beaten up or involved in a high-speed car crash. I'm frightened of the phone ringing or someone knocking on the door in case it's Adele or someone telling me she's been killed on duty. I love both my children equally, Frank, but I live every day in fear of something like this happening. All I've…' She couldn't say any more, as emotion got the better of her.

Frank stood up. He held his wife by the shoulders and pulled her to his chest. Her sobs were loud despite being muffled by Frank's thick sweater. He stroked her hair and apologised.

Adele turned away. She felt uncomfortable, but she was so physically and emotionally drained she didn't have the energy to pull herself up out of her seat and seek comfort elsewhere.

Her phone rang. It was Lucy. She swiped to answer with shaking fingers.

'Lucy, hello.'

'Adele, there's been another shooting.'

Chapter Twenty-One

Derek Simmonds seemed to have all the time in the world. He introduced himself to Scott and Finn and gave them a potted history of his life; how he'd worked in banking for forty years before taking early retirement seven years ago at the age of sixty-three due to an ongoing bowel obstruction, which the DCs heard about in glorious technicolour. Eventually, and with some help from Scott, he got around to telling them what he saw.

'I knew he was trouble the moment I looked up and saw him.'

'What made you think that?' Finn asked.

'The way he walked. He was a man on a mission – large strides, head down, shoulders hunched. And he was talking to himself.'

'Did you hear what he said?'

'No. He was muttering really, but he had a face like thunder.'

'Did you try to speak to him?'

'You're joking! If people leave me alone, I'll leave them alone. I don't want no bother. Hang on, though,' he said, suddenly remembering something. 'I might have him on camera.'

'Sorry?'

'Naming no names,' he said, nodding to the allotment behind him where an elderly man was pretending to dig but was really eavesdropping. 'Some people have got family members with sticky fingers who aren't averse to nabbing what's not theirs to sell for a few quid to buy whatever it is they stick in their veins.' Derek turned around to look over the allotment and smiled when he turned back to the detectives. 'He heard me. His grandson's a little twat, if you pardon my language. Anyway, I had a camera installed. It's running all the time. Come on in.'

Derek led the way into his small shed. Inside, it was perfectly equipped and every available space was utilised in an efficient way. There was a worktop with a kettle, digital radio and a laptop that was plugged in.

'My wife hates all this technology malarkey, but I told her years ago that she'd be left behind if she didn't learn how to use it, and now look where we are. She's scared stiff every time her mobile rings while I've rigged up my shed to capture thieving teenagers with a drug habit.' He smiled as he hammered away confidently on the keyboard.

Finn looked at Scott and gave a tentative smile while Scott rolled his eyes impatiently.

'Here we go. It's only the back view I'm afraid.'

Derek stepped to one side while Finn and Scott viewed the footage of the tall man in combat trousers and an army jacket storm through the allotments. He really did walk like a man on a mission. The backpack he wore looked heavy. What items of death and destruction did he have inside? Was it just limited to guns or was he carrying something more damaging? They watched, transfixed by the screen, until the man disappeared out of shot.

Scott dug in his pocket for a business card and handed it to Derek. 'Can you email this footage to me please?'

'Of course I can. Do you know who he is?'

'I don't, but someone might. Thank you. You've been incredibly helpful.'

'My pleasure. Many injured up there?' he asked as he led them out of the shed.

'I'm afraid so.'

'What kind of world are we living in, eh? I feel sorry for the young ones. Well, only those who plan on doing something with their lives, not the wasters who are out for anything they can get,' he said, raising his voice and aiming his words at the plot behind him once more.

Finn and Scott smiled and walked away.

'Look after yourselves, won't you?' Derek called after them, his face showing the first sign of fear. 'Men with guns are volatile and unpredictable. Don't do anything stupid. I don't want to see your faces on the ten o'clock news tonight.'

They thanked him again and headed back to the Parkway.

———

Before the BBC News van had even come to a complete stop in front of the carnage on the Parkway, Danny Hanson had jumped out of the front passenger seat and headed for the action, leaving Lewis to catch up with his camera equipment.

He looked around him at the broken glass, the bullet-ridden cars, the blood splatter and the covered bodies. This was serious. This was horrifying. This was fucking amazing! He took out his mobile and snapped a few sneaky shots with the camera. He quickly put it away when he locked eyes with DI Brady up ahead.

'Detective Inspector Brady,' he said, putting on his most sincere voice. 'I'm so sorry to hear about what happened this morning. I met ACC Masterson a number of times. She was a wonderful woman.'

'She was,' he said, folding his arms.

'How are you?'

'I'm fine,' he said.

'What's going on here? Is there really a gunman loose in Sheffield?'

'It's early days, Danny. We'll be releasing information through the official channels as and when we get it. Congratulations on the new job, by the way,' he said, despite clearly not meaning it.

'Thanks.' Danny smiled. He turned back and saw Lewis still rummaging around in the back of the van. 'Can you give us anything on what's happened here?' He signalled to the carnage around them.

'Not yet.'

'I don't see DCI Darke here. Is she involved in this case?'

'I really need to get on, Danny,' Christian said, trying to walk away.

'She's been injured, hasn't she?' Brady ignored him. Danny headed after him, snapping his fingers to Lewis to start filming and to keep up. 'Has she been shot? Is she dead?'

Christian stopped and turned on his heels. 'Danny, you're

walking all over a crime scene. If you don't go back to your vehicle right now, I'll have you both arrested.'

Danny stood still. He frowned as he studied the DI's face. 'Something's happened to her, hasn't it?'

'I'm not talking to you anymore.' Christian walked away.

'You may as well turn it off,' Danny said to Lewis and headed back to the van, deep in thought. 'I've got a few people I can ring, but they're not going to tell me if she's dead until it's officially released by the police. But why have they confirmed the ACC has been killed and but no news on Matilda?' he said, talking to himself.

'Maybe they haven't been able to get in touch with her family yet,' Lewis said from behind.

'Matilda doesn't have any family. We need to do some digging.'

'What is it with you and this Matilda woman? Why are you so obsessed?'

Danny smiled. 'Oh, Matilda has been very good for me over the years. She's provided me with some excellent stories. Not only is she a brilliant detective, but she's a liability and her own worst enemy. She's front-page gold.'

'You're not on the papers anymore, Danny.'

'No, I'm not. But I'm not exclusively with the BBC either.'

'What are you talking about?'

'New contract, mate. I'm technically freelance but working primarily with the BBC, which means I can get my own stories and sell them to the highest bidder when I've got a hold on something juicy. Come on,' he said, slapping the roof of the van. 'We need to do some digging. If Matilda is dead, I want to be the first to break the news. Oh, by the way, one more thing, Lewis,' Danny said, half hanging out of the van. 'When we pull up somewhere, and time is of the essence, like it is here, it would really help if you got your fat arse out of first gear and got your camera sorted before what we're covering is yesterday's story.' He shot Lewis a daggered look, then slammed the door on the van.

'Wanker,' Lewis said under his breath.

'I heard that,' Danny called from the front of the van.

Chapter Twenty-Two

'Where's your friend McNally?' Christian asked Sian.
'He's in the canteen having a bite to eat.'
'At the taxpayer's expense,' Aaron said under his breath, but loud enough for all to hear.

They were in the HMET suite, the atmosphere of which was subdued due to the eerily few officers present. Two of their civilian staff had been wounded and were now in hospital, while Ranjeet and Matilda's absences were more deeply felt.

'Actually, no, Aaron. I paid for him to have something to eat out of my own pocket. Not that it's any business of yours,' she chastised him, giving him a deathly stare.

'We've got some images from our CCTV, the office block across the road and the allotment we'd like him to take a look at,' Christian said.

'I'll go and fetch him.' Sian left the suite, her head down and taking long strides.

'Where are we with getting more officers?' Christian asked anyone who'd listen.

'We've got Aaron,' Scott pointed out.

'No offence to Aaron, but one more isn't going to make much of a difference.'

Aaron shrugged. 'None taken.'

'Those left are either going through CCTV footage or taking witness statements here and at the Parkway. There are also the relatives of those injured or dead to be informed, which the Chief Constable is saying is a priority before it's leaked to the media,' Scott said, running his fingers through his hair. He looked tired and harassed.

'Can't we get people in on leave?'

'We already have done. Jennifer Moore is on her honeymoon in Greece and Ellen Devonport is still on her recuperating backpacking tour of the Far East. This, right here, is all we've got.'

'Fuck,' Christian said. He leaned over the desk, biting his bottom lip. His eyes darted rapidly back and forth as he tried to think, tried to make some kind of sense of what was happening and where to go next. He took a deep breath and wished he had a bottle of something alcoholic hidden in his desk drawer. He suddenly realised why Matilda often suffered panic attacks.

'Aaron, we need to find out who this gunman is,' Christian began. 'He's a good shot, he'll have to have practised at some point. You don't just wake up, find a gun and suddenly become a crack shot at it. Look through the licensing register and see if any owners match the description we have of the gunman. Cross-reference that with anyone who's had a military background. We could be looking at a disgruntled soldier here.'

'Really? You're giving me DC-level stuff to do? Look, I know—'

'No, *you* look, Aaron,' Christian said, raising his voice.

'We're two DCs down. I don't have the luxury of delegating jobs to the correct rank, so anyone standing around with his hands in his pockets is going to get something to do, even if that's popping to the shop for a pint of fucking milk. Do you understand me, DS Connolly?'

Their eyes locked. It was a battle to see who would turn away first. Eventually, Aaron sucked his teeth, turned and headed over to his former desk.

Christian wasn't the type of person to raise his voice and shout at a fellow officer, especially in front of others. He didn't believe in that kind of humiliation. However, his fuse was incredibly short today, and getting shorter by the minute.

In Christian's office, Sian took McNally through the CCTV images from the cameras at the office block and the allotment. The gunman was also caught on a camera from HQ overlooking the rear car park.

The gunman knew what he was doing. He knew he was going to be surrounded by CCTV and had kept his face covered and his head down. However, anyone who'd met him, spoken to him, would have been able to recognise him from the images.

'Yes. That's definitely the guy,' McNally said. He had eaten a large cooked breakfast in the canteen, drunk several cups of tea and Sian had asked one of the uniformed officers to sneak him into the changing rooms for a shower. She'd been unable to find him a change of clothes, but he was more than grateful for everything she'd done for him. He looked fresher and more alert than he did when she found him outside the cathedral.

'Are you sure?' Christian asked.

'Yep. Told you – tall and skinny. His eyes were wide, but close together. He was wearing exactly what I said he was, too.' He pointed to the laptop.

'When he spoke to you, how did he sound?'

'I don't know – calm, I suppose. He spoke quiet, low.'

'Any accent?'

'Sheffield, like mine.'

'Was their anything distinguishing about him? Any scars, tattoos?'

McNally thought for a moment, then shook his head. 'No. He had stubble. His left ear had been pierced at some point, but, no, nothing stood out about him. I'm sorry I can't be more help.'

'You've been a big help, McNally,' Sian said, placing a hand on his shoulder. 'Listen, we might need to talk to you again, especially when we catch this bloke.'

'Well, you know where to find me, Sian. If I knew what this guy was planning, I wouldn't have accepted his offer. I really am truly sorry,' he said with genuine sincerity in his voice.

'I know. Thanks. Can he go now, Christian?'

'Sure. Thanks for all your help.'

Sian made eye contact with the DI and signalled towards McNally. Realising what she was trying to say with her eyes, he dug his wallet out of his back pocket and pulled out a twenty-pound note.

'Cheers, mate. Not necessary, but I can rent a bed for tonight now,' McNally said.

'I'll show you out.' Sian left the office with McNally while Christian went into the main suite. Aaron jabbed at the computer, seething, while Scott was just finishing a phone call and Rory was by the window, looking down at the car park longingly.

'Right then.' Christian rubbed his hands together. 'McNally has confirmed the bloke who paid him to set the alarm is the one from the allotments and the rooftop. We've got our man, we just need to identify him. I don't care how you do it, use your informants, knock on doors, ask people in the street, but our number one priority right now is to identify this man. Once we do that, we'll know what his plan is and we'll have some way of trying to catch the bastard.'

Scott spoke up. He wasn't his usual confident self. His voice had an edge of emotion to it. 'I've just been speaking to a uniformed officer who was taking statements from the office block opposite. The gunman used a key card to access the building and gain entry to the roof. It was in the name of Wendy Turton. Last night, she was mugged leaving work and had her handbag stolen. She'd called into work first thing to say she wouldn't be coming in.'

'Ok, Scott, get in touch with this Wendy and get her to tell you everything about her mugging. Did she see the face of the mugger? If not, can she describe him in any way? Find out whereabouts it happened and check out nearby CCTV.'

'He planned this,' Rory said, turning from the window. His eyes were red from where he'd been rubbing them. 'He's been planning to launch an attack on the police for a while. Like you said, sir, he didn't just wake up this morning and decide to shoot us. Someone else should have known what he was up to.'

'Not necessarily. Gunmen are notorious for being loners. They sort of detach themselves from reality. I mean, any normal person, upon hearing people screaming and dying, would react with some kind of remorse, but when you're in the kind of mental state he'll be in, it won't register at all,' Christian said, his hands on his hips.

'He's a psychopath,' Scott said.

'He is,' Christian agreed.

'Does that make him more difficult to catch?' Rory asked, looking hopefully between the two.

'No, but it makes him more deadly.'

'What do you mean?'

Christian looked around the room at the wide eyes glaring back at him. 'Nothing,' he said. He turned and went into his office, closing the door behind him.

'What did he mean?' Rory asked the room at large.

'He meant,' Aaron spoke up eventually, 'that by the end of the day, it's possible that there'll be a few more empty desks in this room.'

Chapter Twenty-Three

A dele and Lucy pulled up at the Parkway but neither of them moved from the car as they looked out at the devastation ahead of them. An invasion of white-suited forensic officers were working hard as bodies were covered, markers were laid down and bullet casings collected.

Adele felt sick. She was shaking and would give anything for a drink right now. She closed her eyes tight and tried to compose herself. It didn't work. Her heart was pumping loudly in her chest, blood thundering through her ears. Inside, she felt like she was screaming.

She had never reacted like this to attending a crime scene before, and as a Home Office pathologist, she had been requested at some of the most high-profile crimes around the country. In May 2017, she'd been the chief pathologist on the Manchester Arena bombing and orchestrated the post-mortems on all twenty-three deaths. Less than two weeks later, she was drafted in to help following the terrorist attack at London Bridge, which had resulted in eleven deaths, including those of the perpetrators. On top of these extraordinary events, she'd had her regular work to contend with which, as chief pathologist covering the whole of Yorkshire and the majority of Derbyshire, accounted for many deaths and procedures coming to her attention. Vulnerable children killed by members of their own families; teenagers needlessly stabbed to death; drug deaths on the increase; elderly people dying in their homes, with charities and governmental departments wanting to know if this was due to austerity cuts. Her email inbox was increasingly full of questions asking her to verify a death, quantify deaths and contribute to reports.

In order to stop her mind from overthinking the day's work while at home in the evenings, she'd succumbed to a glass of wine or two, sometimes three ... and occasionally a whole bottle. She was aware she was on a slippery slope, but hoped she was sensible enough to know when enough was enough.

'Do you get the feeling this is going to be the worst day of your life?' Lucy asked.

'It already is,' Adele said, unable to take her eyes off the carnage.

'Happy birthday to me,' Lucy said under her breath.

They eventually took off their seat belts and stepped out into the gloomy, dank Sheffield air. They set about collecting what they needed from the boot before heading over to the Crime Scene Manager, Sebastian Flowers, who looked as horrified by events as everyone around him.

'Adele, thank goodness you're here,' he said by way of a greeting. 'You're going to have your work cut out.'

'I already have. What can you tell me?' she asked, subdued.

'Eighteen dead at the scene. I've no idea how many have been sent to hospital, but I've been informed two more have since died. Any news on Matilda?'

'Nothing yet.'

He looked from Adele to Lucy and back again, reading their blank expressions.

'Well, I'll leave you two to it. Give me a shout if you need anything.'

'A plane ticket on the next flight to the Bahamas would do nicely about now,' Lucy said as she suited up.

'I'd settle for a time machine taking me back to before all this happened.' Sebastian smiled sadly.

'We're going to struggle with space back at the mortuary. Lucy, get on to Simon Browes. He should be at Watery Street by now. Tell him there's been a second shooting and there are at least twenty more bodies coming in. Ask him to give Nutwells a call. We're going to need a temporary body-storage facility bringing over, and can he contact a few other pathologists to see if they can help out with the post-mortems, either at Sheffield or close by?'

'Will do.'

'While you're at it, ask him to check on supplies, too. I know we only had a delivery last week, but we'll be going through gloves like nobody's business.' Adele squeezed the bridge of her nose and took a deep breath.

'Are you all right?' Lucy asked, placing a comforting hand on her shoulder.

'No, Lucy. To be perfectly honest with you, I'm scared out of my mind. My best friend is undergoing brain surgery that she may not survive, and even if she does, her life will dramatically change for ever. We've got bodies piling up right, left and centre, and my son's boyfriend is chasing around Sheffield looking for a madman with a gun.'

Lucy stood in awkward silence next to her boss. 'I'm sorry. I wish there was something I could say.'

Adele shook her head. 'There's nothing anyone can say. We

just have to try to find a way to get through this nightmare and out the other end in one piece.' She looked down at a body covered with a white sheet not three feet in front of her. 'We're still here, though. We can help those who aren't. Will you get my bag?'

'Sure.'

Lucy patted her boss on the back and went to the boot of the car to retrieve Adele's kit.

Adele put on a pair of latex gloves and walked to the first body. She knelt down, the hard tarmac of the Parkway digging into her knees. She carefully pulled back the sheet and revealed the face of the deceased beneath. The body was of a young girl, around eight years old, with blonde hair tied in bunches. She was wearing a pink flowery dress, a jean jacket over the top and black shoes. There was a large hole in her chest where a bullet had hit her heart directly; blood had oozed out of her, soaked up by her clothing. Adele looked at her face. She was pretty, a line of freckles running across the bridge of her nose and under her eyes. She had studs in her ears and a silver chain around her neck. She was just a child.

Adele lifted up the girl's arm and held her hand. It was cold, soft and pale, small and smooth. The fingernails had been painted a light pink. Adele looked back to the face. She could never understand why people looked at the dead and thought they were sleeping. To Adele, they were bodies. Whatever had been inside them that had made them who they were was gone. This was no longer a person, simply a dead body. A cadaver. Unfortunately, this was the cadaver of a small child whose short life had only just begun and had been snatched from her in the cruellest of ways.

Adele couldn't handle this. Tears poured from her. She looked up and saw the body of a dead woman lying not too far from the girl. She was on her front, her arm stretched out as if reaching for someone. Adele looked back down to the little girl and up to the woman again. They looked alike. She wondered if this was mother and daughter, running for their lives beneath a barrage of bullets. Who had been hit first? Did the mother fall, the daughter stop and was hit as she tried to help her mum? Did the mum reach out to her dying little girl only to be hit once again before she could reach her?

Adele closed her eyes. She could feel her stomach churning. She felt her body buckling from beneath her. She fell forward, her gloved hands hitting the tarmac to stop herself from collapsing. She gasped for breath as her vision blurred. She leaned back, opened her mouth and let out a painful wail.

Lucy and Sebastian ran towards her. Lucy grabbed her, held her in her arms while Sebastian covered up the body of the girl.

'What's wrong with her?' Sebastian asked, his eyes wide with worry.

'I don't know. She's been strange for a while. Adele, what's wrong? Are you all right?'

Adele couldn't speak. She screamed and cried out as weeks and months and years of keeping everything locked up inside came rushing out of her.

Chapter Twenty-Four

Simon Browes was well known for his abrupt temperament and sharp tongue. Of average height, with soft features and warm-looking eyes, he gave the impression he was friendly and approachable. However, within minutes of first meeting him, it quickly became evident he was socially awkward and had absolutely no idea how to communicate with people. His professionalism was constantly switched on, and any social event he had to endure, even a friendly drink in a pub with a colleague, was conducted as if he was having a one-on-one meet with a student.

He wasn't a people person and struggled to maintain personal relationships, but academically, he was at the very top of his field. He was an excellent pathologist and his expertise was much sought after around the country. However, he knew the situation he was walking into in Sheffield and had had a word with himself on the journey over to adapt his manner.

He was met by Claire Alexander and he greeted her with a warm smile, which she likely found disconcerting having already been acquainted with his unique manner, but today, nothing made much sense.

'I hear we have people dead who were known to you?' he asked while he took off his Barbour coat and flat cap.

'Yes. Several police officers have been killed this morning.'

'How are you feeling?' The question did not sound natural coming from his lips.

'Numb. To say the least.'

'And Adele? How is she?'

'I've no idea. Adele is great at masking her emotions. However, when she lets go, she really does let go.'

'Oh dear. Then I suppose my duty is to pick up the slack and give her breathing space.' He gave that uncomfortable-feeling smile again.

'That would be very useful.'

'Well, I'll scrub up and you can get the conveyor belt started. Uh, sorry,' he immediately apologised for his crass comment. 'I've had Lucy Dauman on the phone. She tells me there's been a second shooting and there are eighteen more bodies due in.'

'That's right. There are also two more coming from hospital.'

'Gunshot wounds. How terribly pedestrian. As you know, Claire, I'm not a fan of the digital autopsies, but it would be very useful for me if you could perform them on those that come through and give me a clear indication of where I should target my expertise.'

Claire gave a hint of a smile. 'I knew you'd come around to the digital world eventually.'

'These are highly unusual circumstances. Once back to normal I shall return to sticking pins into a little effigy I've had made of you.'

Claire's smile dropped.

'Ah, sorry. That was my attempt at humour. Should I not?'

'Perhaps not today.'

Claire turned and walked away, leaving Simon alone in the corridor. He looked at the trolleys lined up in front of him. There were so many bodies and not enough staff to process them and put them into the fridges. Simon rolled up his sleeve. He felt a calmness waft over him; he was in his element.

Chapter Twenty-Five

Jake Harrison was parked up in his dirty white Ford van in a supermarket car park close to the Sheffield Parkway.

When his brother Steve had first suggested the plan, he'd spent many days on the computer researching mass shootings. He wasn't worried about having the courage to squeeze the trigger and kill a person, but it was the psychological effects of the aftermath that caused him a few sleepless nights. How would he react when he heard people screaming and running for their lives? Would it trigger something inside him, telling him it was wrong and to stop?

Jake wasn't a very dynamic person. He wasn't deep or confident and was easily led. Since he was a child, his younger brother had taken control and been the dominant one of the two. It didn't help that Jake was six foot before he was even a teenager and the subject of jokes at school. It also didn't help that he could eat for England yet wouldn't put on weight. He was always lanky and had gone through life being called 'beanpole', 'skinny ribs', 'long streak of piss', 'Lurch' and other cruel jibes people would throw at him. He tried not to let it get to him – sticks and stones and all that – but the constant bullying every single day of his childhood took its toll. Yes, he was tall and stick-thin, but why did people have to make fun of him because of it? He couldn't help his height any more than he could help the colour of his skin or what day of the week it was.

By the time he left school, he resigned himself to the fact he was going to be a loner. Nobody would want to date someone like him. Everyone he'd asked out had turned him down; and they hadn't just said no either, they'd said it with revulsion, as if the very idea of going on a date with Jake Harrison was beyond repugnant. When he finally met his future wife, well, that was like being hit by a thunderbolt.

They'd met at college. She was studying for her A Levels and he was retaking the GCSEs he hadn't concentrated on at school. It wasn't love at first sight. It was an incredibly slow-burning relationship. They met one evening when the heavens had opened and the rain was lashing down. Jake was leaving the building, umbrella held aloft, waterproof coat zipped up to the neck; he was always organised. Standing in the doorway was the most beautiful girl he'd ever seen. She had a look of worry on her face as she stared out at the deluge, wearing only a thin sweater, no coat, no umbrella, no protection from the elements.

'Would you like me to walk you to the bus stop?'

'Would you?' she asked, her face lighting up as she smiled at her saviour.

'Of course.'

'You're a star.'

They walked at a pace. Jake towered over her and he kept looking down and smiling. And she smiled back. He racked his brain for something to say, anything, but all he could think of was something dumb and stupid that would make him look ridiculous. How was your day? Crap weather, isn't it? Do you study here? Stupid.

Once at the bus stop and in the dry and safety of the shelter, Jake closed the umbrella.

'Thank you so, so much,' she said, hand on her chest. 'You can't trust the weather in this country, can you? Light showers, it said on breakfast TV this morning. How is this a light shower?'

Jake found himself smiling as he watched her talk. She had beautiful lips, twinkling eyes, and dimples appeared in her cheeks when she smiled.

'It was—'

'Oh, my bus is here,' she interrupted. 'I would have missed this if it hadn't been for you. Thank you, again. You're a life saver.' She touched his arm and jumped on the bus and out of his life.

He saw her a few times again around the college after that. They smiled, waved, said hello, but nothing happened between them. Not until they both happened to be in the local pub one evening. If memory served him correctly, it had been raining that night, too…

'…nearby schools are being placed in lockdown.'

The voice from the radio in the van brought Jake back from his daydream. Although, it transpired, it was more like a nightmare, considering the way things had ended between them. He shook the thought from his mind and turned up the radio.

'South Yorkshire Police must be working on the assumption the two shootings are related. If that is the case, what next for the Steel City? Is there a sniper on the loose? Is the force adept enough to cope with such an incident especially with their number depleted? The

Prime Minister has been informed and is keeping a close eye on the developing story.'

He turned the radio off. If the Prime Minister had been involved, that meant his actions had attracted national interest, possibly international. Gun crime was associated with America and warzones in the Middle East, not England, and certainly not Sheffield. This was a highly unusual crime for this small island. The eyes of the world would be watching.

He reached into the glove box. His hand touched something sharp. He pulled it out and looked at his fingers. A small dot of blood appeared. He squeezed the fingertip and watched as the blood began to pool. It was the first time he'd seen his own blood since the diagnosis. It hadn't changed – it was still a deep red, a thick liquid. He hesitated, then sucked his finger. His blood was diseased. Strangely, it didn't taste any different.

He took his mobile out of the glove box and turned it on. #SheffieldGunman and #Sheffield were the top trending hashtags on Twitter. He couldn't help but smile at that. He scrolled through some of the postings.

@CoffeeCurls Second shooting @ Sheff Parkway. Closed in both directions. Bodies lying in the streets. Fucking scary. I'm not going to work today. #Sheffield #SheffieldGunman

@Pete_Ash68 This country is getting more like America every day. I could hear shots and screaming from Parkway from my house. Helicopter overheard. This is scary stuff. #SheffieldGunman

@annebonnybook Please don't post any pictures on Twitter of the victims of the #Sheffield gun attack. These are people's family members. Have some respect.

@hkist Does anyone know if the schools will be letting the kids out early? Not sure if best place is locked in school or at home. #Sheffield

@saffron1623 Stuck in traffic just off Parkway. Chaos. Police and marksmen everywhere. Someone's gone mad with a gun and shot the whole place up. #SheffieldGunman

@HarrowMorgue News are saying there could be as many as 50 dead. #StandingwithSheffield

@TheQuietKnitter This is the view from our office overlooking SY Police HQ. Bodies everywhere. #Sheffield

@hellywellytaff Very quiet in #Sheffield city centre. Police cars driving slowly looking for gunman. #NoH8

Jake smiled. Steve had told him this would happen. He warned him to prepare to be the most important man in the country once he got started, but he had to rein in his emotions. He couldn't let the excitement, the danger, the adrenaline go to his head. He had a job to do. And he was going to make sure he finished it.

———

Steve Harrison was back in his cell. The news channels were covering the breaking story of the shootings in Sheffield, but they were being careful not to get their fingers burnt by reporting something that might not be true later and end up getting sued. They were playing their cards very close to their chests. He couldn't stand listening to that wanker Danny

Hanson on a loop, mugging it to the camera. He had targeted the journalist while he was on his killing spree in Sheffield. He coveted the press coverage and used Danny to promote his crimes. In doing so, he'd elevated Danny to a TV reporter. He'd benefited from Steve's murders and he was going to benefit from this too. Maybe Steve should remind him of the fact that he'd helped his career. It could be useful to have a journalist in his pocket at some point in the future.

From under his mattress, Steve took out an old iPhone that had seen better days. It was scratched to death, the screen was cracked, and it was far from the latest model, but it wasn't easy to get such things in prison. Considering how they had to be smuggled in, not many people were willing to shove an XR Max up their arse.

He turned the phone on. The time stated it was a little before one o'clock. It was roughly the agreed time to make his call. He scrolled for a number and dialled. It was answered on the second ring.

'You're doing good, kidder,' Steve said as a way of a greeting. He could be found with the phone at any moment. Every second was precious.

'Cheers.'

'How are you feeling?'

'I'm ok.'

'You sure?'

'Yes. No sweat.'

'Good man. Tell me about Matilda.'

'You should have seen her, Steve. Everyone goes running back into the station. I mean, they're charging around like headless chickens and she's just stood there in the middle of the car park. She's looking around to see where I'm shooting from. When she clocks me, she just stands still. Staring at me.'

Jake's words were falling over each other he was speaking so fast.

Steve took a breath. The thought of looking through the eye of a gun and seeing Matilda Darke on the other end gave him goosebumps.

'Did she look scared?' Steve asked.

'Oh yes,' he said with a smile in his voice.

'Tell me what you did.'

'I shot her in the shoulder. She staggered back. I waited a few seconds until she righted herself then, bang! Another shot to the head.'

'You got her in the head?' Steve wanted to shout in excitement but couldn't risk being overheard.

'Yes. The back of her skull actually came off. I saw it. Bang. Hit. Splatter. Down she went like a sack of shit.'

'Jake, you're a fucking star. I love you, man.'

'You too, brother. Listen, I'm done now, yes?'

'Of course you are, mate. You've done me a massive favour and I'll never be able to thank you enough. It's all yours now, mate. Enjoy your-fucking-self.'

'I intend to.'

Steve paused. He knew this was possibly the last time he'd be speaking to his brother, and the sense of occasion was not lost on him.

'Jake,' he said after swallowing hard. 'I know you've had a rough deal lately, but you've always been there for me, mate. You've always come through for me. I couldn't have asked for a better brother. I want you to know that.'

'Cheers, man,' Jake replied, almost nonchalantly.

'I better be going now before someone comes looking for me. I'll be keeping an eye on the news. You'll take care, won't you?'

'Of course, man. Blaze of glory, mate.'

The line went dead.

Steve hid the phone under the mattress and lay down on top of the bed. He was the first to admit that he was a serial killer, a mass murderer, but he blamed Matilda Darke for turning him into one. She was a smug, supercilious bitch who stopped him from getting on when he tried to better himself and get a promotion. There was nothing he could do from prison, but he knew Jake would be easily won over. And, surprisingly, it had been easier than he thought.

Steve received letters and cards from people all around the country. He had fans. People loved the idea of talking to a real-life serial killer. The letters from women were sometimes pure filth, telling him what they'd like him to do to them. He often sold those to the sad loners who needed wanking material. Others wanted to marry him, mother him, look after him. Some were seriously fucked-up. However, he read every single letter he received because sometimes a letter arrived from a true fan, from someone who could be helpful on the outside. When he saw the photo that accompanied the letter, Steve knew he'd found his new right-hand man to act as a conduit between himself and Jake.

Today was a long time in the planning. This required baby steps. But Steve was a very patient man. He drip-fed his new best friend what he needed. He told him to introduce himself to his brother, to develop a relationship and build up a bond. Once that was in place, it was all systems go.

Apparently, when asked if Jake would get a gun and shoot Matilda for Steve, he'd agreed without hesitation. He hadn't even blinked. He said yes, as if he'd been asked if he wanted a cup of tea.

As the weeks went on and the conversations developed,

Steve began plotting the plan of action. It had to be studied from every angle, and a contingency plan had to be put in place should anything go wrong. As Jake was going to get hold of a gun and shoot a copper, he'd most likely be shot dead by police or end up in prison for the rest of his life. Either way, his life would change dramatically because of one tiny little gunshot. So, if your main target is someone high up in the pecking order, why not have some fun? Killing a copper isn't going to get you a few years in prison then out on licence; no, Jake will be in for life. So if you're going to get life for one murder, what else can the courts do to you for a dozen murders?

Once Steve was informed who else Jake wanted to target, he felt more relaxed. His brother was taking this seriously. He wouldn't be backing out at the last minute. He'd given this careful thought.

'I can see his reasoning. I've no problem with that,' Steve had said. He'd leaned forward and lowered his voice so the prison guards couldn't overhear the conversation with his new best friend. 'However, once the police know his identity, they're going to know where he's heading next. He needs to throw them off the scent after the first shooting.'

'How?'

'Instead of just knocking on Matilda's door and shooting her in the face when she opens it, he's going to need to go all sniper on them. Shoot up the whole fucking station. Then, distract them with a second attack in another part of Sheffield. Lie low for a bit, let the cops think he's finished or moved on. Give it a few hours for them to scratch their heads wondering how the two events can be related. Then … Columbine!' he'd said with a grin.

Chapter Twenty-Six

When the call ended, Jake suddenly realised that was possibly the last time he was going to talk to his brother. He'd killed a lot of people today. He'd killed coppers, for crying out loud. There was no way he'd be walking away from this. Once they worked out who he was, and they found him, they wouldn't be interested in taking him in for questioning, it would be like the final act of Bonnie and Clyde.

He wished he'd said more to Steve, something potent and meaningful, perhaps. They were like chalk and cheese but Jake had a great deal of respect for Steve. He loved him. He should have told him that. He looked at the phone and wondered if he should risk calling him back. No. Steve would kick off if he did. 'Under no circumstances should Jake phone me.' That was the first rule.

From the glove box, Jake took out a sandwich box. He removed the lid and breathed in the rancid aroma of corned beef, his favourite sandwich filling. He was hungry. Killing obviously gave you an appetite.

He sat back in his seat and took a couple of large bites.

Looking out of the windscreen, he watched as life in Sheffield seemed to continue as normal. Traffic was teeming along at a normal pace; people were going in and out of shops to buy what they needed. Life hadn't changed much. Did they know there was a gunman on the loose? Maybe they hadn't heard or maybe they just didn't care. People were so complacent these days. If something didn't directly involve them, they didn't take the slightest bit of interest. That's what pissed Jake off. That's why the UK was in turmoil over Brexit, because people only thought about themselves when voting. They didn't look at the bigger picture. Bastards. The lot of them. Selfish, ungrateful, immature, self-centred…

His phone pinged with an incoming text. He hoped it would be from Steve. He'd like to message back, telling him that he loved him and say a proper goodbye.

He recognised the number, but he'd been told not to save contact details, so was not quite sure who was texting him.

Matilda Darke is NOT dead! She's been moved to the Hallamshire.
Think she's being operated on.

'Fuck!' Jake called out, punching the steering wheel. He'd watched her through the gun. He'd pulled the trigger. The back of her head had exploded. How could that not have killed her? Who is she, the fucking Terminator?

He smiled to himself as he put the last of the sandwich in his mouth, put on his seat belt and started the engine. Steve had said to have a back-up plan just in case something went awry. He'd been right. As usual.

Jake drove out of the supermarket car park and headed back the way he'd come. It was time to pick up his insurance policy.

Chapter Twenty-Seven

A dele was no use to anyone at the crime scene at the Sheffield Parkway, and she couldn't bring herself to go back to Watery Street and help Simon Browes with the post-mortems. Every time she thought of them, she pictured Valerie and Ranjeet and the tears would flow once more.

The pathologist had a strange relationship with death. She dealt with it on a daily basis and for the last twenty-plus years of her career, she'd told herself not to get too close to the people she cut open. The more she thought of them as people, as having lives, jobs, friendships, hobbies, the more she felt like she was working on someone she knew. Once the procedure was over and she was writing up her report, the background to the individual was necessary, sometimes, to determine how they died. Learning snippets about them then didn't seem to bother her.

Recently, Adele had found herself becoming more emotional regarding the people who came to her mortuary. Lucy Dauman was relatively new to the profession, and she was slowly becoming hardened to the realities, seeing the dead as puzzles to be solved. Adele had taught her well, yet it seemed she herself was heading in the opposite direction. Maybe it was time to rethink her career.

She had always coveted such a prestigious position but now, something had changed. And she knew exactly what. Last November, she'd performed an autopsy on a thirty-seven-year-old woman, Francesca Mary Rhodes, who had died after falling down the stairs during a confrontation with a burglar. Adele had performed the initial post-mortem and had answered the many questions Francesca's husband, Roger, had about his wife's death. Roger had told Adele all about his wife, the amazing adventures she'd packed into her thirty-seven years, and Adele found herself admiring the woman.

When the burglar was arrested and the case went to court, his defence requested a second post-mortem. Simon Browes was due to perform it, but his car broke down on the M1. Everything was set up, so Adele stepped in at the last minute. When she looked down at the dead expression of Francesca Rhodes, everything she had learned about her came to the surface. It was like cutting open a relative. Adele performed her task with the utmost professionalism, but she was scarred in the aftermath. Every autopsy afterwards was tainted. Whenever she looked at a person on the slab, she invented a fiction for them: married or unmarried, children or none, job, hobbies, favourite films, music, books, food. That initial incision was like sinking the blade into the chest of a close friend.

Adele was sat behind the wheel of her car on the Parkway, too close to the crime scene for her liking. She looked out of the windscreen at the sea of bodies on the ground and cried. Her eyes blurred with tears, but she was still able to see Lucy working alongside Sebastian Flowers with professional ease.

Adele had worked on huge crime scenes with a high body count on many occasions – perhaps too many. She always thought she was in control, though. Her friendship with Matilda had helped a great deal. Whenever one of them had a particularly troubling or harrowing day, they had the other to support them. With Matilda as her rock, the prospect of falling apart, of cracking up, never came into her mind. Now, her meltdown came at a time when she was needed the most, and she had no option to give in to it. Her body was telling her she'd endured too much in the past few years.

The thought of losing her best friend, her confidant, added to the deaths of Valerie, who'd been struggling with the health of her husband of thirty years, and Ranjeet, whose first child wasn't even a year old yet, all contributed to her very public collapse.

As much as Adele wanted to retreat to the safety of her home, plunge under the duvet and sleep for ever, she was needed elsewhere. Matilda needed her. Not caring whether she was in a fit state to drive or not, she put the car into reverse and performed a handbrake turn at speed before charging up the Parkway away from the crime scene.

———————

Adele parked in a side street around the corner from the Royal Hallamshire Hospital, as there were no spaces available in the car park. As she walked towards the entrance, she looked up and saw a pub, aptly named The Doctor's Orders. She felt like a small drink of something strong would steady her nerves, stop her hands from shaking and silence the miasma of voices shouting in her head.

She pulled open the door and entered the dimly lit building. It was relatively busy for early afternoon. She found a space at the bar and slumped against it.

'Whisky. Make it a double,' she said to the student barman as she rifled through her handbag for her wallet.

'What kind? We've got Jack Daniels, Glen Ness, Jameson...'

'I really don't care,' she said, giving him a dead-eyed look.

'Ok.'

Adele watched him slowly prepare her drink. He placed the glass on a red paper napkin in front of her. She couldn't snatch it up fast enough. She slugged it back in one gulp. It burnt her throat and she hated the taste, but it was like a shot of adrenaline to the heart; it was exactly what she needed.

'Same again,' she said as she slapped the empty glass down on the counter.

Once at the hospital, Adele felt lightheaded. On an empty stomach, two double whiskies will do that to anyone. Before going to see Matilda's parents, she went into the toilets to splash some water on her face and compose herself. When she looked up at her reflection in the mirror, she was shocked to see who was staring back at her. She didn't recognise this wreck of an old woman with lank, lifeless hair, dry, wrinkled skin, and the pain and suffering of a countless number of dead people in her eyes. The tears came, and they refused to stop. She crumbled and was found ten minutes later by Penny Doyle.

'Adele! Oh my God! What's happened?' Matilda's mother

ran over to her, squatted and grabbed her by the shoulders, pulling her into a tight embrace. 'Has there been any news? Have you heard anything? She's not… Please don't tell me she's…' Penny couldn't finish her barrage of questions before she, too, was overcome with tears. Together, they sat in a heap on the cold, dirty floor of the ladies' toilets, sobbing in each other's arms.

'I just … I don't know,' Adele eventually said as she pulled herself out of Penny's hold. As comforting as it was, her overpowering perfume could only be endured for so long. She looked up into Penny's eyes, saw the anguish and hurt she was feeling, and decided the mother of someone undergoing emergency brain surgery to remove a bullet was not the person to open up to about her own pain. 'I just needed a few minutes,' she said.

Adele pulled herself up and went back to the sink to wash away the tears. She made every effort not to look at her reflection in the stained mirror.

'I find crying helps,' Penny said. 'I do it more than I like to admit.'

'Really?' Adele asked, turning around.

'People think I'm this cold, hard woman. Frank does. And I know Matilda does, too, but I'm really not.' She tried to smile through the pain. 'I worry every single day about Matilda – more so since James died. I try to bury my head in the sand, act like I don't know what's going on. If I don't ask how her day's been, then I've nothing to worry about. But all I'm doing is driving a wedge between myself and my daughter.'

'You're not,' Adele tried to reassure her.

'I am.' Penny looked at herself in the mirror. She shook her head. 'On the odd occasion Matilda does come for a visit, things are very strained between us. The conversation is stilted. I see her and Frank having a laugh and a joke – we don't have that kind of relationship. I'm the uncaring, unfeeling, emotionless mother.'

'But you do care.'

'Of course I do.'

'You should have told her.'

'I know. Now it looks like I've left it too late,' she said. Her bottom lip began to wobble, and the tears rained down her face, leaving tracks in the recently touched-up make-up.

'It's not,' Adele said, unconvincingly.

'You can't say that. I doubt many people survive a bullet to the head.'

'Matilda's a fighter.'

'If James was still alive, I'd agree with you. Since he died, though … she's lost her will to survive.'

'I don't agree with you.' Adele wiped her nose. 'She loves her job. She loves her colleagues. She's in an exciting new relationship. She has a great deal to live for.'

'She also has a great deal to die for, too.'

Adele gave a half-laugh. 'Matilda doesn't believe in an afterlife. She knows she isn't going to be reunited with James again.'

'Neither did my mother. She was widowed for fifteen years. When she was diagnosed with lung cancer, she didn't want any treatment. She'd had enough. I'll never forget her final day. I sat by her bed, held her hand, and we talked. In her last few minutes she spoke of George, my dad. She said she could see him. I'd never seen her look so content. She died with a smile on her lips, thinking she was going to be with George again. Maybe that's what happens when we die. Maybe Matilda's on that operating table, right now, waiting for James to come for her.'

Adele swallowed her emotion. It was difficult for her to accept the notion of an afterlife, but nobody knows what happens in our final moments. As a woman of science, Adele always believed that when we died, that was it, game over. Was there something more? Penny's mother certainly thought so. She just hoped Matilda didn't.

Chapter Twenty-Eight

The Homicide and Major Enquiry Team suite was a hive of activity, and Christian felt the change in atmosphere the moment he stepped through the glass doors.

Civilian and uniformed staff were busy answering phones and logging any information into the HOLMES2 system, as well as putting the more urgent information on the board at the top of the room. Calls seemed to be coming in all the time; whether they were genuine sightings, paranoid members of the public believing what they saw or suspicious or cruel hoax calls remained to be seen. Either way, every single call needed to be followed up.

'Wendy Turton has given us a good description of the man who mugged her,' Scott said, jumping up from his desk as soon as he saw Christian.

'Why are we dealing with a mugging?'

'She works in the building opposite. Her key card was used by the gunman to gain access. You asked me to follow up, sir.'

'Of course. Sorry, Scott, my memory froze for a moment

there.' He headed for his office, indicating for Scott to follow. 'Go on.'

'She was working late, putting in some overtime, so when she left it was pitch-dark, and there weren't many people around. She was going to her car when this bloke came from nowhere. He jumped her from behind, threw her to the ground, snatched her bag and ran. Now, here's the interesting bit; he runs away, but stops. Looking back after what's happened this morning, Wendy thinks he realised she was wearing her lanyard around her neck and it wasn't in her bag as he must have originally thought. He came back towards her, grabbed hold of the ID and yanked it from her.'

'And she saw his face when he came back?'

'She did,' Scott replied with a smile.

'Excellent.'

'She's given me a description and I've asked if she'll come in to speak to someone about putting together a composite. I thought she'd have refused – she was feeling very sorry for herself – but when I told her about how many officers we'd lost, she said she'd come straight in. She's downstairs now.'

'Brilliant work, Scott. We need to run it by Sian's homeless friend.' Christian leaned on his desk for support. He looked overworked and stressed. He'd already loosened his tie and rolled the sleeves up on his shirt. He was always well turned out and professional in his appearance.

'Since the press conference, the phones have been ringing like crazy, but not with anything useful,' Scott said.

'Any sightings of our gunman?'

'Nothing concrete. There's a team going door to door either side of the Parkway but CCTV from there only shows the traffic on the roads and not on the bridge. Some of those who were injured in the shooting have been questioned and have dashboard cameras in their cars. We're getting the footage from those. But, like you say, until we know the name of this bloke, it's going to be useless.'

'I'll have a word with the Chief Constable,' Christian said after releasing a heavy sigh. 'We need the public to see images of this man. Somebody has got to know who he is.'

'Not necessarily if he's a loner.'

'He'll still have family. Parents. And neighbours. Somebody will recognise him.' Christian sounded determined, even though his face belied his words. 'Any news from the hospital?'

'No. I'm guessing she'll be in theatre for a long time yet.'

Christian looked out into the main suite. Sian was at her desk. She was talking on her mobile, head down, wiping her nose with a saturated tissue. Rory was stood by the window, looking down into the car park below, which was still a closed crime scene. Aaron was next to him. Neither of them were talking. There didn't seem to be anything to say.

'I phoned to check on Kesinka,' Scott said to break the silence. 'Her mother answered. She seems nice. She told me that she'd put Kesinka to bed and was taking care of the baby for a while. I said I'd call back, keep in touch, that kind of thing. I was thinking, should we organise some kind of whip-round or something?'

'That's a good idea, Scott,' Christian said with a hint of a smile. 'Maybe something to talk about on another day.'

'Yes, of course. A lot to do today.'

'Yes.'

Christian's phone rang. He quickly snatched it up. 'DI Brady.' He listened for a while. His eyes widened. He closed them and slumped down in his seat. 'Right. Thanks for letting me know.' He hung up.

'More bad news?' Scott asked.

Christian's eyes had filled with tears. It took him a moment to speak. 'That was Janice, the Chief Constable's secretary. Valerie's husband, Arthur, died this morning. He had another stroke in his sleep.'

'Bloody hell. That poor family.'

'I know.'

'I wonder if he knew.'

'Sorry?'

'Some people, when they've been together for so long, they have a connection, don't they? Maybe on some unconscious level, Arthur knew what had happened to his wife and just let himself go.'

'Whatever helps you sleep at night, Scott,' he said, rolling his eyes. 'Right, plan of action. We don't know who the gunman is yet, but we need to be seen to be on top of this. That means a presence on the streets. I'm seeing far too many officers around the station standing around, doing nothing. I want as many cars out there as possible.'

'The thing is the phones are ringing all the time. Schools and colleges are asking if they should send their students home. We've had someone high up at Meadowhall asking what's going on and Bramall Lane have called three times asking about their charity event tonight. We can't answer all these calls and be out there at the same time.'

'Our number one priority is to catch this gunman before he has a chance to strike again. We can't do that by answering sodding phones,' Christian said, getting riled.

'But we don't know where's he's going to strike again.'

'We can't just sit back and wait for him to kill more people. Why is it taking so fucking long to find out who he is?'

Christian exclaimed, kicking the underside of his desk. He stood up and went over to the window.

The view looked out onto the sprawl of Sheffield and out towards the countryside. Before the expanse of green, there was a palette of different shades of grey from the concrete buildings that made up Sheffield's city centre. Shops, offices, hotels, new and old, some of them abandoned, awaiting demolition or just decaying. In a city of over half a million people, one man was out there with a gun. He had all the power to change every one of those lives for ever. And right now, he was winning.

Chapter Twenty-Nine

Matilda had been in surgery for more than two hours. She had a large, comminuted skull fracture with depressed fragments and the small pieces of broken bone needed to be painstakingly removed. Where possible, they would be stuck back together with plates and screws and put back in place in the final stage of the operation, like the last piece of a jigsaw once the swelling had been reduced. That part of the procedure was still a long way off though, and surgeons were working hard to drain blood and monitor the swelling.

At the beginning of the operation, a catheter was inserted. The nurse, a young operating department practitioner, struggled with the amount of blood. She should have called for help but assumed this amount of blood loss was natural from a patient brought in with gunshot wounds. It was only when a senior scrub nurse noticed how long it was taking her to insert the catheter that she intervened. Despite the trauma the body was facing due to being shot, there was no reason why Matilda should be bleeding from her vagina.

Adele was at a vending machine next to the theatres. Frank and Penny had begun arguing once again, this time about Matilda's sister, Harriet, who had recently separated from her husband and moved out of the four-bedroom house with sea views and massive back garden to a temporary flat above a betting shop. Penny, ever the snob, was urging Frank to step in and talk her daughter into returning to the family home, even if the only reason was to keep up appearances. Frank, however, was siding with his daughter. Her husband had been concealing an affair for two years and even managed to keep an eighteen-month-old daughter hidden from his wife. When the affair was exposed, Harriet left, and Frank admired her for giving up so much.

Adele glared at what the vending machine was offering. She wasn't hungry. She felt sick. The garish chocolate wrappers, the sad-looking sandwiches sealed in plastic didn't appeal. Her mind was blank. She jumped when a hand was placed on her shoulder.

'Sorry, I didn't mean to startle you.'

Adele turned. She recognised the middle-aged woman in a blue nurse's uniform but couldn't remember her name.

'That's ok. I was miles away, sorry.'

'I wouldn't recommend any of the sandwiches. I think they've been in there since before the millennium.' She offered a smile that didn't reach her eyes.

'Thanks for the warning,' Adele said, stepping away. 'Is there any news?'

The nurse took Adele by the elbow and led her to a row of empty seats opposite. She sat her down and took the seat next to her.

'Adele, you know Matilda better than anyone. Had she said anything to you lately about her health?'

Adele looked confused. 'Her health? I don't … no. She's fine. Why?'

'When she was brought in she was bleeding. From her vagina. We took a sample of the blood and we've discovered she was pregnant.'

'Oh my God!' Adele exclaimed. Her eyes widened. 'Wait. Was?'

'I'm afraid she miscarried.'

'Jesus…'

'It's not uncommon, when the body suffers a massive trauma like she has, to reject the pregnancy as a way of saving the life of the adult. She may not have even known she was pregnant.'

Adele shook her head. 'I don't think she did. She would have told me. She definitely would have told me.'

'I'm so sorry.' The nurse placed a hand on her shoulder.

'Thanks.'

'I'll leave you to it,' she said, standing up.

'How's the operation going?'

'It's going to plan so far. I'll keep you updated.'

'Thanks…'

'Leah.'

'Of course. I'm sorry,' Adele said, wiping tears from her eyes.

Matilda was pregnant! That was the last thing Adele expected to hear. Matilda had never wanted children. When she and James married, they both decided to live their lives together, doing what they wanted, going on holiday when they wanted, spending time together, and children didn't fit into that plan. When James died, Matilda expressed a hint of regret that they hadn't had children, if only because it would have meant a part of James would still be with her. Her maternal instincts, however, were purely for selfish reasons. She admitted herself on many occasions that she would have been a terrible mother and work would always have come first.

Adele knew the relationship between Matilda and Daniel was blossoming and she had managed to extract some very personal details from Matilda about their love life once she was under the influence of a couple of bottles of Pinot Grigio, but babies were never mentioned. Had Daniel expressed an interest in becoming a father? Had Matilda realised he was her final chance to become a mother and give her a focus in life other than work? No. She would have told Adele.

In the darkness of the glass in the vending machine across the corridor, Adele saw her reflection looking back at her. She could see the desperation and anger etched on her face. She had no idea what was stopping her from smashing her head into the glass.

'Adele!'

She jumped at her name being called and saw Daniel heading towards her down the corridor. His strides were long, his face a map of worry, his eyes glistening with tears. How was she going to explain this to him?

Chapter Thirty

'Introductions are starting. We're going live in two minutes.'

Danny Hanson was back at South Yorkshire Police HQ. He would have preferred to remain at the Parkway and have the impact of the bullet-ridden vehicles, the white-suited forensic team and flashing lights of the emergency vehicles in the background, but the producer of the BBC News at One felt the unassuming police station as a backdrop was more fitting to the seriousness of the situation.

Danny was still relatively new to the world of broadcast journalism and had wanted to argue his point that an active crime scene was more visual. However, before he could express his opinion, he was reminded that it was only one o'clock in the afternoon. People watching this would be eating their lunch. They wouldn't want to see blood splatter and bullet holes while tucking into their Boots meal deals.

The unfolding story was going to be the lead item, and they'd return to Danny in Sheffield at several points during the thirty-minute programme. He'd also be on screen for most of the ten-minute *Look North* bulletin, and then the BBC News channel was going to focus on the rolling breaking news story for most of the afternoon. Danny was going to get plenty of TV exposure.

To say Danny was excited was an understatement. He wanted to be a big player in the industry and working on the local newspaper was not a satisfying job, despite some of the stories he'd worked on thanks to Matilda Darke. It was a gamble moving into the world of broadcast journalism, and he had been worried he'd made a big mistake when his first story revolved around a zebra crossing being removed outside a junior school in Barnsley, and then reporting on a nursing home in Rotherham setting up a GoFundMe page to raise money for basic supplies for its residents due to heavy budget cuts by the council. However, he'd bitten his lip and held his tongue and was grateful for the experience of being in front of the camera. He was learning so much. Now, here he was, about to report on the lead story on a flagship news programme on the most watched channel in the country.

He'd checked his hair in the wing mirror of the van several times, fingering the ruffled, unkempt look it took him ages to perfect. His blue check shirt was clean and crisp and open at the neck. He looked smart and casual with an air of professionalism about him.

'We can now go live to Sheffield for an update on this ongoing story with our North of England correspondent, Danny Hanson,' he heard the newsreader say in his earpiece.

His cameraman, Lewis, gave him the nod to begin.

'Behind me is the headquarters of South Yorkshire Police, where earlier this morning a gunman opened fire, killing six people, including Assistant Chief Constable Valerie Masterson, who was due to retire later this year. Just two hours later, a gunman shot at cars from a bridge over the Sheffield Parkway, where we believe more than twenty people have lost their lives. Detectives from the Homicide and Major Enquiry Team as well as those from CID are working together to try to catch this gunman before he can strike again.'

'What do we know of the gunman, Danny?' the newsreader asked.

'At the moment, we know very little. Chief Constable Martin Featherstone gave a statement at eleven o'clock this morning but didn't reveal much information as to the identity of the perpetrator. Since then, we've received no further updates on who has committed this atrocity or when the next press conference will be.'

'Are police treating this as a terrorist attack?'

'Again, we haven't been given any information as to the gunman's motives, but a source at South Yorkshire Police has told me detectives are struggling to cope due to the personal nature of the incident.'

'Are detectives being drafted in from other forces?'

'Not at present. My source informed me that South Yorkshire Police were already understaffed before today's shooting. An investigation like this is the last thing they needed. What happens today as this story unfolds, and whether more lives are lost, will surely be felt for a long time to come by detectives in the building behind me, and the public at large.'

'Danny Hanson, our North of England correspondent, thank you.'

'What the actual fuck!' Christian Brady exploded.

The remaining members of HMET had gathered around the

television to watch the one o'clock news bulletin. Despite no further statements being given, they wanted to keep an eye on what the media was saying. It was possible the gunman could be watching this and deciding when and where to make his next move depending on what he heard. If he'd seen this, and believed South Yorkshire Police was dangerously understaffed, who knew where his next strike would be.

'Where's he getting this bollocks from?' Christian stood back from the TV, hands on his hips, face red with thunder. 'Who the fuck is his source?'

Sian pointed the remote at the TV and turned it off. The room was plunged into silence. Even the phones seemed to have stopped ringing.

'He made us sound like a bunch of clowns bumbling about like we're fucking clueless.'

'We are,' Aaron said under his breath.

'Was it you?' Christian snapped, turning to him.

'What?'

'Are you his source? Are you pissed off for being removed from HMET so you thought you'd stick the knife in further—'

'Christian, calm down,' Sian interrupted.

'Why would I give that bastard information?' Aaron asked. 'He broke the story about … well, you all know about that. He helped ruin my marriage, for fuck's sake. Do you think I'd give him information to help boost his career?'

Aaron was visibly shaking at the confrontation. He was always a mild-mannered man, never one to cause a scene or stand out. Now, the entire room was staring at him.

'Shit!' Christian said, squeezing the bridge of his nose to calm himself. 'I'm sorry, Aaron. I didn't mean to accuse you, and I know you wouldn't have spoken to the press, least of all that parasite. I'm sorry.'

Aaron nodded. 'I'm going to the toilet.' He stood up and left the room with his head down.

'I'm sorry,' Christian said again, this time to the whole team. 'I'm not accusing anyone, but whatever we discover about this case does not leave these walls. Is that understood?'

There were nods of assent around the room.

'The gunman will have watched that. He'll believe what that shit said. If he is planning a third shooting, this will give him the impetus to step up his game. He's got guns, he's got a van he could use to ram into a crowd. He could have a bomb for all we know. That,' he said, pointing to the blank television screen, 'could have given him everything he needs to launch an attack bigger than anything we've ever seen.'

A phone rang. Scott answered it on the first ring.

Sian stood up from her desk and went over to Christian by the murder boards. 'What do we do?' she asked. Her voice was quiet, almost tearful.

'Where are we with identifying the gunman?'

'All we've got are a few blurred images from CCTV. Nobody has called in claiming to know him or seen anyone running around with a gun.'

'I emailed those images to Featherstone over an hour ago. Why hasn't he released them to the press?' Christian asked.

'Maybe he has.'

'Then why aren't they on the news? Sian get me someone from the BBC on the phone. I'll send them myself.'

'I've got Danny's mobile somewhere,' Sian said, heading back to her desk.

'I'm not talking to that cock. Get me someone who knows what they're talking about.'

'That was the Chief Constable's secretary. He wants to see you,' Scott said, putting down the phone, to Christian.

'I bet he does,' he said with a heavy sigh.

He tucked his shirt into his trousers and tried to neaten himself up for the Chief Constable. He headed for the door with Sian following.

'Christian, ask the Chief Constable about the images before you send them to the press. There may be a reason why he's holding them back.'

'No. This is my investigation. My call. I want this man found. Somebody knows who he is.' He unlocked his phone and handed it to her. 'The images are on there. Send them to the BBC, Sky, ITV and as many newspapers as you can think of and ask them to use them. I want them on TV and slapped all over social media.' He was frustrated at the lack of pace the investigation was taking, and, fuelled with adrenaline and the desire for a result, his words were falling over each other.

'But—'

'Did you ever see Matilda running to ask for permission? No. Neither am I.'

Chapter Thirty-One

Mowson Lane, Worrall

The twenty-minute drive from Rotherham to Worrall was almost doubled thanks to the Parkway being closed and traffic backed up on all the surrounding roads. Janet Crowther was a nervous driver at the best of times and liked to plan her routes meticulously before setting out. The fact she'd had to double back on herself and go down roads she'd never been on before, and had been beeped at by irate drivers desperate to get to their destination, did nothing for her stress levels. At one point, she'd pulled up on a residential street, turned off the engine and took a few minutes to compose herself. She was close to tears and her hands were shaking. She turned on the radio, hoping a bit of classical music might calm her down.

'*...gunman opened fire from a bridge over the Sheffield Parkway leaving at least twenty people dead and dozens more injured. Eyewitnesses say people were fleeing from their cars and dropping like dominoes as the gunman mercilessly picked off his victims one by one.*'

She quickly turned it off. Janet's face paled. If she'd left home at the arranged time, she could have been on the Parkway when the gunman opened fire. She could have been one of those twenty dead.

'Good grief,' she uttered under her breath, performing the sign of the cross and kissing the crucifix she always wore on a chain around her neck.

Life was incredibly precious. Janet knew that more than most people. What her family had gone through lately would have kept *EastEnders* in storylines for years – two cancer battles, a redundancy, two stolen cars, a house burnt down, a hidden affair, three divorces, an attempted suicide, and a serial killer exposed. What this family didn't need was more drama, and that included her being shot at while driving down the Parkway.

She fired off a quick text to her husband, Ronald, telling him about the traffic issues and another to her sister, Vivian, saying she was going to be even later, due to what was happening in Sheffield. She still hadn't replied to her first text yet, but that wasn't unusual. Vivian and technology did not go well together.

Suitably composed, Janet glared at her reflection in the rear-view mirror. She still looked pale and her eyes were wide, but she'd stopped shaking. Always a good sign. She turned on the ignition of the Nissan Micra, carefully pulled out into traffic and headed for Mowson Lane.

———

It wasn't long before she parked outside the detached house. Malcolm's Vauxhall was under the car port and the downstairs curtains were still closed. It wasn't like Vivian to leave the curtains drawn into the middle of the afternoon. It was a very dull day. If she was reading in the living room, perhaps she wanted the big light on and didn't want passers-by nosing in.

From the front passenger seat, she took a bunch of flowers and a plastic tub with a home-made cake inside. Janet never visited someone's home without a gift.

It was a cold and gloomy afternoon. A mist had hung in the air all day and a fine drizzle was falling. She rang the bell, stepped back from the white door and waited. She looked down at the bunch of flowers and smiled. A burst of colour in this dank, dreary month always cheered things up.

No answer.

She rang the bell again.

A gust of wind came from nowhere and made Janet shiver. Wearing light trousers and a fleece jacket, she was chilly and couldn't wait to get into Vivian's house with the real log fire. Hopefully, there was a coffee brewing.

She stepped back from the house and looked up. The upstairs curtains were closed, too. Janet frowned. She put the flowers and cake on the doorstep and dug out her phone. She selected Vivian's mobile and gave it a call. It went straight to voicemail. She decided against leaving a message and tried calling the landline. She could hear it ringing through the front door. She bent down and lifted the letterbox. The phone was in its cradle on the hall table. The doors leading to the living, dining room and kitchen were all closed. The answer machine kicked in and, again, Janet ended the call rather than leave a message.

This was very unlike Vivian. She knew Janet was coming over this afternoon. If there was a problem, she would have called to cancel, not left her sister freezing on the doorstep.

Janet selected Malcolm's mobile number and rang it while

she went around to the back of the house. She squeezed past the Vauxhall and failed to notice the red light of a sensor above her head come on.

————

Jake Harrison looked at the damage to his neck in the mirror in the visor above the front passenger seat of the van. Three scratch marks that had drawn blood. He licked a tissue and dabbed at it. It stung slightly and he winced. He hadn't expected such a cat fight. It was almost funny. He unplugged his mobile phone, charging in the cigarette lighter, and jumped out of the van. He selected the camera, pulled open the back door and took a photograph of his insurance policy tied up in the back. He winked and slammed the door closed.

Back in the front of the van, he was about to send the picture in a text message when a notification alerted him. The sensor he'd placed in the car port had been triggered.

Taking an iPad from his bag, he selected the program that turned on the hidden cameras he'd placed within the house. There were three in the kitchen, two in the hallway, two in his bedroom and one each looking over the front and back entrance to the house. If the sensor above his dad's car had been triggered, that meant someone was making their way to the back of the house.

Jake selected the camera from the drop-down menu and brought it up full screen. There was Aunt Janet, approaching the back door. His smile turned into a grin.

He'd never liked Aunt Janet and Uncle Ronald with their holier-than-thou attitude. They took in kids who needed emergency foster care, set up a foodbank for those in the neighbourhood who had fallen on hard times, helped with the church and their social and fundraising activities. They were so pious and saintly that it had to be a ruse. Surely their God-bothering was masking a darker identity? If not, then he was pleased it was good old Aunt Janet who was going to stumble across her sister and brother-in-law. That would wipe the sanctimonious smile off her face.

He watched as she approached the back door. She cupped her hands around her eyes and leaned into the glass for a good look into the kitchen. It seemed to take an age before she reacted. When she did, it caused Jake to guffaw. He applauded and was thrilled this was recording. He'd be able to watch it over and over again.

Janet couldn't believe what her eyes had witnessed. No. It didn't make sense. It wasn't possible. She'd spoken to Vivian on the phone last night. She'd told her about her test results and how she'd used the wrong flour in the cake and was making a second one. They'd laughed and Vivian brought up the story of spelling Malcolm's name wrong on his fiftieth birthday cake. How did life go from that to seeing her sister on the floor of her kitchen in a pool of blood? It didn't make sense. It wasn't real.

She almost fell off the back doorstep as she recoiled from the horror barely inches away from her. She wanted to be sick. She wanted to scream for help. She had no idea what to do.

Once again, Janet pulled out her phone and dialled her husband's number. While listening to it ring, she paced up and down the back garden. She wanted to look back in the house to make sure she hadn't plunged into a nightmare, but daren't. She didn't want to see her sister like that.

'Ronald, it's me,' she said with a shaking voice. 'I need you to come over to Vivian's right now. I think … Well, I don't know what to think. Something's happened and … oh goodness, Ron, they're dead. They're both dead.'

'What are you talking about?'

The delayed shock was setting in. Janet started crying uncontrollably. She leaned against the side of the house and fell to the floor. Tears were streaming down her face and she gripped the mobile phone, screaming, begging, pleading for her husband to come to her rescue.

———

By the time Ronald arrived, a neighbour had heard Janet's screams and rushed to her aid. Ronald found her being comforted by an elderly man with a look of horror on his face.

'Janet!'

'It's ok. She's had a nasty shock. I've called the police. They're on their way. They might be delayed though after everything that's going on today.'

Ronald stared at him.

'Sorry, Patrick Burton. I live next door.'

'What's happened?' Ronald squatted down to Janet, who was sitting on the doorstep, her hands wrapped around a mug of tea. She hadn't drunk any and her hands were shaking despite the heat coming from the cup.

'She was talking about Malcolm and Vivian being killed,' Patrick continued. 'I'm afraid I didn't quite believe her, so I had a look for myself. She was right. They're just lying there on the floor in the kitchen. I'm no expert, but it looks like they've been shot.'

'What?' Ronald asked, surprise in his voice.

'It's true,' Janet said. She looked up from the mug. Her eyes were full of tears. 'They're dead, Ronald.'

'What was it? A break-in or what?' he asked turning back to the neighbour.

'I can't see any sign of a break-in.'

Ronald turned to his wife. Her face had softened. The tears had dried up.

'What is it? What's the matter?' he asked.

She swallowed hard. 'Where's Jake?'

'Oh my goodness.' Ronald fished around in his pocket. 'I've got the spare key. We should go inside and have a look. He might be injured or something.'

'Shouldn't we wait for the police?' Patrick asked.

'Are you sure they're dead? Did you hear any shots?'

'No, but, my wife's a bit deaf. We have to have the television turned up loud.'

'Ronald, just go and see, please,' Janet pleaded, grabbing hold of his arm. 'They might need help.'

Ronald patted his wife's hand and made his way to the back door.

'I'll come with you,' Patrick said.

Ronald inserted the key and turned it slowly. He pushed the door open and looked inside. He didn't know if he should enter or not. He'd read enough crime fiction novels to know this was a crime scene and not to interfere with any potential evidence. However, they were his family. He couldn't just leave them there, lying in pools of their own blood, especially if they needed urgent medical attention.

'Oh my goodness,' he said, a hand clamped to his mouth. He looked down at the body of his sister-in-law. Vivian Harrison was a good woman. She'd put up with a great deal over the last couple of years. She was always so kind, caring, considerate of other people. Surely she deserved better than to be shot to death in her own home.

'Are they dead?' Patrick asked behind Ronald.

'I don't know. It looks like it.'

He stepped into the house. The neighbour followed.

They didn't notice the red light come on above the door.

Another bleep caused Jake to switch cameras. He turned to the one that gave a view of the whole kitchen. His mother and father were in the same position he'd left them in this morning while it was still pitch dark outside.

He saw Uncle Ron enter the kitchen and that nosy bastard from next door. They walked slowly and carefully through the room, not taking their eyes from the stricken couple.

Jake put the iPad on the front passenger seat and removed the laptop from his bag. He opened it, woke it up, and began frantically hammering at the keyboard. He paused, slammed his finger down on the large enter button, then went back to looking at the iPad. This show was just about to get exciting.

'They're definitely dead,' Ronald said, having checked for a pulse on his brother-in-law. 'Their bodies are cold. They've been dead for some time.'

'Oh my God. We should probably wait outside until the police arrive,' Patrick said.

'You're right,' he said, his voice full of tears.

'I thought they'd have been here by now. I know that— What was that?'

'What?'

'I thought I heard a beeping noise.' He turned and looked around him. 'The microwave's come on.'

'Has it?' Ronald asked.

'Yes. Look. There's something in there.' He crouched to look through the door but couldn't make out what it was. 'Why would it do that?'

The microwave was counting down from thirty seconds. Ten seconds had already lapsed.

Ronald went over to join him.

'Jesus Christ,' he exclaimed.

'What's the matter?' Ronald asked.

'We need to get out.'

'What? Why?'

'I think that's a bomb.'

There was fifteen seconds left on the clock.

Both men ran out of the house, scrambling with each other over who was exiting first.

'Janet, move. We have to move,' Ronald screamed, grabbing his wife from the side of the house and pushing her past Malcolm's Vauxhall. She dropped the mug of tea. It smashed on the ground.

'What's going on?' she screeched, panic etched on her face.

'There's a fucking bomb in the house,' he said, swearing for the first time in his whole married life.

The three of them ran as fast as they could and only made it to the bottom of the drive before the microwave pinged.

Chapter Thirty-Two

The last of the bodies was being removed from the car park at the back of South Yorkshire Police HQ. Sian watched from the window of the Homicide and Major Enquiry suite. She'd never be able to look out of this window again without seeing the strewn bodies of her colleagues. She glanced up to the building behind, where the gunman had fired from. Sian had never felt such hatred, loathing and venom for one person as she had for the bastard who had mercilessly murdered decent, hardworking people in cold blood.

'Who's that?'

Sian jumped and turned to see DC Finn Cotton join her at the window. She looked back down to see the final body being carried to a waiting police van that would take him to the mortuary.

'Sebastian said it was Robin Morley. A PC. I didn't know him,' she said, her voice filled with tears she was clinging on to.

'I did. We called him Batman, for obvious reasons,' he said

with a ghost of a smile on his face. 'He was a lovely bloke. Only in his late twenties. He wanted to work his way up the ladder. He passed his sergeant's' exam just before Christmas. He could eat for England. I was on protection duty with him once; a whole night shift stuck in a car with him. He knew some filthy jokes, which helped pass the time, but bloody hell, he broke wind that could strip the enamel off your teeth.' He smiled at the memory.

'Are you all right?' Sian asked, placing a hand on his shoulder.

'No. I'm not. I knew every one of those that died out there. In the last two years, I've either worked with them, or had good personal conversations with them. They were more than colleagues. Even the ACC was more than just a boss. I've lost six friends today.'

'We've all lost six friends, Finn. Every police officer in the country will be grieving for these guys. But we pull together. We don't suffer in silence. We come out of this stronger and we fight back. We fight back hard,' she said with real determination.

'Sian.'

She turned at the sound of her name being called and saw DI Brady nodding for her to join in him his office.

'Remember that, Finn,' she said, turning back to the detective constable as she rubbed his back. 'None of us are alone in this. That's how we survive – by banding together and showing this wanker we mean business.'

It was rare for Sian to swear, especially in front of a colleague of a lower rank. She always wanted to maintain that air of professionalism about her. However, today, those words she hated were more than justified.

'I'm so sick of trying to be positive,' she said as she entered Christian's office and closed the door behind her.

'Do you want to take a break, have five minutes to yourself?' he asked.

'No. I want to scream. I want to kick something,' she said, her eyes darting left and right as if looking for something to pick up and throw through a window.

'Sian, take a seat, there's something I need to tell you.'

Her gaze fixed on him. She saw the look of hurt on his face and she suspected the worse.

'Oh God, Matilda's died?'

'No. Nothing like that,' he quickly assured her.

'Oh, thank God.' She slapped a hand to her chest and plonked herself down in a squeaking chair. 'What's happened?'

'A couple of things. First of all, I've had a call from Adele at the hospital; Matilda was pregnant. She lost the baby.'

It was a few long seconds before Sian could take in what he'd said. 'She was … oh, Jesus Christ, no. Oh God.' Her head fell forwards into her hands. 'That's … that's just the worst news. The poor woman.'

'According to Adele, she didn't even think Matilda knew she was pregnant. Adele didn't know, and she said Matilda definitely would have told her.'

'Yes, she would. After all she's been through, she's just getting her life back on track and this happens.' She looked up. 'Did Adele say how the operation was going?'

'Slowly. They're removing the skull fragments from the brain, but until the swelling comes down, they can't repair the skull, and they won't know how much damage there's been until she wakes up. If she wakes up.'

'Am I having a nightmare?' she asked. 'Because none of this

seems real. How can Valerie and Ranjeet be dead? How can Matilda be fighting for her life? I can't get my head around any...' She broke down, her words lost to the tears she had been so bravely hanging on to in front of Finn, Rory and Scott.

Christian ran around to her, pulled her from the chair and held her tightly in his arms. He didn't say anything. There was nothing he could say. A comforting hug, an acknowledgement of support said more than any useless placatory words could.

The door to Christian's office was opened without being knocked on. Christian looked up and saw Chief Constable Martin Featherstone standing on the threshold.

'Everything all right?' he asked in his usual strong, commanding voice.

Sian quickly pushed herself out of Christian's embrace and wiped her eyes. 'Everything's fine, sir. I just needed a little cry.'

'Everything isn't fine, Sian. This is one of the most unusual days I think any of us will ever experience. Anyone who claims they haven't shed a tear over what's happened today is either a liar or a psychopath. Now, I'm glad you're both here. A call has come through – two people have been found shot dead at a house in Worrall.'

'Who?' Sian asked.

'I don't know yet. However, the man who called it in has made several calls. We've not been quick on response due to obvious reasons, but his last call was to say that he believed there was a bomb in the house.'

'A bomb?'

'The gunman's house?' Christian asked.

'That was my first thought,' Martin said. 'Until we know more, I'm going along with the assumption that he's shot and killed his family and booby-trapped the house before heading off on his shooting spree.'

'We need to get into that house,' Sian said, making her way towards the door.

'Nobody is going anywhere until the house is secure,' Martin said, stopping her. 'A bomb disposal unit is on its way from Catterick Garrison.'

'That could take ages. What if there is a bomb and it goes off? Vital evidence could be destroyed,' Sian said.

'And if I let you lot go in there and a bomb goes off, I'll lose even more officers. No. Nobody is entering that house until it's secure. In the meantime,' Martin said, turning his attention to Christian, 'I want you and your team in the neighbourhood. I want the whole street evacuated and the neighbours interviewed. We need to know everything we can about the people living there and how it fits in to the narrative of one man waging a war against the police and the people of Sheffield.'

With that, he turned on his heels and marched out of the office. He'd left Christian's door open when he entered, so the majority of those in the open-plan office had heard everything the Chief Constable had told them. The grim faces of the HMET said it all; they were dealing with more than an angry man with a gun and a vendetta. This was a man who had bomb-making capabilities and a whole arsenal of potential lethal weapons up his sleeve. Who the fuck was this man?

Chapter Thirty-Three

Danny Hanson could feel his mobile vibrating in his jacket pocket, but he was too busy repeating the same shit over and over again in a live piece to camera from outside the front entrance of South Yorkshire Police HQ.

He'd watched the BBC News channel on a slow news day where the same story kept getting repeated until even the newsreader looked bored, but he was in the middle of an exciting, developing story. His phone was buzzing from his police contact giving him exclusive information nobody else had, yet he wasn't allowed to act on it because he needed to be in front of the camera to tell the few viewers who were watching at this time of day that a gunman was terrorising the city of Sheffield.

'Danny Hanson, our North of England correspondent, thank you,' the newsreader said.

He remained still, looking grim-faced into the camera until he was told through his earpiece that he was no longer on screen. He rolled his eyes and lowered the microphone. He turned away, fished his phone out of his pocket and saw he had a voicemail and several text messages.

20 now confirmed dead from the Parkway.

Dead at the station are Valerie, DC Ranjeet Deshwal, PC Natasha Tranter, PC Robin Morley, PC Fiona Lavery and Sergeant Julian Price.

Get yourself over to Mowson Lane. It's all kicking off.

'Fuck!' Danny said out loud.

'Problem?' Lewis asked, looking up from his camera.

Danny ignored him and searched for the number of the producer on his phone.

'Hi, Dan, you're doing a great job,' the producer said by way of a greeting.

Danny hated being called *Dan*. 'Thanks. Listen, I've had a contact at the police give me some exclusive information. I need to get out to Worrall.'

'Where's that?'

'The other side of Sheffield.'

'We're doing a recap at quarter past. I need you there.'

'I've repeated the same things for over an hour. Can't you just run that again?'

'Something might happen. It needs to be live.'

'Nothing's happened. If the Chief Constable was going to give another press conference, we'd have been told about it by now.' He ran his fingers through his hair, pulling at it hard to stop himself from saying something he shouldn't.

'We've got the images sent over from South Yorkshire

Police. Calls are coming in all the time. We could have an ID any minute.'

'I just need ten minutes to check this out.'

'What exactly is happening at the Wirral?'

'It's Worrall, and I don't actually know yet. All I know is that it's kicking off.'

'Is it even relevant to the shooting?'

'I … don't … maybe. Possibly,' Danny waffled.

'Get more information from your contact and call me back.'

'But…' The line had already gone dead.

Danny chewed his bottom lip hard as he thought. He looked up at the building of South Yorkshire Police HQ. It looked how it always did on any other day. The only exception was the increasing number of press parked outside. It was frustrating. If he'd still been working on *The Star,* then he'd already be halfway to Worrall by now.

'Lewis,' he said, turning around quickly. 'Can you cover for me?'

'What? How?'

'I need you to say there's a problem with the camera and we can't do a live feed at quarter past.'

'Why?'

'Just … something's come up. It could be big. I don't know, but we need to move now.'

'I'm not lying for you, Danny.'

'Look, Lewis, this is a massive story. It's huge. How often do we get a gunman in England, for fuck's sake? I've got a contact within the police feeding me information,' he said, holding up his phone. 'He's been spot-on about everything so far. If we get this, it could mean big things for us,' he said with wide-eyed excitement.

'And if it's nothing, it could me the sack. My girlfriend's pregnant with twins – I need this job.'

'I need it too. More than half of my salary goes on my sodding rent. But don't you see what's happening here? I've got an in with the police. If we get footage of another shooting or the gunman being arrested or something, who knows where that will lead us.'

He thought for a moment. 'I really don't like this, Danny.'

'You're a journalist, Lewis. We hunt for the best story we can get.'

'No. You're a journalist. I'm a cameraman. I don't even want to be working on news. I've applied for every nature documentary the BBC have done in the last few years and got nowhere.'

'How many more times can we see fucking penguins shivering to death in a huddle in the Antarctic? It's been done so many times, I bet even the penguins roll their eyes when they see David Attenborough get off the plane. We've got the chance to catch a gunman in action!'

'Doesn't that scare you, even a little?'

'No, it doesn't. It's giving me a boner just thinking about it,' he said, slapping him on the arm and heading for the van.

'You need to see a therapist, mate. You're not wired right.'

Chapter Thirty-Four

Two cars carrying what was left of the Homicide and Major Enquiry Team arrived at Worrall. They couldn't get onto Mowson Lane, so had to park around the corner.

Uniformed officers were busy knocking on doors and informing residents of what was happening in their street. Staying indoors was not an option. They had to leave their homes as there was a potential bomb threat. It was organised chaos as people made their way quickly down the road to where they were being transported by bus to a nearby community centre.

'A bomb disposal unit is less than an hour away. We've no idea how long people are going to have to be away from their homes, so we're asking them to take their pets and any medication they may need.' Inspector Porter filled Christian in on the developing situation as the HMET approached the roadblock.

'Any sightings on the gunman?' Christian asked as he watched an overweight woman trotting up the road with a dog on a lead in each hand and a heavy-looking carpet bag under her left arm. She looked scared to death as she glanced over her shoulder at her house, as if for the final time.

'Not so far.'

'It's been three hours since the shooting at the Parkway. Where the bloody hell is he?'

'He's either gone to ground and someone's hiding him, or he's finished and probably topped himself.'

Christian thought for a moment. 'I very much doubt he's finished.'

'I don't think so either. I'll leave you to it then, mate.' He slapped him on the shoulder and made to leave.

'Is everything all right, Gavin?'

'Yes. My sister lives on this road. I just want to make sure she's safe.'

Christian offered him a sympathetic smile. Despite Sheffield being a large city, it was a close one too, and family and friends tended to stick by each other. DI Brady suddenly felt individually responsible for all half a million lives living in the Steel City.

'What do you want from us?' Scott asked.

Christian took a breath. 'Scott, you, Finn and Rory help with the uniformed officers. If there is a bomb in there, we don't know how it's wired, if it's on a timer or anything. We need this road cleared as quickly as possible.'

The three DCs set off. Christian watched Rory as he moved away. He was quiet. He hadn't said a word on the journey and every time Christian had glanced at him through the rear-view mirror, he looked a million miles away. He was probably working on autopilot today, but tomorrow, and the day after, he'd need careful watching.

'What do we know about the people who live there?' Christian asked, nodding towards the house.

Sian looked down at her pad. 'Malcolm and Vivian Harrison. He's a lecturer in engineering at the university. She took early retirement due to ill health.'

'Who found them?'

'Her sister, Janet, Janet's husband, Ronald, and a neighbour, Patrick Burton.'

'Where are they now?'

'They're being taken back to the station to give a statement. Janet's in shock.'

'Ok. They all need interviewing. I want to know everything about this family as soon as we can.'

'I'll give Aaron a call and ask him to get the interviews going straight away.'

'Thanks, Sian.'

Christian turned back to the house. It was a normal, unassuming detached house in the middle of a quiet, unsuspecting street in an affluent area of Sheffield. What the hell had happened behind that white door for someone to shoot both occupants dead and booby-trap it with explosives?

The sky was darkening by the minute as the dull day descended into late afternoon. It was usually pitch-black by four o'clock in early January. Is that what the gunman was waiting for? Was he going to make his next move under the cover of darkness? A stiff icy breeze caused Christian to shiver. He wished he'd worn more layers today.

'According to Rix, Patrick Burton was telling him in the car back to the station that there was something in the microwave that looked like a bomb,' Sian said, as she returned to Christian at the roadblock, putting her phone in her pocket. 'He and Ronald Crowther went into the kitchen and the microwave came on by itself.'

'It sounds like it was wired to a sensor or something.

They'll have triggered it when they entered,' Christian said, wrapping his coat tightly around his chest to keep warm.

'The microwave was counting down from thirty seconds,' Sian continued. 'They ran out of the house, but nothing happened.'

'Did he get a good look at what was in the microwave?'

'No. He said it definitely wasn't food. He saw wires.'

'Then why didn't it go off?' he mused.

'Maybe it was wired wrongly. Maybe it was a dummy,' Sian guessed.

'Possibly. Sian, get back to the station. There's no point in us both being here. Have a chat with Malcolm and Vivian.'

'I've asked Aaron to do that.'

'I know, but I'd prefer you to do it.'

'Why?'

'You're much better at getting under people's skin than he is.'

'I'll take that as a compliment,' she said, giving a hint of a smile.

As Sian made her way back to a marked car to take her to HQ, Christian heard a van screech around the corner and saw the recognisable grin of Danny Hanson in the front passenger seat.

Chapter Thirty-Five

Night's veil had started to draw in on the journey back from Worrall to HQ. Sian shivered as she climbed out of the car at the front of the building. She doubted she'd ever use the rear car park again.

With her head down, she pushed by a swarm of journalists, ignored their questions and was let into the building by a police constable she didn't recognise.

A little way down the corridor she stopped in her tracks. Sian had been with South Yorkshire Police her entire career. She prided herself on knowing everyone, but it turned out she didn't know as many people as she thought. Out of the six dead, she only knew two by name. Of the eight seriously injured, she only knew three. That had to change. She turned back and returned to the petite uniformed officer standing by the door.

'Have the reporters been any trouble?' Sian asked.

'Oh, no. They've been quite patient, actually,' she said in a soft voice. She obviously hadn't expected a plain-clothed officer to talk to her.

'Have you been here long?'

'I started here a few months ago,' she said with a look of sadness on her smooth, pale face.

Sian gave a sympathetic smile. 'Not the start you were hoping for?'

'You could say that.'

'Well, I'm DS Sian Mills. I'm with the Homicide and Major Enquiry Team.' She held out her hand for the young woman to shake.

'Nice to meet you. PC Zofia Nowak.'

'Beautiful name.'

'Thank you.' She gave a genuine smile. 'My parents are Polish.'

'I know today is highly unusual, and it will affect a lot of us in different way, but if you ever need to talk, just pop upstairs. None of us should go through this alone.'

'That's very kind of you. Thank you.'

Sian promised herself to be more open and forthcoming, especially with the next generation of officers. She proffered a sympathetic smile, turned and headed for the stairs.

But stopped dead when she saw a face she knew at the end of the corridor.

'Kesinka!'

Her colleague turned around. Her face was gaunt and wide-eyed. The moment she saw Sian it wrinkled, and the tears flowed.

'Sian!'

'Oh my God.' Sian started crying and headed towards her with her arms outstretched. They held each other tight and cried on each other's shoulder. 'I'm so sorry, Kes. I'm so, so sorry.' Sian's words were muffled, lost in Kesinka's duffel coat. She pulled herself out of the embrace and looked deep into

Kesinka's wet eyes. 'He was a good man. The best. I'm so sorry. What are you doing here? You should be at home.'

'I couldn't stay in the house. I just ... I don't know ... I needed some air, so I went out for a walk, and I ended up here. I don't even know how I got here.'

'Where's Hemant?'

'He's with my mum. Sian, I don't know what I'm going to do without him,' she said, bursting into tears once more.

Sian fumbled in her pocket for a tissue. She pulled a crumpled one out and handed it to the DC. 'I don't know what to say to you, Kes, I wish I did. You're not on your own, that's the main thing. You have your family. You have Hemant, and you have all of us here. We'll look after you. We'll make sure Ranjeet isn't forgotten.'

Kesinka tried to smile but her tears wouldn't allow it. 'I heard about Matilda. How is she?'

'I don't know. Look, Kesinka, why don't you go into the family room. There are some other relatives there and I'll bring you a coffee.'

'Can I...?' She nodded to the stairs leading up to the HMET suite.

'That's not a good idea, Kes. It's an active investigation. We've got photos on the board that you don't need to see.'

She nodded sagely. 'Sian, I'm scared. I can't believe he's gone.'

A door opened at the end of the corridor and a group of uniformed officers headed in their direction. Sian put her arm around Kesinka and took her into a nearby vacant office.

Kesinka collapsed into the seat as if her spine had been removed and there was nothing to hold her up.

Sian knelt down beside her. 'Kes, I know you feel like you're in a nightmare right now, and I'm afraid you are. We all are. But I promise you, it can only get better from here. There are going to be a couple of difficult weeks ahead, but once things have settled down, you'll find a way to cope. The most important thing to remember is that you are not alone. You'll never be alone. You and Hemant are so loved here. By everyone.'

Kesinka's face screwed up as tears rolled down her cheeks. There was nothing else Sian could say. She pulled her into a tight embrace once again.

Chapter Thirty-Six

'BP's dropping.'

'I'm almost finished.'

The operation to remove fragments of shattered skull from Matilda's brain was not an easy one and required a steady hand. Layton McNulty was the second surgeon to work on her, as the painstakingly slow procedure soon took its toll, and a fresh pair of eyes and a steadier hand was required.

When Matilda was shot, the bullet grazed the back of her head leaving a longer track of shattered bone fragments rather than a perfect entry wound. Although a direct hit would have seriously reduced her chance of survival, the repair job to the skull would have been neater and easier.

The operation was stalled when it was discovered Matilda was pregnant. The body had gone into shock and rejected the pregnancy in order to save her life. It was a while before a catheter could be inserted and Matilda stabilised enough for the operation to continue.

Deep in unconsciousness, Matilda was in the right place. There was a full team of surgeons, consultants, doctors and nurses around her, all of whom were constantly checking her vital signs, making sure she was getting enough oxygen and anaesthetic and that her blood pressure was stable.

There was a tube sticking out of her mouth, her eyes were taped closed and a tube inserted in her nose, yet she looked at peace as if she was enjoying a deep sleep.

A machine beeped a warning sound.

'Blood pressure is dropping through the floor.'

'I can't get hold of this last fragment. It's embedded too far,' the surgeon said.

'It might be best to leave it in and come back for it another time, when she's more stable.'

'I can get to it, just give me another minute.'

'More O-neg.'

'BP eighty over forty and falling.'

'There's another tear. She's losing so much blood I can't see what the fuck I'm going here. Suction,' the surgeon shouted.

Blood began to pour out of a fresh wound in Matilda's head. It pooled onto the table then began to drip onto the floor. It wasn't long before the surgeon was standing in a growing pool of red.

'She's going into VF.'

'We need to shock her.'

'Fuck!'

The surgeon took a step back as the crash team took over. One nurse grabbed the defibrillators, while another nurse began removing the gown covering Matilda.

'Charging to one-eighty. Stand by.'

Everyone stepped back from Matilda as her heart was shocked into life. Nothing happened.

'Again. Stand by.'

Still nothing happened.

'Charging to two-forty. Stand by,' the nurse said. Her voice sounded calm and controlled.

Once again everyone stepped back, and more volts were shocked into Matilda's heart. All eyes turned to the monitor to see if her heart was going to react.

'Still nothing.'

'Charging to three-sixty. Stand by, everyone.'

Matilda's body jolted as a shock of electricity surged through her body. Her face didn't acknowledge what was happening and her heart didn't respond.

Chapter Thirty-Seven

Sian had composed herself after leaving Kesinka in the family room. She'd gone into the toilets, splashed some cold water on her face and had a word with herself in the mirror, before sending off a text to her husband, Stuart, telling him how much she loved him. On her way to the interview room, she called Kesinka's mother, having got her number from HR, and asked if she'd come and collect her daughter. The last place she needed to be today was a police station.

'What room are Ronald and Janet Crowther in?' Sian asked Aaron as she caught up with him in the corridor.

'Interview room one. I'm about to go in for a chat now. I was just sorting some refreshments.'

'Excellent.'

'Wait, are you coming in with me?'

'Yes.'

'Why?'

'Because Christian asked me to.'

Aaron stopped walking. 'Don't you think I'm capable of taking a witness statement?' he asked harshly.

'Where did that come from? I'm sitting in with you, that's all.'

'It's because I'm not trusted.'

'I didn't say that.'

'You didn't need to. It's written on your face. Fucking hell, Sian, I've been a DS almost as long as you have. I make one little mistake and suddenly I can't do my job.'

Sian let out an exasperated sigh. 'First of all, it wasn't a "little mistake", it was a monumental cock-up. You slept with a witness and screwed up an entire murder case. Secondly, you're no longer on HMET, and a member of the team needs to be a part of this interview. You can read into that whatever you want to, but the fact of the matter is, I'm going in there with you. If you want to be an arse about this, I'll get someone else from CID to join me.'

Aaron remained silent, though he didn't take his eyes from Sian.

'Which is it to be?' she asked, looking up to him.

He didn't reply, just turned and headed for the interview room.

Ronald and Janet Crowther were sitting next to each other in silence. They both had a mug of tea in front of them, but neither had touched it. Their faces were blank in disbelief at what they had stumbled across this afternoon. Two hardworking people who paid their taxes and had never been involved with the police, never even had a parking ticket, had been plunged into a living nightmare. Two members of their family had been shot to death and a bomb planted in the house. It didn't seem real. How could it?

This was Sheffield, for crying out loud, not a Jack Ryan novel.

'Is there anything else we can get you?' Sian asked as she sat down opposite them.

Janet shook her head.

'I'm fine, thank you,' Ronald answered.

'Now, we're not recording this interview. Neither of you are under arrest. We just need to ask you some questions to try to understand what happened to Malcolm and Vivian,' Sian said slowly so they'd understand among the confusion of thoughts and images racing around their minds.

Neither of them said anything. Sian turned to look at Aaron. He raised his eyebrows. This was going to be a long process.

'Janet, when was the last time you spoke to your sister?' Aaron asked.

It was a while before she answered. She was staring down into her rapidly cooling mug of tea. She licked her dry lips. 'Last night,' she said, barely above a whisper.

'Was this in person or over the phone?'

'Over the phone.'

'And how did she seem?'

'Fine. Like she always was. We had a chat and a laugh.'

'How long did you chat for?'

'About half an hour, I think,' she said, looking to her husband for confirmation.

'Just over half an hour. You missed the whole of *EastEnders*, so we watched it on iPlayer afterwards,' he said, holding her hand and squeezing hard.

Janet gave a weak smile. 'That's right. Viv can't stand the soaps. She says they're too far-fetched. But try as I might, I can't give them up.'

'Was Vivian on her own while you were chatting?' Sian asked.

'No. Malcolm was there. He answered the phone when I rang.'

'Did anything seem amiss?'

'No,' Janet answered more firmly. 'Everything was fine.'

'Did you arrange to go over there this afternoon, or did you go over on a whim?' Aaron asked.

'I was supposed to go over this morning, but I had a text from Vivian asking if I could go after lunch inside.'

'Vivian texted you?'

'Yes.'

'Did you reply?'

'Yes.' She dug out her mobile phone, opened the messages app and showed Sian the conversation.

'She didn't reply to you. It wasn't read either.'

'No. Vivian isn't good with technology. She doesn't like mobile phones. I bought her a Kindle a couple of Christmases back and I think it's still in the box. Shame really as she likes reading… *Liked* reading,' she corrected herself.

Janet turned to Ronald. He leaned into her and put his arm around her shoulder.

Sian handed the phone back to her. 'Janet, is there anything you can tell me about Vivian and Malcolm that could give us some clue as to why they were killed?'

She thought for a moment. 'No. They're good people. They'll do anything for anyone. Well, Vivian would. Malcolm prefers to keep himself to himself.'

'Has there been any arguments, money worries?'

'No. Absolutely not.'

'Any family concerns?'

'There are always concerns with this family.'

Sian leaned forward. 'In what way?'

'I think that's why Viv doesn't like soaps. They remind her too much of our own family. Divorces, affairs, bankruptcy, you name it, it's happened to us, hasn't it?' She turned to her husband again.

'I'm afraid so,' he confirmed. 'Malcolm and Viv had their oldest staying with them. His marriage ended last year, and he wasn't taking it very well. He always was emotional, even as a boy—'

'Sorry,' Sian interrupted. 'Did you say Malcolm and Vivian had their son living with them?'

'Yes. Jake.'

Sian and Aaron exchanged concerned glances.

'Where is he now?' Aaron asked.

'Oh. I don't know. I assumed he was in the house dead along with his parents,' Ronald answered.

'I'll go and check if we've had any updates on the scene,' Aaron said. He stood up and left the room.

'Is Jake their only son?'

'No. There's… I thought you knew,' Ronald said.

'Knew what?'

'Malcolm and Vivian's youngest is Steve. Steve Harrison. He used to be a police officer here. He's in prison for killing six people, including one of your colleagues. That's when everything seemed to go downhill with this family.'

Sian leaned back in her seat. Her eyes were wide with disbelief. When PC Steve Harrison was unmasked as a serial killer, as the man who had killed DC Faith Easter, everyone at the station felt the shock waves it generated, and it was a long time before they could all move on. Were today's events linked to him? It was already going to go down in history as a dark day for Sheffield, but would South Yorkshire Police ever recover from it?

Chapter Thirty-Eight

'It's three o'clock, here are the news headlines: Two separate gun attacks in the northern city of Sheffield have left more than twenty people dead and dozens more injured. In a third incident, a bomb disposal team has been dispatched and an entire neighbourhood evacuated in the Worrall area of the city after the occupants of the house were found shot dead and a suspicious package found in the house. Chief Constable Martin Featherstone is leading the investigation.

'"Today is possibly the darkest day in the history of South Yorkshire Police, and while our number has been significantly reduced, the police officers of this country are one force and we are banding together to bring the perpetrator of these crimes to justice. At present, this is an ongoing investigation, so I am unable to give you much information. To the people of Sheffield, I advise you to stay indoors for your own safety and only travel if absolutely necessary until the gunman is safely in custody. Thank you."

'Meadowhall shopping centre in the north of Sheffield has been advised to close, and many of the city's schools and colleges are in lockdown. *The Prime Minister is being kept informed of the situation and earlier gave a short statement from Number Ten.*

'"*Our thoughts and prayers are with the families, friends, and colleagues of those injured and killed in today's shocking events. I have been speaking with the Chief Constable of South Yorkshire Police and promised him the full cooperation of the government in his handling of the investigation. The safety of the people of Sheffield, and of the whole country, is our paramount concern. I have every faith in the police force and pray this is brought to a swift and peaceful conclusion.*"

'*That was Prime Minister Theresa May. In other news, Brexit negotiations are continuing as...*'

Steve turned off the radio. He lay back on his bed, put his hands behind his head and a broad smile swept across his face.

This was turning into the perfect day. He'd never liked his parents. He thought them too wet, old-fashioned and weak. They were content to allow life to pass them by as if it was something to be scared of. They'd lived in that house on Mowson Lane since they got married more than thirty years ago. They did the same jobs, shopped in the same stores, watched the same type of programmes and films and went to the same places for a holiday every summer. There was no variety. They were dull. It was tragic that the most exciting thing to happen to them was getting murdered by their own son.

For their twenty-fifth wedding anniversary, Steve had wanted to do something special for them. He wanted them to have a holiday of a lifetime. They'd only been abroad once; they went to Spain for their honeymoon, but there had been a heatwave and they couldn't cope with temperatures past thirty degrees, so cut the holiday short. Twenty-five years later, they were still talking about how hot the sand was underfoot. However, Steve wanted to change all that. He wanted them to explore new cultures. He showed them brochure after brochure of trips to New York, Sidney, Cape Town, Moscow, Brazil, Oslo, Rome, Corfu and Morocco. All were met with a lukewarm response. He had to admit defeat, and for their silver wedding anniversary he gave them vouchers for a furniture shop they enjoyed browsing around. They were dull people. Their lives were pointless and would be quickly forgotten when they died. The least he could do for his parents was make their deaths special.

When today was over and the dust settled, Malcolm and Vivian Harrison would be synonymous with the Sheffield Gun Massacre. It all started under the cover of darkness in their twee semi-detached house, and if everything went to plan, it would end in a glorious bloodbath.

Steve looked at his watch. It was almost three o'clock. Jake would be getting ready for the finale.

Chapter Thirty-Nine

Mowson Lane and the surrounding streets had been evacuated. The team from Catterick Garrison had arrived and an expert wearing a full bomb disposal suit made their way very slowly towards the back entrance of Malcolm and Vivian's house.

Christian stood behind the cordon and watched. He couldn't tell if the person in the suit was male or female as they were covered from head to toe in protective equipment. He took a deep breath and looked around at the quiet houses. This was an affluent neighbourhood; residents looked after their homes and gardens. There was no litter, no graffiti, no burnt-out cars, yet it could all be destroyed if there was a bomb inside the house and it went off. He pitied whoever it was in that heavy suit.

'What's going on?' He turned at the question whispered loudly in his ear to find Danny Hanson behind him.

'I thought I told you to go away.'

'You did.'

'So why are you still here?'

'Because it's my job.'

'Your job is to piss off the police?'

'I report the facts as I see them. I'm currently seeing a bomb disposal team enter a house. I want to know whose house that is and if it has anything to do with the two shootings earlier today.'

'Then you'll have to wait for the official press release like every other media outlet.'

'Oh, come on, Christian, help me out here.'

Christian paused as if giving it some thought. 'No,' he answered firmly with a wry smile.

'Where's Matilda?'

Christian ignored him.

'Shouldn't she be here? I've been at the station, I've been at the Parkway and now I'm here, and I don't see the DCI anywhere.'

'I'm not answering any of your questions, Danny. Now if you don't piss off, I'll have you arrested for obstructing an investigation.'

'I'm not obstructing anything. I'm behind the cordon like you. What's happened to Matilda? Has she been suspended?'

'No, she has not.'

'Has she been shot?'

Christian didn't reply.

'She has, hasn't she? She's been shot. Is she dead?'

'Danny, please, fuck off.'

Christian's mobile started ringing, which saved him from another barrage of questions from the reporter. He'd practically told Danny what had happened to Matilda by answering only select questions. Damn, he should have ignored him from the start. He saw it was Sian calling him and swiped to answer.

'You're never going to believe who that house belongs to,' Sian said by way of a greeting.

'The neighbour did say their names. Michael and Vivian, wasn't it?'

'Malcolm and Vivian *Harrison*,' she corrected him. 'Parents to two sons: Jake Harrison and Steve Harrison. The same Steve Harrison who is currently in Wakefield Prison for killing six people including...'

'You don't need to remind me, Sian,' he interrupted. 'I'm aware he killed one of our own. I don't fucking believe this.' He tried to stop himself from shouting, but a few people turned in his direction, including the grinning Danny Hanson.'Jesus Christ.' He ran his fingers through his thinning hair as he thought. 'Ok, get on to Wakefield Prison, make sure Steve is still behind bars and hasn't managed to escape somehow. If he is, I want to know who he's had contact with in the last six months – visitors, letters sent and received, everything.'

'Will do.'

'Also, try to find out where the other son is living.'

'I have. He's recently separated from his wife. He's living back on Mowson Lane.'

'So, what are we thinking? He's either dead in the house or he's the one who shot them and rigged it up with a bomb before going on a shooting spree?'

'It has to be one or the other,' Sian said.

'Right, show Janet and Ronald those CCTV images we have of the gunman, see if they recognise him. If they do and they think it is Jake, get them to give you a proper photo and show it to your friend who set off the fire alarm, see if he can give you a positive ID.'

'This can't be related to Steve, can it?'

'I don't know. If his brother is the gunman, he could have been planning this with him for years. The first target was the same police station he worked at. It wouldn't be surprising if he's harbouring some kind of grudge.'

'But why open fire at the Parkway? Nobody could guess who would be driving along there at that time.'

Christian bit his bottom lip as he thought. 'I know. Look, try to ID the gunman. Check on Steve in prison and we'll go from there. I'll come back to the station. There's not much I can do here.'

Christian ended the call and headed for his car. Danny caught up with him.

'Problem?' the reporter asked.

'I'm not talking to you.'

'Who does the house belong to? I heard you mention someone called Steve. Who is he? Does he live in this house? Is he the gunman? Come on, Christian, give me something.'

Christian stopped in his tracks. 'First of all, it's DI Brady to you. Secondly, get the fuck out of my face,' he spat.

'Just tell me about Matilda. Was she shot at the station today? Is she dead?'

At his car, Christian paused. He turned back. 'Matilda Darke is very much alive.'

'So why isn't she leading this investigation? A double shooting, a bomb scare, surely a DCI should be on the scene?'

'You're the ace reporter, you tell me.'

Christian jumped into the car, slammed the door and drove off at speed, leaving Danny stood in the middle of the street with a perplexed expression on his face.

He dug his phone out of his pocket and made a call. 'It's me. Matilda Darke. Dead or alive?'

'I can't talk right now,' the reply came in a hushed whisper.

'Just answer dead or alive?'

'Alive.'

'Where is she?'

'For fuck's sake, Danny.'

'Look, answer my questions and I'll leave you alone.'

'She's been shot twice. She's being operated on at the Hallamshire.'

The line went dead. He almost put his phone away, but it burst into life. It was his producer.

'I know there's fuck-all wrong with the camera, Danny. I want you live in two minutes or you'll be back on that shitty local paper.'

Danny turned to the BBC News van and saw Lewis stood with the camera on his shoulder and a guilty look on his face.

'Oh, I'm more than ready.' He grinned.

Chapter Forty

Inside the Harrisons' house on Mowson Lane, bomb-disposal expert Liam Fury crouched to look into the microwave. The glass was tinted and didn't give him a good view, but he could see a small brown plastic tub with a white lid. At the corner, the lid was raised, and a white wire was sticking out. He needed to get at the plastic box, remove the lid and access what was inside.

He took a torch from his pocket, which wasn't easy with the heavy gloves he was wearing, and turned it on. He aimed it at the microwave and had a good look at the inside. The tub didn't seem to be connected to the microwave at all, so it had just been placed on the glass turntable inside rather than wired to the appliance. In that case, opening the door and taking it out shouldn't pose a risk.

'I've located the device,' he said into the built-in microphone. 'It's housed in a small Tupperware tub, but until I remove the lid, I can't see what kind of device I'm dealing with.'

He put the torch back in his pocket, placed a finger on the

door release button and slowly pushed. The door clicked open a fraction. Very slowly, he pulled the door fully open and looked at as much of the box as he could without moving it.

The lid was attached to the box apart from one small corner where the wire protruded. In order to see how intricate the device was, he'd need to fully remove the lid.

Liam could feel his heart pounding in his chest. He was sweating inside the heavy suit, which weighed just over eighty-five pounds. His breaths were shallow, and he tried to calm himself down with a few deep breaths.

'I've opened the microwave door. I'm now going to carefully remove the tub and place it on the kitchen work surface next to it.'

He licked his lips and with two giant, gloved hands he reached inside for the tub. He placed them firmly on either side of the box and made sure he had a secure grip before attempting to lift it. Very, very slowly, he picked it up and took tiny steps back from the microwave in order to bring the box out.

Liam swallowed hard a few times, but his mouth was dry. Aged only twenty-four, he'd been on two tours in Afghanistan and successfully deactivated more than fifty improvised explosive devices. Once back home in North Yorkshire, he tried to return to a normal life, which wasn't easy after the things he'd seen in the aftermath of a warzone. What he never expected was to be standing in a kitchen in a house in Sheffield attempting to deactivate a home-made bomb. His surroundings of a normal suburban street added to the pressure. He hadn't felt this nervous when he was looking at the mechanics of a suicide vest strapped to a sixteen-year-old girl in Kandahar, who was hysterical and had changed her mind. Thankfully, the bomb had only been a dummy.

'I've removed the tub from the microwave and placed it on the work surface. I'm now going to remove the lid in order to look at the device.'

His voice was quiet and low, yet the microphone picked up every word. In order for Liam to take the lid off, he'd have to remove his chunky gloves.

His fingers were steady as they touched the plastic. He lifted the corner that was already raised and ran his finger underneath to detach the lid from the tub. It seemed to take an age until it was fully separated, yet he still couldn't see inside. Wires could be attached to the underside of the lid. Until he knew, he couldn't lift it fully away in case it set the bomb off.

Gently, he bent his knees and lowered himself so his eyes were level with the work surface. He squinted and saw more wires in the box, but none of them seemed to be stuck to the lid.

'I'm now going to remove the lid,' he said.

Standing back up, he removed the lid and placed it carefully next to the tub. He looked into the plastic container.

'What the fuck?'

Chapter Forty-One

Jake Harrison parked around the corner from Stannington Secondary School and turned off the engine. He hadn't bothered listening to the news for the last half an hour, so didn't know how far the police were in their investigations. He didn't know if they'd discovered who he was. He looked around him. There was no police presence at the school. Good. No reason to change his plan.

He opened the back of the van and began removing his clothes. It was now fully dark, and the temperature was starting to fall. He could feel the fine rain on his bare skin as he took off his combat trousers and replaced them with black cotton ones. The white shirt was cold against his chest, but the jacket was heavier than he anticipated. That should warm him up. He looked at his reflection in a cracked mirror he'd found and neatened down his hair. He gave himself a smile, which relaxed his features. He squeezed his feet into highly polished black leather shoes. They pinched at his heels slightly, but the adrenaline coursing through his veins would make him forget the pain.

'Right then,' he said to his victim trussed up in the back of the van. 'I won't be long. Then one more stop and you can go home.' He picked up the bag containing his arsenal of weapons from beneath the seat in the front of the van and slammed the door closed. He was ready.

He looked at the phone he'd been using to contact his brother in prison. There were no texts, no voicemails, no missed calls. He turned it off and dropped it down the drain. It landed with a splash.

The school day at Stannington Secondary School didn't finish until four o'clock. He'd heard it had been put into lockdown and wondered what the procedure was for sending kids home in a situation like this. Would parents have to collect them, even the ones in the final year, aged fifteen and sixteen? He looked around. There were no anxious parents by the gates or sitting in parked cars. In fact, all was quiet. There was a deathly silence in the air. Jake couldn't help but smile.

Schools had certainly changed since the days of Jake's education. There were no open gates to simply walk through; even the perimeter of the school field had an eight-foot fence to keep people out. There were intercoms, cameras and notices telling visitors where to report. Over the years, schools had become more mistrustful and paranoid, or had people become more evil and schools were adapting to a disturbed society of kidnappers and paedophiles? The twenty-first century was not a happy place to live.

He pushed the buzzer on the intercom by the gate.

'Hello,' came the crackled reply.

'Good afternoon. My name is PC Steve Harrison. I'm with South Yorkshire Police. I've been sent to make sure you're all right and answer any questions you may have.'

'There's a red dot just above the speakers and a camera to

the right of it. Could you show your identification to the lens, please?' The woman asked.

'Of course.'

Jake removed his brother's old ID from his inside pocket and aimed it at the camera. He didn't look much like his brother. They didn't have the same winning smile and twinkling eyes, but he could pass for him through a poor-resolution camera, which he hoped this was. The wait to be allowed onto the premises seemed to take a long time. He wondered what the woman was doing. Eventually, the lock on the gates clicked. He'd been allowed in.

Jake swung his bag onto his shoulder and made his way down the drive with his head held high, his shoulders back and a spring in his step. He tried to hide the smile that was creeping onto his thin lips. He didn't want to give the game away until he was inside the school.

He looked up at the building as he approached. A relatively new build on two storeys with a gym, drama studio and football pitch at the back. He'd done his research and knew all the staff who worked here. He knew the Ofsted report and the average grades of the students. This was a good school. Any parent would love to send their child here.

Maybe not after today, though.

Chapter Forty-Two

'It was empty?' Sian asked.

'Not quite. It was a plastic tub filled with wires. Nothing else,' Christian said, warming his hands up around a mug of coffee in the HMET suite.

'I don't get it. Why would someone do that?'

'To delay the investigation. Everything he's done has been to delay us, like finding that burner phone switched on in the evidence bag. Now, according to Janet Crowther, she was due to go around there this morning, but she received a text from her sister asking her to go around later in the day instead. However, initial reports suggest that Malcolm and Vivian had been dead long before that text was sent.'

'So the gunman sent the text to delay the bodies being found,' Sian said.

'Exactly. If she'd gone at, say, ten or eleven o'clock as planned, then we'd have found Malcolm and Vivian sooner and worked out who he was a lot quicker.'

'Why would he want to delay us?' Finn asked from where he was making hot drinks for everyone.

'Because he's planning something else,' Christian said. Everyone stopped dead in their tracks at that and turned their attention towards him.

'You think so?' Sian asked.

'I do. The shooting at the Parkway was at eleven o'clock this morning. It's now three o'clock. What's he been doing for the past four hours? If all he intended was to shoot his parents and blow off steam over the Parkway, we'd have found him dead by now. Shooters like him always either kill themselves or go out in a blaze of glory – as they like to see it. We haven't found him dead, which means…' He trailed off, allowing the team to finish the sentence for themselves.

Aaron entered the suite. 'Sian, your homeless friend is downstairs.'

'He has a name, Aaron,' Sian chastised, picking up a file and leaving the room.

'I've shown Janet and Ronald the CCTV photos, and they say the figure looks like Jake. They're not one hundred per cent certain, but they're in the high nineties.'

'Thanks, Aaron.'

'I've also run his name through the PNC. He's not known to us, but there have been some complaints made against him by his wife.'

'Oh?' Christian said, handing his empty cup to Finn and asking for a refill.

Aaron selected the file on his iPad. 'She called 999 on the twenty-fourth of August last year, saying he was outside her flat and wouldn't leave. When they turned up, he wasn't there. Two weeks later, she called again, saying she saw him hanging around outside her flat. She had a brick thrown through her window and wanted him arrested.'

'What happened?'

'Police went around to his parents' house, but he wasn't in. They caught up with him the next day at work and gave him an official warning. Nothing seems to have happened after that.'

'So, that was late August last year,' Christian said, thinking aloud. 'Get contact details for the wife, find out where she lives, we'll pay her a visit.'

Sian re-entered the suite with a grin on her face. 'McNally is downstairs giving a formal statement, but he says the photo of Jake Harrison that Janet Crowther gave us is definitely the same man who paid him to set off our fire alarm this morning.'

'Yes!' Christian hissed. 'We've got him. All we need to do now is find where the bloody hell he is and what his motive is.'

'You make is sound so simple,' Sian said with a smile.

'If only it was.'

———

Adele entered the relatives' room, closed the door behind her and rested against it. Tears fell from her eyes.

'Oh, God,' Penny said, crumbling in her seat. Frank rushed to comfort her.

'What's happened?' Daniel asked, jumping up from his seat. He handed her a box of tissues from the chipboard table. She snatched one and wiped her eyes.

'Sorry,' she said through the emotion. 'I don't know why I'm crying.'

'Has something happened?' Daniel asked again.

Adele took a deep breath to steady herself. 'Ok. I've spoken to one of the consultants who was in the theatre with Matilda. It was touch and go, and they almost lost her...'

'Oh, Jesus Christ,' Penny said. She had her arms wrapped

firmly around herself, and her face contorted with tears as she began rocking back and forth in her seat. Frank was perched on the arm of the chair, holding his wife for comfort, but his face was pale. He looked like he was about to be sick.

'However, they managed to remove all the bone and bullet fragments from her brain and the swelling is slowly going down. They have to leave the skull open until the swelling has reduced, then they can replace the skull fragments with a metal plate.'

'Is she going to be all right?' Daniel asked, his eyes wide.

'They don't know. They've done all they can for her physically. She'll need further surgery to repair the skull and remove the bullet from her shoulder, but they don't expect any complications with that. It's a waiting game to see if there is any brain damage when she wakes up.'

'Oh my God, Frank,' Penny cried.

'She will definitely wake up though?' Daniel asked.

'They think so.'

'When will that be?'

'I don't know.'

'Didn't they say?'

'Daniel, there isn't a switch you flick on and off for someone to wake up. The body needs time to repair itself. She'll wake up when she's ready,' Adele said, getting testy. She went over to the chair where Penny was and sat next to her, rubbing her hand.

'I'm sorry, I just… Can we see her?' Daniel asked.

'Not right now. She's in Recovery, then they'll move her to ITU. Frank and Penny will be able to see her then.'

'Not me?'

Adele stood up. She grabbed Daniel by the elbow, opened the door and pushed him out into the corridor.

'Daniel, I'm sorry, but only the immediate family will be able to see her. Even I won't be allowed in and I've known her for more than twenty years.'

Daniel leaned back against the wall, tears streaming down his rugged face. 'I love her, Adele.'

She stepped forward. 'I know you do, Daniel.'

'I don't know what I'll do if I lose her.'

'You won't. Look, wait until tomorrow. Once Frank and Penny have been in with her, they're bound to let you pop in for a few minutes. I'll ask them for you. Just take a step back.'

He nodded and gave a weak smile. 'I will. Thanks, Adele. I think I'm going to get a coffee from downstairs.'

'Will you get us all one?'

'Sure.'

Adele watched him head for the lifts before she went back into the family room. Penny was stood by the window, looking out over the grey city.

'You try your best with your family,' she said solemnly. 'You put them through school, college and university. You hope they'll get good grades and a good career, maybe settle down and have kids, but it doesn't matter how old they get, you never stop worrying. Look at Matilda, forty-four years old, and I'm still fretting about her. When does it stop?'

'I don't think it ever does,' Adele said. 'I still see my Chris as a child, and he's settled into a job he enjoys and he's in a relationship.'

'They grow up so fast,' Frank said.

Penny turned from the window to face them both. Her eyes were full of tears. 'I've never regretted having kids. I love Matilda and Harriet to bits. But when you look at the state of the world, it makes you worry all the more. I don't want

Matilda to be a detective. I don't want her doing this job anymore,' she said, as the tears started to fall again.

'Penny,' Frank said, moving over to her. 'It's her choice. We have to support her and, when something like this happens, we make sure we're there for her and help to pick up the pieces.'

'I can't,' she choked. 'I can't do this. What if she's brain-damaged? What if she can't walk or talk or feed herself? She wouldn't want me bathing her. She wouldn't want me putting her to bed and dressing her. And, I know I shouldn't say this as her mother, and God forgive me, but I couldn't do that for her either.'

Adele closed her eyes and put her head down. She understood where Penny was coming from, but if she was in that position and Chris needed round-the-clock care, she'd be there for him. She wouldn't give it a second thought. She dug her mobile out of her pocket and sent a text to her son:

Matilda out of surgery. Still not out of the woods yet. Hope you're ok. Love you. XXX

Chapter Forty-Three

Once the 'bomb' inside the plastic tub was seen to be a hoax, a clean sweep of the rest of the Harrisons' house in Mowson Lane was given before bomb-disposal experts handed it over to police for their investigation to begin.

Simon Browes and Lucy Dauman were called out to make an initial assessment of the bodies of Vivian and Malcolm Harrison. The kitchen was sealed off and police searched the rest of the house.

On the first floor, Jake had slept in the second bedroom next to his parents' room. It was a large room with fitted wardrobes, a double bed pressed against the back wall and an oak desk in the corner where a laptop was plugged in and an iPad charging. These were both bagged and taken by forensic officers to be analysed, but there was plenty for DCs Rory Fleming and Scott Andrews to be going on with in the room.

Scott had been keeping a close eye on his best friend all day. Under normal circumstances, following the death of a loved one, Rory would have been sent home, but today was anything but normal and Scott knew Rory would refuse to walk away from the investigation, even if ordered to do so. Rory was usually a bright and bubbly personality, always quick with a joke or a sarcastic remark, but he'd hardly said two words since the shooting at the station this morning. Not surprising. Every time Scott looked to him and took in the expressionless face of his former flatmate, he wondered what was going on inside his head. What was he thinking about? He wished he'd talk, say something, anything that would alert Scott to what he was going through. He supposed, in his own time, Rory would open up. Until then, Scott just had to let him know that he'd always be there for him, whenever he needed him. Maybe he should move back into the apartment with him for a while. He was sure Chris wouldn't mind.

Rory was standing in front of the large wall opposite the wardrobes, which was covered in posters and maps of the city. The pictures depicted various types of guns and Post-it Notes were stuck to them where Jake had made notes in his illegible scrawl. News articles printed from the internet about gun crime and shooting massacres had been stuck up; the headlines highlighted, key information underlined in red.

'Jesus Christ,' Rory said as he stood in front of the grim collage. 'He's certainly done his homework.'

'He's definitely our gunman then,' Scott said from behind him.

'It would seem so.'

'Why?'

'I have no idea. A psychologist would probably have a field day in here.'

'I should ring the DI,' Scott said, fishing his phone out of his pocket.

'Is this linked to Steve? Did Steve put him up to this?'

Scott turned to his colleague whose face was etched with

pain and horror as his eyes danced over the amount of material on the wall.

'I don't know, Rory.'

Suddenly, Rory darted forward, as if something had snapped in his mind. He pulled open drawers in the bed side cabinet and chest of drawers, scrambling among the clothes and underwear.

'Rory, what are you doing?' Scott asked, phone still in hand.

'We need to find out where Jake is. We need to figure out what he's planning. Look at the wall, Scott – if he was just going to shoot us at the station and then over the Parkway, he wouldn't have done this much research. Look here,' he said as he pushed back the door to the fitted wardrobe and scrambled among a plastic box at the bottom. 'He's got books on terrorism, the Unabomber, Dunblane, Columbine, 9/11, the London attacks. And they're well read, look,' he said, holding them up. 'He's plotting something bigger than we've already witnessed today.'

'Scott, Scott, what's going on?'

Scott heard DI Brady's voice coming from his phone. 'Shit, sorry, I forgot I dialled. We're in Jake Harrison's bedroom. I think you're going to need to send someone out here.'

'I don't have anyone to send out, Scott. What do you need?' Christian sounded harassed.

'Jake has got books on terrorism and weapons, and he's got a wall full of press clippings about gun crime.'

'Look at this.' Rory began laying out small crumpled pieces of paper out on the bed. They were notes written in tiny handwriting, some almost impossible to read. 'Jesus, look at this one.' He handed it to Scott.

'"You can't take your eyes off the main target. That's Matilda. Once she's down you can have fun,"' Scott read out into the phone. 'Sir, there's about ten of these letters, maybe more.'

'Bring them all in,' Christian said.

'Listen to this one, "I've rewritten it in order of who you need to kill first. Memorise it then destroy it",' Rory said, holding up another piece of paper. 'I'm going to see if there's any more.'

'He's got a hit list,' Scott said. 'He's not finished, is he?'

'It doesn't look like it,' Christian said.

'Oh my God,' Rory said.

'What is it?'

Rory held up a black book for Scott to see.

'Shit. Sir, we've found a copy of *The Anarchist Cookbook*.'

'Fuck!' Christian said. 'Bag up everything you can quickly and bring it back here. We need to go through his stuff.'

The line went dead.

Scott's face was ashen. He couldn't take his eyes off the book. A person could face criminal charges for just being in possession of that book.

'He's going to blow something up, isn't he?' Scott asked.

Rory flicked through the pages. A folded-up letter Jake had been using as a bookmark fell out. Rory's eyes quickly scanned from left to right as he read it.

'It's worse than we thought.'

'What?'

He held out the letter. 'He's got nothing to lose. Jake's got terminal cancer.'

Chapter Forty-Four

'I t's chilly out there,' Jake said to the receptionist who'd let him in. He'd concealed his bag at the side of the entrance, out of sight. 'PC Harrison,' he said with a smile, holding out his hand. 'You are?'

'Susan Moss. I'm one of the administrators.' She quickly shook his hand then folded her arms tightly against her chest. 'I'm pleased you're here. A lot of the teachers have some questions, especially with the school day almost finished. We weren't quite sure whether to allow the children home on their own or not.' Susan was a short woman, somewhere in her mid-fifties. She had to crane her neck to look up at Jake. She was dressed conservatively in a long skirt, thick tights, a white blouse and a navy jacket over the top. She spoke with a strong voice, but her panicked face belied her words.

'Don't you have a policy you follow during times like this?' Jake asked as he followed her towards the office, smoothing down his ill-fitting police uniform. His eyes casually scanned the corridor. He took in the nearby classrooms, staircase and exits. This was the big test of his strength of character. He'd been planning and plotting this for so long, but now he could actually go through with it. His heart wasn't racing. He wasn't sweating. His hands weren't shaking. He felt calm. Oh yes, he was more than ready.

'We do, but, well, nothing like this has ever happened before. It's fine to read a procedural document and file it away for future reference, but when something actually happens, it throws all logic out of the window.'

'I fully understand,' he said calmly with a soothing smile.

They went into the office. Another woman, cut from the same cloth as the administrator, was sitting behind a desk. The moment she set eyes on a man in police uniform, she visibly relaxed. Salvation was here. She proffered a nervous smile, which Jake reciprocated.

'Is the head teacher around?'

'Yes,' Susan said. 'Julie, could you call for Alan?'

The woman sitting at the desk nodded and picked up the phone.

'Can I get you a coffee or anything?' Susan asked Jake.

'No. I'm fine. Thank you.'

'I'm guessing you've been busy today,' she said, a nervous edge to her voice.

'You could say that.' He smiled and exaggerated rolling his eyes. He looked around the room while the other woman was on the phone. 'Someone's birthday?' he asked, noticing the cards on the bookcase.

'It was Julie's yesterday. The big six-oh,' she whispered.

'Alan's on his way through,' Julie said, replacing the phone.

Jake unbuttoned the top button of his police uniform jacket, reached inside and wrapped his right hand firmly around the handgrip of the Glock 17, fitted with a silencer, that he'd concealed. He pulled it out and didn't give the two women a chance to react. He placed the gun to the temple of the secretary standing beside him. He squeezed the trigger. The back of her head exploded, and she dropped to the floor. Julie, mouth agape, took the second bullet to the centre of her forehead. She fell backwards in her chair, blood and brain matter hitting the wall behind her.

The rush of adrenaline was immense. He looked down at the dead women. He'd killed two people in less than ten seconds. It was exactly how he'd imagined it. Everything seemed to fade away. The mental agony and anguish he'd been in for so long disappeared. His mind was empty, devoid of everything. He was focused on one task, and he was going to succeed brilliantly.

He heard footsteps behind him. He turned and saw the tall, stick-thin figure of the head teacher, Alan Fitzgerald, enter the room. With his large ears and bulbous nose, he looked like the BFG in a cheap suit. His smile froze as he took in the blood spatter on the walls. He looked down at his feet at the dead eyes of his secretary staring back at him. He didn't have time to react before he felt the gun press against his temple.

'Please, don't shoot,' he spat nervously. 'I have a wife and two—' Jake pulled the trigger. The head teacher dropped to the floor like a stone.

Jake replaced the gun in his inside pocket and headed for the main entrance to the school. He picked up his bag from around the corner and went back inside, closing the doors behind him. From the bag, he pulled out a change of shoes, something more comfortable for his rampage, and removed his police uniform jacket.

Among the arsenal of weapons, Jake pulled out a heavy steel chain. He wrapped it around the handles of the doors and secured it with a padlock. He didn't want anyone getting away. He'd done a recce of the school several times over the last few months and knew where all the entrances and exits and fire doors were on the ground floor. He'd chain those as he went about his task.

Back in the front office, he emptied the bag of its weapons. He reloaded the Glock and placed it in his inside pocket. He had two Heckler & Koch rifles. He put the straps over each shoulder and checked the setting was to fire multiple bullets with each squeeze of the trigger. He double-checked he had plenty of ammunition in his bag, which he put on his shoulders.

At the bottom of the large rucksack, he carefully pulled out a small pressure cooker.

'Right, Jake, old boy,' he said to himself. 'This is it. Let's roll.'

Chapter Forty-Five

Rory and Scott had driven back to HQ in record time, breaking every driving rule in the book. A few traffic cameras had flashed at them on the way, but Rory didn't give them a second thought. He wanted to get to Jake Harrison before he caused more death, destruction and mayhem. He wanted to get his hands on him and make him pay for what he'd done to Natasha.

Scott had wanted to ask him to slow down, but every time he looked across at his colleague, he saw the dark look of determination on his face, a thick vein throbbing in his neck. It was best to leave him alone rather than poke the bear unnecessarily.

Once in the HMET suite, Scott plugged his iPhone into his laptop, downloaded the photos he'd taken and put them up on the projector screen DI Brady had pulled down.

Christian, Sian, Finn and Aaron all stood back and looked with wide-eyed horror as Scott scrolled through the pictures showing press clippings of the Dunblane massacre, the

Columbine shooting, the Oklahoma City bombing and the Aurora cinema shooting.

'What does this all mean?' Sian asked as she bit at her fingernails.

'He's obsessed,' Aaron said.

'But something like what he's done today takes planning; it takes organisation. Surely one man can't do all this on his own? How did his parents not know with all this plastered on the walls?' Sian asked.

'We need to move fast on this,' Christian said. 'Sian, bring Ronald and Janet in here. They need to see these photos.'

'Are you sure about that?'

'Yes. Anything they can tell us about him could be vital. He needs finding, and quickly, especially if he's capable of building a bomb.'

'The two lads who did the Columbine shooting had a copy of *The Anarchist Cookbook* in their possession,' Scott said as he scrolled through his laptop. 'So did James Holmes, who shot all those people watching *The Dark Knight Rises* in Colorado.'

'I don't even want to touch that book,' Finn said, looking at it with disdain. 'Who thought it would be a good idea to publish it, for crying out loud?'

'And look at these notes,' Rory said as he began laying them out like he was dealing a deck of cards.

Make sure you've got your insurance policy lined up. Hopefully you won't need it.

Mum and Dad will turn their back on you soon. Dad can take early retirement next year. They'll move and they won't take you with them.

Sorry to hear about the test results. You may as well go out with a bang, Jake. Life is shit. Fuck them all.

You've got a whole day to do this. Take it steady, don't rush. That's when you'll make mistakes.

'What does it mean by "test results"?' Sian asked.

'We found this letter inside a book,' Scott handed it to Sian. 'He's been diagnosed with myelodysplastic syndrome. I googled it in the car on the way back. It's a rare form of blood cancer. According to the letter, it was detected too late and there's not much the doctors can do for him. They give him six months, tops.'

'Sian, did you call Wakefield Prison?' Christian asked.

She didn't hear him as she was engrossed in the letter. He called her name again, louder. 'Sorry. Yes, I did. The governor has removed Steve from his cell, and they're going to keep him isolated until we can get to question him. Apparently, he's a model prisoner. There were a few incidents when he was first put away, but he's settled down and he follows rules and procedures.'

'He could still know about what's happening today. What about visitors and letters?'

'He has a couple of visitors but none of them regular.'

'His brother?'

'No.'

'No?' Christian asked, surprised.

'When he first arrived, Jake visited him once a fortnight as regular as clockwork. After about six months he just stopped coming.'

'Any reason why?'

'Not that he's aware of.'

'Did his parents ever visit?'

'No.'

'We need to find out who his other visitors are.'

'He's going to send me through all the information he's got. I know these notes suggest Steve put Jake up to it, but how did he get them to him if he hasn't visited him?'

'Maybe he has,' Aaron said, looking up from flicking through *The Anarchist Cookbook*. 'Email, letters, via a third party, text from a contraband phone. There are ways and means if you're determined enough.'

Christian thought for a moment and nodded. 'Sian, get back on to the governor. I want Steve Harrison brought here now.'

———————————

The double doors to the HMET suite opened and a fragile-looking Ronald and Janet Crowther were shown in by PC Nowak. Christian headed towards them taking large strides. He didn't want them seeing the boards until they'd been briefed.

'Mr and Mrs Crowther, I'm very sorry to ask you to do this, but as I'm sure you can appreciate, we're against the clock, here.' Their eyes darted around the room, trying to take everything in. 'We believe your nephew Jake killed his parents this morning. We believe he then came here and opened fire on people at this station. Following this attack, he went to the Sheffield Parkway and shot at people in their cars from a bridge. He's killed more than twenty-five people and we need to find him.'

Janet was crying. Her husband had his arm firmly wrapped around her shoulder.

'I don't… What are you saying?' Malcolm asked.

'He wouldn't,' Janet mumbled. 'Viv and Malcolm were helping him.'

'I'd like you to take a look at what we found in his bedroom.'

Christian stepped back and beckoned them towards the boards. Tentatively, they followed his lead. Their blank expressions didn't change as they looked at the photos of press cuttings and articles printed from the internet.

'These are news stories of gun crimes and terrorist attacks from around the world. The Santa Fe shooting in 2018, in which ten people died,' he said, pointing to one. 'The Virginia Tech shooting from 2007, in which thirty-two people were killed. The Sandy Hook shooting in 2012, where twenty-seven people died. I'm sure you remember all of these appearing in the news. Do you have any idea why your nephew would have stories like this pinned to his bedroom wall?'

Janet's face screwed up, and she almost collapsed as she wailed and bellowed. Ronald caught her and sat her down on a chair Finn had approached with.

'Are you sure this is from his room? Vivian and Malcolm never mentioned any of this,' Ronald said.

'Perhaps they didn't know,' Sian hazarded a guess.

Janet sniffled and wiped her nose on a tissue she'd produced from up the sleeve of her sweater. 'Vivian mentioned a few weeks ago how Jake wouldn't let her into his room. She was very house-proud, always liked things neat and tidy, but Jake said he'd clean his room himself. She said she could smell sweat and wanted to air the room, change the sheets, that kind of thing, but Jake wouldn't let her. She said…' Her voice tailed off as more tears came. 'She said she was frightened of him.'

'He tried to take his own life just after Christmas,' Ronald said. He crouched next to his wife and gave her a clean tissue from his pocket. 'I think Vivian blamed herself.'

'She did,' Janet agreed. 'She loved both of her children. When Steve did what he did, she said she had no alternative but to disown him. I don't know if that was the right thing or not. When Jake split up from his wife, she had him move in. She wanted to keep an eye on him, make sure he didn't go down the same road as Steve.'

'Why did Jake's marriage end?' Sian asked.

'Vivian went to see Ruth many times,' Janet said. She'd taken a plastic cup of water offered from Finn, had a few sips and was composing herself. 'Ruth said that after Steve went to prison, Jake changed. He became more volatile, quick-tempered, distant. She'd tried to support him, but he shut her out. She couldn't live with him anymore, so she told him to leave.'

'Do you know where Ruth lives?'

'Yes. She sold the house they shared, and she's in a flat in… Where is it, Ronald? It's not Sharrow, is it?'

'Nether Edge,' he corrected her.

'That's it, Nether Edge. Vivian asked her several times to take Jake back, give him a second chance, but Ruth said it was over. There was no going back.'

'Can you think of anybody Jake might know where he could get his hands on the kind of weapons he's used today?' Christian asked. He asked Scott to put up images of the Heckler & Koch and Glock on the projector screen.

'Oh my God!' Janet said, clutching the crucifix around her neck as she saw the guns. 'Is that what he's used?'

'I'm afraid so.'

'Is that what he used to kill Vivian and…' Her words were lost to more tears.

'This isn't easy, I know,' Sian said, kneeling down to Janet and placing a hand over hers. 'Nobody wants to acknowledge the fact that a family member could do something like this, but after what's happened to Jake over the past couple of years, we don't know his state of mind. He's obviously mentally ill, and we need to understand what's going through his mind at the moment. To do that, we need to know who's helped him. Where could he have got these guns from?'

'I don't know,' Janet answered quickly.

'This is not real, is it?' Ronald asked, his face fixed on the screen. 'Look, we're a normal, ordinary family. Malcolm was a lecturer in engineering. I work in a bank. Janet works for a solicitor. We don't have any connection to guns and violence, or anything like this. This is a whole other world.'

'Mr and Mrs Crowther, do you know anywhere Jake might be hiding out?' Christian asked. It was obvious by his tone he was running out of patience.

'No,' Ronald said. 'In the last few months, he'd more or less isolated himself. He rarely left the house.'

'Are there any friends you can think of we could contact?'

'I don't think he had many. He was always a bit of a loner, even as a child.'

Christian and Sian exchanged glances.

'I'd like you to look at these notes,' Christian said, handing a few of the small pieces of paper to Ronald and Janet. 'Do you recognise the handwriting?'

Ronald took what was offered and read them. Janet just looked and shook her head.

'I don't. I'm sorry,' Ronald handed them back.

Christian let out a loud sigh, clearly frustrated. 'Did Vivian say anything to you about Jake being ill?'

'Ill?' Janet asked. 'As in mental?'

'No. Physically. We've found a letter among his things telling him he has terminal cancer.'

Sian handed Janet the letter. She took it and read it carefully.

'Vivian would have told us,' Ronald spoke up. 'She and Janet were very close. They told each other everything.'

'Ok, you've been very helpful, thank you,' Christian said, though the words belied how he felt. 'Does his wife Ruth work? She may know more about the kind of places he could be hiding.'

Janet looked up from the letter. 'Yes. She's a teacher at Stannington Secondary School,' she said. 'Lovely woman. Jake was a fool for letting her go.'

The room fell silent, and all eyes turned to the photos taken of Jake's bedroom. He was obsessed with school shootings. He'd read about them online, bought books about them, collected information on the types of guns used and made notes in *The Anarchist Cookbook*. Had today been leading up to a Columbine-style shooting in Sheffield?

Chapter Forty-Six

The twinkle was back in Steve Harrison's eyes as he was led from his cell to the governor's office. He'd asked the prison officers what was wrong, but they wouldn't tell him. He'd practised how he'd react to the news of his parents' murder and he could easily produce tears if need be.

Less than half an hour before his cell door had opened, Steve had disassembled the contraband mobile phone. He'd flushed the small battery down the toilet, swallowed the SIM and hidden the empty shell of the phone under the mattress of the elderly bloke in a cell two doors down. There was no way the communications between him and his brother could be discovered.

He walked down the corridor with his hands cuffed in front of him, a prison officer flanking him on either side, with his head high, a bounce in his step and those sparkling eyes smiling. This was the day he had been waiting for. He'd playacted before. He'd inveigled himself into Faith Easter's life, making her believe he was in love with her so she could feed him information on the investigation of the Hangman case, and she'd fallen for it. Everyone at South Yorkshire Police believed him to be a hardworking copper, eager to climb the ladder and protect the public. Bollocks to that. As soon as he realised how good he was at killing, and able to get away with it, it was difficult to stop. He'd murdered people right under DCI Matilda Darke's nose and she hadn't seen it. Well, she was dead now. He'd finally hit the jackpot.

Doors were unlocked. He passed through and was told to wait until they were locked again, before moving on down the corridor to another set of locked doors. The journey was incredibly tedious. Eventually, they arrived at the governor's door.

Steve had only met the governor a couple of times, and those interactions had all been back when he first arrived, and after he'd been beaten and bullied. While putting his plan with Jake into action, he'd performed the role of the model prisoner, which had earned him rewards and a place in the governor's good books.

Craig Lombardi stood as Steve was shown in and gave him a friendly smile. At six foot five, the governor of Wakefield Prison stood head and shoulders above most of the prisoners. His smooth bald head shone under the lights, his dark blue eyes were piercing, and his strong jaw line and broken nose were evidence this was a man not afraid to get stuck in when the occasion required.

'Steve, have a seat,' he said in his deep, gravelly voice.

The office was opulent and had the smell of furniture polish, stale coffee and desperation from whoever had been in here before him. The seat Steve sat in was warm; someone had been given a long talking to.

He looked at the officers still standing either side of him and feigned wonder at what was happening.

'I'm afraid I've received some bad news regarding your brother,' Craig said, sitting down behind his desk and interlocking his thick sausage fingers.

'Jake?'

'Yes. I don't know if you've caught any news on television or the radio today, but there have been a number of shootings in Sheffield. In their investigations, South Yorkshire Police believe your brother is responsible.'

Steve gave out a hollow laugh. 'Jakes's shot someone? That's ridiculous. He wouldn't know how.'

'I'm afraid the evidence suggests otherwise. They also believe your brother shot and killed your parents in the early hours of this morning.'

Steve's mouth dropped open. 'Mum and Dad? Jake's killed them?' he asked with a frown. His bottom lip began to wobble, and tears pricked his eyes.

'I really am terribly sorry, Steve.'

'I can't … I just can't believe it,' he said, his eyes darting from left to right. *And the Academy Award for Best Actor goes to…*

'South Yorkshire Police have put in a request to interview you. Jake is missing and they require as much help as possible in locating him before he strikes again.'

'But I haven't spoken to Jake for … I can't remember how long. It's a good few years. How would I know where he's hiding?'

'They believe you might be able to help. I know you have a history with South Yorkshire Police, but I've granted them permission. A vehicle will take you there now.'

'You want me to leave the prison and actually go to the station?'

'Yes.'

'Well, of course, I'll do anything I can to help, but I doubt there'll be anything I can do,' he said with mock protest.

'You know your brother better than anyone, Steve,' Craig said. 'And any help you can provide will be recognised here. There could be more privileges for you.'

Steve paused for effect, as if he was trying to take in this unbelievable account. 'When do I leave?' The famous smile was back.

Chapter Forty-Seven

'So, how does the change in the way Pip sees Joe Gargery affect the reader?' Chris Kean asked the class of thirty year-ten pupils. He looked out at the sea of blank faces as they all tried to avoid eye contact with him.

'Lisa?' He smiled at one girl at the back of the room. 'As you haven't even opened your copy of *Great Expectations* this lesson, I assume that means you've already read it in your own time and know where the story goes. So, enlighten us about Pip's relationship with Joe Gargery.'

There was a murmur of laugher from around the room.

Lisa adjusted her position on the seat. She looked uncomfortable. 'Well, at the beginning he, like, looked up to him, didn't he? He was like a father figure to him. Then, when Pip goes off to London and he's got some money and new mates and everything, he's embarrassed by him.'

'Ok, you've given us the plot, now tell us how we should feel about that.'

There was a loud bang from somewhere outside the

classroom door, followed by several others. All eyes turned to the door.

Chris recognised the noise straight away. They were gunshots. He stopped breathing momentarily, as he tried to remember his training. He'd been on several courses in first aid and what to do in the event of a terrorist attack or a gun attack, but his mind suddenly blanked on him.

'Sir?' someone called out to him.

A few more shots were heard.

'What is that?' someone asked.

'It sounds like shooting.'

'Don't be thick, Kevin.'

'Everyone, keep quiet,' Chris said. 'Stay where you are. I'll go and see.' He didn't turn to look at the students. He didn't want them to see the fear in his eyes.

He pulled open the door just wide enough to squeeze through and closed it behind him. The corridor was empty. He looked in the room opposite. Ruth was standing by the door, looking out. Her face was pale. She obviously recognised the noise coming from downstairs too. She came out into the corridor.

'Chris, what was that?' she asked in a whisper. 'It sounded like shooting.'

'I know.'

'It wasn't though, was it?'

'I don't know.'

'What's going on?'

They both turned to see Pauline Butters standing in the doorway, her class of students behind her, straining to see what was happening.

'I don't know,' Chris said. 'I'll go and have a look.'

Tentatively, Chris made his way along the corridor to the

stairs. The school was unnaturally quiet. It was growing dark outside and the brilliant white lights on the wall lit up the corridor like an alien invasion.

At the top of the stairs, Chris gripped the railing and slowly leaned over. He couldn't see anything.

Chris swallowed hard. He took a deep breath and carefully edged his way down the stairs so he could get a better look at what was happening on the ground floor of the school. With his back firmly against the wall, he took each step slowly. He could feel the sweat trickling down the back of his shirt. He was shaking, yet he wasn't scared. It was the unknown that bothered him. If he knew what was going on, he'd be able to come up with a plan of action.

As he reached the bottom of the stairs, he angled himself so he could see around the corner without revealing his position. He saw a leg. Someone was on the floor and not moving. A black shoe and black trousers, obviously belonging to a student, as that was the uniform. Chris's breath was shaking. His hands were cold as he firmly gripped the bannister to lean further into the corridor. He saw blood and immediately jumped back.

He clamped a hand over his mouth. There was a pupil on the floor in a pool of blood. What the hell had happened?

He took out his mobile phone from the back pocket of his trousers, turned on the camera and switched it to selfie mode. With a shaking hand, he held it up and out into the corridor before taking a photo. He pulled his hand back and looked at the picture. The image was blurred as he hadn't been able to hold his hand still, but he could easily make out six or seven bodies on the floor of the corridor.

'Oh, Jesus Christ!' he uttered.

Another shot rang out and Chris ran back up the stairs,

three at a time. Ruth and Pauline were waiting for him in the middle of the corridor.

'What did you see?' Ruth asked.

He held up his phone and showed them both the photo.

'Oh my God!' Ruth put a hand to her mouth.

Pauline turned away from the horror.

'Did you see anyone?' Pauline asked.

'No.'

'Do you know how many gunmen there are?'

'No.'

'Shit!'

It was the first time either of them had heard Pauline swear.

'What do we do?' she asked.

It took a few long moments for Chris to arrange his thoughts.

'Ok. Ok, here's what we'll do. Go back into your classrooms, close the doors, turn off the lights and hide in the corner of the room away from the door. Barricade them if you can. Get your students to text, tweet, whatever. We need to let everyone know something is happening. All phones should be put on silent. All we can do is wait.'

Ruth nodded. 'We all have each other's mobiles, don't we? That's how we'll keep in contact with each other. We'll text.' Her voice was shaking with nerves.

'We need to protect the kids,' Pauline said. She turned to head back to her classroom. She stopped at the door and looked back to Chris and Ruth. 'I know we're a generation apart, but I don't want either of you two doing anything stupid and getting yourselves hurt.' She didn't wait for them to say anything in return. She went into her classroom and closed the door firmly behind her.

There was another single shot.

Chris grabbed Ruth by the shoulders. 'Go back in there, keep them all safe. Do as I said. I'll contact Scott and tell him what's happening.'

He waited until Ruth was back in her room before returning to his own.

'Sir, what's going on?'

He turned off the lights and asked a couple of the boys to help him drag a heavy bookcase in front of the door.

'Everyone, I need you to remain calm. It appears that there is a man in the school with a gun.'

The students reacted in disbelief. Some cried, some gasped, some called out.

Chris held up his hands. 'Like I said, you need to stay calm. Now, I know it's scary and you're bound to be frightened – I'm frightened, too – but we can get through this if we try to remain as calm and as sensible as possible.'

'What are we going to do?' someone asked.

'We're going to remain in this room, hide and wait for the police to arrive. I'm going to call my friend Scott who works in the police…'

'Your boyfriend?' someone chimed up.

Chris turned to face them. A few were smiling at him, others looked petrified. This was hardly the right time to come out to his pupils, but if it distracted them, then what the hell.

'Yes, my boyfriend. He's a detective with South Yorkshire Police and he'll know exactly what to do.'

'Sir, some of the others have been posting on Twitter,' one of the students said as he held up his phone. 'Stannington is trending.'

'Shit. Uh, sorry,' he apologised for swearing in front of them. 'Ok, that's another way we can get help. Everyone, turn your phones to silent, but get on Twitter, Facebook, whatever, and tell everyone what's happening.'

'Should we text our parents?' a student named Beth asked.

Chris thought for a moment. 'That's probably a very good idea, Beth. Yes, I think you should all text your parents.'

Chapter Forty-Eight

'This isn't real,' Janet Crowther said, handing back the letter to Sian.

'I know it seems like a nightmare right now—'

'No,' she interrupted. 'This letter. It isn't real. A GP surgery doesn't write to you to tell you you've got terminal cancer. I had breast cancer a few years ago, and they had me go into the surgery. They told me face to face. Also, I'm with the same practice and this isn't their letterhead. The logo is wrong.'

'What?' Sian looked at the letter. 'Are you sure?'

'I'm positive. Ronald had a letter only last week about his diabetes check-up. It's all wrong.'

'Why would someone write a letter like that to tell Jake he had cancer if he didn't?' Sian asked.

Christian grabbed Sian by the elbow and pulled her to one side, out of earshot of Janet and Ronald.

'Jake tried to hang himself just after Christmas. Maybe he was having second thoughts about going on a shooting spree. This letter could have been written to get Jake back on side. By telling him he only had a few months to live, it's like saying you may as well go out in style rather than fade away in agony.'

'You think someone manipulated him by saying he was terminally ill? That's sick,' Sian said.

'And who do we know who is such a sick manipulator?'

'Steve Harrison.' Sian nodded. 'But surely he wouldn't tell his own brother he had cancer if he hadn't. That's a whole different level of sick.'

'I don't think Steve gives a toss about family anymore. It's all about him. He wants to cause death and destruction, and he'll go to any lengths to do it.'

―――――――

DC Scott Andrews watched as Janet and Ronald Crowther shed tears over the callous murder of Malcolm and Vivian Harrison. He couldn't help but feel moved as they tried to make sense of the horrific information they were being given that a member of their own family was on the loose in Sheffield, had conducted two shooting sprees, and could possibly be planning an even bigger atrocity.

His phone started vibrating in his pocket. He pulled it out and saw it was Chris calling. The picture of his boyfriend sticking his tongue out to the camera came up on the screen. It made Scott smile. He'd give anything to be with him right now, curled up in bed together, arms safely wrapped around each other, away from the nightmares and the chaos. He wondered what time he'd be able to get away from here tonight.

Scott turned away from his colleagues and swiped to answer.

'Hello, gorgeous,' he whispered.

'Scott, there's a gunman in the school,' Chris said quietly. His voice was shaking. He sounded petrified.

'What?'

'I can't talk loudly. There's a gunman in the school – I've heard shots. Lots of them.'

'Fuck!' Scott cried out. Everyone turned to look at him.

'What's going on?' Rory asked.

Scott took a deep, shaking breath. 'Shit. Chris, I'm going to put you on speakerphone. I need you to repeat what you just said.'

Scott placed his phone carefully on his desk and stepped back from it. 'Ok, Chris. Go ahead.'

'There's a gunman in the school.'

'Oh my God!' Sian said, slapping a hand to her mouth.

Scott started crying. Rory went over to him and placed a comforting arm around his shoulders.

'Chris, this is DI Christian Brady. Is this Stannington Secondary School you're talking about?'

'Yes, it is.'

'Where are you now?'

'I'm on the first floor. I've told all the other teachers here to barricade themselves in the classrooms, to keep out of view of the door, and to try to remain calm.'

'You did the right thing. Well done, Chris. I'm going to get a team of armed police out to you. Are there any casualties?'

'I think so. I took a photo. I'll send it to Scott.'

Scott closed his eyes tightly shut. He prayed to every single god he could think of that he'd see the man he loved again.

'Ok, Chris, keep your phone handy and stay safe.'

Scott picked up the phone, turned the speakerphone off and went to the other side of the room, away from his colleagues.

'Chris, listen to me,' Scott said, a warning tone in his voice. 'I don't want you to do anything stupid, ok? Don't be brave. Just stay exactly where you are, and we'll come to get you. We've got trained officers who know exactly what they're doing.'

'Ok.'

'We'll be with you as soon as we can, understand?'

'Yes. I understand.'

'Good. I love you so much, Chris,' he said.

There was a pause before Chris replied. 'I've just come out to my English class.' He chuckled.

'You always have to turn these things around to you, don't you?' He gave a nervous laugh. 'How did they react?'

'I don't think they cared.'

'They won't. I'm going to get off the phone now. I'll be coming out to the school with the team. Now, listen to me, Chris, don't do anything foolish and get yourself hurt. I mean it. I need you at home tonight.'

'I'll be there.'

'Good. I love you.'

'I love you too.' Scott's hands were shaking as he ended the call.

'Are you all right?'

Scott jumped as he ended the call. He turned around and saw Rory behind him.

'He's going to do something stupid. I know he is.'

'He won't put himself in harm's way,' Rory said, placing a firm hand on Scott's shoulder.

'He's in a classroom full of fourteen-year-olds. If someone comes in with a gun, he'll jump in front to protect them. I know he will. We need to get into that school, Rory. We need to get in and we need to stop that fucker.'

DI Christian Brady was out of his depth. He knew it. This was an operation nobody of his rank should ever oversee. Thankfully, he wasn't the decision-maker. He'd called Inspector Gavin Porter and told him to send an armed team to Stannington Secondary School. He told Sian, Aaron and the three DCs to wear protective gear and go with them to help with any pupils or teachers who might have been able to escape. Janet and Ronald Crowther were sent to a relatives' room, and Christian headed for ACC Valerie Masterson's old office, which the Chief Constable was using. Meanwhile he texted his wife to fill her in on what was going on.

He knocked on the door and opened it without being instructed. Chief Constable Martin Featherstone was sitting in Valerie's seat, a coffee from her precious machine on the desk in front of him. It seemed strange not seeing the diminutive officer in the oversized chair.

Featherstone wasn't doing anything. He wasn't reading through reports or liaising with armed officers, he was sat in the high-backed chair with a blank expression on his face, staring into infinity. When Christian spoke, he visibly jumped in his seat.

'The gunman's at Stannington Secondary School. Shots have been fired,' he announced with a shaking voice.

'Fuck! Casualties?'

'We don't know yet. Armed Response are on their way.'

'Right.' Featherstone looked calm, but his darting eyes, the drumming of his fingers contradicted his words.

'What do you want me to do?' Christian asked.

'Get ambulance and fire crews on standby. We'll need an incident room close to the site and call a hostage negotiator and criminal psychologist in case we're able to talk to him. Erm, what else?' he asked himself. 'We need a place for parents to go to wait for their kids and so we can give them information. I want all roads surrounding the school closed and a helicopter overhead. As Gold Commander, I need to remain here,' he said, looking at his blank mobile. 'I need you and a team at the school to report directly to me.'

'Yes, sir,' Christian said. He turned to leave the room but was called back.

'Good luck, DI Brady.'

'Thank you, sir.'

Brady left the room, closing the door behind him. Luck? He hoped the solution to this wouldn't involve luck. Police officers in America had procedures for dealing with situations like this. The last shooting at a school in the UK was Dunblane in Scotland in 1996. A response to an attack like this wasn't something British police rehearsed very often. Actions needed to be swift, but they needed to be correct and accurate. One false move could result in the deaths of hundreds of children. With that on his conscience, Christian had no idea how he'd live with himself afterwards. He thought about his own daughters and was glad they were still too young to be attending Stannington Secondary School.

'Stuart, it's me,' Sian said as she ran into the women's changing rooms for her protective equipment.

'Hello, sweetheart, is everything—'

'Listen,' she interrupted him as she tried to put a flak jacket on with one hand. 'There's a shooting at Stannington Secondary School, and I'm being sent out there.'

'Oh my God.'

'Stuart, get the kids out of school. I don't care what their teachers say, I want you to go in, grab them, and take them home.'

'You think there's going to be another attack?'

'I don't know,' she said, wiping tears from her eyes. 'Just get the kids home.'

'What about you?'

'I have to do my job,' she said, her voice shaking.

'Don't do anything stupid, Sian. You're not Armed Response. This isn't your fight. Make sure you stay well back from the action.' Stuart sounded stern, but it was obvious he was scared for his wife.

'I won't. Stuart' – she took a deep breath – 'I love you.'

'Don't say that. Don't say your goodbyes.'

'I'm not.' She pulled the phone away from her ear for a moment as she choked on her emotion. 'It's just … we've lost so many today. This isn't going to end well, I know it, and I need you to know how much I love you. I've always loved you.'

'Sian,' he said softly.

'Tell the kids … tell them how much they mean to me. How I'm incredibly proud of them, and how I love them all so much, even when they're getting on my tits,' she said.

'You'll be able to tell them yourself when you get home tonight.'

'I know. And I intend to. But I need you to tell them in case I don't come home.'

'You *will* be coming home,' he said with determination.

'I love you.'

'I love you, too.'

She ended the call and put the phone in her pocket. She

looked at her reflection in the mirror. Tears were streaming down her face. Her eyes were wide. She looked petrified. She *was* petrified.

There was a loud knock on the door that made Sian jump. 'DS Mills, are you in there?'

'Yes,' she said, wiping her eyes.

'It's PC Rix. DC Fleming asked me to fetch you. He said the car's ready.'

'I'm coming.'

Sian tried to put on a brave face, but she was fooling no one, not even herself. She was terrified of what she was about to walk into.

Chapter Forty-Nine

@jobeone125 Gunman shooting in Stannington School. Trapped inside. Call police.

@RACHELb75 Shooting @StanningtonSecondary school. People trapped. Send help. **#SouthYorkshirePolice**

@ClareJanetMason Shooting @StanningtonSecondary school. Many dead and injured. People trapped. **#Help**

@Choconwaffles Head teacher @StanningtonSecondary has been killed. Others shot. We r all trapped inside. **#SendHelp**

@maxredhall Teachers and students shot dead in corridors of @StanningtonSecondary school. Gunman still shooting. People trapped.

@Ros_Buckley Shooting @StanningtonSecondary school. Miss Henning shot. People dead in the main corridor. Gunman still shooting. **#SOS**

@StanningtonSecondary Gunman in school. Doors chained shut.
Many dead and injured. Please send help. Gunman still active. LD.

'Miss Henning's been shot,' one of the pupils in Chris's class said, looking up from his phone with wide-eyed horror.

'Sunita texted me. She said she saw her get shot in the head. She just dropped down dead,' another said, voice quivering.

'Oh my God!'

Chris, standing by the door, turned to the frightened faces staring at him, looking for help, guidance. Josie Henning was an English teacher, like Chris. She was thirty-six years old, was engaged to Tom, a PE teacher from another school, and spent most of her free periods looking at honeymoon destinations. She was always smiling, even when the kids got on her nerves and couldn't find the same level of excitement she usually found in Shakespeare and Chaucer. Chris liked her. Her energy was infectious. He had seen her less than an hour ago in the staffroom. She was googling how many calories were in a fig biscuit and wondering whether her wedding dress would need to be let out if she didn't cut back on sugar. Now she was dead. How was that possible?

Chris's mouth was dry. He swallowed hard and it hurt. 'Just post your messages and come off Twitter. It's probably best not to read what others are putting,' he said with fear in his voice.

'Oh my God, Mr Fitzgerald's been killed as well,' another pupil shouted.

Chris quietened them down with a hand signal. 'We need to keep as silent as possible. We can't draw attention to ourselves, in case the ki— gunman hears.'

'Sir, people are saying the doors have been chained shut.

We're not going to get out of here, are we?' one girl asked, tears streaming down her face.

Chris looked at her. He looked at all of them. He had no idea what to say. They looked to him to have all the answers, but he didn't. He had too many questions of his own. This was a real nightmare scenario, and he didn't have a clue what was going to happen within the next minute, let alone how he was expected to lead them all to safety.

He stepped away from the door. 'Look,' he began, trying to sound brave and confident. 'I will do everything I can to protect you all. The police are on their way, and as long as we stay in this room and stay quiet, we have a chance of surviving.'

The expression on their faces told Chris they didn't quite believe him. To be honest, he didn't believe himself, either.

Another gunshot from somewhere in the school rang out. Everyone jumped and the huddle of pupils became tighter.

Chris went back to the door. He looked through the window. In the room opposite, Ruth was staring at him through the glass, tears streaming down her face.

He took a deep breath and let it out slowly. What he was about to do could either be construed as brave or utterly stupid. He strained as he pushed the bookcase out of the way and pulled open the door.

———

Rory was driving at speed through the darkening streets of Sheffield towards Stannington Secondary School. Scott was in the front passenger seat. His face was a map of worry at the thought of his boyfriend risking his own life to save the pupils. He kept glancing at his mobile for any new information, hoping to receive a text from Chris saying he was out of the building and safe. The longer the phone remained blank, the more anxious he became.

In the back, Finn was frantically texting. He'd sent messages to his parents, informing them of what was happening in Sheffield today, while also conducting a text chat with his wife, trying to reassure her he was fine, safe and not in harm's way. If she could see where he was, sitting in the back of a rapid-response car wearing a flak jacket and hurtling towards the scene of a school shooting, she would probably have a thousand fits.

'Nobody gave much thought to the female anatomy when they invented these bulletproof jackets, did they?' Sian said. She was in the back of the car next to Finn and uncomfortably adjusting herself. 'Millions spent on research and development, and you'd have thought one of the tests would have involved a woman sitting down in a police car. And people wonder why there aren't many women in Armed Response. They probably try the uniform on and think, screw that, I'm going back to traffic.' She smiled to herself. She was waffling. It wasn't often she was nervous and scared, but when she was, she talked and talked. As long as she was talking, she wasn't thinking about the situation she was about to enter.

'I bought a strapless dress once when we went on holiday to Corfu. This was years ago. I wouldn't dare have my arms on show now. It doesn't matter what I do, I can't tone them up. I suppose that's down to age and gravity. Anyway, I'm wearing this dress and the only bra I can wear with it is a strapless one. You three blokes won't know, but a strapless bra under a strapless dress, in thirty-degree heat, is not—'

'Sian,' Scott interrupted. 'Do you mind?'

'Sorry. I'm running on, aren't I?'

'It's ok,' Finn said, briefly placing a hand on hers before removing it.

Scott's phone beeped with an incoming text message. He quickly unlocked it and read the text. 'Chris says to read Twitter. The pupils are messaging for help. He said two teachers are dead that he knows of. Can't you drive any faster, Rory?' he shouted.

'Scott, calm down,' Sian said, placing a hand on his shoulder, which he quickly shook off.

'Calm down? Are you serious? There's a man with a gun in a school full of kids and my boyfriend is in there. Do you really expect me to be calm?'

'Yes. I expect you to be calm and professional.'

'Like you were just now? Talking about fucking strapless bras!'

'Scott, that's enough!' Rory snapped. 'We've all lost people today. We can't turn on each other. We need to be there for one another.' He quickly looked over his shoulder and gave a hint of a smile to Sian. 'Personally, if Sian wants to give us a full detailed description of her breasts, I think we should let her.'

Sian reached forward and slapped him playfully on the back of the head.

Rory looked over to Scott and gave him a broad grin. He smiled back.

'I'm sorry, Sian.' He put his hand through the gap in the seats, and Sian grabbed it, holding on tight.

The car fell silent as all four concentrated on the road, and the task, ahead.

Chapter Fifty

Chris darted across the silent corridor and pushed open the door Ruth was behind.

'Are you all right?'

She couldn't speak. She kept her back to her pupils and shook her head.

He placed a hand on her shoulder for comfort and could feel her entire body shaking. 'Ok. Everyone, listen up,' he addressed the frightened-looking students huddled at the back of the room. 'I want you all to run very quietly into my classroom. I think it'll be better if we're all together.' None of them moved. 'Come on, now. We have to be quick.'

He stepped out into the corridor, looked left and right to make sure nobody was there and beckoned them all to follow him.

A group of thirty students couldn't be quiet. Their heavy footfalls resounded off the walls and Chris rushed them into his classroom, pushing some. He grabbed Ruth and pulled her across the corridor.

'I'm so sorry,' she said through her tears.

He closed the door behind him and turned around. Two teachers, one of whom was practically hysterical, and almost sixty students. He would not be able to cope with them all on his own, especially as they all seemed to be looking to him as if he had the solution to getting out of the building.

'We need to barricade this door again,' he said quietly. 'Stephen, Craig, help me with the bookcase. Ruth, you go and sit with the others.'

Chris had chosen two of the largest boys to help him push the tall bookcase, laden with textbooks, back in front of the door. Chris wanted a small gap so he'd be able to look through the window.

He went over to the huddle of students in the far corner.

'Shouldn't we be hearing sirens by now?' someone asked.

'They won't use sirens,' Chris said. 'They won't want to draw the gunman's attention.'

'I've looked online and there's nothing about who he is. Don't terrorists usually say who they are and what they're doing?' someone said.

'He might not be a terrorist,' Chris said. 'There are all kinds of reasons why someone would come into a school with a gun.'

'Like what?'

Chris thought for a moment. 'I don't know,' he lied.

He looked over to Ruth. In the dim light, he could see how frightened she looked. She remained quiet so as not to scare the pupils even more with her shaking voice, but it was obvious to everyone she was petrified.

Chris took out his phone and sent a text to Scott:

I'm in room 14 on the first floor. There's me and Ruth and about 60 kids. We've turned the lights off and barricaded the door. How long until you're here?

A reply pinged back straight away:

We're here. Armed police are assessing the situation. I'll find a way to get you out.

From the outside, the scene at Stannington Secondary School looked like any normal school day. Some of the classrooms were in darkness, while others still had lights on. However, there was no movement from any of the windows.

Rory pulled up in the driveway behind a tactical-support vehicle where armed response officers, wearing full protection uniform, were removing Heckler & Koch rifles from the strongbox in the boot of the car. They already had their Glocks holstered.

'God, I hate guns,' Sian said as she climbed out of the vehicle.

'Inspector Porter. Gavin. Tactical Firearms Controller,' the leader of the armed unit said as he approached her.

'DS Sian Mills, Homicide and Major Enquiry Team,' she said, taking his proffered hand.

'What's happened to DI Brady?'

'He's on his way.'

Another two Armed Response vehicles pulled up. Three officers in each jumped out and headed for the boot to get their rifles.

'Right. We're waiting on a hostage negotiator. We'll coordinate and establish a strategy.'

'Ok. Where are they?'

'Stuck in traffic. We've also phoned for the caretaker.

Hopefully he'll have a floor plan of the school, so we know what we're dealing with—'

'So in the meantime we have to just wait here while a gunman is picking them off one by one?' Scott interrupted.

'Inspector Porter, this is DC Scott Andrews. His partner is a teacher in this school.'

'Have you established contact with her?' Gavin asked.

'Him. Yes, I have. He's in room fourteen with another teacher and sixty pupils. We need to get him out of there now.'

'Son, I understand how you're feeling, and we'll do everything we can to make sure as many people are brought out of there alive as possible. A single loss of life is a failure in my book, and I don't like to lose.'

'Lives have already been lost, for fuck's sake.'

'Scott!' Sian admonished.

'What's going on?'

Everyone turned around to see a woman standing behind them. She was wearing jeans and a thin jumper but no coat despite the cold weather and the fine drizzle.

'My Mark just called me. He said there was a gunman in the school. I thought he was joking but when I saw the police cars… Oh my God, is it true?' She crumbled.

Finn stepped forward. He placed his arm around her shoulder and moved her to one side.

Sian turned away, tears building up in her eyes. 'Shit, we need more help here. Rory, get on to Christian, ask him to send as many officers out as he can. Ask him what he's doing about an incident room and somewhere for all the parents who are going to start turning up here any minute.'

'Will do.'

'Also, ask him if anyone's tried to contact this Ruth. Do we know if she's actually at work today?'

Rory took out his phone and walked away.

'Do we know anything about the gunman?' Gavin asked.

'Yes,' Sian said. She was shivering in the cold despite the extra layer of the flak jacket. 'Jake Harrison. Thirty-four years old. He shot his mother and father dead this morning at their home in Worrall. His brother is Steve Harrison, a former police officer who is in Wakefield Prison for killing six people.'

'I remember Steve. What's this guy's motive then?'

'You tell me. We're wondering if it's related to Steve, but they've had no contact for a couple of years as far as we can tell, so we don't actually know.'

'Do you think Steve might be able to help?'

'He's on his way to the station in an armed car breaking every rule in the Highway Code. Hopefully he can shed some light on this. Also,' Sian said, 'we've found a letter that says Jake has terminal cancer, but we think it's a forgery.'

'Why?'

'God knows. However, Jake is under the illusion he's dying. From his point of view, he's got nothing to lose.'

'Thanks for letting me know.'

Sian watched as he walked away and headed to the members of the Armed Response Unit who were tooling up. She would be lying if she said she wasn't scared. She had no idea how many children were in that school, but they were all young and vulnerable, with their whole lives ahead of them. They shouldn't have to be witness to any of this. It was devastating enough when news of a school shooting in America broke, but for it to happen on your own doorstep evoked a level of fear that was unimaginable before now.

'Chris, it's me,' Scott said quietly into his phone. He'd moved to a quiet part of the car park to risk calling his boyfriend, hoping he'd put his phone on silent. He crouched between a Fiat Punto and a Peugeot.

'Thank God. Where are you?' he asked in a loud whisper.

'We're all outside. Armed officers are here. Listen, do you know where the gunman might be?'

'No. He was on the ground floor when I went to look, but that must have been about twenty minutes ago.'

'Have you heard any other shots?'

'Not for a while.'

'Chris, I probably shouldn't be saying this, but we think the gunman is a man called Jake Harrison. He's the brother of Steve Harrison, remember him? He hanged all those people including DC Faith Easter?' Chris didn't respond. 'Chris, are you there?' Scott panicked.

'Yes, sorry, I was moving to the other side of the classroom. Did you say Jake Harrison?'

'Yes. Do you know him?'

'He's Ruth's ex-husband.'

'We know.' Scott froze. The penny finally dropped. 'Oh my God, I didn't realise. My mind's all over the place. I didn't think of your friend Ruth.'

'Remember me telling you she split with her husband because he went all distant and weird and he frightened her? Well, that's him. She said after what happened with his brother he completely changed.'

'I know. I remember. Fuck. I'm sorry. I didn't put the two together.' He wiped away a tear. 'And she's there with you now?'

'Yes.'

'Shit, Chris, I'll ring you back. I need to tell this to the boss.

Stay where you are. We're coming to get you, I promise. I love you.'

'Love you, too.'

As Scott stood up, his eyes widened at the smiling man standing over him.

'Hello, Scott,' Danny Hanson said.

'Jesus Christ! What are you doing creeping about?'

'My job.' He pulled a small dictating machine out of his shirt breast pocket.

'Did you hear all of that?'

'I certainly did,' he said with a maniacal grin. 'So, the gunman is Steve Harrison's brother.'

'Fuck! Danny, you can't breathe a word of this to anyone. People's lives are at stake.'

'I promise to thank you in my awards speech.' He playfully slapped Scott on the side of the face and walked away.

'Oh, fucking hell,' Scott said to himself.

Chapter Fifty-One

Ruth was too nervous to think about putting the pupils before herself. As they huddled in a corner of the room, below the window and remaining as silent as possible, Ruth joined them rather than acting as a tower of strength to give them hope and optimism.

Chris ended his call and stayed at the far side of the room. He frowned and bit his bottom lip as he thought.

The sound of a single shot being fired made them all jump. It sounded like it came from downstairs.

'Ruth, come here,' he said, beckoning her.

As she approached, he saw in the dim light that tears had formed pathways in her made-up face. She wasn't coping with this situation at all. The students seemed calmer.

'What's going on? Was that Scott? What's happening?'

'Ruth, I've got some bad news,' he said, swallowing hard. The words seemed to be sticking in his throat.

'What is it?' she asked. Her eyes were wide, and transfixed on Chris's face.

'The gunman,' he said, quietly so the students couldn't hear him. He swallowed again. His mouth had dried. 'The gunman is … well, the police have told me that it's Jake.'

'Jake? Who's…' The penny dropped. 'Jake. My Jake?'

Chris nodded.

'No. No. It's not. They're wrong. That's not possible. He wouldn't. I mean, he wouldn't know how to get hold of a gun, let alone shoot one,' she said, her voice rising in panic.

Chris hushed her. 'Ruth, keep your voice down. Scott said they were called out to a house in Worrall earlier. He'd shot and killed both of his parents.'

'What? Viv and Malcolm? Oh my God, no.' She leaned on the windowsill to support herself. 'I liked Viv. She was a good woman. Malcolm was quiet, but he loved his family. When Steve… Do you think this has something to do with Steve?'

'They don't know. Look, Ruth, Jake went to the police station this morning and opened fire. He's killed six police officers, and he shot at people from a bridge over the Sheffield Parkway. He's going on some kind of a spree. Do you know why he might do something like that?' he asked, holding her firmly by the shoulders.

'No. I've tried to have as little contact with him as I can. Every time we spoke, he kept trying to get me to go back to him. It was upsetting. My solicitor said to only communicate through him. That's what we've been doing for the past six months.'

'Has your solicitor said anything about his behaviour? Has he changed in any way?'

'He didn't say. We've just been waiting for him to sign the divorce papers. My solicitor kept prompting him, but that's as far as it went. Chris, are you sure it's Jake?'

'That's what Scott said.'

She looked to the door. She took a deep breath. 'I should go and talk to him.'

'What? No,' Chris said, holding on to her even tighter.

'I might be able to stop him from doing anything stupid.'

'Ruth, he's got a gun. He's got several guns by the sound of it. I think he's way beyond the stage of talking.'

'No. He's kept saying we should talk, to sit down and talk through our issues. That's what he wants.'

'Ruth, he's killed people,' he said in a loud whisper. The pupils could now hear what he was saying. 'There are more than twenty people dead. The time for talking has long passed.'

'So what's the alternative? Do we wait here for the police to storm the building? That's going to result in more deaths and Jake… There are things I need to tell him.'

Ruth seemed more confident. The tears had dried up, and she was no longer shaking. She was full of determination now she knew who the gunman was. Was it less stressful knowing the person with his finger on the trigger? Chris didn't think so.

'Ruth, you can't go out there. What if he kills you?'

'He's not going to kill me. He's come here because he wants to talk. So I'll talk to him.'

'The police would never allow it.'

'The police aren't here,' she said, her voice raised. 'They're outside. They're safe. We're not. We're trapped in here, and if I can help to defuse this situation, then I will.'

Chris looked over Ruth's shoulder at the sixty teenagers crouched beneath the window. They were all watching the exchange with worried, tear-filled eyes, their faces lit up by the blue light from their mobile phone screens.

If only they knew what Jake was doing. Was he trawling the corridors, shooting anyone who moved? Was he hoping to get to Ruth in order to talk to her, or worse, to kill her? Then what? Would he put the gun against his head and pull the trigger or continue to fight to the last bullet? There were several hundred children inside this school. Some had already been shot and killed, others would likely be severely injured. Chris needed to try to save as many as he could.

'I'm going to talk to him,' Ruth said, heading for the door. 'Stephen, help me move this bookcase.'

'Sir?' Stephen asked, looking to Chris for guidance.

Chris took a deep breath. He didn't know what to do for the best.

He watched as Ruth pushed the bookcase away from the door. Stephen jumped up to help her. The sound of the wood scraping along the floor rebounded in the quiet room. Chris wondered if Jake had heard the movement from downstairs. Would he come up? Ruth had suddenly exposed all sixty pupils to the gunman.

'Chris.' Ruth came over to him and took his hand. His were cold and shaking, hers were warm and clammy. 'I know him. He won't shoot me.'

'He killed his parents.'

'But he's come here for a reason. He won't shoot me without telling me why he's doing this.'

'And then he'll shoot you?'

'No. I can act as a decoy. While I'm talking to him, you get the kids down the back staircase and out of the fire doors next to the science labs.'

'I don't like this.' Chris shook his head.

'We have no other choice.'

'We should leave it up to the police. They know what they're doing.'

'No. They'll wait for him to make a move and take a shot at him. I need to talk to him, Chris.'

The silence between them was intense. Chris looked into Ruth's eyes. The fear that was there just a few minutes ago had gone. He knew she'd go out to talk to him, but she was waiting for him to give his blessing, to tell her he was behind her every step of the way. He couldn't do that, but he could fake it. He gave a slight nod of the head.

'Promise me you'll not put yourself in any danger,' he said.

'I promise.'

'Tell him you'll only talk to him if he puts his guns down.'

'I will.'

'And any sign that he's about to reach for them or anything, get out of there as quickly as you can.'

'I will. Just get everyone out of here.'

He pulled her towards him and held her in a tight embrace. 'This is madness,' he whispered quietly into her ear.

'It's the only way to save these kids. You know it,' she whispered.

She pushed herself out of his arms and headed for the door.

Chris couldn't take his eyes from his colleague. He didn't want to watch her walk to her death, but he felt he had to. She didn't look back as she stepped through the door and turned right down the corridor.

Chapter Fifty-Two

Outside, now that darkness had fallen, the temperature was plummeting, but all the members of HMET could do was stand around while the Armed Response teams took control of the situation. Inspector Porter was with the caretaker, going over the floor plans and working out the best route into the building. It seemed futile if they didn't know where Jake was. They'd tried calling the office phone, hoping he'd pick up and speak to someone, but it went unanswered.

A car pulled up and Christian climbed out of the front passenger seat before it stopped moving. He headed for Sian as he zipped up his jacket.

'There's something I need to tell you,' Scott said as he approached Christian and Sian. 'I know Ruth. I didn't think back at the station, my mind was all over the place. I've just got off the phone to Chris and he told me that he and Ruth are together. They're in room fourteen with about sixty kids.'

'I'd better tell Porter,' Christian said. He slapped Scott on the back and headed for the incident van.

Despite this break in the case, Scott's face was still worried.

'What is it?' Sian asked.

'I've fucked up.'

'What are you talking about?'

'When I was talking to Chris on the phone, I didn't realise there was someone earwigging.'

'Who?'

Scott took a deep breath. 'Danny fucking Hanson.'

She stepped forward and put a hand on his arm. 'He was bound to find out somehow. Parasite. We'll worry about that later. Right now, we need to concentrate on getting all those kids out.'

Scott's mobile started to vibrate. He pulled it out of his pocket and showed Sian the screen. Chris was calling him.

'Put it on speaker,' Sian instructed him.

He did so but turned the volume down, just in case there was someone lurking in the shadows of the car park listening in.

'It's me. Ruth's gone out to talk to Jake. She seems to think she can distract him while I get the kids out.'

'What the hell?' Sian exclaimed.

'Who's that?' Chris asked.

'It's Sian, don't worry,' Scott said. 'Has she already left to talk to him?'

'Yes.'

'Why didn't you stop her?' Sian asked.

'I tried. She wouldn't hear it. She said it was the only way to get the kids to safety. The thing is, I think she might be right. While she's talking to him, I can bring them down the back staircase and out through the fire door at the back of the building.'

'I'll need to inform Armed Response,' Sian said.

'There's no time. She's out there now. We're going for it.'

The line went dead.

'Shit!' Scott wiped his eyes, pocketed the phone, and ran towards the school.

'Where the hell do you think you're going?' Sian shouted after him.

'To the fire doors. I can help.'

Chapter Fifty-Three

Ruth had never known the school to be so quiet. The corridor was dark and, try as she might, her shoes clacked on the hard floor, echoing against the walls. She walked slowly past classrooms with their doors closed, looked in through the windows and saw terrified teachers looking at her with wide-eyed horror.

When Chris told her the gunman was Jake Harrison, a calmness seemed to wash over her. No, she couldn't believe he would do something like this, but the more she thought about it, the more she understood.

Following Steve's arrest and imprisonment, Jake had fallen to pieces. They were close as brothers, and Jake looked up to Steve – despite being older – as a confident, determined man. Steve knew what he wanted out of life. He'd always worked towards being a police officer from a young age. His dream was to start at the bottom and work his way through the ranks. He saw himself retiring as Chief Constable after thirty years of service, with a healthy pension and still young enough to do something else with his life.

The day Steve started in the police force, the whole family could not have been prouder, and everyone had gathered to have their photograph taken with the handsome young man in his uniform.

Ruth had often looked at the photo of Jake in tight-fitting jeans and a rugby sweater standing next to his brother in a sharp, crisp police constable's uniform. Both had huge smiles, yet there was something about Jake's eyes that gave the picture a sadness. They looked distant, almost cold. Jake didn't have a plan or a career path. He had never known what he wanted to do with his life and went from temporary job to temporary job, hoping something would pique his interest. It never did. Ruth had asked him once why he didn't join the police force with his brother. Jake had replied, sadly, 'That's Steve's thing, not mine.' She had no idea what that meant and didn't push it further.

To Jake, Steve was doing everything right, and he was a man to be admired, so his exposure as a serial killer, and his resulting fall from grace, hit Jake hard. He was disappointed, inconsolable, and could not understand how a man who had everything would so carelessly throw it all away. Jake visited Steve in prison a couple of times, but he didn't get answers to the questions he asked, and following that final visit, he admitted to Ruth that he didn't know who his brother was anymore.

After that, Jake was a changed man. He distanced himself from Ruth, his parents, his friends. He hardly spoke, he ate little, and he spent his days sleeping and his nights pacing the house. Ruth couldn't survive in such a fragile atmosphere and begged Jake to see someone, talk through his issues and save their ailing marriage.

Before long, Ruth realised the relationship was over. Even if

Jake had said he'd go to see a therapist, she'd have still wanted the marriage to end. She no longer loved him, and there were times she was scared to be alone in the house with him. His silence, his distant looks, the emptiness in his eyes made her feel unsafe in her own home.

She didn't tell him she was leaving. She packed what she needed and left while he was asleep in the spare bedroom. She went to see a solicitor and asked to begin divorce proceedings. The first Jake knew of it was when a letter landed on his doormat.

Had the signs been there? She had no idea. Ruth was a maths teacher, not a psychologist. She didn't think to look for signs that her husband was turning into a murderer. Why would she? But could she have done more to help him? She didn't think so. If he wanted help, he needed to seek it out for himself.

Ruth knew it would all come out in the press as the investigation into Jake's crimes unfolded. The parents and families of the dead would blame her for not reporting her husband to the police. They'd all say she should have known he would do something like this. She'd have to move away, change her name, her whole identity and leave everything behind. That wouldn't necessarily be a bad thing.

Ruth eased herself down the stairs. Her hand gripped the bannister firmly as she descended one step at a time to the ground floor. She listened intently to any sound alerting her to where Jake might be, but she couldn't hear anything. As she reached the bottom, she stopped, frozen in terror, as she saw the dead body of a pupil lying face down in a pool of blood.

The girl had blonde hair pulled back into a tight ponytail, tied with a pink bobble. She'd obviously been shot in the back as she was trying to run to the exit. There was a large hole in the centre of her back. A direct hit. Ruth squinted as she bent down to see the girl's face. She couldn't have been more than thirteen. She looked vaguely familiar and Ruth wondered if she'd taught her at some point. Probably.

Tears pricked her eyes. She looked up. More bodies were strewn about the corridor, mostly pupils but also a few teachers. It was like a battlefield; soldiers shot down, long before their time, and left where they lay. This was a place of learning, and it was a happy and friendly environment. Framed photographs and artwork adorned the walls. A cabinet contained all the trophies the school had won in a plethora of events from sporting achievement to spelling competitions. The only sound usually heard was that of laughter and the raucous chattering of teens with no volume button. All that was ruined. She'd never see anything other than dead bodies when she looked down this corridor again. Blood splatter on the trophy cabinet and photographs was an insult to the institute and the people who had dedicated their lives to teaching the next generation of builders, teachers, doctors and accountants.

Ahead, she saw the double doors leading to safety and freedom. They'd been closed, a thick chain wrapped around the handles and a heavy padlock dangling, securing it in place. Jake had purposely locked the doors before going on his spree. He didn't intend for anyone to be able to escape.

She felt sick. Her husband had done this. She'd slept with a man capable of opening fire on innocent children. What the hell was going through his mind when he pulled that trigger?

'Ruth.'

She froze at the sound of her name being called by a familiar voice. Slowly, she turned and saw Jake up ahead. He was wearing black trousers and a dark body warmer over a white shirt. He had a rifle in one hand and a handgun in the other. He had blood on his clothes and spatter on his face. She didn't recognise this man at all.

She opened her mouth to speak, but the words wouldn't come. There was a huge lump in her throat. Back upstairs in the classroom, there was the slightest hint of hope that the police had been wrong, that Jake wasn't the gunman. Now, with dead bodies at her feet and her husband holding weapons firmly in his bloodied hands, there was no doubt. She was married to a multiple murderer.

'Jake,' she squealed. The word was barely audible. She tried to say more. She wanted to say more, but the words wouldn't come. Her mouth was shaking with emotion.

'It's good to see you,' Jake said. 'You're looking well. You've lost weight. It suits you.'

Ruth squeezed her eyes closed and tears ran down her face. There was blood on the walls, dead bodies between them, and he was talking like they were having a latte in Costa to try to iron out their issues.

'Jake, why are you doing this?' she asked.

'Because it's all gone. Everything's gone.'

'What has?'

'You and me.'

'This isn't about you and me, surely?'

'I love you, Ruth,' he said, a catch in his throat.

Ruth buckled. 'How can you say that? Look at what you've done.'

'It doesn't stop me loving you. I thought we had something special.'

'We did.'

'You said you loved me.'

'I did.'

'But not anymore?'

'You changed.'

'We all change.'

'You scared me.' Tears were pouring down her face.

'How?'

'I didn't know you anymore. You shut me out.'

'You wouldn't have understood.'

'You didn't give me the chance,' Ruth said, gaining in confidence. 'I asked you, time and time again, to talk to me, to open up and you refused. What was I supposed to do?'

'I … I lost everything,' he stuttered.

'You didn't lose me. You pushed me away.'

'I've missed you.' He smiled.

She smiled back. 'I've missed you, too.'

———

Upstairs, Chris had watched from the open doorway as Ruth made her way carefully and slowly down the stairs. He listened intently for her to start talking to her husband. Once the muffled conversation began, he leapt into action.

He ran to the classroom next to his as quietly as he could, looked through the glass and saw Pauline Butters crouched in the corner with the kids. He opened the door and whispered to her.

'Pauline, everyone, come on, come with me.'

'What's happening? Is it all over?' she asked.

'No. It's a long story, but Ruth's distracting the gunman and we're going out the back way.'

'She's doing what? And you let her?' she asked, her face soured.

'Like I said, it's a long story. Come on. We don't have much time.'

He left her to rouse her class, then went to knock on the doors of the other classrooms along the corridor. Some had barricaded the doors while others had simply turned out the lights and hid out of sight of the windows. Soon, the corridor was full of staff and pupils.

'Everyone, I want you to make your way to the back staircase very quietly,' Chris said just loud enough for them all the hear. 'Head for the fire exit next to the science labs. I've told the police this is what we're doing, so hopefully someone will be waiting for us. Now, go.'

He stood back as he watched them scrambling to get to the end of the corridor. He kept turning to the stairs he'd seen Ruth disappear down, wondering what she was saying to Jake, and how long she'd be able to keep him distracted for.

———

'You should have told me how you were feeling,' Ruth said.

'I couldn't. I didn't know myself.'

'Then you should have just said anything. I'd have listened. I'd have stuck by you and tried to understand, but you shut me out, Jake. You shut everyone out.'

'I got a letter. I've got cancer. I can't pronounce it. Apparently, it's a rare kind.'

'I'm so sorry,' she said, as more tears ran down her face.

'It's blood cancer. I'm riddled with it.' He tried to smile, but couldn't. 'Everything has turned against me. Even my own body.'

Ruth didn't know what to say. It was like trying to talk to a complete stranger. She looked down. There was blood all over her shoes. 'Is it true you killed Malcolm and Viv?'

Jake blinked a few times. He nodded.

'Why?' she asked through the tears. 'They were trying to help you. They took you in when you had to move out of the house. They were looking after you.'

'They were in league with them,' he said, bitterness in his voice.

'Who?'

'They kept trying to make me go to the doctor. They kept saying I was depressed and should be on medication.'

'Maybe that's what you need.'

'No!' he shouted loudly, causing Ruth to stagger backwards. 'I don't want to take fucking tablets like I'm some kind of nutter.'

'Ok. Ok. It's ok, I'm sorry. Calm down, Jake,' she said, holding her arms out. 'Are you sleeping?'

'No.'

'Eating?'

'Not much.'

'Maybe it would help to talk to a professional. They'll help you to make sense of what you're feeling and thinking.'

Jake looked up. His eyes were wide. Sweat glistened on his forehead. 'Have they been talking to you?'

'Who?'

'Viv and Malcolm.' He didn't call them *Mum* and *Dad*.

'No. I haven't heard from them for a while.'

'You're lying.'

'I'm not. Jake, why would I lie?'

'You think I'm mad like them, don't you?'

'No. I don't. I think you're still upset about Steve going into prison. Angry, even.'

'Don't bring Steve into this. Steve has been the only person who has helped me see what I have to do.'

'What are you talking about?' She frowned.

Jake slowly began to edge closer to Ruth. 'Steve explained it all to me. There are people out there who try to stifle you, to stop you from achieving great things. That bitch Matilda Darke stopped Steve from being a great detective and so turned him into a great criminal. It was her that made him kill all those people. He asked me to kill her for him.'

'But why your mum and dad?' she asked, tears streaming down her face. 'They were helping you.'

'Steve said anyone who gets in your way has to be dealt with. Anyone who hurts you needs to be made to pay.'

Ruth frowned. 'I didn't think you saw Steve anymore. After he went in prison, you said you were disappointed with him, that you didn't know him anymore.'

'Of course I still know him. He's my brother.' He shrugged.

'Have you been plotting this, all this time?'

'No. I haven't. Steve has, though.'

'But if you haven't been seeing him, how have you been talking to each other?'

'I have my ways,' he said, a hint of a smile appearing on his lips.

A door slammed from upstairs. Ruth gave a nervous smile as Jake stopped in his tracks.

'What was that?'

'What?'

'They're all going, aren't they? You came down here so they could all run out another way. Hats off to you, Ruth. Selfless to the end.'

Jake made his way to the stairs, but Ruth got there before him. She stood in front of them, blocking his way.

'Jake, please, enough lives have been lost. You don't have to do this.'

'I'm on a mission.'

'Your mission is complete. You've killed Matilda Darke. That's what Steve wanted, isn't it?'

'Yes.'

'So why are you carrying on?'

'Because I'm enjoying myself so fucking much.' He grabbed Ruth by the throat and pushed her to the wall. She banged her head. He squeezed her neck hard. She tried to scratch at his fingers to get him to release his grip, but it was useless. He was too strong for her.

She was petrified.

She opened her mouth wide to try and gasp for air. She locked eyes with Jake and saw pure evil, pure hatred in them.

Jake grinned. He pushed the Glock into her mouth, past her teeth and to the back of her throat before squeezing the trigger.

Chapter Fifty-Four

Chris heard the sound of the gunshot and stopped in his tracks. He was at the end of the corridor, pushing the kids through the double doors, urging them silently to get out and run for their lives.

Was that Ruth? Had he killed her? No. She was his wife, surely not.

'Sir?' one of the students said as Chris slowly made his way to the stairs.

He wasn't even halfway along the corridor when he saw someone coming up from the ground floor. As he reached the top of the stairs, Chris saw the gunman, a rifle in one hand, a handgun in the other, bloodstains on his clothes.

'Fuck,' Chris said. He was frozen to the spot.

'Oh my God,' one of the pupils behind him said.

The sound of their voice caused Chris to react. He had to save the students at any cost. He turned.

'Go. Run. Go,' he shouted. Following them.

Jake fired off a shot that shattered the glass in the doors, causing Chris and the remaining pupils to duck. It had been far too high to hit anyone, even Chris, who was over six feet tall. Jake was toying with them.

Once through the doors, Chris quickly looked around to see if there was anything he could use as a barricade, but there was nothing there.

'Shit.' He rounded up the students. 'Come on. We have to go. You need to run as fast as you can. Now. Go.' He screamed, panic and fear obvious in his cries.

———————

Downstairs, the sound of a single gunshot had panicked the escaping teachers and pupils, and so Pauline Butters had gone towards the science lab with a group of students to wait until the coast was clear.

Pauline pushed open the door to the lab and stepped inside. It was in darkness and she fumbled on the wall for the light switch. The room lit up in a brilliant, blinding yellow. She turned back.

'Where are the others?' she asked the group of teenagers, no more than twenty of them.

'They went in the other direction.'

Another gunshot was heard from above, along with the sound of breaking glass.

Pauline was scared. She'd been a teacher for almost forty years. She was one of the old guard, and though she knew basic health and safety, she had refused to be trained in what to do in the event of a school shooting or a terrorist attack. This was Sheffield, England, not Sheffield, Alabama. They didn't get mass shootings here. Surely those kinds of training courses were just inciting fear.

Now, she was nervous and had no idea what to do. She was as scared as the students, and she knew it showed.

Once inside the science lab, the only way out of the building was through the windows at the back of the room. She pushed chairs and tables out of her way, making a path to safety for her and the pupils.

'What's that?' someone asked.

Pauline turned to see where they were looking. There was what appeared to be a slow cooker, similar to one she had at home, in the middle of a desk. She frowned but didn't give it a second's thought.

'It doesn't matter. Come on. Liam, I want you to stand on a desk and open the window. Everyone, line up and climb out carefully. Then run as fast as you can to the front car park.'

Liam, the tallest of the group, dragged a desk over to the window and was about to climb on top when the pressure cooker exploded.

Scott ran along the side of the school, keeping his head down below window height. He kept looking up, taking sneaky glances inside the rooms to see if anyone was hiding in there. All the classrooms looked the same to him. Sian followed, staying close and whispering loudly, telling him to go back and leave the rescuing to the armed response officers. He didn't listen.

Around the back of the building, he saw rows and rows of books through the window. The library. The lights came on. He dived to the ground. Sian followed suit.

'Oh my God, it's wet,' she said as she landed on the damp grass.

He shushed her. 'Someone's just come into the library.'

'How do you know that's the library?'

'I've been in there a few times.'

'Why?' She frowned.

'When I've come to the school if Chris has been working late. There's a fire door in the far corner. I'm going to have a look.'

Sian pulled Scott back down just as he was about to stand up. 'Are you insane? What if it's the gunman going into the room? What if he's got hostages? If he sees us standing here in bloody flak jackets with police written across it in big letters, who knows what he'll do.'

'And if it's a class full of frightened kids, we can get them out.'

'Fifty-fifty. I don't like those odds, Scott.'

'Jesus,' he cursed. He fumbled around in his pocket for his phone, unlocked it and opened the camera and turned it to selfie mode. Slowly, he raised the phone until it was just above window level and took a picture.

He quickly brought it back down and he and Sian squinted as they tried to make out the figures in the blurred photo. There were five people in the shot, four of them wearing similar clothes they guessed to be pupils in school uniform. The other they couldn't make out. Scott zoomed in on the adult.

'Does he look like a gunman to you?' Sian asked.

'I can't see any gun,' he replied.

'He could have it concealed on him.'

'Hang on.' He zoomed in further. 'That's one of the teachers.'

'Are you sure?'

'Yes. Oh God, what's her name?'

'It looks like a man to me with that haircut.'

'She had chemotherapy last year. It's only just growing back. I went to her house once with Chris. Fiona! That's it. Fiona Mayhew.' He stood up and Sian pulled him back down again.

'What do you think you're doing? The gunman could be in there with them. If you jump up, knock on the window and start waving, it could be a bloody massacre.'

'You're right.' He sighed.

'Do you have her number?'

'No. Chris has.'

'That's no good then.'

Scott turned around. Crouched on his knees, his cold fingertips on the edge of the windowsill, he slowly eased himself up so he could see inside the library. He squinted at the bright light. He could see a group of pupils, all scared and frightened, but nobody else. Fiona came into view. She ushered the students into the room and went back to the door to bring in more kids.

Scott tapped lightly on the window with his forefinger, but it made hardly any sound. He rapped again, louder, hoping someone would see.

Sian appeared next to him, her warrant card raised, and slapped it against the glass. 'They need to know we're police, that we represent safety.'

Scott tapped again, louder this time. A female student turned, looked at them and screamed. This alerted Fiona Mayhew, who looked to the window. Scott stood up fully and pointed at himself.

Frowning, Fiona glared at him. Suddenly, the penny dropped that she recognised him. She ran over to the window and pushed it open.

'Scott?'

'That's right.'

'Oh, thank God. I'm so glad to see you,' she said, a hand slapped to her chest. 'What's going on?'

'We need to get you all out of there. Go to the fire door.'

'We can't. It's been locked and chained.'

'What?' Sian asked.

'It's been chained up. So have the doors at the front of the school. There's no way out.'

'You'll all have to climb through the window.'

Fiona ushered the students to the window. As quickly as possible she helped them up and Scott helped them down the other side.

Sian dug her mobile out of her pocket and made a call.

'Christian, don't say anything, just listen. Me and Scott are at the back of the school at the library. The fire door has been chained, locking them inside. We're getting some of the kids out through a window. I need you to meet them as they come running towards you.'

'Jesus Christ, Sian.'

'You can give me a warning later,' she said, ending the call. She turned back; three pupils had already made it out of the building. They looked scared, cold and afraid for their lives. 'It's ok, you're safe now,' she said to one with tears streaming down her face. 'What I need you to do is put your hands on your head and run as fast as you can to the car park at the front of the school but give the building a wide berth. They'll be someone waiting for you who'll show you where to go. Do you understand?'

The petrified girl nodded.

'Good. Follow me, I'll show you where to run.'

Sian led the ever-growing group to the corner of the

building. She sneaked a look around and, in the distance, saw Christian looking for her. She raised her arm, and he raised his, acknowledging he'd seen her.

'Did you see that man?'

The girl nodded.

'That's who you need to run towards. What's your name, sweetheart?'

'Isobel,' she said, her teeth chattering.

'Everyone,' Sian spoke to the group building behind her. 'I need you all to follow Isobel. Put your hands on your head and do exactly what she does. Ok, off you go. Run as fast as you can.'

Sian stood back and watched as the group set off. She saw the flash before she heard the explosion. The glass in the windows of the science lab blew out and the fleeing group of students were thrown to the ground as they were hit with flying debris.

Chapter Fifty-Five

'What the fuck was that?' Rory asked.

Christian stood, mouth agape, as he watched the students running towards him fall to the ground as the explosion went off.

'He planted a bomb. The fucker planted a bomb in a school full of kids. The bastard,' Christian exclaimed as he set off in a run.

'Where are you going?' Rory said, springing into action and following him.

They ran, crouched, towards the stricken students. Christian arrived first and bent down to the girl leading the group. She looked up. She was muddy and covered in shattered glass.

'Can you hear me? Are you all right?'

'I don't know,' she said loudly through tears.

'It's ok. You're safe. Is anyone else hurt?'

The other students began to get up, slowly. A few had minor cuts from the flying glass but none appeared to be seriously injured. He quickly told them to continue running and pointed Aaron out, who was waiting to meet them at the incident van.

Rory stood back, looking up at the hole in the building. 'What the fuck is this bloke doing?' he asked Christian.

'I've no idea, Rory. But we need to get as many of these kids to safety as quickly as possible. Who knows what else he's planning.'

When the science lab exploded, everyone was thrown back by the blast. The students screamed in horror and burst into tears. Scott jumped up and leapt into action.

'We need to get out of here, right now.'

No longer was the exodus conducted in orderly fashion, but the students began scrambling over each other to get out. Scott and Sian helped, grabbing them under the armpits and yanking them out of the classroom.

'Run. Go. Now. As fast as you can,' she said as she pushed them towards the middle of the school field where Christian was waiting for them.

'Fiona, where's Chris?' Scott asked as he pulled her out of the building.

'I don't know. He told us all where to go to get out. He was at the back of the group. I thought he'd followed us, but I don't know, Scott. I'm sorry,' she said, tears running down her face.

'It's ok. Don't worry. Knowing him, he'll have gone back for his iPhone.' He laughed, though it was obvious he was worried for his boyfriend.

With everyone gone, there was only Scott and Sian left. Scott headed for the window and started to climb into the room.

'What the hell do you think you're doing?' Sian asked.

'I'm going to get Chris.'

'You're bloody not. That's what the Armed Response team are here for. They'll be storming the building any minute now there's been an explosion. Get back out here now.'

'I'm sorry, Sian. I'm not leaving him in there.'

'Then I'm coming with you,' she said, grabbing hold of the window frame and easing herself up.

'What? Sian, you can't.'

'You need to wait out here. If you refuse to do so, then I'm coming in with you.'

'But you've got four kids. If anything happens—'

'All the more reason to stay out here and wait for the armed response,' she interrupted.

Scott turned away. His bottom lip quivered, and tears began to fall.

'He'll do something stupid, Sian, I know he will. He'll put himself in harm's way to save the kids.'

'He's a sensible bloke, Scott. You both are. He won't do anything to risk being injured.'

'You don't know him. If the only chance he had of saving those kids was him being killed, he wouldn't hesitate to stand up to the gunman.'

'What are you two doing hanging around here for?' Rory said, joining them.

'Chris is still in the building,' Sian replied. 'Scott wants to go in after him.'

'I don't fucking think so,' Rory said, grabbing hold of his best friend. 'I'm not losing you today as well as Nat.'

Scott had no choice. He let himself be led away from the building. He walked with heavy legs, dragging his feet on the wet grass, looking back at the school where his boyfriend was trapped inside.

When they were almost at the car park, Rory's grip loosened on his arm. Scott took his chance and pushed his colleague out of the way, turned back in a sprint towards the library.

———————

The explosion rocked the whole building. Chris and a group of a dozen students froze as the building was plunged into darkness.

'What was that?' someone asked.

'It sounded like a bomb going off.'

'Oh my God, are they blowing the school up?'

'Look, calm down, everyone,' Chris said. 'The police wouldn't blow up the school. Now, we need to get out of here as quickly as possible. Come on, we'll go through the science labs.'

Chris led the group along the corridor, down a short flight of stairs and opened the door to the science block. He stopped when he saw the devastation. The explosion had brought the ceiling down. There was no way they'd be able to escape through there. He closed the doors on the chaos and turned back around. He looked at the horrified faces of the students. He didn't have a clue what to do next. For all he knew he could be leading them into the path of the gunman. He looked over their heads at the corridor that stretched out before him; it looked alien in the dark.

'We need to go back upstairs,' he said.

'But that's where the gunman was.'

'I know that, Kwame, but we can't get out this way.'

'But aren't we just heading straight for him?'

'I promise, I will not let anything happen to any of you.'

'You can't make that promise,' one of the girls said.

'Lacey, while I'm still breathing, nobody will touch any of you. That is my promise.'

At the end of the corridor, the double doors were kicked open. Jake stood in the entrance. He placed the Glock in the waistband of his trousers and aimed the rifle at Chris and the students.

'Like fish in a barrel,' he snarled as he opened fire.

Chapter Fifty-Six

'You are reckless and irresponsible, do you know that?' Rory said as he caught up with Scott at the entrance to the library and spun him around. 'You've spent all day lecturing me on being professional, on making sure we get the gunman alive and bring him to justice, then you throw it all out of the window to act the hero.'

'I'm not acting anything, Rory. I'm trying to save some lives.'

'Chris's life.'

'Yes. His, and those of the students he's with. That's why we do this job, Rory, to help others. And they need my help right now.'

'That's what Armed Response are for. They're equipped to go head to head with a mad gunman. We're not.'

'And their boyfriend isn't up there getting shot at. Mine is.' He shook himself free from Rory's grip and headed out into the dark corridor.

'Scott…'

'If it was Natasha up there, if she was a teacher instead of a police officer and she was trapped upstairs with a group of students, would you seriously be able to stand outside in the cold and dark and just watch? No. You'd be in the thick of it. You'd be where I am right now. And do you know something, I'd be right beside you, because you're my mate, and I'd be happy to help you.'

Rory looked to the floor. 'You're right. I'm sorry. Today has been... Well, it's a fucking nightmare, isn't it? Come on, let's find this gunman. Then you can hold him down while I tear his fucking head off.'

They walked down the corridor, turned a corner and stopped when they saw the sea of dead at their feet. Mostly students, they'd been shot and killed as they'd tried to flee. Neither of the detective constables could comprehend what they were seeing.

They'd both seen dead bodies before. They'd both attended disturbing crime scenes, but this trumped everything they'd ever witnessed. There must have been twenty students mercilessly shot and killed.

Scott looked away and wiped a tear from his eye. 'Why would someone want to do this?' he asked, a catch in his throat.

'I've no idea. Whatever motive these gunmen who open fire in a school give after the fact, it's all bollocks. Nothing can justify this.'

They headed for the stairs and stopped when they both heard a noise from one of the classrooms.

Neither of them were armed, but they couldn't risk walking past a room full of desperate and helpless teenagers. On the other hand, however, it could be the gunman – hiding, lurking, luring them inside in order to open fire and cause more carnage.

Rory lifted a fire extinguisher from a bracket on the wall. He didn't know whether he'd soak the gunman or hit him with it but, either way, it was better to be armed with something than nothing at all.

Slowly, they approached the first classroom on the left. Standing either side of the door, Scott nodded at Rory who nodded back. They were both ready.

Scott's hand was clammy with sweat. He held the brass doorknob and slowly turned it. He pushed open the door and leaned inside. He released the breath he didn't realise he'd been holding. The room was empty.

They went to the next room along and repeated the drill. This time, a group of ten students were huddled inside. They were trying to remain silent but their muffled cries in the stillness of the school had resounded. Scott turned on the light. They screamed louder when they saw him enter the room.

'It's all right,' he said, raising his hands. 'I'm a police officer.'

That didn't help the kids. They continued to scream and scrambled further out of reach even though there was nowhere else to go.

'I'm not armed. I'm here to get you out.'

Rory stood alongside him and lowered the fire extinguisher. 'What's going on?'

'I've no idea. Look, if you come with us, now, we'll take you out through the library. But you need to be quick and be quiet.'

'Are you going to kill us?' one of the girls said. She was sat on the floor, her knees up to her chest, rocking slightly.

'What? No. We're police.'

'So was the other guy.'

Rory and Scott looked at each other.

'What?'

'The one who was shooting. He was wearing a police uniform.'

'Are you sure?'

'Yes.'

'Jesus! Look, we don't know how he got hold of a uniform, but he isn't a policeman, I promise you. We are. And we're here to help,' Rory said.

'How do we know you're not lying?'

'My name is Detective Sergeant Sian Mills,' a voice came from behind them. Where she appeared from, they had no idea, but she pushed past Rory and Scott and entered the room, holding her warrant card aloft. 'I'm with South Yorkshire Police. These are Detective Constables Rory Fleming and Scott Andrews. Here, take my warrant card, have a look.' She walked calmly and professionally up to the group and handed her card to one of the girls. She unzipped her flak jacket and her coat underneath, holding it open. 'I'm not armed. I have no weapon on me. Neither do those two. We don't know whereabouts the gunman is, but there is a safe route out of here if we go through the library, but you need to move now.'

The girl handed back the warrant card and looked towards the group huddled next to her. Their blank faces didn't change. None of them were willing to move.

Sian crouched on her haunches. 'Look, I have four children, two of them are of a similar age to you. I know what must be going through your heads right now. You're frightened, and that's perfectly understandable. But if we don't move, then the gunman could come down here and we'll all be killed. There has been far too much death and destruction today and I don't want there being any more. Now, please, you are literally a two-minute walk away from getting out of this building. That's all it will take.' She held out her hand.

It took a while, but one of the girls eventually reached forward and placed her clammy hand inside Sian's. Sian pulled her up.

'Good.' She smiled. 'Follow me.'

Reluctantly, the other teenagers began to follow. Once they reached the door to the corridor, Sian stopped and turned to the group.

'I don't want any of you turning back once we're out of this room, ok? Many have died today, and it's not something you need to see. Look straight ahead towards the library. Understand?'

There were nods of assent.

'Good. Rory, Scott, stand guard at the door, shield the bodies,' she whispered to them.

Once the detective constables were in place, she led the group out. She pushed each of the students towards the library, telling them to run, climb through the window and head for the front car park. She turned back to Scott and Rory.

'You two have—' She was interrupted by a barrage of gunfire from the floor above.

'Chris!' Scott shouted. He ran for the stairs and took them two at a time.

'Scott, get down here right now,' Sian called out.

'I'll go and get him. You make sure the kids are out.'

'Rory, stay safe, please.'

'I will.' He placed a hand on her arm, smiled, then turned away, heading upstairs after his colleague.

The first-floor corridor was long and stretched the entire length of the school. At the far side, Rory and Scott could make out a mound of bodies by the door. They were dressed the same, so Scott surmised they were students. He hated himself for thinking it, but he was pleased he wasn't looking at Chris's dead body.

'Where the fuck did he go?' Rory said, his voice barely above a whisper.

'I don't know.'

Scott's phone started vibrating. He lifted it out of his pocket. It was Chris. He swiped to answer.

'Chris, where are you?' he whispered.

'He came for us. He started shooting. I grabbed all I could and ran into a classroom. We're upstairs, but I don't know if we're going to get out.' His voice was full of fear.

Tears began to well up inside Scott's throat. He'd never heard Chris sound so frightened before. It was chilling. He swallowed hard.

'Me and Rory are here. We're on the long corridor on the first floor. What number room are you in?'

'I've no idea… Oh, it's B-sixteen. One of the girls has just told me.'

Scott looked at the number of the door they were passing as they edged carefully down the corridor. 'We've just passed B-three.'

'Are we all right to come out to you? Is it safe?'

'We don't know where the gunman is, but we can get to the library from here and out of the window.'

'We're coming now.'

The call ended.

Scott took a deep breath. He was visibly shaking.

At the end of the corridor, a classroom door opened, and

Chris poked his head out. As soon as he saw Scott, his tense face relaxed a fraction. He looked left and right, then stepped fully into the corridor. Eight students followed. One screamed when she looked at the doors behind them and saw three of her friends shot dead, lying in a bloody heap.

'Come on, this way,' Rory called out as quietly as he could.

Chris and the pupils were almost at the top of the stairs where Rory and Scott were waiting for them when the doors at the end of the corridor were pulled open and Jake appeared in the entrance.

'What do I win if I kill the fucking lot of you?' he shouted before laughing. He aimed the rifle and squeezed the trigger.

Chris tried to shield the students, and his body jerked as bullet after bullet pierced his skin. He fell, pulling a couple of pupils down with him. They, too, began to fall as the loud burst of gunfire continued.

Rory grabbed Scott and pulled him into the doorway of one of the classrooms. He held him close and tight until the gunfire stopped. When it did, a heavy silence descended.

Rory and Scott stood nose to nose. They could feel each other's breath on their faces and hear the sound of the other's heartbeat.

A trickle of blood flowed down the corridor and towards the doorway. Rory closed his eyes tight. They were trapped.

'We can't stay here,' Scott mouthed.

'He could still be out there,' Rory mouthed back.

'Chris,' Scott said. If there had been any volume behind the word, it would have been a yell, he said it so forcefully.

Rory shook his head. 'If we go out there now, we'll be shot.'

'I don't care anymore,' Scott whispered.

'Well, I do,' he said, gripping his best friend harder. 'Stay here. I'll have a look.'

Rory took a deep breath. He edged himself out of the doorway slowly, turned and looked down the length of the corridor. There was nobody there.

'He's gone,' Rory whispered.

'What?'

'He's not here.'

'Are you sure?'

'Yes. I'm sure.'

'He saw us, though, right?' Scott asked.

'I assume so.'

They both stepped out from the doorway. Looking down at the floor, they saw a female student seriously injured but still alive. She was crawling along the ground towards them and Rory dropped to his knees to help her.

Scott moved forward and then stopped, stock still. His eyes were fixed on Chris. His back was riddled with bullet holes. His white shirt was saturated with blood. There was no saving him. He dropped to his knees, held Chris's head in his hands and stroked his hair.

'I've got you. Come on. You're going to be all right,' Rory said to the girl. Slowly, he began to lift her to her feet. 'What's your name, love?'

'Rebecca,' she said, quietly. It was clear that she was in a great deal of pain.

'Ok, Rebecca. We're going to—'

A single gunshot rang out, and the girl dropped.

Rory was still holding her in his arms, but she was slumped dead. He looked down at her young face. There was nothing he could do. He looked up and saw Jake standing about five feet in front of him, and Scott, a distant expression on his face. Rory looked back down at Rebecca. He splashed her face with his tears.

'I'm so sorry I couldn't save you,' he said with a catch in his throat, gently placing her back on the floor.

'You bastard,' Scott said with venom, standing up to his full height. 'Why the fuck are you doing all this?'

Rory reached forward, grabbed Scott by the top of his flak jacket and pulled him back so they were stood side by side. He didn't want his friend and colleague doing anything stupid and risking his own life.

'I know you two,' Jake said stepping slowly forward.

'I don't think so,' Rory replied.

'I do. I've studied everyone on Matilda's team. Detective Constables Rory Fleming and Scott Andrews. Now, which one is which? Steve told me all about you both. Two more who don't deserve to be on such a prestigious team. "Not bad to look at, but thick as pig shit, the pair of them." That's how Steve described you both. From where I'm standing, he was spot on. What kind of idiots stare down the barrel of a gun?'

'I may be an idiot, but I'm not scared of you,' Rory said firmly.

'No? You should be.'

'Why? Because you have a gun in your hand? Am I supposed to feel threatened by a little man with a gun? Sorry, you don't frighten me because I know who you are. I know what you are, and you're a pathetic little man, a nobody who wants to be a somebody. Just like your dick of a brother.'

'Is that right?' Jake asked, tightening his grip on the Glock, his knuckles whitening. 'If I'm such a pathetic nobody, then why don't you come and disarm me? There's two of you and only one of me. Surely two hotshot detectives can overpower little, insignificant me.'

'You're a mad man with a gun,' Scott said, fighting to hold

back tears. 'You're volatile. Reckless. You should be fucking destroyed for what you've done today.'

'Oh, the other one *is* capable of speech. Sorry, you're going to have to help me out here. Which one is Rory, and which one is Scott? I'm staring at two cardboard-cut-out detectives and although Steve told me all about you, I'm having trouble telling you apart.'

Scott's eyes were darting all over the place. He kept looking down at Chris, hoping against hope that he wasn't really dead, that, by some miracle, he was still clinging to life.

'Hang on a minute, you're Scott, aren't you?' Jake said, pointing the gun directly at him. 'You're the gay one going out with the teacher. Is that him? He nodded towards Chris. 'Have I just killed your boyfriend?' he asked with a smile.

'Don't answer him,' Rory said out of the corner of his mouth. 'He's trying to make you angry. Don't let him.'

'I have, haven't I? I've just shot and killed your boyfriend in front of you? Wow. There's a bonus I wasn't expecting.'

'You're sick,' Scott said through gritted teeth.

'So that means you must be Rory, the one with the roving eye, a different girl each month, strutting around the station thinking he'd God's gift to women,' he said, turning his gun back on Rory. 'The thing is, I've got a list of people who I'm supposed to kill should I come across them on my journey today. It's all stored up here.' He tapped the side of his head with his gun.

'Why are you doing this?' Scott growled. He was struggling to hold on to his emotions. 'Why are you killing these innocent people?'

'Innocent? Is that what you think?'

'These are *kids*, for crying out loud. They've come to school to learn. Whatever's going on in that fucked-up head of yours has nothing to do with them or anyone else.'

'That's where you're wrong,' he said, stepping forward, the gun held out firm. 'Every single person needs a wake-up call. You're all so selfish in your sad, pathetic lives. You think you're safe and indestructible in your little bubbles. Well, you're not. Life without fear, pain and anarchy is a life wasted.'

'You seriously believe that?' Rory asked. 'Do you think you're some kind of mastermind terrorist? You're nothing. You're a conduit for your brother. You won't be remembered for starting some kind of revolution. If you're doing this for fame or notoriety, then I'm afraid you've failed. Nobody will remember you.'

'Now, that's where you're wrong. I will be remembered. Your mother and father will remember my name every single time they look at your photograph. They'll remember me as the man who killed their son.'

Rory swallowed hard. Despite trying to appear brave, he was scared stiff.

'No. My parents will remember me, and the good life I've led and the people I've helped and loved. They'll remember me with a smile,' he said, a tear rolling down his cheek.

'It's a shame we'll not be able to find out. Still, let's see which one of us is right.'

Jake aimed the Heckler & Koch rifle at Rory's chest and looked him straight in the eye.

Rory licked his lips and braced himself. This was it. The end. If his life was a film, then a troop of armed police officers would burst through the doors, shoot Jake in the head and save Rory's life in the nick of time. He'd be relieved and come up with a corny quip before the final credits rolled.

But life isn't like it is in the movies. There is no such thing as a happy ending. He looked down at Chris's bullet-riddled body. He thought of Natasha as he'd cradled her in the car park of the police station. He pictured Matilda as she was stretchered into the back of an ambulance with half of her head missing.

Rory always knew he'd die in the line of duty. He'd hoped it would have been while doing something heroic. *If only we could pick and choose our ending.*

He could sense Scott by his side. *If he could die knowing he'd saved the life of his best friend, it would be worth it.*

Jake squeezed the trigger. A hail of bullets hit Rory in the chest. He fell backwards and was dead before he hit the floor.

Scott froze to the spot. He felt the explosion ricochet through him, and the splatter of blood and brain matter hit his face. He closed his eyes tightly. When he eventually opened them, Jake had turned the gun onto him.

Scott took a deep breath and prepared himself.

'You can relax. Steve gave me both your names, but told me to only kill one of you, whichever I saw first. He said he thought it would be fun for one to try and survive without the other.'

'What?' Scott said quietly through the tears. He looked down and saw the dead bodies of his best mate and the man he loved.

'I'd buy a ticket for tonight's lottery if I were you. It's obviously your lucky day.'

Jake turned on his heels and headed down the corridor for the exit.

'What? No. No. You can't just leave,' Scott called out. Jake didn't respond and continued walking away. 'Come back here. For fuck's sake, you can't leave me like this. *Come back!*' he screamed. He collapsed to his knees. Tears were rolling down his face. 'Come back here. Kill me. Fucking kill me. *Please*. I'm begging you. *Fucking kill me!*'

His words resounded off the walls. Jake opened the door at the end of the corridor and walked through without looking back.

Scott was left alone surrounded by the dead bodies of complete strangers, his best friend and the only man he'd fallen in love with. He crawled towards Chris, bypassing the dead pupils, wading through the blood of the innocent. He grabbed Chris by the shoulders and tried to lift him up, but he was a dead weight.

'I'm sorry,' he cried as he leaned down over him, stroking his hair with bloodstained hands. 'I'm sorry,' he repeated as tears flowed.

Scott sat back on his haunches and managed to pull Chris towards him so he had his head resting on his lap. They had lain in this position many times during the evenings after a hard day at work, both of them relaxing on the sofa, simply enjoying being together. Chris liked having his hair stroked. So for one last time, that's what Scott did.

'I'm sorry I couldn't save you,' he whispered, choking on his own words.

Chapter Fifty-Seven

N ow it was dark, Steve Harrison only saw his own image reflected back at him when he looked through the window. He'd been enjoying the view of the landscape as the adapted car sped down the M1 to Sheffield.

He sat in the back, handcuffed to Rupert Carter, a burly prison officer with laboured breathing, stubble on his many chins and rancid breath. He looked down at the cuffs. They were loose on him but seemed to be digging into Rupert's fat wrists. Surely he wasn't medically qualified to be a prison officer. He'd be useless in a riot. Driving was Shaun Cox. He was a vicious bastard. His steely looks were enough to strike the fear into anyone. His threats worked because you knew he meant every word. Even Steve was scared of him when he saw that vein throb in the side of his neck. In the front passenger seat, Zoe Cartwright sat staring straight ahead out of the windscreen. He'd flirted with her on many occasions. At first, she'd resisted his charms, but there were times when he thought he was winning her over to his side. She hadn't been at Wakefield long. A few more months and she'd be putty in his hands.

Zoe looked at her watch. She leaned forward and turned on the radio.

'*It's four o'clock. We're going over to the newsroom now for the main headlines with Peter Rouse,*' the Radio Four announcer said.

'*At least twenty people have been killed in two gun attacks in Sheffield. The gunman is currently held up in a school where shots have been fired. We can now go live to our North of England correspondent, Danny Hanson.*'

A smiled spread across Steve's lips as he relaxed into his seat. The events in Sheffield were headline news. Tomorrow, it would be on the front pages of all the newspapers and coverage would fill many of the inside pages too. Gun attacks in the UK were rare. This story would travel the globe. And it was all down to him. He couldn't help but feel proud.

It was apt that Danny Hanson was reporting on these shootings, as he had been the principal journalist in covering his own crimes. In fact, if memory served him correctly, Danny won an award for a feature he wrote about a police constable turned murderer. Maybe he should contact him one day, offer him an exclusive.

'*I'm reporting live from Stannington Secondary School in Sheffield,*' Danny began, '*where less than five minutes ago a huge explosion ripped through the building. Armed police are surrounding the school and several pupils and staff members have been seen running from the rear with their hands on their heads. A police source has told me armed police are now storming the building in order to confront and contain the gunman.*'

'*Danny, this is the third gun attack in Sheffield today. Is this a lone gunman or part of a larger terrorist incident?*' the newsreader asked.

'*Police believe one man is responsible for all three attacks, though his motive remains unclear. A few hours ago police were called to a house in Worrall where the occupants, Malcolm and Vivian Harrison, were found shot dead. Malcolm and Vivian are parents to former Police Constable Steven Harrison, who is currently serving life in prison for six murders he committed in 2017.*'

Steve was itching to cheer at the mention of his name and crimes from the back of the car, but he had to remember he was playing the role of a concerned brother and son. He lowered his head to show he was feeling remorseful, when he was really trying to hide his smile.

'*Are these attacks in any way linked to Steve Harrison?*' the newsreader asked.

'*This is a fast-moving investigation. We've been told a statement will be released at some point this evening. Until then, we don't know.*'

'*What can you tell us of casualties, Danny? We understand a number of police officers have lost their lives today.*'

'*That's right. Assistant Chief Constable Valerie Masterson was killed this morning at South Yorkshire Police Headquarters. ACC Masterson had led the force through some difficult times in recent years including the Hillsborough Inquiry and the inquiry into historical sexual abuse in Rotherham. She was a tough leader of the force and will be greatly missed. Another victim was Detective Chief Inspector Matilda Darke…*'

Steve looked up. He'd been waiting for this confirmation. He hoped that bitch suffered.

'*…DCI Darke was shot twice in the same incident as the Assistant Chief Constable. She is currently undergoing emergency surgery at the city's Royal Hallamshire Hospital where she is in a serious and critical condition…*'

Steve tuned the rest of the broadcast out. She was still alive.

How the fuck was that possible? Jake said he'd shot her in the head. He'd seen the back of her skull explode as she dropped to the ground. How can anyone survive that?

Steve seethed. He could feel his blood boiling. All he'd wanted was to get payback for her stifling his career. She only got the job to be in charge of the prestigious Homicide and Major Enquiry Team because she was a woman and the force needed to show they weren't sexist. She'd handpicked her rag-tag bunch of idiots to support her and none of them deserved to be there. He did. Steve knew he was wasted as a PC, but he had been prepared to work through the ranks. His sergeant had tried to stop him climbing the ladder. He'd sabotaged his chances of passing his sergeants' exams and those bastards on HMET conspired to keep him in uniform.

He clenched his fists hard, digging his nails into the palms of his hands. He was full of rage, anger, fury and vitriol. He could feel the hot blood racing through his body, coursing through his veins, and his heart pounding so loudly in his chest he thought everyone in the car could hear it.

'What's up with you?' Rupert asked as he turned his fat neck to look at him.

'Nothing. Why?' Steve said through almost gritted teeth.

'You've gone bright red. Not trying to fake a heart attack, are you?' He tried to laugh, but it turned into a cough.

'Fuck off,' Steve snarled.

'Language!' he chastised. 'You know this Darke woman then, do you?'

'Just keep out of it. Go back to thinking of cake and biscuits, you fat bastard.'

'I won't tell you again, you little shit.' Rupert yanked hard on the cuffs, pulling Steve towards him.

'What's going on back there?' Shaun asked, looking through the rear-view mirror.

'Just trying to teach this shit some manners.'

'Save your breath. He's evil to the core, that one. Aren't you, Steve?'

'You'd know all about that, Mr Cox,' Steve said, making eye contact with him through the mirror. He sat back in his seat and closed his eyes, blocking out all sounds and sights. He needed to know where to go from here. The plan was for Jake to kill Matilda, divert the police's attention by shooting from a bridge over the Parkway, then for Jake to get his revenge on Ruth. He'd probably killed her, but how could he get a message to Jake to finish Matilda off? Steve had told Jake to consider every possible outcome and to always have a back-up, a contingency plan. Fingers crossed he had listened to him and he was putting that plan into action right now, providing he managed to get out of the school alive.

_____

Chapter Fifty-Eight

Armed police had stormed the building and were sweeping through it room by room, floor by floor. They shouted, 'All clear!' and officers and paramedics were allowed in to rescue those trapped inside and administer medical aid to the injured.

Christian, Sian and Aaron stood at the main entrance to the school. They could see the ground floor littered with bodies. It was a sight that filled them all with horror. All three had young children. To be standing in a school surrounded by dead students was a nightmare scenario none of them wanted to be part of. However, their job was to investigate, to identify the dead and inform the parents and families.

'Where are Scott and Rory?' Aaron asked, breaking the heavy silence between the three of them. His voice was quiet, dulled by raw emotion.

'Knowing Rory he'll have found a vending machine,' Christian said and gave a nervous laugh.

'It'll save him raiding my snack drawer.' Sian tried to smile but she was shaking too much.

'Is there any news on Jake? Is he dead? Have they caught him?' Aaron asked.

'I know as much as you do,' Christian said.

Sian buckled. She bowed her head and allowed the tears to fall. There had been no sound coming from the school after armed police had entered. It could only mean one thing: this whole operation had been a monumental failure, resulting in dozens of dead, including more of their own colleagues.

'Can we have a detective in here, please?' Someone shouted from inside the building.

Christian stepped forward. A paramedic in a green all-in-one suit smeared with blood met Christian just inside the entry. He was tall and solidly built with a messy mount of dark blond hair.

'We have one of your officers upstairs,' he said. 'He seems to be suffering with shock and we're having difficulty moving him. I thought a friendly face may help.'

'Right,' was all Christian could say.

The paramedic led him through the minefield of dead bodies. He stepped around them carefully, taking care not to slip on any spilt blood or stand on a limb. As he looked down, he felt ill, staring into the dead faces of the young. How many had been killed in this school? How would he be able to go home tonight, hug his wife and daughters, and go to bed?

Up the stairs, more bodies were strewn about. This was a crime scene that was going to take days to process. He made a mental note to mention counselling to the Chief Constable. Everybody would be affected by this for years to come.

Through the double doors at the top of the stairs, Christian stopped in his tracks as he came face to face with Rory Fleming's dead body. He felt his heart skip a beat and held his breath. Less than eight hours ago, everyone was joking with

Rory at how happy he was following the announcement of his engagement to PC Natasha Tranter. Now, both had been murdered. Two young lives destroyed.

'Are you all right?' the paramedic asked.

Christian swallowed hard. He felt his bottom lip wobbling as he tried to swallow his emotions, but it was no use. The tears had started to fall. He shook his head.

'Can you cover him?' he said quietly, nodding towards Rory.

'Of course.'

Christian waited while a white sheet was brought over to respectfully cover Rory's face. Christian couldn't take his eyes off him. He was half expecting him to blink, to sit up and say he was fine. As the sheet covered his face and he still didn't move, he knew. Rory was truly gone.

Further down the corridor, Scott Andrews was sitting with his back firmly against the wall. He was drenched in blood. On his lap, he was cradling the dead body of Chris Kean, his boyfriend, stroking his hair.

As Christian approached slowly, he could see the look on Scott's face. There was nothing there, no hint of emotion. His body was there, in the middle of this horror, but his mind had shut down to protect him from the nightmare.

'Scott,' Christian said. It came out barely above a whisper. His mouth was dry, and he was shaking. He licked his lips, swallowed hard a couple of times, and tried again. 'Scott.' He was louder this time, but there was no response from the young DC.

'Scott, it's me, Christian,' he said, stepping forward towards. 'Can you hear me?'

Scott didn't react.

Christian reached out and placed a hand on his shoulder. He was taut, rigid, and didn't move as he shook him slightly.

'Scott. Scott,' he said louder. 'Come on, let's get you outside.'

Eventually, he blinked. He turned slightly and made eye contact with Christian. The DI gave him a brief smile.

'You all right?' he asked before realising it was a bloody stupid question. Scott was visibly shaking. 'He's cold,' he said to the paramedic. 'Do you have a blanket or something?'

'Sure.'

Christian stepped closer. He dropped to his haunches, placed his arm around his colleague and sheltered his vision from the sight of the carnage behind him. 'Scott, can you tell me if you're hurt anywhere?'

It was a while before he responded. There were no words; he just shook his head.

'That's good. Look, we need to move you. You need to come with me outside. We'll take you back to the station and Sian will let you empty her secret snack supplies,' he said with an exaggerated chuckle. Again, Scott didn't react.

The paramedic handed Christian a red cellular blanket, which he wrapped as best as he could around Scott's shoulders. The wall was in the way, but it would give him some warmth for the moment at least.

'Scott, you're cold. Come with me and we'll get you warmed up.' He tried to pull him away from the wall, but he wouldn't budge. 'Scott, look at me. Can you understand what I'm saying?' he asked slowly.

Scott looked and nodded.

'Good. We can't stay here. We need to go back to the station. Will you come with me?'

Again, he nodded.

'That's good. Now, I've got you,' he said, gripping him harder around the shoulders. 'I want you to come with me, stay looking straight ahead, and we'll go downstairs to the car. Can you do that?'

He nodded once.

'Right. Let's go.'

Christian struggled to lift Scott up. The life had been drained out of him and he was a dead weight. As he stood, the paramedic reached forward and grabbed Chris, placing him gently down on the bloodied tile flooring and covering him with a white sheet.

Once Scott was standing, Christian adjusted the blanket, wrapped it around him and held him close with a firm grip. Scott rested his head on his shoulder.

'Now, we're going to take it slowly, ok? One step at a time.'

They walked carefully through the sea of bodies, making sure nobody was stood on or kicked. Christian wanted to scream and cry, but he needed to be strong for Scott. He increased his grip on the young DC and whispered more placatory words.

Once off the corridor and through the double doors, Christian felt himself relax a little and they took the stairs at a steadier pace.

At the bottom, Sian was waiting for them. Her eyes widened in horror when she saw Scott, the amount of blood covering him. A tear fell, and she let it. She looked up with questioning eyes. Christian shook his head, telling her there was no one else left alive. She squeezed her eyes tightly closed. Like Christian, she tried to keep a hold on her emotions, but she also wasn't succeeding, and the tears quickly came.

'Is there a way to get him out of here without stepping over those bodies?' Christian asked quietly.

'Through the library,' she said, her voice breaking. 'They've opened the fire door.'

'Good. Any sign of—'

She shook her head. 'I'm hoping we find him dead in a classroom somewhere.'

As they reached the bottom of the stairs, Sian reached out and took hold of Scott's left hand.

'He's freezing.'

'He's in shock.'

She grabbed him and pulled him into a tight embrace. 'I am so sorry,' she whispered earnestly into his ear. 'I know you'll be thinking you're on your own right now, that you've lost everything, but we are all here for you. I'm here for you. Always. Never forget that.'

Scott hugged her back, wrapping his arms around her. He leaned into her shoulder and started crying loudly, his sobs resounding off the bloodied school walls.

Chapter Fifty-Nine

Frank and Penny were sat either side of Matilda's bed in a single room, high up in the hospital. Adele had tried to look through the window but in between the slats of the Venetian blinds, all she could make out were the monitors Matilda was hooked up to, the tubes and wires feeding into her and a large bandage wrapped around her head. She was still unconscious and would be for some time, but she was stable.

'Come on, Matilda,' she said under her breath. 'You can survive this. I know you can.'

She felt more relaxed now that Matilda was out of surgery. Being able to see her was a relief. She'd tried to remain positive in front of Frank and Penny but had wanted to cry her heart out for her best friend. Now, she found herself smiling. Recovery would be long and arduous, but she would have supportive people around her, which was important.

'I brought you a decent coffee from the shop on the ground floor,' Daniel said.

Adele hadn't heard him approaching and jumped at the

sound of his deep voice. She turned to face him. She had tears in her eyes.

'Is everything all right?' he asked, handing her the cardboard cup.

'The next twenty-four hours are critical. She's survived the initial operation though, that's the main thing.'

'She's a fighter,' he said with a hint of a smile.

'She's had to be. Daniel, come and sit down, there's something I need to tell you.'

Adele went over to the seating area. She lifted the plastic lid off the cup and gave the coffee a sniff. It smelled strong and she thought it a shame that she didn't have a bottle of whisky in her bag so she could pour a tot in.

She sat down on the plastic seat and took a sip of the coffee. Daniel sat opposite her. He looked at her with a sad expression.

Adele took a deep breath and looked down into the swirling brown liquid. 'Daniel, Matilda was pregnant.'

He was silent. Adele had to look up to make sure he'd heard what she said.

'Pregnant?' His eyes seemed to sparkle at the notion.

Adele nodded.

'Why didn't she tell me? Did you know?'

'No. I think it's possible Matilda didn't know either. She wasn't too far gone.'

'Oh. Hang on, you're speaking in the past tense. She's lost it, hasn't she?'

'Her body went into lockdown after she was shot. It rejected the baby so it could focus all its survival skills on saving her. I'm so sorry, Daniel. I thought it best you know,' she said, placing a hand on his knee.

His face was unreadable. 'We never spoke about children.

When you're in your forties, you just assume you're not going to have them. I'm not sure how I feel.'

'Do you have kids?'

'No. Do you think Matilda would have been happy?'

Adele thought for a long moment. She would probably have been horrified at the prospect of becoming a mother at forty-four. 'I don't know,' she answered.

'Maybe we could talk about it when—'

Daniel was interrupted by Adele's phone ringing. She looked at the display, saw it was Lucy calling and made her excuses. She moved away to take the call.

'Lucy, you phoned at exactly the right time. Remind me to buy you a bottle of Prosecco. What's up?'

'I'm sorry, Adele, I think you need to come back to work. We've been informed of a third shooting. There are more bodies coming in.'

'Another? Shit. I'll be there as soon as I can.'

The drive from the Hallamshire Hospital to Watery Street didn't take long. Traffic was hectic on West Street, as usual, but once in the centre of Sheffield, Adele didn't have any trouble getting through. News of the shootings seemed to have kept everyone off the streets. Usually, in the car, Adele would have the radio on, a bit of background music or the news, but she wanted silence for this journey while she marshalled her thoughts. Matilda had survived the surgery, but that was only the first hurdle. She'd need more operations, reconstructive surgery, and then there was physiotherapy and counselling. What would the MRI scans reveal? Would she be brain-damaged? She might not be able to live on her own anymore.

She might have to have round-the-clock care. It was strange to think that less than twenty-four hours ago they were both sitting on the sofa in Matilda's living room, sharing a bottle of wine and taking the piss out of the clothes on an episode of *Columbo* from the 1970s.

When Adele pulled into her regular parking space at the back of the mortuary building, she found she'd been crying the entire journey. Their carefree lives might never be the same again. It had taken Matilda years to be able to laugh and joke after James's death. How would the events of the today shape their lives from this point onward?

She climbed out of the car and wiped her eyes as she saw Simon Browes with some administrative staff putting together a ResponStor temporary body-storage system. The car park was lit up by floodlights. She felt physically sick at the thought of all those dead bodies waiting to be processed. What the hell was wrong with her?

'Nutwells delivered about half an hour ago,' Simon said as she approached. He had his shirt sleeves rolled and his tie tucked inside his collar. 'We had these at the Manchester bombing a couple of years back, remember? We'll have them up in fifteen minutes. Each unit can fit twelve bodies and we've been sent five. I'm hoping it's enough.'

'Really? What do you know about this third shooting?'

'Not much so far. Apparently, the gunman burst his way into a school and opened fire. He even had a home-made bomb that he set off.'

'Bloody hell. Please tell me they've caught him.'

'I've no idea. Lucy took the call. I've got a few technicians going out to the scene, and we're manning the fort here until they can bring them back. Hopefully, we'll be up and running by then. It doesn't help it's the middle of winter and the fridges are already stocked with flu victims. Adele, you couldn't give us a hand with these units, could you? I don't know Sheffield, so I don't know how long it'll take to get the bodies here from Stannington.'

'Yes. I'll just go and get changed into… Hang on, did you say Stannington?'

'Yes. That's where the third shooting was.'

Adele paled. She reached out and placed a hand on Simon's arm to steady herself. 'A school at Stannington?'

'Yes.'

'What was the name of the school?'

'I don't know. Like I said, Lucy took the call. It's a secondary school though, so I'm guessing they'll be young teenagers and—'

Adele didn't wait for him to finish. She headed for the doors, pushed them open and practically fell into the warm building.

The corridors leading to the main post-mortem suites were lined with trolleys, most of them occupied. Simon was wrong; he had to be. Like he said, he didn't know Sheffield. There were several schools in Stannington. It wouldn't be the one Chris worked at.

'Lucy,' she called out.

She pulled open a door and went down the narrow corridor towards the digital autopsy suite. Claire was inside, analysing the results on her computer monitors.

'Claire, have you seen Lucy?'

Claire turned and immediately burst into tears. 'Oh God, Adele, I'm so sorry.'

'Wha…?'

The look on Claire's face said it all.

Adele fell against the wall and collapsed to the floor.

She came round to find Claire and Lucy standing over her, looking down at her with worried expressions.

'Here, drink this.' Lucy proffered a plastic cup of water.

'What's happened? What's going on? Chris?' Adele panicked as she tried to sit up. 'Where am I?'

'Adele, calm down,' Lucy said. 'You're in your office. You fainted, that's all. You're fine.'

Adele's eyes darted rapidly around her. She was indeed in the small space she laughingly called her office, but it looked strange, alien. It was a cramped off-shot room, full of textbooks, charts and files. The work seemed to be never-ending. She often came in here for some alone time after a particularly challenging post-mortem, but right now she felt claustrophobic.

'Chris? Where's Chris?'

Lucy and Claire exchanged an awkward glance.

'Oh my God, no. Please, no,' Adele cried.

'Adele, we don't know anything yet. All we know is that there was a shooting at Stannington Secondary School,' Lucy said slowly. There were tears in her eyes and a catch in her throat. 'We've been told there are many students dead, but we don't know anything about any staff being killed.'

'Where's my bag? I need to call him. I need to make sure he's all right. Will you both let go of me!' she shouted as she scrambled in her bag. She shook them off her and retrieved her phone. 'There's a message,' she said, looking at the screen. 'Chris has left me a voicemail.'

With shaking fingers, Adele accessed her answer service and put it on speaker.

'Mum, it's me. There's a shooting at the school. I'm inside

with some of the students, but we're hiding. I've called Scott and the police are outside. They're trying to find a way to get us all out. I'm sure everything's going to be fine. It's just … if it isn't, I want you to know that I couldn't have asked for a better mum than you. You've been amazing. You brought me up on your own as well as working hard at a career. You're a bloody superhero. I love you. I know I don't say it often, but I do. I love you, Mum.'

The silence in the small room when the message ended was heavy. All three women stood with tears streaming down their faces. None of them looked at one another.

Chris sounded nervous and scared. He was obviously trying to be confident in front of the students he was shielding, but the shaking of his voice was evidence of a man fearing for his life.

'How long ago was that message left?' Claire asked. Her voice was quiet and broken.

Adele looked down at her phone. 'Just after half-past three. Should I call him?' she asked, looking up at her colleagues with wet eyes.

'If the police are in the building, then they've obviously got the gunman. It should be safe for you to call,' Lucy said, giving her a comforting smile.

'I will. I'll ring him,' she said, not making any effort to make the call.

'We'll leave you to it,' Claire said, tapping Lucy on the arm and nodding towards the doors. 'We'll be in my office if you want us.'

They didn't make it to the doors before they were opened by another. DS Sian Mills entered and slowly approached Adele.

She didn't need to say anything. The blank look on her face, the wide, distant eyes and the tear stains on her cheeks told the whole story.

Adele looked up at Sian. She opened her mouth and released a heart-wrenching sound that seemed to come from the centre of her soul. She fell to the floor as she screamed and wailed. Her only child, her lifeline, had been cruelly taken from her.

Chapter Sixty

DC Finn Cotton entered Christian's office carrying a tray with three mugs of tea – one for each of them and another for Aaron Connolly. They were all sat in silence as they tried, and failed, to make sense of what had just happened at Stannington Secondary School, at everything that had happened since early this morning. Seven police officers were now dead, three from their own team. A word had yet to be invented to describe the events of today. Nightmare didn't seem strong enough to cover it anymore.

Finn stood by the door, his hands wrapped around his mug. He took a sip, but it didn't taste of anything. He turned to look out of the room. A few support workers were milling about in silence, going about their tasks, but there were two desks that would remain unoccupied for quite some time. He blinked, and a tear fell from his eye which he quickly swept away.

'Any news on Scott?' Aaron asked.

'I called my sister – she's a nurse at the Northern – and she said that his mother's with him. He's had to be sedated.'

'I didn't know your sister was a nurse,' he said.

'Yes. She works in gynaecology.'

'That's not where Scott is, I hope,' Aaron said, in an attempt at levity to relieve the tension.

Finn flashed the barest hint of a smile. 'No. She goes out with someone who works in A&E, who passed on the news.'

'Ah.'

The room fell silent again and none of them knew what to say.

Christian hadn't touched his drink. He was sat forward on his chair, staring into the distance. He looked physically, mentally and emotionally drained.

'Sir,' Finn said. His voice barely above a whisper. 'DI Brady,' he said louder.

'Christian!' Aaron called, snapping his fingers in front of Christian's face.

'Hmm? What?' he asked, coming back to reality from wherever his mind was.

'What do we do now?' Finn asked. 'Where do we go from here?'

'That's a good question, Finn. I wish I knew the answer.'

'We need to wait until Inspector Porter's finished at the school. If they've killed the gunman, then it's all over. If they arrest him, it's just beginning for us,' Aaron said.

'It's weird, isn't it?' Finn began. 'You don't realise how fragile life is until something like this happens. Just this morning we were taking the piss out of Rory for getting engaged to Natasha, now they're both dead along with Ranjeet and the ACC. In the blink of an eye, all those lives lost.'

'Are you all right?' Christian asked.

'I don't know,' he replied, a heavy frown on his face. 'I

don't know how I feel. It's like ... there's too much going on for me to understand and accept.'

'You're in shock.'

'We all are,' Aaron said.

'Have you called your wife?' Christian asked.

Finn nodded. 'I didn't tell her we'd lost more officers. I didn't want to worry her. She's been watching the news all day. They've taken the regular programmes off BBC One and are doing a news special.'

'Danny Hanson will be loving that,' Aaron said.

'Susannah said that Danny's been trending on Twitter since he made his first broadcast. He's very popular with female viewers, apparently.'

'Really? The twat'll be even more annoying now,' Aaron said.

The door opened. Finn quickly stepped out of the way to stop being squashed against the wall. Chief Constable Martin Featherstone entered. His expression was grave.

'I'm incredibly sorry about DC Fleming,' he said. 'I won't lie and pretend I knew him, because I didn't. But if DCI Darke chose him for her team, then he was obviously a dedicated and professional detective. And I know he'll be missed by you all.'

'He will, sir, thank you,' Christian said.

'I've had Inspector Porter on the phone from the school. They've done a full sweep of the building and they haven't located Jake Harrison.'

'What?' Aaron asked, incredulous.

'He must have got away, somehow, in the melee.'

'An explosion, a gun attack, dozens of lives lost including one of our own – I'd hardly call that a "melee",' Aaron said scathingly.

'You're right. I'm sorry. Poor choice of words.'

A phone rang in the main office.

'That's mine. Excuse me,' Finn said, looking almost relieved to be leaving Christian's office.

'There are two thoughts as to what happens next,' the Chief Constable began. 'Either we'll find Jake dead somewhere, having taken his own life, or he's planning a fourth attack.'

'From what we know of Jake, there's no evidence for where a fourth attack could possibly be,' Christian said. 'He's killed his parents, he's attacked us as a force, and he's killed his wife. What other grievance could he possibly have?'

'Maybe it's entirely random like the shooting at the Parkway,' Featherstone said.

'No. There is nothing about this that's been random. Everything has been planned in the minutest of details.'

'Then what was the motive for the Parkway shooting?' Aaron asked.

'To confuse us,' Christian said. 'To throw us off his scent. To give him more time to plan his strategy and get to the school. We had two massive crime scenes to process, and we were several officers down. While we were sorting ourselves out, he was biding his time until it went dark so he could attack the school and kill his wife.'

'We need him found, Christian, before he strikes again. How is he moving from one location to the other without us knowing about it? Does he have a car or a van? Do we know any of that?' Featherstone asked, almost shouting.

'We know he has a van.'

'Registration number?'

Christian shook his head.

'So, we're looking for a white man driving a van. Well, that really narrows the search down,' Featherstone said with bile.

'Sir—'

'And why is there such a lack of information about a man who has been able to terrorise the city for the best part of eight hours?' Featherstone interrupted.

'Because we don't have the intelligence or the resources. This man is a loner. He doesn't have friends we can call upon. His aunt and uncle haven't a clue what kind of vehicle he's driving and, you may not have noticed, sir,' Christian said, his face reddening in anger, 'but we have lost seven officers from this station today. Seven good men and women. I'm sorry that this team isn't filled with emotionless robots, but we're struggling to process the loss of our colleagues and friends.'

Christian would never have raised his voice to a senior officer before today, which was testament to the unusualness of the situation. He was angry. He was frightened. He was also incredibly protective of the team he'd been put in charge of during Matilda Darke's absence.

There was a light rap on the door. Christian looked around the Chief Constable and barked at Finn to enter.

'Sorry to interrupt. I've had a call from downstairs. Steve Harrison has arrived.'

Chapter Sixty-One

Jake Harrison was sitting behind the wheel of his van. He was breathing deeply and rapidly. His adrenaline was through the roof. His white shirt was splattered with blood, as were his face and hands. He could smell the cordite from the bullets fired and the exploded bomb, which he hadn't expected to work. It had been so simple to put together.

He thought about Ruth. He really did love her. When she walked out on him, abandoned him when he needed her the most, his love quickly turned to hate. They had been good together, but Steve going to prison, his hero turning out to be a serial killer, destroyed all that.

When Jake had been approached by someone Steve trusted and the plan began to form to reap revenge on the police force, Jake knew he'd want to add Ruth to his list. She had to die for leaving him. The look on her face when he rammed the Glock pistol into her mouth was something that would stay with him for a long time. Her eyes widening as she looked at him pleadingly, tears running down her face. As if he was going to let her go. As soon as he fired – as soon as her head exploded –

brain, blood and bone spattered the wall behind her. He let go, and she dropped to the floor with a heavy thud. The bitch was dead.

He couldn't remember much else after that. He remembered shooting one of the coppers on Steve's list and letting the other live. Then, he had turned and calmly walked along the corridor, down the stairs, and out through a window in a storage room on the ground floor. While police were storming the front of the building and kids were fleeing from the back, he was walking over the field, Glock in the back of his trousers, rifle over his shoulder, breathing in the cold, damp air and feeling the drizzle on his face. It was cool and refreshing.

But this was far from over. Matilda Darke was still alive and her being dead was the main point of today. It didn't matter how many people he killed, including his own parents and wife, it would still be a failure if Matilda remained alive. Being in a coma or a vegetable would not be enough for Steve. He wanted her dead.

From the glove box, he took out another iPhone and turned it on. Nobody had this number. He'd use it once, then destroy it.

He climbed out of the van, opened the back door and saw his hostage tied up in the back. Her face was stained with tears. She looked to be in pain as the gag around her mouth was rubbing at the skin.

'I need you to shut the fuck up,' he said, pointing the Glock at her with one hand while he dialled with the other.

It was a while before the call was answered.

'Listen carefully,' he began. 'Don't say anything until I've finished. Matilda Darke is still alive, and she needs to be dead. I'm going to the Hallamshire Hospital to finish her off. You need to make sure I'm not challenged. Do you understand?' There was no reply. 'I said, do you understand?'

'Yes,' came the weak reply.

He held the phone out and placed it next to his hostage. She whimpered and tried to speak, but the gag wouldn't allow it.

'Did you hear that?' Jake asked.

'I did.'

'She's still alive. If I see one copper at the hospital, I will fucking kill her, and she'll know it's your fault. Understand?'

'Yes.'

'Good man.'

He ended the call. He removed the battery and SIM and dropped them down a nearby drain.

'It's nearly over, love,' he said, winking at his hostage before slamming the van door closed.

Chapter Sixty-Two

Steve smiled at the familiar building when the car turned and pulled into the visitors' car park at the front of the police station. He'd only worked in there for two years, but he knew every inch of it.

Growing up, he'd passed the place many times, hoping, one day, to be working there. He felt proud to wear the uniform, to be out on the streets representing South Yorkshire Police. It didn't take long for the feeling to sour once he realised the politics involved, the brown-nosing, the sucking up. If your face didn't fit, and Steve's obviously didn't, there was no chance of promotion, of being among the elite. You were just a statistic, a face in the crowd, a uniformed nobody to police a Sheffield United match, guard the crowds during Armistice celebrations and patrol the lanes of Meadowhall at Christmas to pacify the shoppers that their safety was paramount.

He hated this building and every fucker in it.

The car door opened and Steve, still handcuffed, was

helped out. He looked up and wondered how many of his former colleagues would be looking down at him. He needed to play the role of a repentant man, of the grieving son, of the shocked brother. This wasn't going to be easy.

Once inside the building, he couldn't help but take in his surroundings and smile. He never thought he'd be back in here again. He was pushed down into a hard, plastic chair and told to wait. He had no intention of going anywhere. They could have removed his cuffs, left the door open and the car engine running, and he wouldn't have escaped. There was plenty more drama left in the day and he didn't want to miss out on a single minute of it.

The door opened and DI Christian Brady entered the reception. He looked older than the last time Steve had seen him. He was softer around the middle and his hair was a lot thinner. He looked tired, haggard, and there was a redness to his eyes. He'd obviously been crying.

'Steve,' Christian said as a form of greeting. There was no pleasure to his voice.

Steve nodded but didn't say anything.

'Can I get you anything? A tea or coffee, perhaps?' he asked, though it seemed to pain him to be polite.

'A coffee would be nice,' he replied, refusing to say thank you. 'Black, strong, one sugar,' he said with a friendly smile.

Christian seemed to bite his lip to stop him from reaching for Steve's throat and squeezing the life out of him. He turned to the desk sergeant and asked him to set up an interview room while he went and made the coffee. As he left, Steve saw Christian's eyes burning into him. This was going to be so much fun.

'Sian, I didn't expect you back so soon,' Christian said as he stepped into the corridor from the men's toilets.

After meeting Steve again after all this time, Christian had needed a few minutes alone. He couldn't help but think of all the pain and suffering the former constable had caused, and how he'd duped DC Faith Easter into thinking he was in love with her just to get closer to the investigation. He hadn't needed to kill her. She was a good detective, a genuinely decent person. It angered Christian that she had been used so despicably.

'How's Adele?'

'Devastated,' she replied. Sian's face looked dry, but her eyes were red, likely from crying alongside the pathologist. 'Claire's taken her home. I think she's going to stay with her overnight. I just...' She shook her head and swallowed her tears. 'I have no idea how she's going to get through this.'

'We'll be there for her. All of us,' he said, squeezing the top of her arm. 'Look, Steve's arrived from Wakefield Prison. Do you want to interview him with me, or shall I get Aaron to sit in?'

'No,' she said, her face hardening. 'I'll come with you. Can you give me a few minutes though?'

'Sure.'

Interview room one had been set aside for Steve Harrison. He sat at the table and took a leisurely sip of his coffee. It was the best he'd had in a long time. He made the most of his time in prison – there was nothing he could do about his incarceration, so he didn't fight it – however, there was the odd luxury he missed: a decent cup of coffee, takeaway food, going to the coast, getting pissed at the weekends and a good shag. But if he dwelt on what he missed, he'd go mad. The best and only way to get through the slog of a prison sentence is simply to accept it. Don't think of what you no longer have, adapt to what's available and make the best of the situation. Once he'd settled, he was much happier with his surroundings.

Sitting next to him in the interview room was Shaun Cox. He sat with his back straight, his massive arms folded across his chest and his huge legs spread apart in front of him. His face was craggy and set permanently to scowl. He radiated malevolence. It was as though Steve could feel the seething mass of rage blistering from him.

'Enjoying your day out?' Steve asked.

Shaun didn't reply.

'You can relax, you know. It's me in for questioning, not you.' He looked across and saw the thick vein throbbing in the prison officer's neck. 'How do you relax, by the way? You always look like a lion in the jungle ready to pounce on a zebra. I bet you spend your evenings sharpening your weapons waiting for the zombie apocalypse.'

The door opened and Christian entered with DS Sian Mills behind him. Steve sat up straight, licked his lips and shifted in his seat. It was show time.

'Sian, lovely to see you again.'

'I'd say the same, but we'd both know it would be a massive lie,' she said.

'Not still upset about me punching you in the mouth, are you?'

'I was more upset about you killing one of my friends.'

'Shall we get started?' Christian said, pulling out a chair

and sitting down. 'Steve, you're not under arrest. However, this conversation will be filmed and recorded. As you know, your parents were killed this morning and we believe you brother shot them in their home. I truly am very sorry for your loss.'

Steve looked up into Christian's eyes and saw the sentiment was genuine. 'Thank you.'

'We've looked at the record of people coming to visit you in prison and saw that Jake was a regular visitor in the first six months but then suddenly stopped. Why was that?'

Steve paused for effect. He knew time wasn't on the police's side, but he had no hurry to get back to Wakefield Prison. He could quite happily spend the night here. He took a sip of his coffee, leaned back in his chair and thought about his reply.

'The thing you need to know about Jake,' he began, 'is that he looked up to me. He idolised me. He's three years older than me, but he put me on a pedestal. I was always the confident, happy one, even as children. He followed me around and always wanted to play with me and my mates rather than get friends of his own. Me going to prison sort of burst the bubble.'

'He was disappointed with you?' Sian asked.

'Disappointed. Upset. Angry. He wanted to know why, when I seemed to have everything, did I turn to, well, the dark side, I suppose you'd call it,' he said with a slight smile.

'What did you say to that?' Sian was struggling to compose herself. Steve Harrison had caused the deaths of so many people today – police officers, school teachers and pupils – and his contempt for them was causing a rage to build inside her she'd never felt before. Sian had never known true hatred. She did now.

Again, Steve took his time to think of a reply. 'I don't think I did. I couldn't give him the answers he was looking for because I didn't know them.'

'You do, though, don't you?' Sian said. 'You killed all those people because you thought they hadn't served enough time for the crimes they'd committed. You believed they should have been given tougher prison sentences. You took the law into your own hands and hanged them. You were the judge, jury and executioner.'

'If you say so.'

'What would you say?'

'I'd say that's your interpretation of the events.'

'Are you saying I'm wrong?'

'No. Theories aren't wrong until they've been proven so,' he said, leaning forward on the table. 'This is lovely coffee, by the way.'

'Enlighten me, Steve,' Sian said, matching his body language and leaning forward. 'If you weren't killing to seek justice, why were you doing it? What was the motive behind your crimes? Come on, you have a captive audience here. Give us an insight into your mind.'

'Ok,' he cleared his throat. 'I killed the first victim, that paedophile, because he deserved to die. The rest... I did it because I enjoyed it.'

Sian swallowed hard. She leaned back in her seat as if trying to put as much distance between herself and Steve as she could.

'Why did you kill Faith Easter?'

'I just said; because I enjoyed it,' he said slowly. 'Although, with Faith, there was a second reason.'

'Go on.'

'I wanted to see Matilda suffer. You should have seen her

face when I threw Faith over the bannister and she fell, the rope tightening around her neck. Matilda actually reached out to catch her. Silly cow. She'll have made Faith's death take longer. If she'd have let her drop, she'd have snapped her neck and it would have been lights out in seconds. I like to think Matilda spends her nights thinking of that moment. I like to think she has nightmares about it.' There was a satisfied smile on Steve's lips and he knew the twinkle in his eyes was back.

'You felt hatred towards Matilda?' Sian asked.

'Oh, absolutely.'

'Is that what today has all been about?'

Steve's face dropped. He'd been tricked into moving away from talking about his brother's one-man gun fight. If he'd been genuinely upset by his parents' murder and Jake's actions, he wouldn't have been able to revel in his own crimes and taunt Sian as much as he had.

'You're good,' he said, admitting defeat. 'You're very good, Sian. I underestimated you.'

'You knew today was going to happen, didn't you? You knew Jake was going to kill your parents and attempt to murder DCI Darke. Did you put him up to it?'

'No comment,' he said, sitting back and folding his arms.

'Did you tell him where to get the guns from and how to make a bomb?'

'No comment.'

'Was it your idea to have a random shooting from the Parkway to throw us off the scent?'

'No comment.'

'Where is he going next, Steve?' Christian asked. 'Where's the next attack going to be?'

'No comment.'

'Answer the fucking questions,' Shaun Cox said, swiftly elbowing Steve in the face, knocking him off his chair.

Christian and Sian jumped up from their seats.

'Sorry,' Shaun said. 'I can't stand narcissistic wankers.'

Chapter Sixty-Three

J ake was parked in the corner of the car park at the Royal Hallamshire Hospital. His dirty white van was sheltered by trees on one side and the darkness of the evening on the other. He hunkered down in his seat, watching and waiting.

It was a large hospital and the number of spaces available in the car park did not equal the number of staff and visitors, which meant it was always full, day and night, so Jake had been lucky to grab this spot. He had no intention of moving. Not just yet.

Jake removed his seat belt and stepped out of the van. It was a cold evening; it had finally stopped drizzling, and the sky was beginning to clear. The clouds were dispersing, the stars were twinkling, and the full moon was lighting up the sky. He loved the winter. He loved the cold. He spent many a night in the back garden just looking up at the moon, wondering what it would be like to leave Earth, leave all these hateful bastards behind and start from scratch on another planet.

He pulled open the sliding doors at the side of the van. It was dark inside, but he could make out the shadow of his victim. He took a mobile phone from his back pocket, turned it on and switched on the torch. He aimed it directly into her face. She squinted. She was filthy. Her face was wet from crying and she looked to be in pain. Her wrists and ankles were firmly tied together with rope.

'Are you all right?' he asked. There was a sadness to his voice, as if, finally, the events of the day, the horror he'd inflicted on the city, had sunk in.

She squealed and shook her head.

'Are you in pain?'

She nodded.

Jake climbed into the van. She tried to get away from him but there was no room and she was severely restricted. He nudged up to her, put his left arm around her shoulders and told her to look into the camera. He smiled as he leaned his head towards her and took a selfie. He stared at it for a long time before showing it to her.

'I hate having my photo taken, don't you?' he said. 'I remember Ruth saying I had a nice smile. Not as nice as Steve's, obviously, but it made my eyes sparkle, apparently. What do you think?' He looked at her, but she didn't react. 'It's all bollocks, though, really, isn't it? People say what they want you to hear. It's false flattery to lure you into their trust. Do you believe in happy endings?'

She didn't answer. She couldn't. The tape around her mouth was restricting her speech to moans and squeaks. With dirty fingers, blood beneath his nails, he slowly pulled the tape away.

She gasped for breath, taking in the cold air from outside of the open van. She licked her lips and tried to get moisture back into her dry mouth.

'Do you think you could untie my wrists? I'm very uncomfortable.'

'Sorry, love. I can't do that. I was told to get an insurance policy, and that's what you are.'

'Who told you? Who put you up to this?'

'Don't. Ask. Questions,' he said, his eyes closed tightly, a vein throbbing in the side of his neck. 'If all goes well, you'll be back home in your own bed tonight.'

'You don't really want to do this, do you? I can see it in your eyes. This isn't the real you.'

He half laughed. 'I don't know what the real me is. I've no idea who I am. I've never fitted in anywhere, not at school or with my family. I've always been an outsider. Everything I do fails.'

'I'm sure that's not true.'

'It is. So, do you believe in happy endings?'

She nodded. There were tears in her eyes.

'How can you? We all have one thing in common; we die. It doesn't matter how long we live for, what we achieve, we all die in the end. That's not a happy ending.'

'I don't think that matters,' she said softly. 'It's what we do while we're alive that counts. If you can look back in your final moments and see that you've been happy, you've made others happy, you've made a difference to people's lives, then it doesn't matter if you die aged twenty-three or ninety-three.'

'Let's say today is your last day. Let's say your husband doesn't get here in time and I kill you. Knowing that, can you look back on your life and say you've been happy, that you've made others happy?'

Tears rolled down her face. She tried to speak a couple of

times, but her emotions wouldn't let her. Jake leaned towards her and wiped her eyes with the edge of his sleeve.

'Yes. I think I can,' she eventually answered. 'I'm married. We have a very happy marriage. I have two daughters whom I love very much, and I know they love me. They're growing up to respect others, and I know they're going to become good-natured young women. They'll be a credit to me and my husband.'

'But is that enough? You're just doing what society expects of you – to get married and have kids. Is that really enough?'

She smiled. 'I've never been an ambitious person. I've never wanted to climb a mountain or run a huge business. My family was very poor when I was a child and all I wanted was to have a nice house with a big garden and enough money to live comfortably. I've got that. I've achieved what I set out to do. So, yes, I'm happy.' Again, she smiled through the tears.

'I wanted a wife and children, too,' he said wistfully. 'I found the wife. Ruth. She was beautiful. But when ... well, when things happened, she turned her back on me. She wouldn't help me when I needed her. I can't trust anyone.'

'Look,' she said, shuffling closer to him. 'I know we haven't met under the most normal of situations, but I'd like to think I'm a good judge of character, and I can see you've been dealt a very bad hand. You're not an evil person. You can turn this around.'

He turned to her. His eyes were wide and cold. 'I've lost count of the amount of people I've killed today. I murdered my parents. I put a gun in my wife's mouth and pulled the trigger. I chained the doors of a school then walked along the corridors shooting people at random. My brother is Steve Harrison. He's in prison for murdering six people. There is evil running through us both. Nothing can change that.'

She was shaking from pure fear, though she pretended it was the cold air. 'You are stronger than you give yourself credit for. You can change. You don't have to kill any more people.' She placed her hands on his arm. 'I'm not going to lie to you and say you won't go to prison, you will, but help is available. I think you're misunderstood, and you need someone to talk to. People will listen. I'll listen.'

A clock chimed somewhere. Jake looked at his watch. They'd been chatting for over half an hour.

'Sorry, I don't have time for this right now.' He moved and jumped out of the van.

'Wait. Wait. Talk to me. I'll listen. We can sort something out between us.'

He picked up a roll of duct tape and tore off a strip. 'There's no point in talking. I have a very rare form of blood cancer. It's flowing all around me, eating away at me from the inside. I'll be dead before the summer. I don't want a long-drawn-out death.' He secured the tape across her mouth.

From a bag, he took out a Glock pistol and loaded a full magazine. He checked the ammunition in the Heckler & Koch rifle and slung it over his shoulder.

'I have enjoyed this chat, though. Thank you.'

Chapter Sixty-Four

'I don't understand how Steve could have known Jake was planning all this if they haven't had any contact for over two years,' Sian said.

Christian and Sian were in the HMET suite with Aaron and prisoner officer Shaun Cox. Finn was making them all a coffee. Following the chat and Shaun elbowing Steve in the face, it was decided a break was needed. Steve wasn't in a state to continue anyway with a broken nose. He was currently being assessed by a doctor with the other two prison officers standing guard.

'All of Steve's letters into and out of the prison get thoroughly checked,' Shaun said. 'He gets a lot of mail.'

'Really? Who from?' Aaron asked. He lifted Sian's snack supply out of her desk and placed it on top. He told Shaun to help himself.

'Mostly women. They send him cards, photos, love letters. They come from all over the world. And when it's his birthday or Christmas or Valentine's Day, well, we're inundated. I'm telling you, he's a popular bloke.'

'I've never understood why people write to serial killers,' Finn said, handing around the drinks. 'He's killed six people. Why are woman attracted to someone like that?'

'Hybristophilia,' Sian said.

'Sorry?'

'That's what it's called when a woman is attracted to a man known to have committed some outrage such as murder. Hybristophilia.'

'How the hell do you know that?'

'It was a question in a pub quiz a few weeks back,' she said with a smile. 'Some women probably believe they can be the one to change him from his evil ways. Others may see him as a little lost boy that they can nurture. A few likely want to share the media spotlight in the hopes of getting on the chat-show circuit or maybe even writing a book. And then there's the notion that an incarcerated male is actually the perfect boyfriend. She knows where he is every night, he's not going to be out drinking and chatting up other women, and she doesn't have to wash his pants.'

'Weirdos. Every single one of them,' Shaun said. 'I've read some of the letters Steve's received. Some of them make even me blush.'

'But he's received nothing from Jake?' Christian asked. He was rummaging around the snack drawer but pulled his hand out without picking anything. He had no appetite.

'Hand on heart, none whatsoever.'

'So we're back to my original question,' Sian said. 'How could Steve have known?'

'Maybe he didn't,' Aaron suggested. 'Don't forget, this is a change from the humdrum for Steve. He's out of prison for the first time in years. He's going to want to make the most of it. By saying he's helped his brother, or knows of what's going to happen next, he's keeping himself useful to us. He's got the power back that he had when he was committing his crimes.'

'That's true,' Sian agreed.

'So, what do we do? Do we ignore what he's saying, send him back to the prison and try and find Jake ourselves?' Christian asked.

Shaun Cox's mobile rang. He made his excuses and went to the other side of the room to answer it.

'I think it's more than likely that he's killed himself,' Sian said. 'Don't gunmen usually do that after they've been on a shooting spree?'

Chief Constable Martin Featherstone pulled the door open and entered the suite. His jacket was unbuttoned, as were the first two on his shirt. His tie was loose, and he looked harassed.

'That Danny Hanson is like a sodding Jack Russell nipping at your ankles,' he said.

'You have to admire his stamina,' Sian said.

'Little shit,' he said, perching next to Sian on one of the desks. 'I've been speaking with Inspector Porter – Gavin, is it? – I've told him to remain at Stannington Secondary School for the foreseeable. There are still a lot of victims on site, and maybe Jake has killed himself and they just haven't found him yet, I've no idea. What's the thought process you're all mulling over here?'

'Sorry to interrupt,' Shaun said. 'DS Mills, have you got an email address the governor can send some photos of Steve's visitors to?'

'Sure.' Sian jumped down from the table and went over to him.

'There are two thoughts,' Christian began. 'Either Jake has shot himself and he's still in the school, or he's gone off somewhere else to do it – either way he'll be dead. Or there's a chance he's planning a fourth attack.' He felt his mobile vibrate in his pocket. He took it out, looked at the screen and put it back.

'Do you need to get that?' Featherstone asked.

'No. It's fine. If he is planning a fourth attack, we need to know where. Now, the first one was, we're assuming, in revenge for his brother by targeting the police force. The second was random to keep us occupied while he could get to the school undetected in order to kill his wife. If there is to be a fourth attack, we've no idea where that could be as he seems to have achieved his goals.'

'The ones that we know about,' Aaron added.

'Unless … no,' Finn said, then quickly retracted.

'Go on,' Christian said.

'I was just thinking on what Steve was saying. He has a real grudge against the police force, DCI Darke in particular, seeing as she caught him. If this is a revenge thing, then it's not worked, as Matilda is still alive.'

'And that prick Danny Hanson has been all over TV and radio saying she's survived the attack,' Aaron said.

'His next attack could be at the hospital to kill Matilda for his brother,' Finn continued.

'I'll get on to Inspector Porter,' Featherstone said, getting off the desk and heading for the door. 'Christian, we can't have another shitstorm like we had at the school. I don't want any police there unless necessary. This needs to be an extremely covert operation.'

'Agreed.'

'What's going on?' Sian asked when she came back to the group.

'We think Jake's going after Matilda at the hospital.'

'Bloody hell! Shouldn't we warn them?'

'Featherstone's doing that.'

'So, what are we supposed to do? Sit around here twiddling out thumbs while Aaron empties my snack drawer?'

Aaron threw an unopened Mars back into the drawer.

'There's nothing we can do,' Christian said.

'There bloody is. We've lost too many of our officers today and I'm not going to sit back while we lose another.'

'Where are you going?'

'To the Hallamshire,' she said, snatching up her coat from the back of her chair.

Chapter Sixty-Five

Alone in a cubicle in the toilets on the ground floor of the police station, he took out his phone and looked at the screen. The message was from an unknown number, as were all the others he'd received today. His hands were shaking as he unlocked the phone. He took a deep breath and opened the message.

He clamped a hand to his mouth as he saw the photograph of Jake grinning to the camera with his arm around his wife, who was bound and gagged. She was crying. She looked scared, frightened, and in pain. What had that bastard done to her? A worse thought: what was that bastard planning to do to her next?

The message attached to the photo read:

At the hospital now. It'll all be over within the next half an hour.

He hoped so. It pained him seeing his wife in such distress. He wanted her back. He needed her back. He couldn't live without her. If he had to allow Matilda to die in order for his wife to live, then so be it. She didn't have any children, and she was still struggling following James's death. Her parents were still alive, and she had a sister, but they'd understand if she was killed in the line of duty. How would his girls cope without their mother?

He turned off the phone and put it back in his pocket. He lifted the lid on the toilet and vomited.

Chapter Sixty-Six

'Can you believe any of this is happening?' Sian said from the front passenger seat, staring out of the window at the dark Sheffield streets.

Aaron had stepped outside the police station for some fresh air and saw Sian's car was still in the car park. He went over, leaned down to look in the driver's side window and saw his colleague in floods of tears. The emotion of the last few hours had finally caught up with her. He opened the door, pulled her out and held her tight against his chest. When she'd finished crying, he saw that her tears had soaked his jumper. He told her to get in the passenger seat and he'd drive her to the hospital.

'All those kids in that school,' Sian said as they pulled out the police car park. 'There must have been more than twenty dead. To do something like that is beyond evil,' she said, her voice filled with tears.

'Are you sure you're all right? I can take you home to Stuart if you'd prefer.'

'Of course I'd prefer to go home. I want nothing more to go

to bed, snuggle up to Stuart and wake up tomorrow to find this has been a horrible dream. But … I can't. I need to see this through. I'm not going to rest until I know that bastard is either in a cell or on a mortuary slab.'

She dug in her pocket for a tissue and blew her nose. She turned to Aaron. 'How are you?'

'Numb,' he answered quickly.

'We haven't spoken much lately, have we?'

'We don't work together anymore.'

'How are things with you and Katrina?'

'Over.'

'I'm sorry.'

'So am I. But, like you said at the time, it was of my own doing. I've only myself to blame.'

'I shouldn't have said that.'

'Yes, you should. You were right. I cheated on my wife with a woman who obviously had a few screws loose. She kept asking me to leave Katrina and move in with her, but I wouldn't, so she took her revenge. She lied about being pregnant, got her story in the papers and ruined my marriage.' They pulled up at a red traffic light, which lit up the whole interior of the car. Aaron turned to Sian. 'No. *I* ruined my marriage and I'm paying for it. It's my fault. Nobody else's.'

'I'm sorry,' she said again.

'So am I.'

Sian's mobile pinged with the sound of an incoming email. She took out her phone and unlocked the screen. She cast her eyes along the message.

'Oh my God,' she exclaimed.

'What is it?'

'Shaun said the governor of Wakefield Prison had got images of all the people who have been visiting Steve Harrison since he's been inside. There haven't been that many, but he's emailed them through to me. Look who's been to see him every two weeks for the past year!' she said holding up her phone.

'Fuck me!' Aaron said.

Chapter Sixty-Seven

'PC Steve Harrison. Can you tell me what ward Matilda Darke is on please?' Jake said. He stood at the reception desk on the ground floor of the Royal Hallamshire Hospital. He held his brother's warrant card and was wearing his brother's police uniform, though he'd had to change the shirt to hide the bloodstains. He tried his hardest not to look up at the CCTV cameras.

While waiting, he used the hand sanitiser provided and smiled at the woman next to him in the queue for information. He was the very image of the dedicated copper.

'She's in the Neuro Critical Care Unit on K floor. The lifts are through the double doors on your left.' The receptionist smiled.

'Thank you,' Jake said. He picked up the rucksack at his feet and headed for the lifts.

A slow-moving lift and people getting on and off at every floor meant it seemed to take an age for Jake to reach K floor. Whenever someone entered, they looked at Jake as if they'd never seen a police officer before, giving him a lingering look before relaxing their face and proffering a reassuring smile as if they felt safer in the presence of a constable. They would all have heard of the shootings around the city today and would no doubt feel nervous about being away from the safety of their homes. However, getting into a lift with a copper seemed to give them a sense of security and their smiles were warm and genuine. Jake couldn't help but smile back. He even helped one little old lady when she dropped her shopping bag and several packets of biscuits fell out.

'Thank you, young man. They're for my Henry. He's got such a sweet touch.'

'You're welcome,' Jake said, putting on his best sickly voice.

The journey continued and finally the lift pinged, signalling K floor. He was glad to get out of the lift. It was warm in there. He could feel sweat running down his back and prickling his armpits. Was it the heat from being in such a confined space or was it the sense that he was nearing the end? He knew he'd never be able to escape from the hospital alive. Hopefully he'd done enough so he could get to Matilda in time before the police did. He could die happy knowing Matilda was dead and his brother had his revenge.

The waiting area outside the bank of lifts was empty. Once the doors had closed behind him, he stood in the middle and allowed the silence, the warmth, the closeness to envelope him. This was an old hospital and badly in need of decorating. It was a depressing place. No wonder people walked around with glum expressions. All they had to cheer them up was generic lifeless prints on the dull walls, uncomfortable seats and an out-of-order vending machine.

He went over to the map on the wall, found where the Neuro Critical Care department was, and set off down the maze of corridors.

Chapter Sixty-Eight

Aaron entered the car park at speed. They were both tossed about as they went over a speed bump. He didn't bother parking, he merely pulled up and stopped outside the entrance. He and Sian jumped out and ran into the police station.

'Where's he likely to be?' she asked.

'I've no idea.' He looked at his watch. 'Try the canteen first?'

'Good a place as any.'

They headed for the canteen. Despite not being very tall, Sian charged off with such determination that six-foot Aaron had to trot to keep up with her. Sian was on a mission, and she refused to accept failure as an option.

She pushed open the double doors with such force they slammed against the walls on either side. The canteen wasn't packed, but those in there enjoying a much-needed cup of tea or a comforting bite to eat to keep them fuelled for whatever the rest of the day had to throw at them turned to look at the noise.

Sian spotted him straight away. He was alone by the window, a mug of tea in front of him and a look of angst and worry on his young face.

Sian had never felt such rage and anger before in her life. If she was plugged in, she could power the entire station for a week. Everything around her seemed to fade away as she took short steps towards him. Her eyes didn't leave him once. His couldn't settle on her, they were frantically darting around the large room.

When she reached the table he was sitting at, she stopped and glared at him with a deathly stare.

'Give me one good reason why I shouldn't put your head through that window right now,' she said. Despite her body physically shaking, her voice was cool and calm, though there was a great anger waiting to erupt any moment.

He didn't say anything. A tear rolled down his cheek.

'Don't you dare. Don't you dare cry after what you've caused today.'

Aaron stepped forward. 'Justin Rix, I am arresting you for conspiracy to murder. You do not have to say anything, but it may harm your defence if you do not mention, when questioned, something you later rely on in court. Anything you do say may be given in evidence.'

'I really am sorry,' he said, his voice cracking with emotion.

Aaron grabbed him by the elbow and lifted him out of the seat. As they headed for the doors, all eyes were on the young PC. One of their own had been involved in a murderous rampage that had caused the senseless death of seven of their colleagues. It didn't seem possible.

Chapter Sixty-Nine

PC Justin Rix was twenty-three years old. At six foot one, he looked clumsy, with large ears and a large nose in the centre of his pale face. His thick white-blond hair was stylishly spiked, and his complexion was smooth, as if a razor had never scraped across his chin.

He sat at the table in the interview room in his uniform, his back straight, his eyes facing forwards. There wasn't a single hint of emotion on his face.

'I'm not saying anything until my solicitor gets here,' he said. His voice was soft, and he refused to look up and make eye contact with Christian and Sian. He was leaning over the table, knotting his fingers together nervously.

Christian slapped the photographs on the table in front of him. 'You can't deny this is you visiting Steve Harrison in Wakefield Prison.'

Justin didn't say anything.

'Why?'

'I'm perfectly allowed to visit anyone I like,' he stated.

'Why Steve?'

He glanced quickly from Christian to Sian and back but didn't answer.

'Are you related to him?'

'No.'

'Why have you been visiting him every two weeks for the past year?' Christian barked.

Sian placed a hand on Christian's arm, telling him to step back. She pulled out a chair and sat at the table. Time was of the essence. It was important they located Jake before he could launch another attack, but it was obvious Justin was scared and shouting at him wasn't going to get him to open up and reveal everything he knew. She hoped Featherstone was pulling out all the stops to protect Matilda. She couldn't lose anyone else today.

'You love him, don't you?' Sian said, her voice quiet and calm, almost serene. 'You've been writing to him for a while and you've been acting as a messenger between Steve and Jake, setting up everything that's happened today. I'm right, aren't I?'

Justin couldn't hide his smile. 'I do love him. He loves me too. He's said so. We're going to get married.'

'For God's sake,' Christian said. He pulled out a chair and sat next to Sian.

'You don't know. You don't understand,' Justin exclaimed. 'Steve is an intelligent, warm and loving bloke. He writes such beautiful letters. It was ages before he replied to me after I started writing, but once we got talking to each other, everything seemed to – I don't know – fall into place.'

'Did you tell him you were in the police force before his first letter to you?' Sian asked.

'Yes. I sent him a photo of me in my uniform. That's when he wrote back. He told me I looked very smart and handsome.

I think I'm awkward-looking, but Steve Harrison said I was handsome. I couldn't believe it. I mean, have you seen him? He's gorgeous. That smile.' Justin's face was beaming.

'You weren't at South Yorkshire Police then, were you?'

'No. I was at West Yorkshire Police. It was Steve who said I should get a transfer here.'

'Did he say why?'

'He said it was a good station. He also said I'd be closer to his brother. He wanted me to look out for him.'

'You passed messages to him?'

'Yes. There's nothing wrong with that, is there?'

'Did you read the messages?'

'No. They were in a sealed envelope.'

'Did you have any idea what was going to happen today?' Christian asked.

'No,' he answered quickly. 'Hand on heart. I had no idea what was going to happen today. I was passing notes to Jake. I thought they were just Steve trying to get Jake to visit him again. I didn't…'

He words were lost to his tears. Sian reached forward and placed a hand on his arm.

'Justin, did Steve ask you to forge a letter from a GP saying he had a rare cancer?'

Eventually, Justin looked up. He nodded.

'Why?'

'He didn't say.'

'Didn't you question him?'

'No.'

'Why not? Didn't you think it was cruel to say someone had cancer when they didn't?'

'I did, but then I thought maybe it was Steve's way of

getting Jake to visit. If Jake thought he didn't have long left to live then maybe he'd want to see Steve to say a final goodbye.'

'Oh my God,' Christian said, turning away.

Sian took a deep breath. 'When did you realise Jake was behind the events of today?'

He wiped his eyes with his sleeves like a naughty schoolboy would. 'Just after dinner time. He asked me if it was true that Matilda wasn't dead. I said it was. He said Steve wanted her dead.'

'Didn't you ask why?'

He shook his head.

'The shooting at the Parkway was a distraction, wasn't it?' Christian asked.

He nodded.

'And what happened at the school?'

'He wanted to kill his wife,' Justin said quietly, looking down at the table.

Sian took a deep breath. 'Where is he now?'

'I don't know.'

'Do you have a number for him?'

'No. Every time he calls it's from a different number.'

'I think he's going to go to the hospital and try to kill Matilda. Am I right?'

Justin didn't say anything, just looked down at the table and continued to play with his bony fingers. Sian jumped up to leave.

'You can't stop him,' Justin shouted.

Sian and Christian both turned back from where they stood in the doorway.

'If he doesn't kill her, then Steve will see it as a failure. He'll think I haven't done my job properly. He won't want to be with me anymore,' he said. There was a look of loss and desperation in his eyes.

'I've got news for you, Justin,' Christian spat.

'We don't have time for this.' Sian grabbed Christian by the arm and pulled him out of the interview room.

———

Justin Rix was to be charged with conspiracy to murder, and nobody was showing any compassion to a man who had orchestrated the cold murder of their friends and colleagues.

'What was that word you used to describe people who love serial killers?' Christian asked.

'Hybristophilia.'

'So, Justin fancied Steve, and Steve exploited the fact to suit his own ends.'

Christian and Sian were still in the interview room. Neither of them wanted to return to the HMET suite. It didn't feel the same anymore, having lost so many of their team that day.

'He's a great manipulator. We know that from the way he treated Faith Easter.'

'I feel absolutely drained.' Sian rubbed the temples on the side of her head firmly, trying to stave off an encroaching headache.

'If Jake has gone to the hospital to kill Matilda, let's hope Porter's got there before he has,' Christian said.

There was a light knock on the door. Finn Cotton was standing in the doorway with a mobile phone in his hand.

'I've been through Justin's mobile,' he said, holding it aloft. 'There have been a lot of calls and texts to Danny Hanson today.'

'Shit,' Christian said, bowing his head. 'He's been feeding

information to the press. I bet that was Steve's idea, too. That man is going to be in so much shit. Finn, get everything you can from that phone.'

'Will do.'

Sian looked at her watch. The waiting was the hardest part. She felt sick. Her heart was in her mouth with what could possibly be happening right now at the Royal Hallamshire Hospital.

'I should be there.'

'And risk what happened to Rory happening to you? I don't think so. You're better off here.'

'I can't sit around waiting.' She kicked out at a chair, sending it toppling to the ground. 'Matilda's parents are there. Daniel is there. What if he's got another bomb, Christian? What if he's got a hand grenade or something? Who knows how many innocent people are going to die.'

She turned and looked out of the window. It was dark, but the floodlights outside lit up the car park. It had been cleared of the dead bodies of her colleagues, but she could still see them in her mind's eye. She turned around, putting her back to the scene of carnage, but it was in front of her too.

Everything about this job, this station, was tainted now. It would never be the same again. Sian had no idea how she'd be able to get out of bed tomorrow morning and come to work in the aftermath of all this.

The sound of screaming and shouting from the custody suite echoed down the corridor.

'What the hell's going on?' Christian asked.

He walked towards the noise, Sian following, and they saw uniformed officers clinging onto Justin as he pleaded and begged for Steve Harrison to help him as he was led through by Shaun Cox.

'Steve, I did everything you wanted me to,' Justin screamed. 'I gave Jake all the notes and letters. I've done my part. We can be together now, Steve. We can be together.'

Sian watched in horror as Justin was pulled away while Steve simply stood at the side of the room with a smirk on his face.

'Fans can get so clingy sometimes, can't they?' he said. The famous twinkle in his eyes was back.

'You really don't care who you destroy, do you?' Sian asked, walking up to him.

He leaned forward, as far as he could being handcuffed to Shaun. He looked Sian up and down and licked his lips.

'Don't worry, sweetheart,' he said quietly. 'I won't destroy you.' He licked her face.

Shaun Cox grabbed him and pulled him away.

'Don't let him see you cry.' Christian put his arm around Sian but it was too late as a single tear rolled down her cheek.

Chapter Seventy

S ian had needed a breather, a few minutes alone to scrub her face and call her husband for him to say the right things to help her calm down and try to make sense of all this madness. She ended the call, and as she came out of the toilet cubicle, she caught her reflection in the stained mirrors above the sinks. There was the smallest hint of a smile on her face, which quickly disappeared. Stuart always knew what to say whenever she'd had a bad day or was feeling down. He always managed to perk her up. However, she felt guilty for having a moment of happiness when she was surrounded by such devastation.

She left the toilets, almost bumping into Inspector Porter in the corridor.

'Jesus, Gavin, you scared the life out of me. How did it go? Did you catch him?'

'Who?' he asked.

'Jake. At the hospital?'

'What are you talking about? I've been at the school all

afternoon. There's not much more we can do at the moment until—'

Sian cut him off. 'The Chief Constable said he was calling you to send you to the Hallamshire.'

'He didn't.'

'He got on his phone as he was leaving HMET. I saw him do it.'

'Well, he didn't call me.'

Sian's eyes widened as realisation dawned. 'Bloody hell! Come with me, Gavin.'

They ran to the HMET suite where Christian was in his office talking on the phone to his wife. He had tears in his eyes. He quickly ended the call as Sian launched into an explanation of what she suspected was going on. Together, all three ran towards Valerie's old office and burst in.

Martin Featherstone was sat at the desk. He looked gaunt, as if all life had been drained out of him. There were tearstains on his face. He was staring down at his mobile phone in the middle of the desk.

'Martin,' Sian said, stepping tentatively closer to the desk. 'What's going on?'

He looked up slowly.

'You didn't send an armed response team to the hospital, did you?'

A wave of emotions ran across his face. His bottom lip wobbled, and more tears fell. He shook his head.

'I couldn't,' he croaked. 'He's got Roisin. He said he'd kill her if anything stopped him. I can't lose her. She's been through so much lately.'

'What?' Christian asked, stepping forward.

Martin unlocked his phone, opened the text messaging app and turned it around on his desk, pushing it towards him.

The DI stepped forward. He picked it up, looked at the photo of the CC's wife trussed up in the back of a van, tears streaming down her dirty face. He handed it to Sian.

'How long have you known about this?'

He shook his head and said nothing.

'He's been calling you, hasn't he?'

He nodded. 'He wants Matilda dead. He told me if I didn't keep the police off his back until he'd done it, then he'd kill Roisin, film it and send the video to my kids. I couldn't … I…' He choked on his words. He was a shell of the man they knew him to be.

'You're allowing him to murder DCI Darke to save your wife?' Sian asked, venom in her voice.

'I can't lose her,' he said softly. He looked at his watch. 'It'll be over now. I'm just waiting for his call to tell me where Roisin is. I'm so sorry.'

'You bastard,' Sian said. There was pure hatred in her voice.

'I'll call security at the hospital and send a team out,' Gavin said, turning and storming out of the office.

'Sian, come on,' Christian said, grabbing her by the shoulder and trying to pull her away from the death stare she had fixed on the Chief Constable.

She ignored him. 'It's not just Matilda who's at the hospital. Her parents are there. Her boyfriend is there. Do you think he's just going to walk in, shoot her, then walk back out again? He'll kill them all. Not to mention the doctors and nurses who'll try to help. Do you have any idea what you've done, how many people will have died because of you?'

'Sian, leave it, come on. It might not be too late,' Christian said.

'I can't lose Roisin,' he said again through a torrent of tears.

'Do you honestly think he's going to let her go? He's killed dozens of people today. One more won't make any difference.' She stepped forward, placed her hands on the desk and leaned close to him. 'You should have come to us. As a team we could have worked together to have stopped this going so far if we'd been given all the facts earlier. You know that. How the fuck did you get to be Chief Constable in the first place?' she screamed.

'Sian, now is not the time.' Christian practically had to pick her up to drag her out of the room.

'If Matilda's dead, it'll be all your fault,' Sian screamed as she was pushed through the door.

The Chief Constable was left in silence. He looked down at the phone and pressed the screen, bringing it to life.

'Come on, you bastard, ring. Tell me where she is.'

Chapter Seventy-One

Jake Harrison found the Neuro Critical Care Unit after taking several wrong turns. Why did hospitals have to be so difficult to navigate? The door to the unit was closed and locked, accessible only by punching in the correct code number. He rang the bell above it and waited impatiently.

He'd been watching Chief Constable Martin Featherstone and his wife for some time. They were a couple who liked their routine, and it wasn't long before Jake learned their daily schedules by heart. There was one snag. Martin and Roisin seemed to be living separate lives.

Martin left the house early and didn't come back until late. Roisin worked regular hours, but she often went out for a drink or a meal with colleagues after work, and at weekends she spent time with her daughters rather than her husband. Did they even sleep in the same bed? How often did they have a meal together or sit down in front of the TV and chat about their day? If Roisin was to be his insurance policy, he needed Martin to want to save her life. The only way to do that was to remind Martin what he stood to lose.

So Jake had played the waiting game. He followed Roisin. He learned her schedule, her routine, her route to work and back. He spent weeks on her tail, and she had no idea. When the time was right, he launched his attack.

It was a dark night. The clouds were thick and heavy, hiding the moon. The new streetlamps Sheffield City Council had erected were next to useless unless you were standing directly beneath one. In the shadows of the trees, Jake grabbed Roisin from behind and threw her to the ground. He wanted to make it look like a violent mugging. He hadn't expected Roisin to put up much of a fight, but he'd underestimated her.

From her coat pocket, she pulled out her keys and swiped at his neck, scratching him with the rough end of a Yale key. He yelled out in pain and could feel the blood dripping down his shirt. Her feistiness made him angry. He kicked her in the stomach. She rolled over to protect herself, pulling her knees up to her chest. He kicked her in the back several times and jumped on her legs. He could hear the bones breaking beneath the heavy grips of his walking shoes. He didn't want her dead, but he wanted the bitch damaged.

As he walked away, he looked through her bag. He took her purse and mobile phone out and tossed the bag into bushes. He looked back and saw the prostate Roisin Featherstone curled up in the darkness.

It was a couple of days before the 'horror attack' made the newspapers. The journalist focused hard on the victim being the wife of a Chief Constable, and Martin gave a statement declaring his undying love to his wife, mother of his children and his best friend. It was touching and heartfelt. It almost made Jake sick.

Jake's stalking of the Featherstones continued. He watched as a worried-looking Martin spent long days and nights at the hospital. When Roisin was released after four weeks, she was led carefully to the car on crutches. In the following weeks, Martin accompanied his wife to all of her physiotherapy appointments, and they seemed to be spending more leisure time together, too. He followed them to restaurants, the theatre, days out at the coast. The attack had brought them together. They were in love again. They were right where Jake wanted them. He just hoped, now, that Martin had kept his side of the bargain. If he valued his wife as much as he said he did, he'd keep the police at bay long enough for him to finish Matilda off.

It was a while before a large nurse waddled down the corridor to the door. She squinted through the glass at Jake.

'We're in lockdown,' she said loudly.

'I'm police.' He stood back so she could see his uniform through the small window.

'I can see that,' she said with a smile. 'We've been informed not to let anyone in under any circumstance. This is a secure ward. Apart from fire exits, this is the only way in. We're all safe so there's no need for you to enter.'

'I appreciate that, ma'am. However, I need to see for myself everyone is safe. For all I know, you could be being held hostage and told to tell me everything is normal.'

'I'm sorry. I've had my orders,' she said, holding her hands out.

And I've had mine, he thought.

He pulled the Glock out of the rucksack he'd taken off his shoulders and was holding in front of him. The silencer was already screwed on. He held it up and fired twice. The first bullet shattered the glass, the second hit the nurse in the face. She was thrown backwards and hit the floor with a heavy thud.

Jake reached in through the hole in the door and unlocked it from the inside. As he stepped into the overheated ward, he saw people coming out of rooms to investigate the sound of glass breaking. He aimed the gun and fired.

He ignored the screams and allowed some of the medical staff to flee and hide. He knew he wasn't going to make it out of the ward alive, or in handcuffs, but he had a task to do and he couldn't let his brother down.

He walked up to the reception desk where two nurses were huddled behind.

'Where's Matilda Darke?' he asked. His voice was as calm and steady as if he were a visitor looking for a family member.

Neither of the young nurses reacted. He rolled his eyes and pointed the gun at one of the women.

'I will shoot her in the head right now if you don't tell me what room Matilda Darke is in,' he said, looking to the other nurse.

The nurse held her hands up and slowly stood up. She went over to the computer and, with shaking fingers, typed onto the keyboard. She was crying and made several mistakes, cursing herself and apologising.

'She's in B11,' she cried.

'Where's that?'

'Down the corridor. Turn left. It's the last door on the left.'

'Thank you,' he said with a smile. 'You've just saved your friend's life. Not yours, unfortunately.'

He aimed the gun at the nurse who'd help him and squeezed the trigger. Her head exploded. She dropped to the floor and the nurse who was already cowering was splattered with the blood and brain matter of her dead colleague.

Jake listened to her screaming as he made his way down the corridor.

'What the hell is going on out there?' Frank asked Penny.

They were both sat either side of Matilda's bed, watching her chest rise and fall as the machines breathed for her. They'd heard the sound of screams and assumed it was a patient in pain, but the terrifying sounds continued.

Penny was holding her daughter's hand. She looked up with tears in her eyes.

'Leave it, Frank. It's nothing to do with us.'

The door burst open, and Daniel Harbison almost fell into the room, slamming the door behind him and standing firmly in front of it.

'There's a gunman out there. I overheard him asking for Matilda. Then he shot a bunch of people.'

'What?' Frank asked, standing up.

'The attacks didn't stop at the police station this morning – there have been more all day. I think he's come to shoot Matilda.'

'Oh my God, Frank!' Penny said, descending into hysteria. Frank went over to her and held her in his arms.

'What are we going to do? Is there any way we can move her?' Frank asked.

'I doubt it. Not without a medical team,' Daniel said, looking at the bank of monitors and machines keeping Matilda alive.

Someone tried to open the door, but Daniel was blocking it. He turned and saw a doctor he had been speaking to in the corridor earlier through the glass. He was banging frantically on the door.

'Let me in! Let me in!'

Daniel opened the door, dragged the doctor in and closed it again.

The young doctor had blood on his striped shirt and spatter on his face. 'I've just seen three nurses gunned down. I've pressed the panic buttons and alerted security, but I don't think they'll be able to get here in time.'

Penny was shaking, in floods of tears as Frank held on to her tightly.

'Where is he?' Daniel asked the doctor.

'I don't know. He was at the nurses' station. There's a door at the end of this corridor between us and them that can be locked but I don't think we'll be able to close it without him seeing us.'

'It's worth a chance,' Daniel said. He looked to Matilda's parents who were looking at him with hopeful eyes. 'Do you have the numbers of any of Matilda's colleagues?'

'Yes. Sian's,' Penny said.

'Call her. Tell her what's happening.' He glanced over to Matilda. They hadn't officially been dating long, but his feelings for her ran deep. He wasn't going to let this madman kill her.

Without giving a second thought to his own safety, he opened the door and ran out into the corridor.

He headed for the open door at the end of the long corridor. Through it, he could see a nurse on the floor, lying in a pool of her own blood. He'd never seen a dead body before and lost crucial seconds registering the horror of the sight before he took off at speed.

He reached the door without knowing where the gunman was. He closed it, but it wouldn't fully shut. He pushed harder, but there was an obstruction. He looked down and saw the dead nurse's arm blocking it.

'Oh my God,' he said under his breath. He'd been slamming the door against someone's arm. He opened the door and senselessly kicked the arm out of the way. 'I'm so sorry,' he said, slamming the door closed. The mechanism locked. The only way for it to be opened now was with a code on the keypad on the other side.

Picking up a fire extinguisher, he slammed it down on the handle which fell off in one swift movement. There was no way the door could be opened from this side, even if the gunman shot the glass and reached inside.

He was headed back for Matilda's room when he heard the glass break behind him. He turned around and saw a man aiming a gun at him through the hole in the door. They made eye contact. The gunman smiled as he squeezed the trigger.

Chapter Seventy-Two

O nce again, Sian was on Glossop Road hurtling through the traffic towards the hospital. This time Christian was driving, and Aaron and Finn were in the back.

Sian was still seething from the confrontation with the Chief Constable. She had no idea what the fallout from all this would be, but surely he would have to answer some very serious questions. She doubted he'd still be Chief Constable at the end of the day. Life at South Yorkshire Police was never going to be the same again once all this was over.

Sian's mobile started ringing, bringing her out of her dark reverie. She struggled to pull it out from her coat pocket, which was being squashed under the weight of the flak jacket she was wearing over the top. She saw it was Matilda's mother calling and braced herself for the worst. She swiped to answer and put it on speaker so the others in the car could hear.

'Sian, it's Penny. Matilda's mum,' she said with a shaking voice. 'We're trapped. There's a gunman in the ward. He's shooting doctors and nurses. Daniel heard him asking for Matilda at the front desk. You need to send someone out here.'

'Penny, calm down,' Sian said. It was a stupid thing to say, but what else *could* she say. 'An armed response team is already on site and we're literally minutes away.'

'It's going to be too late,' she said, tears evident in her voice.

'Jesus Christ,' Finn said from the back seat.

'It's not,' Sian said. She too was struggling to hold back the tears. 'Penny, armed police are already in the building. We're going to contact them and let them know exactly where the gunman is. Just sit tight. I promise you we'll get you out of there.'

'I'm calling Gavin. It's ringing,' Aaron said.

Christian and Sian exchanged nervous glances. Both of them knew it was likely already too late.

Chapter Seventy-Three

The door to Matilda's room burst open and Daniel staggered inside, clutching his shoulder, blood seeping out through his fingers.

'Oh my God, Daniel's been shot,' Penny screamed into her phone.

The doctor leapt into action and grabbed hold of Daniel. He sat him down and looked at the wound.

'There's an exit wound. The bullet has gone straight through. I don't think there's any nerve damage, but we need to stem the blood flow. Can you pass me that towel?'

Frank handed the doctor a towel from Matilda's bedside locker, and he tied it tightly around the wound in Daniel's shoulder.

'Keep it in place, apply pressure and don't move.'

'It doesn't hurt. I'm fine,' Daniel said, almost calm.

'You're in shock.'

A barrage of gunfire was heard from the corridor.

Jake smashed the glass in the door, reached through and struggled to locate the handle. When he saw it lying on the floor, he had to smile. They certainly weren't making it easy for him to finish his job. He placed the Glock in his bag and took out the Heckler & Koch rifle. He changed the setting to continuously fire whenever he had his finger pressed on the trigger. He checked he had a full magazine, stood back and began firing around the hinges on the door.

In the rest of the hospital, as many people were being evacuated as possible. Doctors, nurses and administrative staff were calmly directing patients and visitors out of the building. It was a logistical nightmare but in the face of a gunman, there was no alternative. Those who were able to walk were told to do so. Wheelchairs were used for those less able patients, and in the most urgent of cases, patients were being wheeled out on their beds.

Christian pulled up, and all four climbed out of the car amid the melee of people aimlessly wandering about, not knowing where to go for their own safety.

He located Inspector Porter and headed for him with Sian and the others in tow.

'I've got a team heading up there right now. They can hear gunfire,' Porter said. He was wearing a headset so he could speak directly to his armed team. 'Is this really all about someone wanting to kill Matilda Darke?'

'Partly,' Sian said.

She looked up at the imposing twenty-one-storey concrete block. Almost every window was lit up. From the inside, she knew it gave glorious views of the whole city on a clear day.

The 1970s structure was a place of healing and safety. Now, it was the scene of a terrifying armed siege. Jake Harrison was volatile and unpredictable. There was no way anyone could foresee how this was going to end, or how many innocent people he would kill before he was done.

———————

Jake stopped shooting. With a swift kick, the door toppled. He walked steadily over the pile of spent cartridges and headed down the corridor towards room B11 where Matilda and her family were hiding. He'd kill the fucking lot of them. He stopped at the door and looked through the toughened glass. He heard a woman scream, probably Matilda's mother, and all eyes turned to face him. He smiled. He placed his hand on the door handle—

'Armed police! Drop your weapon.'

Jake turned to see a team of armed officers in armoured gear standing not ten feet away from him. All had guns aimed in his direction.

———————

The lift pinged, and the doors opened. Christian, Sian and Gavin stepped out into the corridor and walked in silence down the maze of corridors before they reached the entrance to the Neuro Critical Care Unit. They saw the carnage at their feet. Dead bodies littered the floor, riddled with bullet holes and surrounded by blood. These were doctors and nurses who had dedicated their lives to helping and saving others, who worked in difficult conditions and faced tightening budgets and poor wages on a daily basis, yet still continued to work for the good of the patients, and they'd been mercilessly gunned down.

'Do you have access to a hostage negotiator?' Gavin said as he stepped over bodies.

'We called for one earlier at the school, but I'm not sure if they ever turned up,' Christian said.

'I'd have thought the time for negotiating had long since passed,' Sian said. 'He doesn't want to talk. He just wants to kill.'

They approached the standoff between armed police and Jake Harrison but remained well back. In the ensuring chaos, Jake had taken a hostage. Standing in the corridor outside Matilda's room, he had his left arm wrapped around her father's throat, and a Glock pistol in his right hand, pressed firmly against Frank's temple. He was using him as a human shield.

Gavin was handed a mouthpiece attached to a loudspeaker. He cleared his throat.

'Jake, my name is Inspector Gavin Porter. I'm here to talk to you.'

'I can't see you,' Jake shouted his reply.

Gavin lowered the mouthpiece and took a deep breath. 'Looks like I'm going to have to do this face to face.'

'You go down that corridor and he'll shoot you,' Christian said.

'He's not going to talk to me like this.'

'He's not interested in talking. Like Sian said, he's past all that. Tell one of your men to shoot him in the knee or something.'

'He's holding a gun to Frank Doyle's head. There are four other people in that room and who knows how many others trapped in rooms down that corridor! He had a bomb at

Stannington School. There could be one in there with him. We need to assess the situation before anything happens,' Gavin said.

'Are you still there, Inspector Gavin Porter?' Jake said in an almost sing-song voice, taunting the police by showing he was in charge.

'Fuck,' Gavin said under his breath.

He looked from Sian to Christian before turning and heading for his team of officers at the top of the corridor. He gently made his way to the front.

'There you are. I was beginning to think you were one of those who sits behind a desk giving orders without seeing any real action,' Jake said.

'Not at all. What can I do for you, Jake?'

'You can call your men off.'

'You know I can't do that.'

'Then I'm afraid these good people are going to die,' he said, pressing the gun harder against Frank's head, causing him to call out in pain.

'Why are you doing this, Jake? You're not seeking revenge for your brother. It goes deeper than that.'

'Please don't try to psychoanalyse me. We'll be here for days if you try to understand what the fuck is going on in here,' he said, tapping the side of his head with the Glock.

'Then why don't you enlighten me? Share with me, Jake.'

He released a sigh. 'I'm really not interested in talking anymore. I've had enough.'

'Of what?'

'Of this. You try to do the right thing and you just get kicked in the teeth. Look at my brother. He was a good man. He wanted to be a policeman since he was a child. He wanted to help and save people, until you lot got your hands on him and turned him into a killer.'

'That's not what happened, Jake.'

'You poisoned him. He wasn't prepared to play the game and lick people's boots, so he had to be got rid of.'

'Jake, I'm Sian Mills,' Sian said, pushing through the crowd and stepping in front of Gavin. He tried to stop her, but she shook him off. 'I work with Matilda Darke. I knew your brother.'

Jake's eyes lit up in recognition. 'Yes. Steve mentioned you.'

She smiled. 'Steve was a good man, a good copper. He went down a different path and things went very dark for him. They don't need to go dark for you, too.'

'Take a look around you, Sian. It's pitch-black. I've killed so many people today. I've destroyed so much. Don't try to placate me by saying I can put all this behind me and move on.'

'Jake, this isn't you. You've been brainwashed. You're not a killer.'

'Why do people keep saying that?' he shouted through gritted teeth. 'Suddenly, everyone is an expert in who I am. Where were they last year, five years ago, ten years ago?'

The corridor was narrow. Sian could easily have touched the walls on either side with her arms outstretched. It was windowless and oppressive. She could hear Frank's laboured breathing as Jake's armed gripped him tight around the throat. Behind her, the collective breaths of the Armed Response team whistled in her ear. Yet, despite the close proximity, she felt completely alone as she looked Jake straight in the eye.

'Why did you try to kill yourself on Boxing Day?' Sian asked.

His face dropped. 'I...'

'You'd had enough, hadn't you? You didn't want to go ahead with Steve's plan anymore. It was too much. You didn't agree with what he intended, and you thought that by killing yourself, it would put a stop to it.'

A flurry of emotions swept across Jake's face, as if he was trying to make sense of what was before him, of where he suddenly found himself, of what had brought him to this point. It was a while before he spoke.

'I wanted to be like Steve for so long,' he said quietly.

'But you didn't want to be a killer, did you?' Sian asked.

He shook his head as tears rolled down his cheeks.

'Jake, the letter you received from the doctor saying you had cancer. It was forged.'

'What?'

'The man who's been passing you notes from your brother, Justin, forged the letter. Steve told him to. He wanted you to think you didn't have much time left so you'd do something like this rather than fade away in a hospice. You don't have cancer, Jake. Steve lied to you.'

'He … wouldn't. He's been good to me.'

Sian shook her head. 'He's been manipulating you from day one. Don't give in to his demands. Don't let him think he's won. You can be the bigger person, here, the better brother.'

Chapter Seventy-Four

Danny Hanson's contact was no longer answering his phone. There was no more news coming out of the police station, and standing around in the cold and dark with his fellow reporters on the off-chance someone might make a statement was not his idea of fun. When he saw Sian and Christian driving away at speed, he knew something was happening and decided to follow. The gunman hadn't been killed in the school shooting, which meant this was still a developing story. While the other members of the press were either still at the school or doing a piece to camera in front of South Yorkshire Police HQ, Danny was forcing Lewis to pack away his camera and get back in the van.

'Where are we going?' he asked.

'I haven't got a fucking clue,' Danny said as he looked in all directions out of the window.

Just then, an unmarked car shot past them at speed.

'I've always wanted to say this – follow that car!' He grinned.

'You're a prick, do you know that?' Lewis asked.

The roads were full of rush-hour traffic as people made their way home from work, and the journey to the hospital was on a busy route passing shops and offices and university buildings. Buses were parked in the middle of the road while passengers got on and off, and traffic lights stayed on red for a long time so more vehicles could join from side roads and trams could cross.

'Ignore the lights,' Danny shouted as Lewis began to slow down for a red light.

'Fuck off, we'll get smashed into.'

'Not if you put your foot down.'

'I'm not getting killed on your say-so, Danny,' he said as he came to a stop.

'You're a real pussy, do you know that?' Danny asked, turning to his cameraman.

'And you're a psychopath. There's more to life than work.'

The lights changed to green and Lewis set off.

'The polar bears are going to eat you alive if you ever get to the South Pole,' Danny said scornfully.

'Polar bears are at the North Pole, you ignorant prick.'

'Like it matters,' he huffed.

They had to stop just before the hospital as a police cordon had been put in place and traffic was being diverted.

'Something's definitely going on in the hospital,' Danny said, looking up at the concrete eyesore. 'Drive round the back.'

There was nowhere for them to go. Parked cars lined both sides of the road.

'Ok. Just pull up anywhere. Get your camera ready. I'll go and see if I can find out what's going on.'

Danny jumped out of the van. He looked at his watch. There was going to be a BBC News Special in less than half an hour, and Danny was needed to give a live update.

He ran down to the front of the hospital, bypassing doctors and nurses as they rushed patients to safety. The hospital was obviously being evacuated. This was big. Danny was struggling to suppress his smile. He didn't want to waste time asking someone medical what was happening, as they were known for being tight-lipped. So when he clocked an old lady in a dressing gown smoking a cigarette and looking up at the building, he made his way over. She looked the gossiping type.

'Excuse me, I'm Danny Hanson from BBC News—'

'Oh, yes, I've been watching you all day,' she interrupted, her face lighting up as she recognised him. 'You're a lovely-looking lad.'

'Thank you.' He felt himself blush. 'What's going on here at the hospital?'

'You're not going to put me on the telly, are you? I'm in my dressing gown and I've not combed my hair today.'

'No, I'm not. Don't worry.'

'Thank God for that. They say telly makes you look fat as well and these tablets I'm on have already made me put on half a stone.'

Danny's smile was stuck, though he was rapidly losing patience. 'What's going on inside?'

'Well, apparently, that gunman they've been looking for has gone in there and started shooting the place up. He's looking for a detective, I think the nurse said, the one who brought me out. I don't know why we had to evacuate. I'm only one floor up and they're all on K floor.'

'K floor?' he asked, looking up at the building.

'Yes. I'm missing *Eggheads* standing out here.'

Danny ignored her. He saw Lewis approaching with his camera and headed for him. 'We need to find a back way in. Everything's kicking off on K floor.'

Chapter Seventy-Five

Sian edged closer to Jake, taking baby steps. She knew she had the weight of armed response behind her, but it wouldn't be much help if Jake turned on her and fired. She looked to Frank Doyle. He seemed to be calm. His face was expressionless. He'd smiled at Sian a couple of times when they'd made eye contact, as if telling her he was fine.

'Jake, tell me what you want. We can't be here all night, can we? How do you want to resolve this?'

He looked down, sniffled, then back up to Sian. 'I don't know.'

'Shall I tell you what could happen? If you shoot Frank, then those men behind me will shoot you and you'll be dead before you hit the ground. I really don't want that to happen,' she said, stepping closer. 'But if you let Frank go and put your gun down, I'll take you to the police station. We'll have a sit down and a good chat and you can unburden yourself. I bet you haven't eaten all day, have you?'

'Not really.' He shook his head.

'I missed lunch myself.' She smiled. 'The canteen will

probably be closed, but we can send out for pizza or something.'

A smile appeared on Jake's face. Sian felt herself begin to relax slightly. There was an end in sight.

'I'm not a lawyer, Jake, I can't tell you what will happen to you, but I know for a fact that you're not one hundred per cent responsible for what's happened today. You've been lied to. Other people have manipulated you. This can all be sorted without any more people having to die.'

———

The lifts in the hospital were all being used to evacuate the patients, so Danny and Lewis had to take the stairs to climb the eleven flights to K floor. Danny started by taking them two at a time, but soon stopped when his breathing became laboured. Lewis was way behind, hampered by a heavy camera on his shoulders.

At the entrance to F floor, Danny stopped to take a breather and allow Lewis to catch him up.

'Don't you have to be fit to go to the Arctic?' Danny asked as Lewis turned the corner. His face was red and a sheen of sweat covered his forehead.

'I'm going to throw something at you in a minute.'

'A hissy-fit, probably.'

Danny left his cameraman behind and headed for the next floor.

'Bastard,' Lewis said under his breath.

'I heard that.'

———

'I killed my wife,' Jake said. 'What was I thinking? I loved her. Steve said to make a list of all the people who'd abandoned me, who didn't love me anymore. Ruth was at the top of my list. I still loved her though. She was the only person who ever said they love me.' Tears pricked his eyes.

'That just goes to prove my point, Jake,' Sian said, getting even closer. She was almost within touching distance. 'None of this was your choice. Other people have tricked you into doing their work for them. Lawyers and judges will see that. They'll understand.'

'I've never been a confident person. I've always been led by others.'

'Jake, I'm the same. I'm fine at work but make me go to a party and I fall apart. I never know what to say.'

'Neither do I.' He smiled. 'Even among my own family, I sometimes feel like I don't fit in.'

'Same here. You sit there, surrounded by them all, and they're laughing and joking and it's like nobody's told you what the joke is.'

'Exactly,' he said. 'You get it, don't you?'

'I do. But, you know, we can do things to make ourselves better,' she said, taking another step closer. 'There are groups and courses to help us be stronger people.'

'Have you been on one?'

'I'm looking into it. I don't really fancy going on my own.'

'I... No.'

'What?'

'I could ... I could come with you,' he said quietly, hesitantly.

'That could work.' She smiled. 'We could help each other out.'

'I'd like that.'

'Me too. So, shall we go and have a chat and a pizza and go from there?'

He nodded.

There was a bang from somewhere behind Jake. He increased his grip on Frank, whose face reddened. He winced as the gun was pressed firmer against his temple.

'What was that?' Jake asked.

'I don't know, Jake. It was probably a door slamming or something.'

He backed away down the corridor, dragging Frank with him. Sian followed.

'Jake, give me the gun. Come on, let's go somewhere warmer and more comfortable to talk about this.'

At the end of the corridor, Jake turned. He saw Danny Hanson and his cameraman enter from the fire exit. He saw the BBC logo on Danny's jacket and the camera on the other man's shoulder.

'You fucking bitch. You lied,' Jake screamed.

The gun went off. Frank's head exploded, splattering Jake and Sian with blood, brain and bone fragment.

'Sian! Down!'

Sian couldn't move. She froze. She was back in the car park again, watching her colleagues fall. She felt someone grab her and pull her to the floor.

'Put the fucking gun down, now!' Someone yelled.

Jake was using Sian as a shield. He was kicking out, pulling Sian with him, trying to put some distance between himself and the armed officers aiming at him.

The floor was covered in the blood leaking from Frank's body. Jake was skidding in it as he tried to maintain a hold on Sian and the gun.

Sian could feel the warmth of Frank's blood rolling down

her face. She could smell it, taste it. It was everywhere. The thick viscous liquid was running through her fingers.

'You lied to me,' he whispered in her ear. 'You don't give a fuck about me. You just wanted me to put the gun down.'

'Drop your weapon now!' Porter shouted.

Jake kicked at the floor again as he tried to get away from the approaching armed team. Sian was on top of him, his arm around her throat, the gun pressed against her head. She could feel it burning her flesh, the heat caused by the shot that killed Frank making the barrel feel like a flame.

'Of course I did,' she whispered with anger. 'Did you honestly think you and me were going to pop to the college for a course in confidence? You were falling for it, though,' she seethed. 'You were believing everything I was saying because you're weak and you need people to tell you what to do.'

'Shut up,' he screamed.

'No. If you want to kill me, then go ahead. But those men there will riddle your body with bullets, and you'll be dead just like me. What will you have achieved then, eh? Nothing. But that's been the story of your life, hasn't it? You're nothing. A nobody.'

'I swear to God, I will fucking kill you,' he shouted in her ear.

'This is your final warning, drop your weapon!' Porter shouted.

'You need me. If you were going to shoot, you would have done so by now. You don't want to die any more than I do. You know that if you kill me, you'll be dead within seconds. You need me to get out of here, you little prick.'

A shot rang out.

Sian slumped to the floor.

Chapter Seventy-Six

Outside the hospital, Jake's van had been located in the corner of the car park. CCTV footage and ANPR cameras backtracked Jake's entry into the hospital and discovered the vehicle he'd climbed out of. DS Aaron Connolly and DC Finn Cotton stood well back while bomb-disposal officers checked out the van to make sure there were no hidden devices or traps. A fine drizzle had started to fall. Both detectives were wet and freezing cold.

'Have you spoken to your wife today?' Finn asked.

'I called around lunchtime. She didn't answer, but I left her a message; told her everything that was going on,' he said, arms folded, glaring straight ahead.

'Did you hear back from her?'

'She sent a text telling me to stay safe. That's all.'

'That's a step in the right direction. Maybe she's beginning to thaw.'

He looked down at the young DC. 'No. She made her feelings perfectly clear. She won't have me back.'

'Have you asked her?'

'Until I'm blue in the face.'

'Ah.'

'Would you have your wife back if she cheated on you?'

Finn thought for a moment. 'No. I don't think I would.'

'There you go then. Anyway, she's started divorce proceedings. It's my own fault. I can't turn the clock back. Come on, it looks like they're giving us the go-ahead.'

'Either that or they're wanting to use us as the canary,' Finn said with a smile.

As they approached the van, one of the team began removing the bomb-disposal suit with the help of a colleague.

'Fresh air,' he said with a smile. 'We've done a sweep of the van. There's nothing underneath it, nothing under the bonnet and we've not detected any kind of explosive material inside the vehicle.'

'I sense a but,' Finn said.

'We don't know what's inside the van. The handle could be rigged to trigger some kind of air compression system that explodes a nail bomb or something,' he said, hazarding a guess.

'So, it's not safe for us to just open it?' Aaron asked.

'No. Not here.'

'Can't you remove it and take it elsewhere?'

'What we need to remove it wouldn't get in this space. We're going to fit a small charge to the lock on the back of the van, powerful enough to blow the doors open. Hopefully that will give us the opportunity to look inside.'

'You want us to make sure everyone is well back?'

'Please.'

As they walked away, Aaron noticed Finn smiling.

'What are you grinning at?'

'I just heard Michael Caine in my head saying, "You were

only supposed to blow the bloody doors off."' He laughed. 'Sorry,' he said when he noticed Aaron's grim expression.

The car park was empty of people and all police were ushered back while bomb-disposal experts placed a small charge on the lock of the van. They carefully unrolled the wire until they were a safe distance away, pressed a button on a remote control, and a muffled bang echoed around the open space. The doors immediately flew open.

'I was expecting more of a bang than that,' Finn said.

'You just wanted to quote Michael Caine again, didn't you?'

'I can't do the accent.'

'You're telling me.'

They were beckoned over to the van. A powerful torch was aimed inside the vehicle, lighting up the space. It was a while before their eyes adjusted.

'Oh my God,' Finn said.

'Do you know who that is?' a bomb-disposal expert asked.

'Roisin? Is that you?' Aaron asked, climbing, carefully, into the van.

She looked up. Her wrists and ankles were tied, tape secured her mouth closed. Her face was mucky, her clothes were torn and tears rolled down her face. She nodded.

He reached forward and gently removed the tape. 'I'm DS Aaron Connolly. We met, very briefly, around Christmas.'

'I remember,' she said quietly with a smile. 'Is it all over?'

'I've no idea. But you're safe. That's the main thing.'

Chapter Seventy-Seven

Inspector Gavin Porter and DI Christian Brady ran over to Sian. She was slumped in the corner of the corridor, caked in blood and brain matter. Porter kicked Jake's gun away while Christian squatted in front of his DS.

'Sian, Sian, can you hear me?'

She looked up at him. Her eyes were wide and unfocused. Her face was pale.

'Is it over?'

Christian glanced to one side, saw Jake Harrison propped up against the wall with half his head missing, his eyes wide open.

'Yes,' he said.

'Everything's muffled,' she said.

'That'll be the gunshot. Your hearing will come back soon. Are you hurt?'

'No. I don't think so.'

He helped her up. 'I am so incredibly proud of you.'

She couldn't help but smile. 'Really? I was staring down the barrel of a gun. I'm an idiot.'

'Well, yes, that too.'

She turned and looked down at Jake. 'How can one man cause so much destruction?'

'It wasn't just one man, though, was it? His brother takes a lot of blame for this. Come on, let's get you a drink.'

He helped her to her feet. She looked down at herself, at the amount of blood she was covered in. Another outfit ruined.

Slowly, Christian walked Sian down the corridor to the lifts. They passed Frank's lifeless body. She looked into Matilda's room. The DCI was lying in the bed, unconscious, oblivious to all the drama going on around her. Penny was in tears, screaming and wailing, though to Sian it was muffled. A female armed response officer was trying to calm her down. Daniel Harbison was having his gunshot wound checked by a nurse.

The further down the corridor they went, Sian took in the aftermath of the carnage. Spent bullet cartridges, doctors and nurses lying on the floor where they'd been gunned down. This really was a nightmare from which there was no waking up.

Chapter Seventy-Eight

Sian's clothes were evidence. She had to sit in the blood-drenched pieces while samples were taken from her and she was photographed from every angle. She was then cut out of her clothes, which were placed in evidence bags and sealed. She was allowed to have a wash in the nurses' changing room at the hospital before being given a white forensic suit to change into.

Christian stayed with her every step of the way. He wanted to call Stuart for her, to come and be with her, but she said she needed time to process what had happened first. After a long, hot shower, she was ready to return to the station.

'Are you all right?' Christian asked for what felt like the thousandth time.

She nodded.

They were in the back of a marked car being driven by PC Nowak.

'Roisin Featherstone was found alive,' he said.

'That's good news.'

'Martin's on his way here now.'

'He'll have a lot of questions to answer.'

Nowak cleared her throat. 'Sorry to interrupt, I overheard the Chief Constable on the phone at the station. He's handed in his resignation.'

'I can't say I'm surprised,' Sian said.

'He'll still have a lot of questions to answer,' Christian said. 'We all will.'

Back at the station, Christian and Sian went straight to the interview suite where Steve Harrison was still waiting. In the car on the way back, Sian asked if she could break the news to him. Before opening the door, she composed herself, took a breath, then burst in.

Steve jumped. He looked up, saw Sian in her forensic suit and laughed.

'Oh dear, got a bit of blood on your clothes?' he asked.

'They were caked in it,' she said, standing in the doorway, a slight smile on her lips. 'Still, a ruined jumper and trousers are a small price to pay for the death of a killer.'

Steve's face dropped.

'Oh, haven't you heard? How remiss of me,' she said, her words oozing with sarcasm. 'I should have sent someone down to tell you that Jake was killed. Not before he spent about ten minutes crying, telling me how nobody had ever loved him and how he didn't have the confidence to make anything of his life, blah, blah, blah. It was all very embarrassing.'

Steve remained impassive. He looked at Sian with smiling eyes, a smirk on his lips, totally unfazed by the death of his brother.

'You see, today has all been for nothing,' Sian said, leaning down on the table. 'Matilda is still very much alive. The operation to remove bone fragments from her fractured skull was a complete success. She'll make a full recovery and she'll be back at work before the end of the year, mark my words. You failed, Steve. You'll be charged with incitement to commit murder. Any privileges you had at the prison will be removed, and you can kiss goodbye to your minimum term. You'll never see daylight again.'

She looked up at Shaun Cox and gave him the nod to take Steve away. He'd be going back to Wakefield Prison tonight. They knew where to find him when they needed to question him again.

'I haven't failed,' Steve said. He stopped in the doorway and turned back around. 'Matilda might still be alive but look how many have died today. You've lost detectives, people you work with and care about. You've seen things today you thought you'd never witness. Both of you.' He looked from Sian to Christian. 'In fact, every single one of you will have nightmares and flashbacks. You'll be in therapy for a very long time. I did that. Me. I'm in your head now. And I've no intention of ever leaving.'

Chapter Seventy-Nine

'Today has been one of the darkest days in Sheffield's history. The events of Tuesday the eighth of January 2019 will be remembered for years to come as the day a lone gunman took to the streets of Britain's fourth largest city and went on a killing spree, mercilessly massacring men, women and children. He was finally stopped here, at the Royal Hallamshire Hospital, where he was cornered and gunned down by armed response officers. In a very brief statement released by South Yorkshire Police, we can officially reveal the gunman was identified as thirty-four-year-old Jake Harrison, brother of former police officer Steven Harrison, who killed six people in 2017. The death toll from today is not yet known and it will take several days before all the crime scenes are processed, but together, these two brothers have murdered more than thirty people and will go down in history as Britain's most prolific sibling killers. Danny Hanson, BBC News, Sheffield.'

Christian pointed the remote at the television screen on the wall and turned it off.

'Wanker,' he said. 'You know he's going to write a book about them, don't you?'

'Did you see the look in his eye?' Sian said. 'He was practically smiling. He's loved every minute of today.'

Two hours had passed since the events at the Hallamshire Hospital and they were currently sat in the Homicide and Major Enquiry suite. They were the only ones remaining. A few desk lights were on, but they were in virtual darkness. Finn and Aaron couldn't get out of the station fast enough when Christian said they could leave for the day. For some reason though, despite wanting to be with his family, Christian felt the need to stay, just for a little while longer.

From a drawer in Valerie Masterson's filing cabinet, Christian had taken a bottle of whisky and two glasses and poured himself and Sian a large measure each.

'Can you believe any of what we've been through today?' Sian said, fighting back the tears, looking at the empty desks in front of her, some of which would still be empty tomorrow morning when work resumed.

'It's going to be a while before it sinks in.'

'Christian, tell me we can come back from this,' she said, turning to face him. She had had only one Mars bar from her snack drawer all day, and the effects of the alcohol were quickly sinking in. Her head lolloped to one side.

'We can. It's whether we want to, that's the question.'

'What do you mean?'

'Well, do you still want to be a police officer after today?'

'Yes. Of course,' she replied firmly. 'More than ever. I consider it my duty to serve in the memory of those we've lost today. Please don't tell me you're thinking of leaving.'

'I need to speak to my wife,' he finally said. His voice was heavy with emotion. 'It's not only my decision to make.'

'I can't do this without you,' she said, a single tear falling down her cheek. 'We've lost so many good officers today.

You're needed here.' She reached out a hand and placed it on his arm. 'I need you here.'

He turned and smiled at her. 'Have you phoned Stuart?'

'Yes. He's coming to collect me.'

'Will you tell him everything that's happened today?'

She nodded as more tears fell.

'We're lucky really, aren't we? We've both got people we can share these things with,' he said.

'Stuart is a very understanding and sympathetic man. I couldn't wish for a better husband.'

'But who have Scott, Kesinka, Matilda and Adele got?'

'They've got us. And they've got each other,' she said, slurring her words slightly. 'The only way we can defeat people like Steve and Jake is by growing stronger together.'

Her mobile on the desk in front of her began vibrating. She picked it up and smiled when she saw Stuart's face. She swiped to answer. 'Hello … Ok. I'll be right down … No, well, I may have had one. See you soon.' She ended the call and tried to stand up but stumbled.

'Have you had anything substantial to eat today?' he asked.

'I don't think so.'

'Maybe you should.'

'Maybe. Right, well, I'd better be getting off.' She held her arms out for a hug.

Christian stood up and obliged, holding her tight.

'Promise me you'll come in to work tomorrow,' she said, her head against his chest.

'I promise.'

'We need to stick together, Christian. If we don't, they've won.' There were tears in her eyes and a catch in her voice.

'I know.'

She stepped out of his embrace, picked up her coat and bag and walked unsteadily towards the doors. She turned back.

'A new day tomorrow, Christian.'

'A new day.' He smiled.

He waited until she was gone, and he was alone in the suite. He looked around him. So much had happened. He was surrounded by darkness and silence, but the atmosphere was heavy. He pictured Rory sat at his desk, having a playful argument with Sian about the contents of her snack drawer, and how she would tease him about cutting him off if he didn't contribute. He couldn't see the levity returning to this room. It was tainted. Everything had changed today. Life for the remaining members of the Homicide and Major Enquiry Team would never be the same again.

Chapter Eighty

Penny Doyle was alone in Matilda's hospital room. It was lit only by a small lamp attached to the wall, and the various screens Matilda was hooked up to.

Penny held her daughter's hand in both of hers. She looked at her with tear-filled eyes. It was a good thing Matilda was unconscious because Penny had no idea what words to use to tell her everything that had happened today. It still didn't seem real. Frank was gone. How was that possible?

'Matilda, I'm so sorry.' She sniffled. 'I've been a terrible mother to you. I've been so scared of losing you that I thought if there was this barrier between us, then I wouldn't be hurt so much if … well, if you were injured like this. I was being selfish. But I get it now. Why you do what you do. I understand. People like this Jake character, well, they're everywhere, aren't they? You turn on the news and someone's been beaten to death for the sake of a mobile phone, or a child's been killed by their father to spite the mother when they split up. There are bad people everywhere, and we need people like you to stop them. You're one of the good guys. I always knew you were, but I selfishly wanted you to be safe.

'I love you so much, Matilda. I always have. I need you to wake up. Please, Matilda, for me, for your dad, wake up.'

She looked at the monitors. She had no idea what any of them meant, or what the flashing green numbers and the red lines were saying. It was alien to her.

Penny looked back at her daughter, glaring at her, willing her to wake up.

Nothing happened.

Nothing happened.

Nothing happened.

Epilogue

Tuesday, April 23rd 2019

Dear Friend,

Thank you for your letters. I've been researching you and looking into your background. At first I was sceptical, but now I believe you're in a prime position to help me, and I'm the perfect man to help you.

You need to prepare yourself, mentally, for the journey ahead, as it's going to be a long one. We have a great deal to plan. Matilda is an interesting adversary and one we must keep an eye on. My brother came incredibly close to killing her, but he fell at the final hurdle. However, he achieved greatness in his task and that is something we must emulate.

Matilda has a long road of recovery, and we can allow her that. I've been keeping an eye on the news and seen the way her 'ordeal' has been documented so candidly. Let's give her some breathing space. Let's give her time to relax, recuperate and recover from her injuries.

I will send you a visiting order so you can come and see me, and we can talk about our plans. Time has passed since you last had any dealings with Matilda and as you only met her briefly, I'm guessing she won't recognise you at all, even when you're right in front of her.

You can be my eyes and ears on the outside, and I have plenty of contacts I can manipulate. Time is on our side. If we rush, we will make a mistake. Let Matilda relax, return to work, rebuild her team and start to enjoy life again. That's when we will strike.

Remember, Deuteronomy 32:35 – 'Vengeance is mine, and recompense, for the time when their foot shall slip; for the day of their calamity is at hand, and their doom comes swiftly.'

Yours,

Steve Harrison

Acknowledgments

This book was written and produced during the first lockdown of 2020 and I would like to say a huge thank you to the entire team at One More Chapter and HarperCollins who were working from home yet still managed to put a whole book together. Not just mine, but the whole output from HarperCollins. Their efforts during this strange and frightening time were nothing short of amazing and their professionalism never wavered. Particular mentions to Charlotte Ledger, Hannah Todd, Bethan Morgan and Rebecca Millar. Thank you for taking care of me and Matilda.

I'd also like to thank my agent, Jamie Cowen, and the team at Ampersand for their ongoing work in my writing career.

Now, for the technical people who helped to bring this book together:

Philip Lumb: eminent pathologist, who, despite being incredibly busy, always finds time to furnish me with fascinating and gruesome information. A wave here for Carolyn and Elizabeth, too.

Simon Browes: an incredibly busy man who had a shocking

2020 and is doing Herculean work within the NHS to make sure we're all vaccinated against Covid-19.

Andy Barrett: for his insight into all things crime scene related.

Neil Lancaster and Mr Tidd: for their information regarding police procedure.

I thank you all and any errors within this book are entirely mine for the purpose of fiction and nothing to do with the professionalism of the experts.

I'd like to say a big thank you to Nutwells who gave me a great deal of information regarding what equipment was needed during mass crime scenes.

A special thank you to the people of Twitter who allowed me to use their Twitter names in this book. The characters who are screaming out for help or fearing for their lives are real people.

To the readers, reviewers and the bloggers, so many thank yous to you all.

Finally, there are some people who would turn me into one of my victims if I didn't mention them: my mum (thanks for the cakes), Christopher Human (thanks for the random chats), Kevin the Beagle (thanks for the photos), Big Squishy Max (thanks for being big and squishy), Jonas Alexander (thanks for the moustaches, and we are definitely seeing Scream at the cinema), Chris Simmons (thanks for the books).

ONE MORE CHAPTER

One More Chapter is an
award-winning global
division of HarperCollins.

Sign up to our newsletter to get our
latest eBook deals and stay up to date
with our weekly Book Club!
<u>Subscribe here.</u>

Meet the team at
<u>www.onemorechapter.com</u>

Follow us!

 <u>@OneMoreChapter_</u>
 <u>@OneMoreChapter</u>
📷 <u>@onemorechapterhc</u>

Do you write unputdownable fiction?
We love to hear from new voices.
Find out how to submit your novel at
<u>www.onemorechapter.com/submissions</u>